J.P.

(5)

M. Morris —
London / July '84 —
On a visit to Craig.

D1431228

# A SENSE OF PLACE

*By Maisie Mosco and available from New English Library*

ALMONDS AND RAISINS
SCATTERED SEED
CHILDREN'S CHILDREN

BETWEEN TWO WORLDS
A SENSE OF PLACE

# A SENSE OF PLACE

Maisie Mosco

NEW ENGLISH LIBRARY

The author wishes to thank Linda S. Price and Carola Edmond for editorial advice, and Tanya Ossack for assistance with research.

The Author and Publishers gratefully acknowledge
permission to include an extract from 'Burnt Norton'
in *The Four Quartets* by T. S. Eliot, by permission of
Faber and Faber Ltd.

First published in Great Britain in 1984 by
New English Library, Mill Road, Dunton Green, Sevenoaks, Kent.
Editorial office: 47 Bedford Square, London WC1B 3DP.

Typeset by Hewer Text Composition Services, Edinburgh.
Printed in Great Britain by Biddles Ltd, Guildford and King's Lynn.

British Library Cataloguing in Publication Data
Mosco, Maisie
   A sense of place.
   I. Title
   823'.914[F]        PR6063.0/

ISBN: 0 450 06055 1

*For*
JUNE *and* TOM PAXMAN,
*whose New England hospitality
enriched this book*

# *Part One*

Footfalls echo in the memory
Down the passage which we did not take
Towards the door we never opened
Into the rose garden.

                              *T. S. Eliot*

# CHAPTER ONE

ALISON CAME offstage in a daze and threaded her way through the cluttered wings, the scent of the red roses she was carrying rising sweetly to her nostrils, the thunder of applause still echoing in her ears. Playing St Joan was a nightly challenge. Exhilarating and exhausting.

By the time she reached her dressing room, only the exhaustion remained. She felt like a wound-down clock and was thankful that it was Saturday. Two days of rest stretched ahead of her before she need wind herself up again.

She put the bouquet on the sofa. Apart from the floor, there was nowhere else to put it. The dressing room was crammed with red roses, and Alison, for whom they had in her youth represented love, at thirty associated them with success.

She summoned the energy to change into a wrapper and remove her make-up, and was brushing her hair when the stagedoor-keeper came to tell her that she had visitors.

'A Mr and Mrs Battersby, Miss Plantaine. The gentleman says he's an old friend of yours.'

Alison would not have described Albert Battersby in quite that way. He had been her girlhood sweetheart, but they had never been friends.

'Shall I tell 'em you're not receivin' tonight?' the stagedoor-keeper said. Alison's silence was making him feel uncomfortable.

'No. Please ask them to come in.'

Alison had not encountered Albert since their affair ended, in 1919. It was now 1930. She eyed her reflection in the mirror and thought how the intervening years had sped by, and of the romantic girl she had once been.

But not romantic enough to put marriage before her career. Albert had forced her to choose, and by doing so had lost her, she was thinking when he entered with his wife.

'How nice to see you again,' Alison said to him, though this was not an accurate assessment of her feelings. How did she feel? As if a ghost had risen from her past.

Albert's appearance did not match that metaphor. The lanky lad Alison remembered had turned into a portly man.

'Same here, Alison,' he replied to her greeting.

His wife seemed momentarily struck dumb.

'Don't look so nervous, Doreen love. Alison isn't going to bite you!' Albert joked.

Doreen found her voice. 'It's just that I've never been in a theatre dressing room before.'

'Well, make the most of it, love,' Albert told her. 'I don't suppose you ever will be again.'

'I'm afraid it's terribly untidy,' said Alison unnecessarily. 'But do sit down, and we'll have some sherry.'

'Haven't you got a maid?' Doreen asked her. 'I thought famous actresses always had.'

Alison laughed ruefully. 'I've never managed to find one who'll put up with me.'

Doreen glanced at the spilled powder on the dressing table, and at the general disarray. 'I'm not surprised.'

This was not construed by Alison as rudeness. Since making her London debut, work had kept her in the capital, but in her childhood and youth, touring the provinces with the Plantaine Players had taught her that Lancashire folk always called a spade a spade.

She was pouring the sherry and paused with the decanter in her hand, briefly touched by nostalgia. Nowadays, Alison rarely thought of the family company. She had gone her own way, but the elder Plantaines still worked side by side, in Hastings where they had settled during the Great War. And occasionally, seeing a mention of them in *The Stage* conjured up for her a picture of her mother and grandparents, and her Aunt Ruby and Uncle Oliver, taking a curtain call together. Though Alison's grandparents were now creaking with age, from time to time they still appeared onstage.

Albert switched Alison's thoughts to her paternal relatives, who lived in his home town. 'You don't visit Oldham very often, do you?' he remarked. 'Your cousin Conrad said they only seem to see you at funerals.'

'He was joking, Albert,' Doreen said.

'But I bet he didn't think it was funny when Alison didn't go to his wedding.'

Alison sipped some sherry. 'Did you come backstage to tick me off, Albert?' she said lightly. Inwardly, she was seething and recalled that he had always had the knack of getting her back up. He had not even said he had enjoyed the play!

He did so now and Alison managed to stem her anger, but was unable to cast aside the accompanying guilt. But what she was guilty of was unavoidable, she told herself. Her work came first. And Conrad Stein – who was Albert's friend – had been married on a working day. Alison could not miss a performance to attend a wedding. This, the Plantaines would understand. But the Steins were not theatricals.

As a girl, Alison had come to think of her maternal and paternal relatives as her two worlds. Each was steeped in its own tradition. The Plantaines held nothing more dear than their thespian heritage. The Steins' Jewish heritage had conditioned them to place family ties above all else.

Alison was a Christian, like her mother. But her father's blood, too, flowed strongly in her veins and it was to his family she had run with her youthful troubles. What a long time ago that seemed. And, as she had just been reminded, some of her visits in recent years had been to attend funerals.

In 1924, her grandparents died within weeks of each other. The following year, Alison's father, too, had been laid to rest in the Jewish cemetery at nearby Failsworth. He had not practised his faith since marrying outside it, but had wanted to be buried as a Jew, beside the parents from whom he had been estranged for much of his life.

'Cheer up, Alison,' Doreen said kindly. 'Albert didn't mean to upset you.'

5

Alison put a smile on her face. 'I'm sure he didn't.' But he had succeeded in doing so. A ghost from the past he certainly was, bringing with him a motley of memories so poignant, Alison wanted to weep.

Instead, she must sit here chatting with the overbearing man he had become. Put on a performance for him and his well-meaning, dumpy wife, with whom Alison did not even have the past in common. They had been briefly introduced when they were girls, and Doreen a typist at the Battersby cotton mill.

'What brings you two to London?' Alison inquired.

'Business,' Albert informed her.

'I've never been to London before, so Albert let me come with him,' said Doreen, eyeing him fondly.

'Let' would be the key word for Albert Battersby's wife, Alison thought, and the difference between her personal freedom and Doreen's domestic bondage struck her forcibly. Yet Doreen did not seem bowed down by it. On the contrary, there was about her an air of quiet contentment which Alison found hard to reconcile with her dreary lot.

'We arrived last night and I've been looking round the shops all day – my feet're killing me!' Doreen said, glancing down at her lizard-skin shoes. 'Not that I bought much. Only a toy each, for the kids – we've left them with Albert's mam. We're being careful with our pennies just now, aren't we, Albert?'

'Got no choice, love, have we? The extra it cost to fetch you along has set us back enough.' Albert finished his sherry and went to put the empty glass on the dressing table. 'I spent the day trying to drum up some orders,' he told Alison. 'As you must've heard, the textile trade's in the doldrums, along with everything else.'

He glanced at his wife's musquash coat. 'Lucky I bought Doreen that fur before times started to get bad!'

'And I'm ashamed to walk past the dole queues wearing it,' Doreen declared. 'I was surprised to see the theatre so full tonight, Alison. I'm sure the folk up north couldn't afford the price of the tickets.'

'Well, the theatre's for the nobs, isn't it, love?' said Albert disparagingly. 'You'n me were the only ones not wearing evening dress.'

In the eyes of their millworkers, the Battersbys were what Albert called 'nobs', but Alison refrained from saying so. She changed the subject. 'How old are your children?'

'Our Billy's four, and Katie will be three next month,' Doreen told her.

Albert brought some snapshots of them from his pocket. 'I never lose the opportunity to show 'em off.'

Alison scanned the two snub-nosed little faces. They looked like Albert's mother. Whom would her own children resemble? – if she ever had any, which seemed unlikely.

'They're delightful,' she pronounced.

Albert and Doreen exchanged a proud, parental glance.

'The kids are our be-all and end-all, aren't they, Albert?' Doreen said.

'Needless to say, love. It wouldn't suit you, of course, Alison, but to me and Doreen, that's what life is all about.'

There was no snideness in Albert's tone, and Alison knew that none was intended. He had been stating a fact. The one on which their romance had foundered, and Alison did not regret that it had.

What did she regret? she asked herself when the Battersbys had gone. For regret was the aftermath of their visit, and, too, a loneliness of which she had not been conscious before they came.

Alison's solitary state was her own choice. Many men had proposed to her in the years since she made her London debut, and without the curtailment of her career that Albert had required. But Alison had not met a man with whom she wanted to share her life.

Not even her manager, the powerful impresario Maxwell Morton, had succeeded in capturing her. It was not for the want of trying. His was a sturdy shoulder to lean on, and Alison did not hesitate to do so, as she once had on her father. But she had not allowed herself to slip into a less daughterly relationship with Morton. He remained her trusted friend.

These were Alison's thoughts while she carefully dressed to go home. Once, she had been casual about her attire, but had by now accepted what her mother had fruitlessly tried to teach her: that an actress must retain her glamour offstage.

Accordingly, it was a strikingly attractive woman, in a chic black velvet suit and a matching, eye-veiled hat, who paused to sign autograph books outside the stage door. She was carrying the bouquet of red roses, for effect.

When Alison arrived at her flat, the new loneliness was still assailing her. The spacious drawing room that over-looked Hyde Park seemed to be echoing with emptiness. Only her cat was here to greet her. It gave her a cursory 'miaow' and went back to sleep.

I'll ring up Maxwell and ask him to take me to supper, Alison decided, though she had told Morton she intended to have a quiet weekend. A coy female voice answered his telephone. Alison replaced the receiver, without surprise. Morton's being in love with her did not stop him from finding elsewhere what she continued to deny him.

She took off her hat and went to the kitchen to make herself a sandwich. When she had done so, she could not eat it. 'Look, you don't have to sit here by yourself,' she said aloud. There were several after-the-show parties to which she had been invited. But if she went to one of them, she would still return, eventually, to this elegant, empty apartment.

As Alison's life was, of all but her career. She'd been too immersed in getting to the top to see that she was heading, too, for this desolate moment of truth. You couldn't be as single-minded as Alison was without being wrapped up in yourself. But if you lived for yourself alone, alone was how you ended up. Meeting the right man might have saved her, but the few romantic entanglements she had allowed herself had, for one reason or another, palled. And her friendships were the casual kind, born of nothing more than the social-ising in which theatricals indulged.

'But that isn't my fault,' she told the cat which had joined her in the kitchen. 'When I first came to London, I trusted everyone, but one after the other people let me down. And how can there be true friendship without trust?'

She bent down to stroke her furry companion, remembering her first big disillusionment. A girl she had thought was her pal had offered to sleep with Maxwell, to get a part he was considering offering to Alison. 'In the end, neither of us got it,' she said to the cat. 'But when I heard on the grapevine that she'd tried to stab me in the back, I was more upset about that than about not getting the part. The trouble with my profession, puss, is that most people will do anything to further their own career – and it's hard to know who your real friends are. And don't you believe it, if anyone tells you that Alison Plantaine got where she is overnight.'

On the contrary, Alison thought, resting her back against the sink and wryly reliving her uphill climb. The initial shock of discovering that her distinguished thespian name meant little in the competitive London theatre; that away from the family company she was just another struggling young actress. The slow realisation that Morton's taking her under his managerial wing was not an automatic passport to success. The disappointment when roles she had coveted went to others, and lesser ones to herself. And the years in a Bloomsbury bedsitter, when only her father's generosity saved her from going hungry on the pittance she then earned; there were those who dined out with stagedoor-Johnnies, but Alison never had.

She recalled, too, a long-running production in which Morton had asked her to understudy the star – whom everyone knew was his current mistress – and Alison had said a nightly prayer for that lady to fall ill.

'I even thought of slipping some strong laxative pills into her tea,' she confessed to the cat, 'to keep her offstage for just one performance. But unlike some others, I don't play dirty tricks.'

Eventually, Alison had accused Morton of not giving her a leading role because he wasn't interested in bedding her, and had been curtly told she would get her chance when she was ready and the right vehicle in which to launch her came along.

It had taken some time for it to seep through to her that

she was special to him and he respected her. When after her first starring role he proposed to her, she had been tempted to say yes.

'But I can't marry a man I don't love,' she declared to her pet. 'Kind to me though he is.'

Instead, here she was – talking to a cat. She removed the sardine filling from the sandwich she had made, put it into the animal's dish and threw away the bread. Moments of truth might be good for the soul, but where did they get you? And why had the self-sufficiency she'd worn like an armour gone from her tonight? Coming home to an empty flat was nothing new and she'd been fine before the Battersbys walked in on her.

But their visit had had a jarring effect. Suddenly, Alison Plantaine, who had thought she had everything, had been brought up short, made to take stock of herself and her shallow existence – which she had not known was shallow. Until now.

The regret Alison had felt in the dressing room stirred in her again. But no longer inexplicably. Don't be a fool, she told herself. Domesticity was not for Alison, as Albert had reminded her tonight. But by eschewing it, she had denied herself the simple pleasures and warm, human contacts which were for others part of living. It was as though she had just learned she was only half-alive.

She returned to the drawing room and switched on the electric fire, but its glow could not remove the chill pervading her spirits. If she had had some sleeping pills, she would probably, and unprecedentedly, have resorted to drugging herself into temporary oblivion.

She was tempted to take a drink, but did not succumb. Alison was not in the habit of drinking alone. Too many of her acquaintances had demonstrated the folly of setting forth along that road.

Her gaze drifted around the room. There wasn't a crease in the apricot silk cushions, carefully propped at the other end of the sofa upon which she was seated. A neat pile of unread magazines lay beside a lacquered box on the coffee table, placed there by the cleaning lady. Like a stage set,

Alison thought, as if nobody lives here. But I'm rarely at home.

The emerald silk shawl she had worn to parties in the Twenties was draped on the grand piano. The shawl had been her father's gift to her when she made her West End début, and she got up to look at his photograph. Oh how she missed him!

There was no picture of Alison's mother among the silver-framed collection on the piano. Hermione Plantaine had allowed her detestation of her husband's family to keep her from his funeral, and Alison had not forgiven her for it. But there were many things for which Alison could not forgive her mother.

Why am I standing here raking up the past? she thought. Because it had been that kind of night. Once something switched your mind backwards, the memories came thick and fast.

She blotted them out and went to gaze through the window. Late-night traffic was trickling along Bayswater Road. She could see the tall trees in the park being whipped by the wind, and the rain-soaked pavements gleaming gold in the lamplight. A few pedestrians were struggling to prevent their umbrellas from being blown inside out.

Her bird's-eye view from the top floor increased Alison's feeling of being cut off from the mainstream of life. She felt like a captive in an ivory tower. But it was of her own making, she thought, turning from the window to restlessly roam the flat.

Only her bedroom looked lived-in, she registered, eyeing the garments she had not bothered to rehang after selecting her outfit for this evening. And her cousin Emma Stein would have a fit, if she saw all those expensive gowns lying in a heap on the bed, Alison thought. Emma was neatness personified.

It was not uncommon for Alison to think how Emma would react to this or that. Though they did not see each other often, the friendship established in their youth had survived.

A moment later, Alison was making a telephone call to

11

Oldham, tapping her foot impatiently while she waited for the operator to put her through.

'I'm coming to see you, Emma,' she said when her cousin answered the phone.

'That's wonderful, Alison! When?'

'Now, of course. I just said to myself, "Wouldn't it be lovely to see the family up north." '

Emma laughed. 'And with you, Alison, it's no sooner said than done.' For Emma, Alison was impulsiveness personified. 'But you've missed the last train, haven't you?' she added practically.

'My dear, darling Emma! Have you never heard of a hired car?'

'It would cost you a fortune, Alison!'

'So what?'

'And how can you hire a car at this hour? It's midnight.'

Alison could hear the grandfather clock chiming in the Steins' hall – and what a heartening picture it conjured up. 'This is London, darling!' she reminded Emma. 'Some people are just thinking of calling it a night when you are getting up. I shall phone the firm Maxwell uses and they'll send a car round here *tout de suite*. Did I drag you from your bed?'

'What do you think?'

'You'll have to forgive me.'

'There's nothing to forgive, Alison.'

Alison smiled. How many times, over the years, she had heard Emma say that.

'But it's a good job the phone didn't waken Mam and Dad,' Emma added. 'Not that they'd have dared to answer it. For us to get a phone call late at night, someone has to be dying or dead.'

Alison's Jewish relatives were conventional people. And eminently ordinary, as she had recognised when she first met them. But this was the quality that made them, for Alison, so very reassuring. Knowing that the Steins were there if she needed them provided the only stability in her life. They were the anchor her parents had been unable to provide.

On the long journey north, her mind again swooped backwards. This time to her childhood and youth, and the succession of theatrical lodgings that had been her transient homes. Not until she went to stay with the Steins had Alison experienced home life in its true sense.

And I've yearned for it ever since, she thought while the car bowled smoothly along. This secret yearning was the root cause of Alison's present bleakness. But it did not fit in with what her art had decreed for her, and she must stamp it out.

Meanwhile, she could look forward to a warming interlude with the Steins and was cheered by the prospect. Just talking on the telephone to Emma had made her feel better.

Not for a moment did Alison doubt her welcome. Nor had she allowed herself to feel ashamed that, once again, she was turning to the Steins for comfort, but would not be heading north now had that need not been there.

Alison's egocentricity enabled her to excuse her own behaviour, while making no concessions to that of others. Those who had achieved lasting closeness with her – and they were few – had done so only because they were prepared to accept her as she was.

Lottie and Lionel Stein, and their son Conrad, had succumbed to Alison's charm when she was only fourteen, and fled to Oldham after quarrelling with her mother, while her father was serving in the war. But Lottie would have opened her heart to her brother's child even had Alison not been endowed with the special charisma that was hers.

For Emma Stein, Alison could do no wrong. They were the same age, and Alison epitomised for Emma all that she herself was not and could never be.

Conversely, Emma's elder sister Clara, who rated herself as glamorous as Alison, had never liked her. The antipathy was mutual, and Alison was hoping that Clara would not choose this weekend to drop in on her parents.

'Would you like me to pull up at the next transport café and fetch you some tea, Miss Plantaine?' the chauffeur asked as they approached Stoke-on-Trent.

'No, thank you. I'm in a hurry to get to Oldham.'

The man increased speed. His parched throat and bursting bladder would have to wait until then. Actresses! he thought. He had never driven Alison Plantaine before, and had heard from his mates who had that she was a friendly lady. But she'd hardly spoken a word to him. Must have something on her mind, he reckoned, eyeing her expression in the rear-view mirror.

Alison was gazing at the tall factory chimneys looming on the horizon. They were no feast for the eye, she thought. But, as always, it was good to be heading north. Technically, Alison was a southerner. Her mother had given birth to her in Plymouth, when the company happened to be playing there. But her father's roots were in the north and it was to them that Alison clung.

# CHAPTER TWO

L OTTIE S TEIN stirred her kitchen fire to a cheerful blaze and glanced at the clock. 'I may as well start cooking the breakfast,' she said.

Emma was laying the table. 'But Alison isn't here yet, Mam.'

'What we already know, she's telling us!' her father exclaimed. 'I'm not on edge enough already because, in weather like this, Alison is travelling by road!'

November fog was blanketing the trees in the rear garden, and the houses that stood back to back with the Steins' villa were barely visible.

Lionel shifted his attention to the *News of the World* to shut out a vision of his only niece lying injured in a mangled motor car.

'If Alison isn't here when the breakfast is ready, I can keep it warm in the oven,' Lottie decided. 'Better that way, than she should have to wait for me to cook it.'

A visit from Alison was always an event. The magic aura of the theatre entered the house with her and lingered like her perfume after she was gone. Meanwhile, the household was bristling with excitement because she was coming.

'Why don't you go upstairs and brighten yourself up a bit, love?' Lottie said to Emma.

Lionel raised his eyes from his newspaper. 'Your mother is right, Emma. Alison is sure to have on a smart dress.'

Emma laughed. 'You want me to enter into competition with Alison, all of a sudden?'

'Don't be ridiculous,' her father said. 'But why must you always wear brown?'

'If I didn't,' said Emma comfortably, 'I should probably wear grey.'

'It's no wonder she gets called the family sparrow!' Lionel exclaimed to Lottie. 'What with her clothes, and her meek and mild nature.'

Alison's arrival put an end to the discussion.

She was greeted with love and kisses, as she had known she would be. And by a delicious aroma of frying kippers, when she entered the kitchen.

'I expected to get here long before now. Then we ran into fog and had to crawl for the last thirty miles. I'm absolutely ravenous!' she said, watching Lottie dish up the breakfast.

'And you look as if a good meal wouldn't do you any harm,' Lottie declared, appraising her. 'You've lost weight since we last saw you, Alison.'

'While she's here, she'll put it back on,' said Lionel.

Alison sat down at the table and eyed the heaped plate her aunt put before her. 'I don't doubt it, Uncle!'

Lionel seated himself beside Alison and gave her cheek an affectionate pinch. 'So how is my niece the actress?' he inquired with a smile.

'Not getting any younger!'

'Me neither,' Emma said.

They exchanged a smile and Alison noted that Emma had begun to look her age – which Alison did not. It used to be the other way round, she thought. Emma was tiny, and in her teens and twenties had looked like a little girl wearing grown-up clothes. Alison's tall figure had matured early, which had made her appear older than her years.

Lottie was admiring her niece's sleek, shoulder-length coiffure. 'Your hair looks lovely, Alison. I wish our Emma would change her style, instead of wearing it in a bun, like a schoolmarm.'

'I wouldn't have minded being one,' Emma said.

Her parents looked taken aback.

As Alison was. 'You never told me that teaching was your ambition, Emma.'

Emma went on removing the backbone from her kipper. 'It wasn't my ambition, Alison.'

'Then what you just said doesn't make sense,' Lionel declared.

In Alison's view, ambition was what Emma had always lacked. But it was not in her character to strive for things, Alison thought. Emma was the kind who hoped for the best, but didn't expect to get it.

'It's just that I think teaching might have been right for me,' Emma went on, 'as I'm fond of children. But it's too late now, isn't it? And anyway, Dad never wanted me, or our Clara, to have a job.'

'Clara wouldn't have dreamt of taking a job. All she ever wanted was a lady's life,' said Alison scathingly.

Nobody contradicted this. The truth was the truth.

'And now she's got what she always wanted,' Lionel said, exchanging a glance with Lottie. 'And she hardly ever comes here. But that's our Clara!'

'Does that mean we shan't be seeing her this weekend?' Alison asked hopefully.

Lionel sighed. 'I'd say that it's highly unlikely.'

'She's too busy arranging a big *Bar Mitzvah* party for Percy,' Lottie informed Alison.

'What – already?' said Alison. 'It seems like yesterday that I sat here watching Emma spoonfeed Percy in his high chair. Do you remember the time he threw his dish of potatoes and gravy at you, Emma?'

'That wasn't the only time he did it, Alison.'

'I can believe it!' Alison's recollections of Clara's son were of an obstreperous, whining toddler. 'I hope he's not as spoiled now as he was then,' she said.

'He hasn't turned out too badly, all things considered,' Lottie replied. 'As you'll see for yourself, Alison. You'll be getting an invitation to his *Bar Mitzvah*.'

'Probably.'

'There's no probably about it!'

Even though Clara dislikes me, Alison reflected. But she had had time to learn that kinship took precedence over dislike when guest lists for Jewish family functions were compiled.

Outright vendettas were another matter. 'I bet Clara doesn't invite her first husband's parents,' Alison said.

'Why would she?' Lionel answered. 'She's kept them away from their only grandchild for nearly thirteen years. Ever since the boy was born. Not letting them see him confirmed will be her biggest triumph.'

Clara's feud with her first husband's parents dated from his death in the war. She had blamed them for his having joined up, and was still enjoying her revenge. She was now the wife of an affluent solicitor, many years her senior. Alison had met him at the family funerals and thought him a nice man.

Too good for Clara, she reflected, aware of a heaviness in the atmosphere, which mention of the Steins' elder daughter invariably evoked. There were times in this house when Alison felt Clara's presence as one does that of an offstage character in a play. Today was one of those times.

She picked at the remains of her kipper and studied her aunt and uncle.

Lottie was wearing a smart burgundy frock beneath the apron she had forgotten to take off when she sat down to eat. She had always dressed with style, and Alison could not remember ever seeing her look less than immaculate.

How old was she now? Fifty-five? And still a handsome woman. That's how I'll look, Alison thought, when I'm Aunt Lottie's age. Alison had always strongly resembled her aunt. But Lottie's hair was now silver. Streaks of it had begun to appear before she was forty – put there by Clara. And Lionel's stocky figure looked bowed down with care.

'It's time you wrote Clara off!' Alison told them with feeling.

They looked immensely shocked. Emma too.

'Well, she hasn't treated you very well, has she?' Alison persisted. 'After all you've done for her.'

'Parents don't expect repayment for what they do for their children, Alison,' Lottie said with a smile. 'As you'll know if you ever have any.'

'Which I doubt.'

Lionel cleared his throat. 'That, I don't like to hear from

you, Alison. But on the subject of Clara, what upsets us most is what her boy's other grandparents have been deprived of.'

'One day, Percy will go and see them,' Alison wagered, 'even though his mother's forbidden him to. He'll take matters into his own hands.'

'Like you did, eh, Alison?' Lottie reminisced.

'And aren't we glad she did!' Lionel declared.

Alison got up to give them each a hug. 'I hope Percy finds the courage to do it. I wouldn't want him not to have the joy that knowing my father's family has given me.'

'It's nice that you feel that way, Alison. But now let's get back to discussing ambition.' Lionel looked sternly from his niece to his daughter. 'The only ambition I'm interested in you two having is to find yourselves a husband.'

Alison giggled. 'What? One between us?'

'A joke it isn't,' her uncle informed her.

Emma had flushed with embarrassment. 'Please don't go on about it, Dad.'

'If I don't tell you, who will?'

'When they're eating kippers isn't the time,' said Lottie. 'They could choke on a bone if you upset them.'

'I am not in the least upset,' Alison put in.

But Emma clearly was. 'If Alison wanted to be married, I'm sure she would be, by now,' she said stiffly to her father. 'As for me, like I've told you, I don't mind one way or the other.'

Lionel sighed. 'When did you ever? About anything?' Emma's placid nature was a pleasure to live with, he thought, but not an asset to herself. A plain young woman like her would not get a husband unless she made up her mind to do so – and possibly not even then. The only sure way was an arranged marriage; Lionel could provide a good dowry. But Emma had refused to hear of it.

For this, Lottie – who was a romantic – did not blame her daughter. Had the Steins lived in Manchester, there might have been more chance for Emma, Lottie thought now. There, Emma could have attended the Jews' School, and her childhood friendships with those of her own faith would have extended into her adult life. As it was, Emma had no Jewish friends, while the Christian girls with whom she had gone to school in Oldham were, by now, married. So, too, were the young men and women with whom Emma found herself seated at table when the Steins were invited to *Bar Mitzvah* and wedding receptions in Manchester. Time and opportunity had passed Emma by, and Lottie had watched her settle for spinsterhood.

But Lionel would not allow her to settle for it. 'What will you do when your mother and I are gone?' he demanded. 'Alison at least has her profession. But what will become of you, Emma?'

Emma got up and left the room.

It took Alison a moment or two to recover from the shock of her cousin's uncharacteristic exit. But she, too, felt the need to escape. 'If you'll excuse me, I'll go and join Emma.'

'Why not? The two of you are a good pair!' Lionel flung at her, as she headed for the door.

Alison found Emma in her bedroom, gazing through the window though there was nothing to see but fog.

'I'm sorry this happened while you're here, Alison,' Emma said. 'I didn't want you to know about it.'

Alison went to stand beside her. 'It isn't exactly news to me, Emma, that your parents would like you to be married.'

'That wasn't what I meant. Of course you know that. It's what all parents want, and expect, for their daughters. But I didn't want you to see Dad going on at me about it – which he does all the time.'

She sat down at the dressing table and studied her reflection in the mirror. 'I've always known I probably wouldn't get married, Alison. And I'm quite happy not being.'

'Are you?'

'Except for the motherhood part, it really doesn't matter to me. I would like to have children, but I've never met a man I'd want to father them.'

Alison smiled. 'Me neither, Emma. Which is another way of saying I have never really been in love.'

'But if you met the right man, Alison, he'd be sure to fall in love with you.' Emma avoided Alison's eye. 'Dad knows, as I do, that I'm not the kind men fall for – and when do I ever meet any single ones, anyway? So he wants to approach a matchmaker about me —'

'What!' Alison was outraged.

'It's me Dad's thinking of,' Emma said.

'Don't apologise for him! I never heard of anything more humiliating.'

'But Jews don't see it that way. Our Shrager grandparents' marriage was an arranged one, and Grandma once told me that her parents only met once before their wedding day – when they were introduced.'

'Good God!'

'Which doesn't mean I'd like that to happen to me.' Emma tucked a wisp of hair into her bun and secured it with a hairpin.

'Then don't let it, Emma.'

Emma looked troubled. 'But my being single is such a worry for my parents, isn't it, Alison? Dad probably lies awake at night, wondering who will take care of me in my old age.'

'You and I will take care of each other,' said Alison impulsively. 'In fact, we could start now, Emma,' she added.

'I beg your pardon, Alison?'

'I've just had a brilliant idea, darling! Come and sit beside me on the bed, like we did when we were kids, while we talk about it.'

'I mean, there am I living in London, by myself,' Alison said, when they had settled themselves with Emma's chintz eiderdown tucked warmly around them. 'And here are you, Emma, with nothing special to keep you in Oldham. So why not come and share my flat? To tell you the truth, darling, I was suddenly so desolate last night, I felt like jumping into the Thames.'

'But I always thought you had hundreds of friends.'

'Acquaintances is the right word for the place they occupy in my life. Except for Maxwell Morton, of course. I'd go so far as to say that he and you are my only real friends.'

Alison scanned her cousin's thoughtful expression. 'Well, Emma?'

'Well what?'

'I'd like an answer to my proposal.'

Emma laughed. 'It's the only kind I'm likely to get! And it sounds wonderful, Alison. But Mam and Dad would be broken-hearted if I left home.'

'If marriage were the reason,' Alison reminded her, 'they would be very happy for you. Even if your husband was from another town, and you had to go and live there.'

'That's different, Alison.'

'No, it isn't. You are entitled to your own life, married or not. That's what I am trying to make you see.'

'But if I came to London, how would I fit in with your life, Alison?' Emma smiled wryly. 'I mean – well, someone as dull as me?'

Alison got up to pace the room. 'It pains me to hear you say that, Emma.'

'It's what everyone thinks about me.'

'How can they not, when that is your opinion of yourself?'

Alison recalled all the sound advice about this and that she had received from Emma over the years, and the fun they had had together when they were girls.

'In fact, Emma,' she declared with feeling, 'you are a highly intelligent person, and capable of being amusing and witty – though I must say I've seen no evidence of that for some time.'

'And you'll arrive here one day and find me in the vegetable rack. I'll have turned into a cabbage,' was Emma's dry reply.

'If your father doesn't talk you into a loveless marriage first, which I fear he may.'

'So do I,' Emma admitted. 'He's wearing me down.'

'Then you must come with me when I leave tomorrow. She who hesitates is lost.'

Emma squared her shoulders. 'Don't worry, Alison. I'm coming. I've made up my mind.'

Alison's father had once told her he thought Emma was equipped with a quiet strength she herself did not yet know was in her. Alison was about to see it emerge.

Emma stood her ground against her parents' protestations. 'It has all been decided,' she told them. 'There's nothing to discuss.'

Lionel rose to poke the fire, needing to busy himself. 'Is this what you came for?' he flashed to Alison.

'No, Uncle.'

'I believe her,' Lottie said.

So, grudgingly, did Lionel. 'Then how did this notion arise?'

'From the things Alison heard you say to me, and my reaction to them,' Emma replied.

'And also from my personal need,' Alison added, feeling that nothing less than honesty was called for.

'And what might that be?' her uncle wanted to know.

'Alison doesn't have to explain herself to you,' Emma intervened. 'She's a grown woman, Dad. And so, may I remind you, am I.'

Lionel returned himself to his chair. 'Is this really our Emma talking?' he asked Lottie – who, like himself, appeared to be suffering from shock. 'All of a sudden she's learned how to speak up for herself? So how come?'

Emma answered his question. 'Perhaps because this is the first time there's ever been anything I really want to do, Dad. And I'm going to do it,' she said, exchanging a smile with Alison.

'I don't believe this is happening,' Lionel declared.

Nor did Lottie. But she had always regretted Emma's lack of spirit, and hoped that her daughter's sudden boldness would last. 'Let the girls give it a trial,' she said to Lionel. 'What is there to lose?'

And that was that.

Or so Alison thought, until Conrad arrived that afternoon. Emma and Alison were packing Emma's clothes when Conrad came into the room.

'Dad told me on the phone what's going on, but I could hardly imagine it was true,' Conrad said.

'Well, now you can see it is,' Emma smiled and added her nightdress case to the contents of a suitcase.

'Have you gone crackers, our Em?'

'No, I've come to my senses. You haven't said hello to Alison yet.'

'But he did give me a glare,' said Alison dryly. 'In lieu.'

'Is Zelda with you?' Emma inquired. 'Since Alison hasn't met your wife, this would be a good opportunity.'

'Zelda's got a sore throat and a temperature – or she certainly would have come with me as there's a family crisis!'

'Don't be melodramatic, Conrad,' Alison said. 'And, frankly, I'm disappointed in you.'

'Is that so?'

'I would have expected you to applaud what Emma has decided to do.'

'With a little help from you, Alison. Our Emma never decided anything on her own in her life.'

'Don't you think it's time she started to?'

'Sure. I always have.'

'Then what is all this fuss about?'

'The wisdom of the decision.'

Conrad toyed with his watch chain and leaned his tall frame against the door. 'You and I once promised we'd always be honest with each other, didn't we, Alison?'

'Yes, I believe we did.'

'We were only youngsters at the time. You came to Oldham on one of your impulsive, unheralded visits,' Conrad recalled.

'And found the family away, and you home on embarkation leave. I remember the occasion quite clearly,' Alison said. 'But what has this to do with Emma's coming to live with me, Conrad?'

'I'm hoping your promise to be honest with me still holds. Why do you want Emma with you, Alison?'

Again, Emma would not have Alison questioned. 'That's quite enough,' she told Conrad firmly. 'For me, it's a blessing that Alison does.' She gentled her voice. 'If it doesn't work out, Conrad love, I can come back.'

But she never will, Conrad thought, watching her carefully fold the selection of neat lace collars with which she enlivened her drab frocks. Emma would make it work out by bending to Alison's personality, as she had been doing with those around her for as long as Conrad could remember.

'We must buy you some new clothes when we get to London, Emma,' Alison said. 'From now on, you'll be mixing in fashionable circles.'

Conrad looked at his sister, who was very dear to him. Only her clear hazel eyes relieved her nondescript appearance. New clothes or not, Emma would fade into the woodwork in the ambience Alison's words had conjured up.

Conrad's glance moved to his cousin, who was more stunning each time he saw her. He was aware, too, of Alison's personal magnetism. There was about her a vibrancy few would be able to resist. Conrad was not surprised that Emma had been so easily lured.

He noted that Alison was not actually helping Emma pack, but approving, or discarding, the things Emma proposed taking to London. Which epitomised their friendship, Conrad reflected. Alison would always call the tune.

It was Conrad who had first dubbed Emma 'the sparrow', and the circumstances now vividly returned to him as he observed Emma and Alison together on the brink of a shared life.

Conrad and Emma had just seen Alison off at the railway station, after her first visit to Oldham.

'If Alison were a bird, she'd be a peacock,' Emma had declared.

'Don't you mean a peahen?' he had answered.

But he had agreed with the imagery, and had jokingly told his little sister which bird she would be.

Conrad now had cause to wonder how the sparrow would fare in the gilded cage into which she was about to fly.

'Don't look so worried, Conrad darling!' Alison said. 'Everything is going to be fine.'

Emma went to give her brother a hug. 'I can't tell you how much I'm looking forward to my new life.'

Conrad straightened his tie, ran a hand through his thinning brown hair, and managed to smile. 'I believe you, our Em.' At least it was a cage in which his sister wanted to be.

# CHAPTER THREE

MAXWELL MORTON lit his first cigar of the day and pressed the intercom switch.

'Get me Miss Plantaine, would you, Mollie?'

'Disturb her at 10 a.m., Mr Morton? Is that wise?'

'Probably not, but I want to check that she's all right. She never goes away for the weekend without letting me know, but there's been no reply when I've tried to call her.'

'All the same,' said Mollie, 'I'd leave it until later if I were you. I'd hate to be the one to wake her with a phone call if she's in bed asleep.'

'OK. You win!' Knowing Alison's temperament, it was sound advice.

Mollie's desk in the reception area faced an array of actresses' signed pictures. Some of them, she suspected, had on their way up shared her employer's bed. But there was one who definitely had not, and she silently applauded Alison Plantaine, whom talent alone had got where she now was.

It was no secret to Mollie that Alison could, if she wished, be Mrs Maxwell Morton. Mollie had been his secretary for twenty years, and before Alison's arrival on the scene had witnessed his infatuation with a succession of young women. But they had been brief interludes in Morton's busy life. Even while the infatuation lasted, he had not displayed the protectiveness he had, from the first, shown to Alison Plantaine.

It had begun when Alison left her family company to make her West End début in a Morton production. He had asked Mollie to find respectable lodgings for Alison, and to instruct the landlady to keep an eye on her.

It struck Mollie now that Morton himself had been doing

just that, ever since. Meanwhile, Miss Plantaine's absence was causing him to delay dealing with his correspondence. He usually asked Mollie to come in with her notepad long before now. She would be late getting home tonight, thanks to Miss Plantaine!

Morton was standing by his office window, watching a lone cab wend its way along Shaftesbury Avenue. Cabbies did not expect to find fares here at this time in the morning, when theatreland was quiet as the grave.

At night this part of London took on an atmosphere all its own, as Broadway did. Morton, who was just back from seeing its current offerings, recalled that Times Square, too, was deserted early in the day. There, as here, the theatre lights which in daytime looked like dead eyes, sprang to life and the pavements were thronged with those who came to enjoy the plays.

It was not unusual for Morton, hard-headed businessman though he was, to reflect on the pleasure that theatre brought to people's lives. This was to him as rewarding as the affluence that purveying theatre had brought him.

And his father before him, he thought. On the window through which he was gazing was printed MORTON THEATRICAL ENTERPRISES, but it was the late Henry Morton who founded the firm. On his death, it had passed to his son – and Maxwell had hoped to pass it to a son of his own.

This returned his mind full circle to Alison. He was still young enough to watch a son grow to manhood, and would not give up hope that Alison would change her mind and marry him, unless she married someone else.

Once, Morton had feared that he had irrevocably lost her. Just before her father's death, Alison had become involved with a costume designer. The boy – which was how Morton had thought of him – was tall and handsome, and Alison's age.

Morton could still recall the agonies of jealousy he had suffered during the few months the affair had lasted, and the self-denigration that comparing the boy's appearance with his own had evoked. Why should Alison be interested in a man with a broad torso and stumpy legs, when she can

28

have an Adonis? he had mentally flagellated himself. His leonine head and uneven features reflected in the bathroom mirror when he shaved had, at the time, seemed monstrous to him.

For that brief period, Morton, whose looks had never proved to be a disadvantage where women were concerned, had allowed himself to wallow in despair because of them.

Only when Alison's romance ended did he recover his equilibrium. She had returned to London after her father's funeral wanting to see nobody but Morton, as though the young designer had ceased to exist for her. It was then that Morton had recognised that he occupied a special place in Alison's personal life, as well as in her professional one. He was aware of her closeness to her relatives in Oldham, but in London he was the person to whom she turned.

He had since come to realise that she regarded him with genuine affection. But it was that of a young woman for a respected, older man and for Morton it was not enough.

He brushed this final thought aside. Until Alison said yes to him – and even if she never did – it would have to be enough.

By two-thirty that afternoon, his anxiety about her had mounted. He had cancelled a luncheon appointment, and Mollie had sent out for sandwiches for both of them. She had been calling Alison's number non-stop since eleven o'clock. There was still no reply.

Mollie entered his office with her shorthand pad and pencil. She smoothed her black wool skirt over her bulging hips and noted the unopened paper bag on Morton's desk. 'You haven't eaten a bite!'

'Kindly stop mothering me!' Morton retorted. 'You haven't done it in all the years you've worked for me, and I'd rather you didn't start now.'

'It hasn't been necessary till now. And we really can't leave it any later than this to deal with your mail, Mr Morton.'

'Can't you deal with it?'

'Certainly. I do when you're away.'

'Then consider me away now. And keep trying Miss Plantaine's number.'

An hour later, Mollie spoke to Morton on the intercom. 'I've got through. But whoever answered the phone won't let you speak to Miss Plantaine.'

Morton bristled. 'Indeed!' He was not accustomed to such peremptory treatment. 'I'll have a word with that person, Mollie.'

'Certainly. But I doubt that you'll get her to bring Miss Plantaine to the phone. She was very firm with me.'

'To whom am I speaking?' said Morton briskly, when Mollie put him through.

'I'm Alison's cousin. Emma Stein.'

'How do you do, Miss Stein. Now let me talk to Alison, would you?'

'I would rather not disturb her, Mr Morton.'

'I see.'

'Alison has been staying with my family, up north, over the weekend,' Emma told him. 'We've just arrived back and Alison was exhausted from the journey. I made her rest in bed before going to the theatre.'

Made her? thought Morton. He had never before met the person who could make Alison Plantaine do anything. Apparently he had now. He had gathered from Alison that her cousin Emma was a paragon of all the virtues, which had made her seem to him a young woman too sweet to be wholesome. Her gentle voice went with the image. He knew, too, that Alison had immense respect for Emma Stein, and sought her advice in personal matters – as she did Morton's.

'I believe you were away in America when I visited Alison two years ago,' Emma said pleasantly.

'Perhaps we shall meet on this occasion,' Morton replied.

'This time I am here to stay, Mr Morton. Alison has asked me to share her flat.'

'How very nice for both of you.' Something told Morton it might not be nice for him. Would he find himself relegated to the lesser role of solely professional adviser, now that Emma Stein had stepped from the wings to centre-stage? Not if he could help it!

Emma broke the moment of silence. 'Are you still there, Mr Morton?'

'Yes.' And I intend to remain so, thought Morton. 'I am as concerned for Alison's welfare as you are, Miss Stein,' he said, 'but that, you have yet to learn. Her career puts a great strain upon her, and I make it a rule not to telephone her too early in the mornings. Nobody knows better than I that Alison needs plenty of sleep. She seldom rests in the afternoons, as you'll find out, and it is merely to allow herself to relax, on the odd occasion when she does. I'm surprised she didn't pick up her bedside telephone when the bell rang.'

'I switched off the bell, Mr Morton, as I am now here to answer the phone.'

'Then kindly go and tell her I wish to speak to her.'

'Is it very important?'

'That isn't the point. She would want to talk to me if she knew I was on the line.'

'It's best not to disturb her, Mr Morton. I'll ask her to call you back later. Goodbye.'

Morton was left with the feeling that from now on, Emma Stein would always be telling him what was best for Alison, and that the ridiculous verbal wrangle that had just taken place was the beginning of a contest between them. In which Emma had won the first round.


Emma had experienced no sense of triumph when she replaced the receiver. Asserting herself was not in her nature, and she would not have thought herself capable of the firmness she had just displayed. Nor of the strength she had mustered to deal with her father's objections to her coming to London, she reflected.

But now she was here, she would watch over Alison – even if being firm with people was a necessary part of it. Alison was the kind who gave her all to everything she did. Emma would try to make sure she didn't burn herself out; do her best to protect Alison from some of the strains Mr Morton had mentioned – which included disturbing her rest with phone calls from himself.

Emma removed a wilted leaf from the ivy that stood beside the telephone and gazed disconsolately at the black and white tiles that gave the hall floor a chequerboard appearance. She had offended Mr Morton; of that there was no doubt. He probably thought her a bossy-breeches. But when he got to know her, everything would be all right.

# CHAPTER FOUR

SEVERAL MONTHS had sped by since Emma's move to London. The trees in Hyde Park, at which she loved to gaze through the drawing-room window, had lost the winter-weary appearance with which they had greeted her, and were joyfully heralding spring.

In the interim, Alison's cheerless apartment had undergone a transformation. As Alison's gift was acting, Emma's was homemaking.

She had begun by rearranging the furniture, dispelling the formal atmosphere. The sofa and armchairs were now grouped around the hearth, instead of lining the walls as they previously had. The piano had been brought from its lonely corner to fill the empty space.

To Alison, the drawing room now looked half its size and much less grand, but she liked the cosiness Emma had managed to contrive.

Alison had not bothered furnishing the dining room. It had seemed pointless to do so. She could not cook, and inviting people for drinks was as far as her entertaining went. But allowing guests to leave without feeding them was not Emma's way. She had asked her mother to send to her and Alison their late grandparents' dining furniture which was stored in the Steins' attic. Now, the carved mahogany pieces were put to good use; the occasional Sunday lunch at Alison's was something to which her acquaintances looked forward.

Lottie had also sent them some smaller items from their grandparents' house. It had been willed to Conrad, who was living in it, but his wife had not wanted the furniture and bric-à-brac.

'Mam was keeping these things to give me when I got

married,' Emma had told Alison, when they opened the packing case. 'It looks as if she's given up hope!'

'Where on earth are we going to put them all?' Alison had exclaimed.

But Emma had found a place for everything.

The twisted brass candlesticks, in which their grandmother had lit her Sabbath candles, looked perfect on the dining table. Her bunch of purple wax grapes and a small copper jug enhanced the sideboard. Above it, Emma had hung some framed flower prints, which had come from their grandfather's bedroom. In his declining years he had developed a passion for flowers, and had died while watering some geraniums. Two Victorian doorstops, orbs of glass with floral centres, were now serving on the writing desk as paperweights – and to remind Alison and Emma that their grandma had used them to prop open the doors of her dining room and parlour, to air the rarely used rooms. In the kitchen, where they ate their meals *à deux*, some blue and white china from their grandparents' hall plate-rack was displayed on a shelf beside Emma's saucepans and cookpots.

Thus it was that Alison and Emma began their homelife with mementoes of their mutual forebears all around them, which provided a shared stability it might otherwise have taken them years to achieve. For Alison, it was as though the straw on the wind to which she had likened herself in her unsettled childhood and youth had finally come to rest. At last she had a real home, and with it the sense of place she had hitherto lacked.

'Your coming to live here is the best thing that's ever happened to me,' she said to Emma one morning.

'To me, too, Alison.'

Emma was watching Alison put the finishing touches to her make-up before going out to lunch. Initially, she had participated in the social round Alison's career demanded. But little by little she had withdrawn into a routine of her own.

By now they had established a pattern that suited both. Alison came and went. Emma occupied herself with

34

housekeeping. Twice a week, she shopped for food, and occasionally went for a short stroll in the park, but was always there when Alison returned.

'Your stocking seams are crooked,' Emma noted when Alison took off her kimono to step into the skirt of a pale grey suit.

Alison straightened them. 'How did I manage without you?'

'That's what I keep wondering.' Emma hung up the kimono and handed Alison the white silk blouse she had just ironed for her.

What a comforting little person she is, Alison thought, standing over me in her gingham apron like a mother hen. 'Don't worry, I didn't forget to put my knickers on, Emma!' she joked.

'I should hope not!'

Emma watched Alison button her jacket, and suggested that she wear a scarf.

'As I go everywhere by cab, Emma darling, I am unlikely to catch cold.'

A mother hen was right, thought Alison with a smile. Taking care of people was Emma's natural role. She had always been this way with Alison, and Alison had grown accustomed to it, as she had, in their girlhood, to Emma standing contentedly by while Alison had all the fun.

'Isn't it today you're lunching with your stepcousins?' Emma said.

Alison nodded and grimaced. Seeing Luke and Lucy would be the opposite of fun. 'The terrible twins!'

'Why do you call them that?'

Alison put on her hat and tilted the brim to a fetching angle. 'Because that's what they are.'

'I thought they were nice, when we ran into them that afternoon.'

'Thinking people are nice is your speciality, Emma darling. Even when they're not. Come on, you can walk me to the lift. It will be an outing for you!'

Alison had arranged a fitting for some new evening dresses that afternoon, but had not bothered asking Emma

35

to accompany her, or to meet her for tea, later. She knew what Emma's answer would be.

'What time will you be back?' Emma asked. 'Will you be eating at home tonight, Alison?'

Alison was at present between plays and was taking the opportunity to do some theatre-going. Emma was not interested in going with her; her sole interest in theatre was Alison's being an actress.

Emma had seen only two plays since coming to London. Alison had prised her from the fireside to see the final performance of *St Joan*. The other occasion was when Morton took them both to see the new Noël Coward play, Alison now recalled.

Morton, who liked to keep abreast of the international theatre scene, was just back from seeing what the *Comédie-Française* was currently offering.

'I promised to see Maxwell this evening,' Alison replied to Emma. 'It seems that while he was away, a new play landed on his desk, which he thinks may be right for me. I was thinking of inviting him to eat with us.'

'We have plenty of food,' Emma said.

Alison had just stepped into the lift, and paused with her hand on the gate. 'I won't if you'd rather not, darling.'

Emma bent down to stroke the cat, which had followed them out of the apartment. 'I don't mind, Alison.'

But Alison knew that she did, and that Morton would accept the invitation reluctantly. The manner in which they had reacted to each other was a source of distress to Alison. A puzzle, too.

Morton was adept at putting people at their ease, but had not tried to do so with Emma. Nor did he seem able to relax in her presence. For some reason, he was brusque and formal with her. Alison had never known him be that way with anyone else.

Just as inexplicable was Emma's strained demeanour with Morton. Though his manner towards her could not be described as likeable, Emma had always made allowances for what others would not. It was a family joke that there was nobody whom Emma could not manage to like.

36

And that included Luke and Lucy Plantaine, thought Alison, in the taxi taking her to the Ritz where she was to meet them. Only Emma would have ignored their overt condescension, when Alison introduced her to them. That chance encounter with her stepcousins had occurred some months ago, in December, but Alison still burned on Emma's behalf, remembering it.

Alison and Emma had gone to Harrods food department to buy a Christmas pudding. The twins were treating themselves to some sweetmeats, and had made snide jokes about Emma's never having heard of *marrons glacés*. Also about her north-country pronunciation of the word 'pudding', Alison recalled. But they had always enjoyed ridiculing those whom they considered fair game. Initially, they had tried it with Alison, but had quickly realised their mistake.

Alison glanced through the taxi window at the cosmopolitan elegance of Park Lane, which familiarity had allowed her to take for granted. How long ago it seemed since she lived in a little seaside town, under the same roof as the twins.

They had entered Alison's life when her Uncle Oliver Plantaine married their widowed mother. Alison was then fourteen, a lonesome, only child, and had hoped that she and her stepcousins would be friends. It had not taken her long to learn that the twins were friends to nobody but each other.

As the Plantaines not only worked side by side but lodged together, Alison had seen a good deal more of Luke and Lucy than she cared to. She would have preferred, after leaving the company, never to see them again.

Inevitably, their paths had crossed. The twins had left for London shortly after Alison did, and from time to time she had run into them at the Ivy, or in some other rendezvous which theatre people frequented to see and be seen.

And they are never less than charming to me, Alison recalled now, with a grim smile. Charm was the veneer beneath which they hid their envy of Alison's success. She would not have agreed to lunch with them, had Luke not said on the telephone that there was an urgent family matter they must discuss with her.

Family, my foot! Alison thought as she entered the hotel dining room and saw them awaiting her. They had chosen, for the sake of their careers, to adopt their stepfather's distinguished thespian name. They didn't care a fig for the Plantaines.

Luke rose to greet her with a kiss. 'My dearest Alison, how very entrancing you look.'

Alison gave him an actressy smile. 'How kind of you to say so.'

'I was about to say the same,' Lucy gushed, as she and Alison touched cheeks.

They're the same cunning double-act they always were, thought Alison. What do they want of me? she wondered while Luke was ordering the meal.

While they ate their smoked salmon, she pondered, too, on how Luke could afford to pay for it. He had not had a part in a West End play for some time. Nor had Lucy, come to that. Both had recently done a stint as guest-players with the Plantaines in Hastings, Alison remembered reading in *The Stage*, but they would not have done so had anything better been available.

Alison picked at her food and studied them surreptitiously. In their youth, they had looked like a pair of sea-sprites – as her Uncle Oliver, who adored them, had been fond of saying. Both were slight, with tawny hair and arresting green eyes. Viewed from afar, they could still be taken for the sixteen-year-olds they were when Alison first met them. At close quarters, they looked older than their thirty-two years.

There was now a jaded air about them which Alison, much as she disliked them, found pathetic. But she was not in the least surprised. When all three were still with the Plantaine Players, the twins had been the centre of a wild young set. Alison did not doubt that they had led the same kind of life in the capital during the frenetic Twenties. She would not have put it past them to have indulged in sniffing cocaine, which was considered by their kind the fashionable thing to do.

The main course was served and eaten without the twins

having told Alison what they wished to discuss. But direct-ness was not their style. On the contrary: deviousness was second nature to them, Alison thought.

'Shall we come to the point of this meeting?' she said crisply.

'By all means,' Luke answered. 'It was good of you to spare us the time, Alison darling.'

'We really appreciate your coming,' Lucy said.

Alison paused while their plates were removed, some crumbs brushed from the table, and the order taken for Luke and Lucy's dessert.

'Are you sure you won't have something, Alison?' Luke asked solicitously.

'Quite sure, thank you.'

'Well, if you're certain. But we wanted to give our illus-trious relative a good lunch.'

'Kindly stop buttering me up! Now what did you want to talk to me about?'

The twins exchanged a glance.

'Uncle Oliver's health hasn't worsened, has it?' Alison said as that possibility occurred to her. Their stepfather had a heart condition, and Alison was very fond of him.

Luke set her mind at rest. 'Heavens no! The dear man couldn't be better.' He smiled ruefully. 'Which is more than can be said for our financial position. Right, Lucy?'

'Only too right, Luke.'

Were they going to ask her for a handout? It would not surprise Alison if they had, by now, milked their mother dry.

Luke toyed with his watch chain. 'Did you know that our late father had set up a trust fund for us, Alison?'

'No.'

'We thought you might have learned about it via the family grapevine. He did it when we were born — '

'And being the kill-joy he was, arranged that we shouldn't receive the money until we're thirty-five,' Lucy chipped in, with a frosty smile. 'Luke and I are not likely to forget the kind of childhood we had, thanks to him. Luke sent away to school, and me having to live in his big, dingy house in

39

Epping – with an old crone housekeeper spying on me the time.'

'Lucy and I only saw each other when I went home f school holidays,' Luke told Alison. 'And as Mother was always away touring, we rarely saw her. It was as if Father had made up his mind to protect us from Mother's influence.'

Alison could well believe this. The late William Appleby had been well into his sixties when he married the flamboyant young actress Ruby May. Alison had no doubt that Ruby had married him for his money, or that Appleby had spent the rest of his life regretting his folly. Ruby was a woman who exuded sex and knew it. Her scandalous reputation had not receded until she became Mrs Oliver Plantaine.

But Alison had not known until now that the twins had hated their father, and wondered if that perhaps accounted for them being the twisted people she knew they were. Nobody is born bad, her Jewish grandmother had once said to her; something has to have made them that way.

'However,' Luke cut into her cogitation, 'the trustees are empowered to release a substantial sum to us in advance, at their discretion. Which boils down to them having to approve of what we wish to do with it. Mother is one of the trustees and the other is Father's solicitor.'

'Who, needless to say, Mother has eating out of her hand,' said Lucy. 'They have flatly refused to let us have the cash we've asked for, so we must wait three years before we can get our hands on a penny.'

'I see,' Alison said warily.

Luke gave her his boyish smile. 'As you well know, Alison, that's a long time in the theatre. We need cash now, to back a West End play. Directed by me, of course, with Lucy in the cast.'

Luke had tried his hand at directing with the family company years ago, and Alison had recognised then that he had both talent and flair. But what he and Lucy proposed to do was foolhardy to say the least, she thought.

'Mother's hoping that by the time we do get our money,

40

we'll have changed our minds about staking it in a production,' Lucy told Alison.

'Of course she is. She knows the risk you would be taking. If the play flopped, you'd lose your shirts – and part of your inheritance. I can quite understand Aunt Ruby's refusal to let you take that risk.'

'But it wouldn't flop if you starred in it, Alison,' Luke said.

'Everything you do is a sure-fire box-office success,' Lucy declared. 'Mother would change her tune if you agreed to do the play.'

Alison was stunned by the twins' audacity, and by the depths of their scheming. They were even more wily than she had supposed.

'We happen to know that you haven't lined up your next play yet,' Luke said.

'You've certainly done your homework.'

'An impresario has to, and that's what I aim to become. I've found the perfect vehicle for you, Alison.'

Alison fixed her gaze upon a lady in a red hat at the next table. She could not bear to look at the twins. 'Oh yes?'

'It's by a new dramatist – of the Coward genre.'

Trying to emulate the inimitable was, in Alison's view, the road to failure. Though he had emerged as a playwright less than ten years ago, Coward had – as Luke's words confirmed – already established his own genre. He would live on in the theatre long after his imitators had faded from the scene, Alison wagered.

Luke was encouraged by her thoughtful expression. 'The play is a three-hander, darling. Two women and a man. I'd take the male role, to keep down our expenses.'

'And I would be happy to play the supporting female role – with you starring, Alison, like we said,' Lucy sweetly added.

Even though it would kill you to play second fiddle to me, thought Alison. But Lucy would do it, to give her ambitious brother his break.

'So you see, Alison darling, it would be a Plantaine

cast,' Luke enthused. 'Just like the old days at Hastings. Remember?'

Alison was unlikely to forget her experience of working with Luke and Lucy. She recalled, among other things, their habit of deliberately upstaging her so that they, not she, faced the audience. Actors and actresses sometimes did this, to enhance their own performances, but Alison had sensed vindictiveness in the twins' consistently upstaging her.

'Well, darling?' Luke prodded her with a friendly smile.

'For me there are just two things to be considered in this matter,' she said evenly. 'One is that I work exclusively for Maxwell Morton — '

'That's common knowledge, my love,' Luke cut in, 'but surely he would release you for just this one production? And we wouldn't expect you to stay for the run of the play; just long enough to get us rolling.'

At which point, thought Alison, Lucy would step into the star role – and when advance bookings stretched way ahead. Cunning wasn't the word for it! But all this was hypothetical.

'Mr Morton would certainly release me,' she said. 'If I asked him to. But you interrupted me, Luke, before I had reached the second consideration. Why should I do this for you?'

'Because we are Plantaines, darling. That's why we said it was a family matter.'

'Stuff and nonsense!' Alison exclaimed. 'You bear the name solely because you chose to.'

'So did your father,' Luke reminded her. 'He was born Horace Shrager, wasn't he?'

Alison's cheeks flamed. 'Kindly do not compare yourselves with a man whose honour was unquestionable.'

'And what is that supposed to mean?' Lucy inquired sharply.

'Exactly what it implies.'

Luke cautioned his sister with a glance. 'If I said something that upset you, I'm sorry,' he assured Alison.

Lucy took her cue from him. 'The last thing we want to do is upset you, darling. We are very fond of you.'

42

Uggh! thought Alison. Lucy's expression of affection was as genuine as the fake pearls around her neck.

'I am not in the least upset,' Alison said calmly.

But her dark eyes reflected her anger. How dare this pair of arch-plotters prey upon her family feeling to get her here, then involve her – in public – in a scene like this!

Because she was Alison Plantaine, she was the focus of attention wherever she went. Even the sophisticates who lunched at the Ritz were affected by her presence. People had been eyeing her throughout the meal. Though Luke and Lucy were less successful than Alison, they too were familiar faces to the public. Their cool, blond looks were a perfect foil for Alison's brunette colouring. And those beholding us are doubtless thinking what an attractive picture the Plantaine cousins make, and that we're having a friendly get-together, Alison dryly surmised.

And so it must continue to appear. Had this meeting taken place in private, Alison – the way she felt now – might have banged the twins' scheming heads together.

Her Uncle Oliver had once said, jokingly, that Luke and Lucy had contrived to introduce him to their mother. Alison could now believe it was true. That ploy had gained them entrance to the Plantaine Players, and launched them on the stage career both had passionately desired.

She eyed the twins' studiedly innocent expressions. If she didn't get out of their company fast, she was going to be sick!

Luke broke the silence. 'You've had a few minutes to think things over, darling. What have you to say?'

Alison put a pleasant expression on her face, for the benefit of those who were watching her. The reply she gave to Luke was anything but. 'Only that you and your sister are a couple of slimy toads.'

Lucy bit back a sharp retort. Luke had kicked her ankle when she opened her mouth to utter.

He gave Alison a rueful smile. 'Aren't you being a little too dramatic, my love? Didn't you tell us you weren't in the least upset by what I said?'

'You and Lucy don't have the power to upset me, Luke.

43

Only to disgust me. I thought I had seen the full range of your machinations when we were young. Evidently I hadn't.'

'Machinations?' Luke addressed his sister. 'What on earth is dear Alison talking about?'

'Come, come,' said Alison. 'I'm your beloved cousin, who's known you a long time – remember? And isn't it just like you to try to brazen things out!'

The twins were momentarily reduced to silence. Lucy sat fingering the artificial camellia adorning her baby-blue hat. Luke carefully smoothed his mane of hair.

'Did you really hope to manipulate me into saying yes to your proposition?' Alison asked them.

Luke shrugged in the manner of a man who has gambled and lost. 'It was worth a try.'

'And you two would try anything, wouldn't you?' said Alison with contempt. 'Also stop at nothing, to get where you want to be. If you were true Plantaines, you'd rely on your artistry, as I did.'

Lucy turned nasty. 'Do you expect us to believe that sleeping with Maxwell Morton didn't get you where you are?'

'You may believe what you wish, Lucy; artistic integrity is a quality you know nothing about. And if the pinnacle of our profession can be reached by performing in the right bedrooms, you should surely be a great star by now.'

Alison pulled on her gloves and rose from the table.

Luke, whose manners were usually impeccable, did not bother to rise. 'So be it, Alison,' he said quietly. 'We are unlikely to forget that you refused to help us.'

Lucy echoed his ominous tone. 'And the day may come when the boot is on the other foot.'

'I doubt it. And meanwhile, thank you for lunch.'

Alison made a dignified exit, taking with her a mental picture of two pairs of narrowed green eyes, which was still with her when she emerged on to Piccadilly. So, too, was the feeling that if looks could kill she would now be dead.

It was not yet time for her dress fitting. Perhaps some fresh air would help her recover from the distasteful encounter. Mingling with the distaste was regret that friendship between herself and her stepcousins was prohibited by them being the kind they were. Had that not been so, Alison would happily have lent them a helping hand.

There was no doubt about who had come off best. She had seen Luke and Lucy grovel because they wanted something from her, and had finally dashed their hopes to the ground. She drew no pleasure from it. Malice was their speciality, not hers. And, as Luke had said, they would not forget. Somehow, they would find a way to hit back at her, even if it took them years to do it.

Think about something else, she ordered herself, entering Green Park which lay like a peaceful oasis amid the West End's thronged thoroughfares. But the matter that came immediately to her mind was no more cheering. How was she to cope with the strained situation between Maxwell Morton and Emma?

# CHAPTER FIVE

ALISON HAD gone ahead with her plan to invite Morton to dinner. The meal Emma served was, as always, delicious. But the atmosphere in the dining room! It's a toss-up as to which of them is displaying the stiffest smile, Alison thought: Emma, who was seated opposite her, or Morton, who looked like a captive placed strategically between them.

Alison swallowed down her food and chattered on about this and that, which she found easier than breaking the silences that kept gathering. She was aware of Morton watching Emma from beneath his hooded eyelids, and of Emma pretending not to be conscious of it.

It had not occurred to Alison that Morton was jealous of Emma, or that Emma's coolness to him stemmed from his treatment of her. Alison's egocentricity allowed her to see no further than the effects of their behaviour upon herself. Sooner or later, they must warm to each other – nothing else was conceivable, as they were the two people closest to her.

Morton's resentment had continued to prevent this. He could not have remained unaware of Emma's many fine qualities, or that she was good for Alison and a stabilising influence in her life. Yet he could not bring himself to unbend with Emma.

Emma had not lost her aptitude for adapting to vicissitudes major and minor, but in this instance she had done so with a heavy heart. She had concluded that Morton was not going to give her a second chance; that she had cooked her goose with him on the telephone, and that was that.

Only for Alison would she have endured the torture of Morton's presence. He was the one blot on her new horizon.

46

Inexplicably, she was fascinated by him, too. She could feel the power of his personality now, as if it were a magnet drawing her towards him, and could not drag her gaze from his tapering hands which were the only beautiful thing about him.

She made herself do so and went to the kitchen to fetch the dessert. When she returned, Morton was laughing at something Alison had said. His laughter petered out when Emma rejoined them at the table.

Emma served the pudding in silence and saw that Alison's expression had darkened. It was as though an electric storm was brewing, Emma thought.

'Would you mind passing the sugar, Miss Stein?' Morton said brusquely.

'I'm sorry my apple charlotte isn't to your taste, Mr Morton.'

A moment later the storm broke. Morton had picked up the sugar bowl from where Emma had placed it. Alison dashed it from his hand.

'How dare you, Maxwell!' she exploded.

'How dare I what?' he asked when he found his voice.

'You ought not to require telling! When a lady cooks you a meal, and apologises for something not being to your taste, the least you can do is refrain from allowing the apology to appear necessary. To anyone but Emma, you would have been gracious enough to explain that you have an overly sweet tooth!'

Morton sat staring down at the upturned sugar bowl, which had toppled to the floor.

'Leave it where it is!' said Alison when Emma bent to retrieve it. 'He made me knock it out of his hand, so he can pick it up.'

'Don't be silly,' Emma protested.

Alison snatched the bowl from her and returned it to the floor.

Emma was assailed by a feeling of unreality. People did not behave this way in her world – and she had never seen Alison do so before. It struck her now that there was a side of Alison she did not know. Over the years, Emma had seen in her flashes of the temperament expected of actresses – but this?

Morton's expression was akin to that of a whipped dog. There was no other way to describe it.

'I am waiting for you to pick up the bowl and deal with the spilled sugar,' Alison said to him curtly.

To Emma's astonishment, Morton got down on his knees and did so. She felt her cheeks flush with shame on his behalf. She could not bear to see this powerful man reduced to servility. She wanted to run from the room, but was rooted to the spot. What was Alison thinking of, inflicting such humiliation on Morton? And why was he subjecting himself to it?

The answer to the first question was that Alison had not paused to think – she rarely did, Emma reflected with the part of her mind that was not frozen with shock. And the second question? If you loved Alison – and people either loved her or loathed her – you were putty in her hands. Emma had been since they were young girls but she had not known, until now, that Morton was.

She could hear the clink of the spoon, as he scooped the sugar from the floor into the bowl. There was no other sound in the room. It was a scene she would not forget: Alison in a flame-coloured evening gown, her hair gleaming like black satin in the lamplight, standing imperiously beside Morton's abject figure. And as though she were outside of it, looking in, Emma saw herself in the position she had always occupied. An insignificant brown-clad person merging into the background.

'Thank you, Maxwell,' Alison said when Morton got to his feet. 'Now that's over, I'll go and make us some coffee.' She was already regretting her outburst, and the way she had degraded him.

'I'll make the coffee,' Emma said stiffly.

'No. You can stay here with Maxwell. I need to be alone for a few minutes. Between you, you've been making me thoroughly miserable. Why do you suppose I let fly like that?'

This was the nearest thing to an apology that Alison

could bring herself to make. And it would have to do, she thought as she left the room.

Morton sat down at the table and peeled a pear, so he need not look at Emma. What must she think of him for not standing up to Alison? He forced himself to say something. 'Does Alison know how to make coffee?'

Emma managed to smile. 'I doubt it. She never remembers to warm the pot when she makes tea.'

'She isn't in the habit of volunteering to make either.'

'Which is probably as well,' said Emma, 'as both coffee and tea need to be carefully made. But why are we talking about coffee and tea, Mr Morton?'

'What would you like to talk about, Miss Stein?'

'The matter that's occupying both our minds: the way Alison behaved just now. It might be over for Alison, whose temperament is like the weather, but I haven't yet recovered from it. And I'm sure you haven't.'

'I'm sorry you had to be present to witness my embarrassment, Miss Stein. And if you wouldn't mind, I'd rather not discuss it.'

'What is the point of us not discussing it, Mr Morton? I was present. And I don't believe in brushing things under the rug.'

'Especially not sugar,' said Morton dryly. 'For my part,' he added, 'I have always found it easier to humour Alison than to argue with her.'

'Me too. But I don't think we should go on doing so. What Alison needs is a good spanking!'

'But nobody is ever going to give her one, are they?' Morton answered ruefully. 'Least of all you or I.'

The first glance of rapport they had ever exchanged now passed between them. Then Morton returned his attention to his pear.

'I can understand how we've been making her miserable,' said Emma carefully. 'She wanted us to like each other.'

Morton quartered the pear. 'With the benefit of hindsight, Miss Stein, I can't blame you for not liking me.'

'You didn't give me a chance to. And to tell you the truth, I've dreaded your coming here, Mr Morton.'

'No more than I have resented your being here, Miss Stein.'

Emma surveyed him thoughtfully. 'I've made you feel pushed out, haven't I?' she said gently.

'How very perceptive you are.'

They fell silent and Morton stared at the fruit bowl. Was this sympathetic little person the same woman who had got his back up, on the telephone?

'I want to marry Alison,' he found himself telling her, 'but she won't have me.'

'Maybe she will one day.'

'No,' Morton declared with conviction. 'I had hoped that she would eventually. Even famous actresses need someone by their side when they're old and grey,' he added with a smile. 'Though I hadn't reckoned on Alison keeping me waiting quite that long. But now she has you to keep her company, I don't think she will ever marry.'

'I doubt that the man exists who could take precedence in Alison's life over her career,' Emma said.

'Then you know her as well as I do,' Morton replied. 'What you just said has been plain to me since I first met Alison. In effect, she is wedded to her career and always will be. And the intensity of her emotional involvement with her dramatic roles sometimes causes me to fear for her.'

Morton gazed unseeingly at the tablecloth. 'She doesn't just play them, Emma. She lives them. Alison feels every pang and pain decreed for the character she is portraying – and makes the audience feel them, too. That's what makes her a great actress.'

'You called me Emma.'

'So I did. But it's time we dropped the formality, isn't it?'

'It'll be a relief to do so. Up north, we don't know from formality. You're the only person who's ever addressed me as Miss Stein. Do you ever get called Max, for short?'

'My mother called me Max.'

'Would you mind if I did? Maxwell is such a mouthful.'

'Not at all. If you wish. Nobody has since my mother died.' Morton's eyes shadowed with memory. 'That was a long time ago, and it seems like another life,' he said, collecting himself. 'When I was a youngster, in Canada.'

'Alison told me you were born there.'

'It was my mother's death that brought my father and me to England. Father was a one-woman man – like me,' said Morton with a wry smile. 'He sold his timber business and came here to try to recover from losing the wife he adored. But he never really did. Why am I telling you all this, Emma?'

'People always tell me things.'

Morton surveyed her kindly expression. 'I can understand why.'

'I thought your father was an impresario, like you,' Emma said.

'Timber was how he got the money to become one. I come from a long line of lumberjacks,' Morton said whimsically. 'Which probably accounts for my broad shoulders.'

'A person needs them, to cope with our dear Alison.'

'Too true!' Morton eyed Emma's tiny frame. 'It's a good thing that, metaphorically speaking, you are not lacking in strength yourself.'

Emma fingered the cameo brooch pinned to her collar. 'I used to think I did lack strength. It's only recently that I've found I can make myself do whatever has to be done.'

'Including being bossy on the phone with frosty gentlemen!'

Emma returned his smile. 'If it's in Alison's interests, yes. If you and I, who care deeply for her, don't watch over her, who will, Max? You said there are times when you fear for her. So do I, and not just because her work takes so much out of her. Her impulsiveness scares me stiff.'

'Me too,' Morton replied. 'I once arrived back from America in the nick of time to stop her from adopting a child,' he recalled.

'Alison loves children.'

'But she is in no position to look after one, is she? And could you imagine her doing so? She'd have to employ a nanny.'

'No, she wouldn't. She's got me.'

'Let's not waste our breath on hypothesis, Emma! I am fond of children myself – I'd hoped to have a son. But I'm also a realist, which Alison very definitely is not. So she hears about this little kid, whose parents had perished in a fire, and makes up her mind there and then to adopt it.'

'Were there no other relatives?' Emma asked.

'Only an elderly grandfather. He was the stagedoor-keeper at the theatre where Alison happened to be playing. That's how she heard of the tragedy.'

'I'd have felt like giving that child a home,' said Emma.

'But you'd have slept on it and made a sensible decision. Alison, on the other hand — '

'You don't have to say any more,' Emma cut in.

'I wouldn't have mentioned it at all, had we not been discussing Alison's impulsiveness.'

Emma went to gaze through the window at the trees silhouetted against the night sky. 'Another example of it is the way Alison decided on the spur of the moment to invite me to live with her. And I have to confess that I didn't bother to sleep on that. I allowed Alison to sweep me along.

'It's turned out to be good for both Alison and me. But that isn't the point. The point is that I mustn't let Alison sweep me along on her waves of excitement, like she has done since we were girls. You and I are going to have to be a pair of wet blankets, Max.'

'I'll drink to that.'

Alison's arrival with the coffee put an end to their conversation.

She set the tray on the table and gave them a happy smile. 'I expected to find you in opposite corners of the room, glaring at each other. But you seem to have broken the ice at last. Have you been talking about me behind my back?'

'If we have, it is what you deserve,' said Morton with mock severity.

'But I didn't deserve my two dearest people to be chilling to each other, did I?'

They told her in unison: 'We're sorry about that.'

'From strife to solidarity in one fell swoop!' Alison exclaimed. 'I shall have to watch out.'

Emma lifted the lid off the coffee pot and peered at the contents. 'As we expected, Max. The grounds are afloat on top.'

Alison giggled. 'Max, eh? That's going a bit far, isn't it, Emma dear? Is he going to call you "our Em", like your brother does?'

'He'd better not!'

'I adore her,' Alison told Morton when Emma had departed to make some drinkable coffee. 'That's why I want you to.'

'My darling girl,' he said emotionally, 'there is only one person I shall ever adore. But I am now prepared to admit that "our Em" is a very good sort.'

Later, they drank the coffee in the drawing room, seated beside the hearth. Emma had brought her knitting and sat busily clicking her needles, while Morton told Alison about the play he had found for her.

'How does the play strike you, Emma?' he asked when he had outlined the story and Alison began glancing through the manuscript.

'On plays I'm not an expert, Max. Recipes are more in my line.'

Seeing them so relaxed together was to Alison as though someone had waved a magic wand. She could not have been more content than she was that night. The cosy three-some she had envisaged had come to pass.

In truth, it was nothing of the kind, but the beginning of a precarious, three-cornered relationship, and Alison its sole *raison d'être*.

# CHAPTER SIX

EMMA WAS peeling vegetables when the doorbell rang. She rinsed her hands and picked up her purse; it was probably the milkman, who called for his money on Fridays.

She opened the door and gaped.

'Aren't you going to invite me in, Emma?'

'Of course. But what are you doing here, Clara?'

'Visiting my sister.'

'Take off your coat and come into the kitchen.'

'Is the living room reserved for Alison's friends?'

'I was busy at the sink when you rang the bell — '

'Well, you would be, wouldn't you?'

'I think I left the tap running,' Emma went on, ignoring Clara's second snide remark within the space of a minute. 'And,' she added, 'I don't usually go and sit in the best room with my pinafore on.'

Clara patted her blonde Marcel waves, after removing her model hat. 'When haven't you got a pinafore on!'

Her unexpected intrusion into Emma's new life was a bleak reminder of the one she had left behind her, but Emma managed to smile. 'And I can't recall ever seeing you wearing one.'

'Alison either, I bet. And I don't think it's right, Emma, that you're doing for her what you should be doing for Mam,' Clara said, watching Emma head toward the kitchen. 'That's what I've come to tell you,' she declared, following her. 'And a few other things, too.'

'I don't doubt it. But you're wasting your breath, Clara.'

'That's what our Conrad said your answer would be. But I decided to have my say anyway – as I wasn't there to speak my mind before you upped and left home. Is Bond Street far from here, by the way?' Clara asked irrelevantly.

Emma laughed.

'What's so funny?'

'Trust you to combine your mission of mercy with a shopping spree.'

'You might not be sorry for your deserted parents, Emma, but everyone else is. And if you'd seen our Conrad's wife rushing up and downstairs looking after Mam when she had 'flu, and having to run her own house as well, you wouldn't have thought that was funny!'

Emma cleared the vegetable peelings from the sink and dumped them in the rubbish bin. 'Then why did you let her do it?'

'She offered to. Zelda's a very kind-hearted girl.'

'There's no need to tell me that.'

'She takes her family responsibilities seriously, Emma, and I used to think you did.'

'Yours are exactly the same as mine, Clara. And you live a good deal nearer to our parents than I now do. They haven't stopped running trains between Manchester and Oldham, and it isn't a long journey. You could have gone to Mam's every day to look after her – if you'd wanted to.'

Clara looked outraged. 'Why should I have to? When I've got an unmarried sister – who didn't have to leave home?'

They looked at each other across the chasm that had, over the years, widened between them. They had never been close – but nor had they, until now, exchanged cold words. Because I didn't argue with Clara, Emma thought. Nothing had seemed important enough – but this was.

'You had no right, Emma, to desert Mam and Dad in their old age,' Clara declaimed.

Emma tried to control her anger. 'They're not that old.'

'But that won't always be the case, will it? And what will happen then?' Clara smoothed the skirt of her chic black frock and fingered the diamond brooch her husband had given her when their little daughter was born. She watched Emma fill the kettle, to make some tea. 'When Mam needed nursing, it made me think about the future. And you and I must get things settled between us now, Emma. As you're single, it will be your place, not mine, to look after Mam and Dad.'

Emma slammed the milk jug down on the table. 'Don't keep going on about me being single, as though it's a disabling disease, and all I'm fit for is to sit by the fire with my parents!'

'You didn't have such a sharp tongue before you came to live with Alison,' Clara retorted, springing up from her chair and rocking the table in the process. The milk jug rocked, too, spilling some of its contents on Clara's dress. 'Now look what you've made me do!'

She grabbed a tea towel to mop her milk-stained garment. 'And you've got too big for your boots, our Emma, just because you live in London now! Some of the things you're coming out with – like what you just said – sound more like Alison than you.'

'Alison's certainly opened my eyes to a thing or two, if that's what you mean.'

'And got herself an unpaid skivvy.'

Emma's eyes blazed. 'How dare you say that!'

'Somebody has to, as you can't see it for yourself.' Clara was still dabbing at her frock. 'I came here to have a sisterly chat with you – and sat for five hours on a train, to do it – and all you can do is make me ruin my lovely new dress!'

They stood glaring at each other, and Emma was reminded of the incident between Alison and Morton at the dinner table: ostensibly about a bowl of spilled sugar, but the acrimony voiced on that occasion was no more attributable to spilled sugar than Clara's was to milk being spilt on her frock.

Clara made one last try. 'Mam and Dad really miss you, Emma. It's pitiful to see.'

'But I doubt that you see it often – as you seldom go to see them. It would be strange if they didn't miss me. I miss them.'

'Then why not go home? It would save a lot of trouble, all round.'

Emma bristled again, but remained silent.

56

'To tell you the truth, I'm being driven potty,' Clara said. 'Since you left, Mam phones me ten times a day.'

'Why?'

'There's nobody there for her to talk to, is there?'

'I'm surprised that she finds you at home when she rings up.'

'If I'm not, she chats to the maid. One day, I came back from the hairdresser's and found the ironing wasn't done, Betsy had been too busy telling Mam her boyfriend-troubles on the phone!'

Clara sat down and sipped the tea Emma had poured for her. And added: 'That remark you just made wasn't very nice, Emma. You didn't use to be so sarcastic.'

Nor had Emma known she was capable of it.

'Are you ever sarcastic with Alison?'

'She doesn't give me cause to be.'

'Knows which side her bread is buttered, I suppose.'

They lapsed into silence, then Clara gave Emma a wan smile. 'Believe it or not, I do care about you, Emma.'

'And me about you. But we've never spoken the same language, have we?'

'Perhaps because we never wanted the same things. I've always thought life was meant to be enjoyed. But you — '

'There's more than one way of enjoying it.'

'But give me my way, anytime.'

And selfish is the word for it, Emma thought. 'Are you happy with your second husband?' she said.

'Lew is very good to me and I'm short of nothing. But if you mean am I in love with him, the answer is no.' Clara rose to admire her reflection in the kitchen mirror, as Emma had often seen her do when they were girls. 'If romance came first with me, I'd have remarried long before I did. Before Lew came along, I met more than one man I could have fallen for, but I didn't let myself. They didn't have the wherewithal.'

'How can you be so mercenary!' Emma exclaimed.

Clara licked her finger to secure a kiss curl on her forehead. 'That's what you call it. Me, I call it being sensible. But I didn't come here to talk about myself, Emma.'

'And shall I tell you something, Clara? This is the first real, honest conversation you and I have ever had. In some ways, we've been like strangers. Not like sisters at all.'

'Well, that certainly applies since Alison came on the scene!' Clara flashed. 'From the day she first crossed our doorstep and Mam and Dad accepted her as one of the family – though she's only half-Jewish – you've preferred Alison to me.'

'What has her being only half-Jewish got to do with this?'

'Never mind!' Clara's long-standing animosity towards Alison embaced everything about her and she could not have rationalised it even had she been prepared to try. 'She took you away from me, Emma, and made me feel I couldn't trust you. That's why we never confided in each other, the way sisters do. When we were younger, I often felt like telling you things, but I was afraid you'd tell them to Alison and I didn't want her sniggering behind my back. And finally, she succeeded in taking you away from Mam and Dad.'

'If they'd really needed me, I wouldn't have gone.'

'But the longer you stay here, the harder it will be if you ever have to disentangle yourself from Alison and go home.'

Clara's words had an ominously prophetic ring. Suddenly, Emma could bear her presence no longer. Was it because she knew that what her sister had just said was true? Or because her own conscience still pricked about having left home to live her own life? A moment ago, she had been regretting that she and Clara had never been friends, wondering if it was too late to put things right. Now, she wanted to bundle her out of the flat.

'Well, I'd better get going if I'm to do some shopping before I catch my train,' Clara fortuitously said.

'Tell Mam and Dad I'll visit them soon.'

'A fine thing for an unmarried daughter to become only a visitor, they'll reply. And I agree.'

# CHAPTER SEVEN

ALISON'S NEW play, *Over The Moon*, turned out to be the one that Luke Plantaine had wanted to produce. Had she known this before committing herself to it, she would certainly have turned it down. She had no wish to increase the twins' enmity towards her.

By the time she made the discovery, rehearsals had begun. The information was conveyed to her in a letter from Luke, which Alison read while she and Emma were eating breakfast.

Emma stopped buttering her toast and scanned Alison's expression. 'Have you received some bad news?'

'I wouldn't call it good news.'

She showed Emma the unpleasant epistle, in which Luke had accused her of starring in the play solely to spite himself and Lucy.

'If that's what they want to think, let them think it,' said Emma. 'Take it from where it comes.'

'That's the trouble. I do. And they absolutely hate me.'

'Well, you hate them, don't you?'

'But not in the same way. I just want them to stay away from me so I can forget they exist. I don't want to harm them. With the twins, it's different; they get their knife into you and keep it there until they've done some real damage.'

Emma shuddered. 'Lessons in hate she's giving me with my breakfast! Have some toast and honey, Alison, and another cup of tea. It will make you feel better.'

Alison gave her a wan smile. 'Sometimes you sound just like your mother.'

Emma smiled too. 'Sarah Sandberg – she's a friend of Mam's from Manchester – calls food "Jewish comfort".'

59

'But it isn't the answer to all ills,' said Alison, rising moodily to pace the kitchen.

Emma now eyed her anxiously. 'What ills are you talking about, Alison?'

'Not physical ones, so don't ask me to put out my tongue and say "ah"! But one day the twins are going to do something terrible to me, Emma. I feel it in my bones.'

'What could they possibly do to you?'

'I don't know. But you wait and see. They will.'

Emma picked up Luke's letter and threw it into the rubbish bin. 'Go and get dressed, Alison, or you'll be late for rehearsal.'

'I wish I'd never agreed to do the damned play!' Alison gave the sash of her dressing-gown an edgy twitch and went to gaze through the window.

'But you did. And if you don't get a move on, the other actors will be wasting Max's money, sitting waiting for you.'

'It's his fault I'm in this mess!' Alison flashed.

'How come?' said Emma with one eye on the clock. 'And what mess?' Alison's conversation was sometimes like a Chinese puzzle.

Alison turned to face her. 'I'm not keen on the play, Emma. I never was, really. But Maxwell thought I should do it, and I've always trusted his judgement. Finding out that it's the one Luke had up his sleeve has put the tin lid on it, so far as I am concerned.'

Alison watched Emma don her pinafore and stack the dishes on the draining board. 'And that is another thing,' she went on hotly. 'I shall have something to say to young Justin Henry when I see him!'

Emma filled the sink with water. 'Who is Justin Henry?'

'He came to that cocktail party I gave, before we went into rehearsal. Don't you remember?'

'I was too busy serving snacks to notice who was there.'

'He's the playwright, Emma.'

But it wasn't surprising that Emma didn't know, thought Alison dryly. Most women would grasp at the chance to be part of the theatrical crowd, enjoy rubbing shoulders with celebrities. But Emma would always remain on the fringe.

Alison surveyed her with affection. Though technically she was now living in the capital, and the companion of a well-known actress, in effect Emma lived on an island that was a little bit of her own homespun world, with someone who was just her cousin Alison.

'You'll never change,' Alison said to her.

'It's enough that one of us is like the weather. Max is right when he says that about you, Alison. A person never knows how you are going to be from one minute to the next.'

'I can't help it, darling.'

'Did I say you could?'

Alison gave her a hug. 'It's so lovely to have you here.'

'And it's time you were not here, Alison.'

'All right, I'm going. And heaven help Justin Henry, when I get there!'

'I'm sorry for him in advance. What has he done?'

'You wouldn't understand, darling. But I intend to make sure that he does.'

The playwright recoiled from Alison's thunderous expression when she strode to his side during the morning coffee-break. This was her first opportunity to tackle him, and her anger no less for the waiting.

He was standing in a corner of the rehearsal room with the director and designer. Alison did him the favour of not reprimanding him in their presence.

'Please come with me, Justin. I want a word with you,' she said, leading him out to the corridor.

'Don't you like the rewrites I've done for you, Miss Plantaine?' he asked nervously, when Alison's gaze had pinned him to the wall.

'No, as a matter of fact. But I didn't bring you out here to talk about that. I wish to tell you that I am shocked by your unethical behaviour.'

The freckle-faced young man looked taken aback. 'I beg your pardon, Miss Plantaine?'

'And so you should. Mr Morton's, too. You had better

learn now, at the beginning of your career, that it isn't done to offer your work to more than one manager at a time – unless you make it clear that you have done so.'

'I'm afraid I don't know what you are talking about, Miss Plantaine.'

'Kindly don't add lies to your other transgression.'

'I am guilty of neither.'

'Then how was it possible for my stepcousin, Luke Plantaine, to ask me to star in *Over The Moon*? At a time when the play was lying on Mr Morton's desk?'

Justin looked confused. 'I didn't even know that Luke was a manager — '

'He isn't,' Alison interrupted. 'He is trying to become one. And he is as duplicit as you are.'

'I am nothing of the kind!' Justin retorted. 'But I see now that Luke most certainly is. I allowed him to read the play. He and his sister used to lodge where I do, and Luke sometimes popped into my room when I was working. It would have seemed uncivil of me to say no when he asked to see the finished script. That is the truth, Miss Plantaine. I swear it.'

Alison believed him. And one up for the twins! she thought. They had offered her a part in a play on which they did not hold an option, and had caused her to upbraid this nice young man for something he hadn't done.

How can such a beautiful lady be so cuttingly unkind? Justin was thinking. Like all the young men with whom she came in contact, Justin was dazzled by Alison's charisma. It was hard for him to relate the charming smile she was now giving him to the harshness she had just displayed.

'I owe you an apology,' said Alison sincerely.

Justin did not reply.

'I was extremely angry, and you must forgive me, darling.'

'But did you mean what you said about not liking my rewrites? Or did you just say that because you were furious with me about the other matter?'

Alison thrust her hands into the pockets of her cashmere coat and gave him a direct glance. 'I said it because I meant it, Justin. If you get to know me better, you'll discover that

I always say what I mean, with regard to my work. You were probably up all night doing those rewrites — '

'I was.'

'But we are all going to have to work hard, darling, if the play is to be a success.'

'Yes, Miss Plantaine.'

'You must learn to take criticism, darling. As we all must, in this business.' Alison kissed his cheek. 'And also how to kiss and make up.'

Justin blushed and gave her a grateful smile, though a few minutes before he had felt like throttling her. But she was that kind of woman, he thought. The kind a chap could not stay angry with for long.

'Next time I run into Luke, I'll give him a piece of my mind,' he told Alison.

'Make sure that you do. And be careful who you allow to read your work, in future. You are not afloat in a sea without sharks, Justin dear. Regrettably, my stepcousin is one of them. Now let's go and have some coffee together, shall we?'

'I'll bear all your advice in mind. It was jolly nice of you to give it to me,' Justin said.

'You better had, if you are to survive in the theatre.'


Justin Henry was not destined to survive in the theatre. *Over The Moon* proved to be his first and last play. The reviews tore it to shreds and the playwright afterwards sank without trace, as had others before him who lacked the stamina to try again.

Morton closed the production after a week.

'That poor boy,' Alison said to him when he took her out to supper after the final performance.

'I am as sorry for him as you are, my dear,' Morton answered.

'Then why did you close so soon? We weren't exactly short of advance bookings.'

'Naturally. As you were starring. But I can't allow you to continue appearing in a poor play, Alison. It wouldn't enhance your reputation. The public expects everything you do to be a huge success. I made a mistake. But I shall try to make sure that you are never associated with a critical failure again.'

Alison sipped some wine and laughed. 'You're not God, darling!'

'But I am your guardian angel.'

Alison surveyed him for a moment. As always, he was immaculate, and evening dress added to his distinguished appearance. Alison had once thought him ugly – which, physically, he was – but he had become for her a beautiful person, and the nearest thing to a father she now had.

'Yes, darling,' she said to him. 'My guardian angel is certainly what you are.'

The waiter served them with pork chops, for which Alison had little appetite, though pork was nowadays a treat for her. Emma's one proviso when she moved in with Alison was that she be allowed to keep a *kosher* house. Alison noted that Morton, too, had no enthusiasm for his meal. Like Alison, he was depressed because *Over The Moon* had failed. Alison would have preferred to eat at home tonight, but Morton had insisted that they go to the Ivy and show their faces. They were putting up a front, as theatre people must.

Charles Bligh, who was one of Morton's fellow impresarios, came to their table to commiserate. He was a brash and showy-looking man whom neither Alison nor Morton cared for. Weak puns were his style and he made one now: 'Over the moon that it's over, are we?'

He laughed at his own joke and clapped Morton on the shoulder. 'I would be, old man, if I'd bought that pig in a poke.'

Morton gave him a bland smile.

'Thank you so much for your sympathy, Charles,' Alison said politely.

Bligh's gaze roved to the deep décolletage of her black silk dinner gown. 'Mourning suits you, sweetheart. And you can have my sympathy any time. I almost sent you a wreath instead of flowers on the opening night.'

64

'It was kind of you to come over and have a word with us,' said Morton insincerely.

Bligh shifted his cigar from one side of his mouth to the other. 'The pleasure is mine.'

I bet! thought Alison. Bligh liked nothing better than saying 'I told you so'. But without having read *Over The Moon*, how could he have known it was a poor play? – which his remark about the wreath had implied.

Bligh was about to supply the answer. 'It could have been me, sitting where you are,' he told Morton. 'Those engaging cousins of Alison's brought me a copy of the play, before you bought it.'

'Stepcousins,' Alison curtly corrected him. Luke must have had a copy typed, when Justin let him read it, and had taken it to Bligh after Alison turned the proposition down.

Alison glanced at the corner table where Bligh's noisy party was sitting, and saw with shock that the twins were seated one on either side of the chair their host had just vacated. Lucy, who knew how to make the most of her assets, had on a green dress that matched her eyes, and looked as if she had been poured into it. Luke was talking animatedly to Bligh's dowdy wife.

Morton, to whom Alison had not confided her feelings about the twins, wondered why she had suddenly paled.

Neither of her stepcousins had cast a glance in her direction. But to Alison it was as though they had begun to contrive for their venom to reach out and touch her from afar.

'I didn't know that Luke and Lucy were friends of yours,' she said to Bligh.

'Since they brought me *Over The Moon*, I've taken a shine to them – ha, ha!' he replied. 'All they want to do – and I must say I find it immensely touching – is to live up to the Plantaine family name.'

They are much more likely to dishonour it, Alison thought with disgust. But she made herself smile.

'Luke is burning to direct, as I'm sure you're aware,' Bligh said to Alison, 'and dear little Lucy has set her heart on following in your footsteps. But you must know how they feel about you, Alison.'

'I certainly do.'

'They didn't come over with me to speak to you because they can't bear to see you when you're down, sweetheart.'

Morton stiffened. 'I would hardly put it that way, Charles. The critics panned the play, not Alison.'

'I was merely repeating what her cousins, bless them, said.'

'Stepcousins,' she corrected him again.

'I'm getting the feeling you don't love them!'

Alison managed to remain silent.

Bligh smoothed his well-brilliantined hair and gave Alison and Morton an equally oily smile. 'Look, my dears. You don't have to pretend with your friends. A flop is a flop.'

'And as they say on the other side of the Atlantic, with friends like him, who needs enemies!' Morton exclaimed when Bligh had kissed Alison and departed. 'Bligh is one of the most slippery customers in the business,' he added with distaste.

'Tonight he's in the right company,' said Alison.

Morton eyed her tense expression. 'I'd gathered that you weren't too keen on the twins, but — '

'That is putting it mildly!'

'What have they done to you, darling?'

'It's what they've tried to do, Maxwell. One way and another. Over the years.' Alison glanced at Bligh's table. 'Now that Charles has taken them under his wing – and he obviously has – they've moved into my circles. Our paths will be crossing all the time.'

Morton ordered coffee. They had barely touched their main course, and neither was in the mood to enjoy dessert. Alison had averted her eyes from the twins and was staring down at the tablecloth.

'There's Gertie,' Morton said to distract her.

He waved to Gertrude Lawrence, who had just entered with Noël Coward. 'How I'd like to get hold of a new Coward play for you, Alison. But Gertie has the monopoly.'

Alison had not met Miss Lawrence, but admired her

work. 'I don't have her unique talent for contemporary comedy,' she said. 'She is a born comedienne. I am basically a classical actress. How could I not be, when I imbibed Shakespeare with my mother's milk? Did I ever tell you, Maxwell, that I knew all the Bard's texts by heart before I was twelve?'

'No, darling. But it doesn't surprise me, as you are Gregory Plantaine's grand-daughter.'

Alison smiled reminiscently. 'I used to sit on a high stool in the wings, mouthing Shakespeare's lines with the actors. And once, on my birthday, Grandpa gave me a special treat – he allowed me to prompt,' she recalled. 'And I was able to do so without looking at the book. I can remember being scared stiff, though, because it was one of the nights when my Uncle Oliver had been at the whisky before curtain-up.'

'I heard he stopped drinking when he married the twins' mother,' Morton said.

'Yes. The marriage was good for him, though not for the rest of us, I'm afraid.'

Morton looked surprised. 'But the company benefited from the capital Ruby put into it, didn't it? Wasn't that how the Plantaine Players got their own theatre?'

Alison nodded. 'But I don't have to tell you that my grandfather has no interest in money. Plays that smacked of the commercial were always anathema to him. When I was a child, my father tried to make Grandpa see sense, but he gave up in the end.'

Alison stirred her coffee, a faraway look in her eye. A picture had just risen before her of herself aged twelve, nervously crumpling her frilly pinafore because her parents were quarrelling – about company policy. Her mother had always taken her grandfather's side.

'But eventually, a commercial policy was imposed on Grandpa by Aunt Ruby,' she said, collecting herself. 'She is a hard-headed businesswoman, Maxwell, and made sure, legally, that she got the upper hand in the company in return for her capital. That's why the Plantaines' repertoire is no longer solely Shakespearean. Everything changed with Aunt Ruby's coming – and I loathed her for it, at the time.'

67

'And now?'

'I've grown up, Maxwell.'

Morton, who sometimes doubted that, smiled.

'I have to admit that what Aunt Ruby did was necessary, or the company would not have survived.' Alison toyed with her topaz ring, which her Uncle Oliver had given her on her début night. 'But sometimes I miss the old days,' she went on, 'before Ruby and her despicable offspring came on the scene. The Plantaines were never a happy family, but they were united in their art. Everyone was dedicated to the same thing.'

'And you still are, Alison,' said Morton. 'In many respects, you are out of your element in the commercial theatre, darling. You suffer it for the sake of your art. You don't enjoy it.'

'And I never shall.'

'But your art cannot be purveyed without money to back it,' Morton gently reminded her. 'That is where philistines like Bligh and me come in.'

'Kindly don't compare yourself with that man!' Alison said with feeling. 'As I require a philistine in my working life, I would rather it were you than him.'

Morton laughed. 'I've had some dubious compliments in my time!' He paused and took Alison's hand. 'I am sorry to have let you down on this occasion, my dearest girl.'

'Anyone – even you, darling – can make a mistake about a play.'

'And thank you for being so gracious about it, Alison. But we must get you back on the boards as soon as possible, before the public has time to register that Alison Plantaine appeared in this year's biggest flop.'

'I would love to do some Shakespeare,' said Alison wistfully. 'It's been ages since I did.'

Morton fingered his chin and looked thoughtful. The public could get all the Shakespeare they wanted at the Old Vic, and were prepared to trek to the Waterloo Road to see it; and, too, to see the opera and ballet Miss Lilian Baylis was now staging at Sadler's Wells.

Alison had been invited to play at the Old Vic, as many

of England's finest actors from time to time did. But she had remained loyal to Morton, though he had never asked her to sign an exclusive contract. There was between them an unwritten agreement born of their mutual respect.

Alison cut into Morton's thoughts. 'I said I'd love to do some Shakespeare, darling.'

'I'd prefer you to do some Shaw,' he declared as that decision clicked in his mind.

'Not *St Joan* again?'

'I know how much *St Joan* took out of you, Alison. I'm not thinking of including it in the season.'

'What season?'

Morton's mind was racing ahead. 'I shall lease a theatre and put on a whole season of Shaw's social-conscience plays. The economic climate is right for them. And you, my darling, will play all the female leads.'

Alison sagged. 'Are you trying to kill me?'

'Nonsense, my dear girl! You will absolutely love it. I don't believe it has been done before, using just one leading actress.'

Alison sipped some coffee. 'You realise, of course, that I shall get absolutely no rest? While one play is in performance, the next will be in rehearsal.'

'You were accustomed to that when you were with the Plantaine Players,' Morton reminded her.

'But Lucy and I alternated the leading roles.'

'I could, if you wish, engage another actress to share the load with you?' Morton offered, knowing what Alison's answer would be.

'Certainly not! I'll do it if I drop. But I don't know what Emma will say when she hears what you're planning for me.'

'Leave Emma to me.'


The matter precipitated Morton and Emma's first quarrel. As Emma had never in her life quarrelled with anyone, doing so was more painful for her than for him.

Morton called at the flat the following morning, when

he knew that Alison would not yet have risen from her bed. Though Alison's professional commitments were not Emma's concern, he felt honour-bound to discuss the Shaw project with her. She, too, would have to cope with the strain it would put upon Alison.

'Let me get this clear, Max,' Emma said. 'Are you telling me that Alison is going to have to work all day, as well as perform on the stage at night?'

'That's inevitable,' Morton replied, 'when plays are performed in repertoire.'

'But why must Alison be in all of them?' Emma demanded.

'Because that's the object of the exercise, Emma. The season will be a showcase for Alison Plantaine.'

Emma had made them some lemon tea for which Morton had developed a taste. Emma drank a little of hers. 'I don't like the sound of it, Max,' she said bluntly. 'Alison will be half-dead by the end of the season.'

'Physically, perhaps,' he conceded, 'but artistically, it is the kind of stimulation she needs. Alison is capable of getting stale, Emma.'

'I beg your pardon?'

Morton added more sugar to his tea. 'Stardom can become a rut. Once you are at the top, what is there left to strive for? is what I'm really saying. I've seen other stars affected that way – and it could happen to Alison.'

'Never!' said Emma emphatically.

'Why not? I think she already believes she has reached the pinnacle of her career.'

'And you don't?'

'What I think isn't important. It is bad for Alison, at the age of thirty, to believe she has no further to go. That was why I staged *St Joan* for her. To present her with a challenge. *Over The Moon* was intended to give her a working-rest. I knew it wouldn't tax either her strength or her artistry: I deliberately chose an undemanding play for her. But I shall never do so again. Alison thrives on challenge, Emma.'

'I'm pleased if you're pleased, Max. But one right after

the other? Why can't you arrange for her to rest between challenges?'

They were back to square one.

Emma got up to peep into the oven. When Morton dropped in to chat with her, the kitchen was where they sat – as daytime visitors did in the Steins' home in Oldham.

'I mustn't let my strudel burn,' she explained, returning to her chair.

'Never mind your strudel!' Morton exclaimed. 'How am I going to make you understand?'

'Understand what? That you're more concerned about Alison's career than you are about her well-being? I can see that without you drawing me a picture, Max. What I can't understand, is why. It doesn't fit in with what you said the night we had our first chat about Alison – that you feared for what her involvement with her acting might do to her.'

'Are you accusing me of handing you a line?'

'Please don't speak to me in American! Each time you go to New York, you come back saying things I can't make head nor tail of. What does handing you a line mean?'

'Giving you a convenient story,' Morton translated. 'And you should know me better than that.'

'I thought I did. But now I'm wondering if I know you at all.'

'Now you look here, Emma!'

'No! You look here, Max!' Emma heard herself shout. 'It seemed to me that we'd agreed to share responsibility for Alison, because somebody has to watch over her. If there wasn't that understanding between us, you wouldn't be here talking to me about her now. And I have to say that the last person I thought it would be necessary to protect her from was you!'

Morton turned scarlet with anger. 'I am afraid, Emma, that what you just said cuts both ways! It didn't occur to me that you would try to come between Alison and her career. And I won't have you trying to influence her against doing the Shaw season!'

'That is exactly what I intend to do!'

They glared at each other for a moment. Emma would

not have thought herself capable of the anger coursing through her. Then she smelled burning, which exacerbated it.

'Now you've made me ruin my baking!'

Morton watched her remove the singed strudel from the oven. 'I'm sorry.'

'You should be. I made this specially for Alison. She's lost two pounds in weight since the newspapers wrote those spiteful things about *Over The Moon*, and I'm trying to feed her up.'

Morton was surprised that Emma knew the title of the play. 'It's a pity you are not so attuned to the rest of Alison's well-being,' he said. 'Making sure she eats well, and rests, is only part of what she requires, Emma. But I should have known I'd be wasting my breath telling you about her artistic need.'

'Then why did you bother telling me?'

'Because Alison will do the Shaw season whether you approve or not.'

'I know.'

'So what's the point of letting her know you disapprove, Emma?'

Morton finished his tea and straightened his Brooks Brothers tie – he wore Savile Row suits, but bought his shirts and ties in New York.

Emma was trying to remove the strudel from the baking tray without breaking it, which gave her an excuse not to look at Morton.

'There was a time when I wouldn't have told her I don't approve,' she said. 'When I didn't think what Alison did was my business. Now I'm living with her, it is.'

'But it won't do her any good to feel she's doing something you've warned is not advisable,' Morton declared. 'I had hoped to make you see that.'

'Something she wouldn't be doing if it weren't for you,' Emma countered.

Square one again! Morton thought.

'Look,' he appealed to her, 'you and Alison can take a holiday immediately the Shaw season closes. Perhaps in the

South of France. You could stay at the Carlton in Cannes. It's one of the world's finest hotels, Emma.' Would cajolery succeed where pressure had failed? Morton wondered.

He ought to have known better.

'Who are you trying to *shmooze*, Max?' Emma said. 'And who will pay our bill at one of the world's finest hotels?'

'I will, Emma. Happily. But didn't you know that Alison is by now quite a wealthy lady?'

'I never gave a thought to my cousin's bank balance. Why should I?'

Of course not, Morton thought. Emma was not that kind.

'I have a regular allowance from my father,' said Emma proudly. 'It's a very generous one – considering how I just upped and left home. But it wouldn't run to the kind of hotel you were talking about.'

Morton trod carefully, lest he offend her further. 'As Alison's companion, you will probably be called upon to travel with her from time to time, Emma. But it will be paid for out of her business account – or mine.'

'We'll see about that when the time comes.'

Meanwhile, Emma decided, Morton was right about the other matter. It wouldn't be good for Alison to know that Emma was against her doing what Max was planning for her.

'You win,' she told him. 'I won't say a word to Alison when she tells me what she's going to do next.'

'I'm very grateful to you,' he said with relief.

'Don't be. It isn't for your sake that I'll hold my tongue. But it's as well you came round to warn me.'

'Believe it or not, that wasn't why I came. I simply thought you and I should talk about it.'

'You mean you knew you'd have to talk me round,' she replied with her customary bluntness. 'But you won't talk me into going to the South of France, Max. I've never been out of England. I haven't even got a passport.'

'Then you'd better get yourself one. When Alison appears on Broadway she will want you to go with her, and I'm sure you won't let her down. If the Shaw season is the success I expect it to be, I shall arrange to transfer it to the States. Alison hasn't yet played there, and it's time she did. It's important to her career.'

Morton smiled at the panic-stricken expression on Emma's face. 'Would you like a drop of brandy?' he teased her.

'Do me a favour, Max! Go to your office and leave me alone!' All Emma had ever wanted was an ordinary home life. Foreign travel was not for the likes of her. What had she let herself in for when she came to live with Alison?

# CHAPTER EIGHT

THE SHAW season opened with *Major Barbara*, in which Alison had once played Barbara in a Plantaine Players production.

Her grandparents came up to town from Hastings to attend the first night. Morton brought them backstage after the performance and Alison found it difficult to conceal her emotion when they entered her dressing room.

'It was lovely of you to come,' she said when they had congratulated her.

It was years since they had seen her perform and she had been delighted when they accepted her invitation for tonight. She had reserved rooms for them at Brown's Hotel and hoped to have them with her at the opening-night party.

'It's long past our bedtime, Alison dear,' her grandmother said, 'so you will have to excuse us.'

'Would that we were still the age for late-night revels,' her grandfather added wistfully.

Old Jessica Plantaine, in whom it was still possible to discern the fragile beauty she was in her youth, gave Alison a smile of pride. 'But we would not have missed this evening for anything, my dear. It was an effort to make the journey, but this is rather special, isn't it? Alison Plantaine with a season of her very own.'

Gregory Plantaine was still a striking figure, despite the stoop that marked his advanced years. He too was bursting with pride, and said to Morton, 'When I saw my dear grand-daughter off to London, to make her West End début, I prophesied that she would bring glory upon our fair name. And for me, this evening is the zenith of our family's achievement.'

Alison was overwhelmed. 'Even though I am appearing in Shaw, not Shakespeare, Grandpa?'

'I have come to think, Alison, that Shaw is the Shakespeare of his age.'

When the old people had left, Morton sat down on the sofa beside Alison and took her hand. 'If anyone else talked about "bringing glory on our fair name", it would sound ridiculous,' he said with a smile. 'Only Gregory Plantaine could get away with it.'

'Courtliness – for want of a better way of putting it – has always been Grandpa's style. He is part of a bygone age.'

Alison gazed pensively into space. 'You don't know what it means to me, Maxwell, to have heard him say what he did. I had never really rid myself of guilt because I left the family company to go my own way – even though Grandpa released me with a good heart. No other blood-Plantaine has ever done what I did.'

She blinked away a tear. 'But I feel now that I have wiped out my defection. I could weep for joy.'

'You haven't time to, dearest. I left instructions at the stagedoor that you were not to be disturbed until your grandparents had left. Your dressing room will be awash with people any second now.'

Alison's joy fled when the twins arrived with Charles Bligh. Emma entered behind them and gave her an encouraging wink.

'I shall try my best to follow your shining example, Alison darling, and get to the top of the tree,' said Lucy when the false kissing session was over.

It won't be your fault if you don't, Alison thought – but not by following my example. Lucy was hanging on to Bligh's arm as if she owned him. Luke, too, behaved toward Alison as though their confrontation at the Ritz had never taken place, nor his venomous letter to her been written. The depths of the twins' duplicity had to be seen to be believed. Emma's expression told Alison that she agreed.

She felt like telling them to leave, but controlled the urge which meant that she too was being two-faced. Not because she wanted to be. Once again, it was necessary to put up a front. Others had streamed into the dressing room to congratulate her and she must not create an offstage scene. Alison Plantaine must maintain her public façade.

The party that followed was marred for Alison by the twins' presence. Charles Bligh's wife was conspicuously absent, and Alison had learned from Morton that Lucy was Bligh's constant companion. Also that Luke was to direct a play that Bligh was mounting for a provincial tour, in which Lucy would play the lead. The twins had not made their mark upon the West End yet, but Alison knew that they would. They never gave up until they had done what they set out to do. Which includes harming me, she thought.

Nobody could have divined Alison's troubled thoughts as she stood at the centre of an admiring group. But she had her grandfather's words of praise to hearten her. The twins could not take that away.

'How beautiful Alison looks tonight,' Morton said to Emma.

As usual, Emma had positioned herself on the fringe of the crowd. Morton, who was hosting the party, had deserted his guests to have a word with her.

'Why are you sitting here by yourself?' he asked, briefly transferring his gaze from Alison to Emma.

'You know me, Max,' she replied with a smile and a shrug.

But he had already returned his attention to Alison. 'It isn't just her beauty that captivates people, is it? It's something indefinable that only Alison has.'

Emma, who had succumbed to that indefinable something the moment she first met Alison, remained silent. That wintry day in 1914 was engraved upon her memory. She had opened the door of her parents' house, wondering who could be calling on them so early in the morning.

'How do you do? I am Alison. And you must be Emma,' the cousin with whom she corresponded but had not met, said to her with a smile that had made Emma her slave from then on.

Alison had arrived on the Steins' doorstep travel-weary but undishevelled after her impulsive night-journey north.

Emma could still recall how elegant she had looked in her winter coat, with an emerald tam-o'-shanter on her head and a little fur tippet around her neck. Emma had felt herself shrink into insignificance beside her, but had not minded in the least.

The pattern of their relationship was forged then, when they were fourteen years old. And next summer we'll be thirty-two, Emma thought.

She smoothed the skirt of the new evening gown Alison had insisted upon her buying for tonight, and surveyed Alison's flowing white chiffon, in which she looked like a Greek goddess.

'You're wearing brown again,' Morton remarked, munching some *hors d'oeuvres* a waiter had just served to them.

Emma was surprised that he had noticed what she was wearing. 'Go and talk to your guests, Max! You don't have to sit here with me.'

She watched him rejoin Alison, as she had known he would. If Alison was in the room, Morton could not stay away from her, and his eyes remained on her if he did briefly leave her side.

'Our Em has just snapped at me,' Morton whispered to Alison with a smile.

'For some reason you're the only person she ever does snap at,' Alison replied.

Emma saw Morton put an arm around Alison's shoulders, and a feeling she did not recognise stirred within her. Alison is all that Max and I ever discuss, she thought simultaneously. He only came to speak to me just now because I'm the one person he is able to talk to about her.

Then a feeling Emma did recognise assailed her: pity. For Morton who loved a woman who would not have him. What a rare kind of love it was, into which self did not enter – or he wouldn't allow Alison to keep him on a string.

It struck Emma then that Alison was using Morton. She chided herself for the thought, but it lodged at the back of her mind, and later returned to the forefront when she saw Alison flirting outrageously with a young actor. Emma had

78

not seen her behave that way before. How could Max bear it?

Morton met Emma's gaze across the room and knew what she was thinking, but managed to smile.

Alison was now as bubbly as the champagne she had imbibed. 'Pete wants us to go on to a night-club, darling,' she called to Morton, who was beside the door saying farewell to some friends.

'Then by all means do, my love,' he replied brightly. 'But include me out. I've had a long day.'

Alison went to give him an exuberant kiss. 'Thank you for my lovely party, Maxwell dear. Will you see Emma home?'

'Of course.'

Alison blew a kiss to Emma. 'See you tomorrow, darling!'

'It's tomorrow already,' Emma said to Morton, when Alison and her entourage had departed and they were left alone in the littered room.

'And time you and I went to find ourselves a cab,' he said with a rueful smile.

Again Emma was moved to compassion for him. 'I'm sure Alison enjoyed the party you gave for her, Max,' was the only comforting thing she could think of to say.

'But she didn't begin to relax until after Charles Bligh and the Plantaine twins had left.'

He's aware of Alison's every mood, Emma thought. 'I liked Alison's grandparents,' she said.

Morton looked surprised. 'Had you not met them before?'

Emma shook her head. 'I was introduced to them during the interval. And they were just as I had always imagined them, Max. As different from Alison's other grandparents – who were also mine, of course – as oil from water.'

Morton smiled. 'Don't you mean chalk from cheese?' he asked when they were in the taxi.

'I said oil and water because they don't mix. And it's a wonder to me how my late Uncle Horace, Alison's father, ever fitted into the Plantaine family.'

Morton recalled the polished gentleman Horace was. 'I don't understand what you mean, Emma.'

79

'You would if you knew my family – and Uncle Horace was one of them. He must have made himself into what the Plantaines expected their son-in-law to be,' Emma said shrewdly. 'As he was an actor, it probably wasn't too difficult.'

In the latter respect Emma was wrong, though she could not have known it. Alison had not told her that Horace had remained an outsider so far as the Plantaines were concerned. Nor did Alison herself know that her father had discovered, too late, that his metamorphosis from a Jew of immigrant stock to a member of an English theatrical family was only skin deep.

Morton gazed thoughtfully at the trees on Park Lane, as the cab rumbled past them. 'Alison never mentions her mother, does she?'

'No. And I haven't met her, either.'

'When her grandparents came backstage, Alison didn't even ask them how her mother is,' Morton recalled, though the omission had not registered with him at the time.

'That doesn't surprise me.'

'Why? Has Alison quarrelled with her mother?'

'I think her relationship with her mother has been one long quarrel.' Emma sighed, for she loved nothing better than peace. 'During the war, when Alison's father was serving in France, she was always rushing up north to us, without letting us know she was coming.'

Morton smiled. 'Well, that's Alison, isn't it?'

'Sure. But I always had the feeling it was to get away from her mother.'

'I've only met Hermione Plantaine a few times,' said Morton, 'and a long while ago, but she struck me as being a most delightful lady. Though she hasn't the warmth her daughter has, she is extremely charming as all the Plantaines are.'

'There must be something special about her, Max,' Emma answered, 'or my Uncle Horace wouldn't have married out of his religion for her. It's very rare for a Jew to do that.'

'So I understand, Emma.'

'And I don't think my grandparents ever really forgave

80

him,' Emma went on. 'Though they papered over the rift as well as they could, in the end.'

'I didn't know there was a rift.'

'Hasn't Alison ever told you how her life was affected by it? She bears the scars to this day.'

Morton shook his head. And it occurred to him that there was a good deal he did not know about Alison. That she presented different aspects of herself to different people, and kept hidden the person she really was, scars and all.

'I have often wondered why Alison never visits her family in Hastings,' Morton said.

'Then stop wondering, Max. There is definitely some mystery about Alison and her mother. And whatever it is must hurt her very much, as she can't bear to talk about it even to me.'

They had arrived at the apartment block and Emma was relieved when Morton declined to come in for a nightcap. She had had enough, for one evening, of discussing Alison with him – and was still chiding herself for feeling like that, when she put her weary bones to bed and fell asleep.

# CHAPTER NINE

WHEN THE Shaw plays transferred to Broadway in the spring of 1932, Alison and Emma stayed at the Algonquin. Morton was unable to join them until the final week of the run. A crisis affecting another of his productions had kept him in England, but his disappointment was compensated for by the knowledge that Emma was with Alison.

Alison had not been to New York before, and insisted upon Emma accompanying her when she wandered abroad. They window-gazed on Fifth Avenue, strolled in Central Park, lunched in Greenwich Village, visited Chinatown, and one day found themselves on the Lower East Side, where Emma saw more of her co-religionists than she had imagined there were in the whole world.

This matched her overall impression of New York. She was bemused by the city's larger-than-life quality, and deafened by the cacophony of motor horns on the thronged streets. The traffic terrified her. And, too, the pace at which people went about their business. It was as though nobody in New York had a moment to spare.

Alison found their excursions fascinating, but Emma was always relieved to return to the hotel.

'It's a pleasure to come back here,' she said to Alison one afternoon, when they were having tea in their suite after a shopping spree.

'I'm delighted that something is a pleasure to you in New York,' Alison teased her.

'So I'm not the big-city kind,' said Emma with a shrug. 'Though I quite like London.'

Alison laughed. 'The bit you've seen of it. And if I didn't drag you out, you'd see nothing here except the inside of this hotel.'

82

Emma got up to remove a wilted leaf from the vase of flowers on the window sill, as she would have done at home. 'I feel comfortable here, Alison. This isn't like a hotel room, is it? It's more like a sitting room in a house – and reminds me a bit of my parents' parlour.'

She returned contentedly to her comfy velvet armchair and fed some milk to the hotel cat, which knew a cat-lover when it met one and had taken to following her. 'Max couldn't have found a more suitable hotel for someone like me,' she declared.

'And only you, Emma,' said Alison fondly, 'could have stayed here without knowing that you're rubbing shoulders with some of America's literary élite. The Algonquin is where they get together.'

'Why didn't you tell me?'

'I once told you the Prince of Wales was coming to see me in a play – and you just went on rolling pastry for your strudel. So why would I bother mentioning that this morning we shared the lift with Ernest Hemingway? Or that the lady touching up her lipstick beside us in the cloakroom yesterday was Dorothy Parker?'

Emma smiled. 'You've made your point.'

'But now you know, you can include it with your memories of staying here. Along with the strawberry shortcake we have with our tea,' Alison added, helping herself to a slice, 'and the cat.'

For Emma, the hotel would retain a more personal significance. It was there, on the penultimate night in New York, that she realised she was in love with Morton. That the feeling she had experienced at his party in London was jealousy of Alison, and she had not let herself recognise it.

The three were eating a late supper together, when these realisations hit Emma like a double blow.

It was a moment she would remember always. The tinkle of silver and glass, and the murmur of the diners' conversation, in the mellow Oak Room restaurant. Her beautiful cousin, dazzling in a rich burgundy gown, her sculptured features emphasised by the sophisticated turban framing her face. Morton, gazing adoringly at Alison, who would

83

not have him. And herself, outwardly the same, but inwardly aching with love for him; no longer the passive third party.

Emma had not thought that love for a man would ever, now, be aroused in her. Nor was she the kind to whom it could happen in a flash. What she felt for Morton was like a slow-burning fire that had suddenly burst into flame. Why did it have to be Max who had stirred in her this painful emotion? And jealousy of Alison seemed inconceivable. How could you be jealous of someone so dear to you?

'I'd like a brandy,' she heard herself say.

Morton raised his eyebrows. 'With your soup?'

'Are you feeling ill, Emma?' Alison inquired anxiously.

'No.' Ill wasn't the word for it.

'Then why do you want a brandy? You don't drink.'

'You don't smoke, but if you suddenly asked for a cigarette nobody would make a fuss about it. Why does there have to be a fuss about my asking for a drink?'

Alison smiled. 'Because you are you, Emma. And I am me.'

Exactly, Emma thought. And the way Alison and Max were looking at her was as though she'd told them she'd decided to dye her hair green.

'If you want to experiment with drink, our Em,' said Morton, 'with a meal I would recommend a drop of wine.'

Why had she asked for a drink? It would take more than alcohol to deaden her pain. Her heart had ceased its wild thudding, and her thoughts their frantic whirling, but the contented-with-her-lot creature she was before the thunderbolt hit her was gone forever.

She watched Morton pour some hock for her, then told him she didn't want it. 'I've changed my mind.'

'That's something every woman is allowed to do. Even you, Emma,' he said, with a warm smile.

Alison reached for some melba toast. 'What were we discussing, Maxwell, when Emma had her mad moment?'

'Pirandello's *Six Characters In Search Of An Author*. I was telling you it was revived here, last year, at the Bijou Theatre – and only ran for thirteen performances.'

They went on discussing it. But listening to their theatre-talk was nothing new for Emma. It had never made her feel excluded, nor did it tonight.

'Are we boring you, Emma?' Morton asked, as he occasionally did.

'No more than usual.' How was she managing to smile?

She wanted to escape to her room, be alone with her terrible, new self-knowledge. She curbed the impulse. This was how it would be from now on and she would have to live with it. Nothing had changed for the other two, only for her, and she must not let them know that it had.

It did not occur to her to disentangle her life from theirs. As always, Emma adapted herself to the existing situation.

By the time they returned to London she had stemmed her jealousy. But her love for Morton, once unleashed, strengthened day by day, and the way Alison, who did not want him as Emma did, took him for granted, evoked in Emma a feeling of injustice.

Though Alison and Morton detected no change in her, the balance of the relationship had shifted irretrievably. There were now times when Emma, who had once put Alison first, could shake her for her thoughtlessness toward Morton. Despite her continuing affection for her cousin, Emma had hardened toward Alison.

But which human situation ever stands still? The less so, when one of its participants is Alison Plantaine, ever oblivious to the effects of her personality upon those whom she would not want to hurt.

Alison would not have thought of the threesome as a situation. Nor would Morton, who had other pre-occupations. Had either viewed it, with their greater experience of life, from Emma's point of the triangle, they would have seen that a triangle was what it had become. A triangle in which unrequited love and the seeds of bitterness vied with the mutual esteem and loyalty that held it together.

It is perhaps remarkable that Emma, the least likely of the trio to do so, introduced to the situation the explosive potential it now had. But the old saying that still waters run deep had proved to be true in Emma's case. She had just begun to plumb her own depths. And Destiny was waiting in the wings to put her loyalty to the test.

# CHAPTER TEN

ALISON AND Emma celebrated their thirty-second birthday with a picnic lunch on Hampstead Heath.

We were born on the same day, but not under the same star, Emma thought with the wryness that helped keep her jealousy of Alison at bay. She glanced at Morton, who disliked picnics. Only for Alison would he be sitting uncomfortably on a canvas chair, brushing insects away from his face.

It isn't surprising that Emma and I are twin-souls, Alison was thinking with affection. She had always attached significance to their coming into the world simultaneously.

Briefly, Alison thought, too, of the woman who had given her life. How was it possible that three decades later it was as though that unseverable bond between herself and her mother did not exist? Was Hermione Plantaine thinking, on this date, of her only child? Remembering the long-ago August evening when she was rushed from a theatre in Plymouth to the hospital where she had almost died, giving birth?

There was never a card from her mother among the pile Alison received on her birthday morn. But Alison did not send greetings to Hermione on her birthday. Since her father's death, she and her mother had each wiped the other from her horizon. Once he had gone, there remained no reason for pretence.

Alison switched her mind to the present, which was infinitely more pleasant than the past of which her mother had long been part. 'It couldn't be a more perfect day,' she said delightedly, gazing up at the cloudless sky. 'And aren't we having a lovely time?'

Morton grunted. 'Speak for yourself, my darling.'

87

Alison giggled. 'Don't be a grumpy old thing, Maxwell. What could be nicer than eating al fresco with the sun shining down on you?'

'And the gnats biting him,' said Emma, when Morton swatted one that had settled on the back of his hand.

'They always seem to go for me.'

'That must be because you're so sweet,' said Alison.

'Enough of your flattery! As I was cajoled into suffering this, let's get on with it. What else is there to eat?'

Emma surveyed the mouthwatering array of delicacies in the hamper Morton had ordered from Fortnum's. 'Anything you care to mention. What would you like?'

'I'll let you choose for me.'

'Some pâté de foie? Which I hadn't even heard of before I came to London! And I'm not allowed to eat because it isn't *kosher*,' said Emma, spreading some on a water-biscuit for Morton.

'I ordered smoked salmon. And hard-boiled eggs, Emma. Specially for you.'

'Thank you for thinking of me, Max.'

'It's your birthday, too.'

Or he wouldn't have thought of me, Emma registered. No, she corrected herself, that wasn't so. Max was a thoughtful man.

She handed him the bottle of wine that went with the food and watched him deftly open it, fascinated as always by his beautiful hands. How strong and dependable he was; the sort who would never let you down. Emma was fortunate to have him for a friend. Friendship would have to be enough.

'Before we drink a birthday toast, let's tell Emma our news, Alison,' Morton said with a smile.

'We've been keeping a secret from you, Emma darling,' Alison added.

Emma felt as though a dagger had stabbed her heart. Were they going to tell her that Alison had finally agreed to marry Max? And ask her, of course, to keep house for them? To which Emma would be fool enough to say yes!

'Alison is going to appear in an international theatre festival, next week, Emma,' Morton said.

Emma wondered if her relief showed on her face.

'If I'm going to have to pack my case again, I'm not surprised that you left it until the last minute to tell me,' she said, recovering.

'Alison's too, needless to say,' Morton laughed.

'And where are we off to this time?' Emma asked. 'Timbuctoo?'

'No further than the Continent,' Morton reassured her. 'Berlin. And you'll only be away from your kitchen for three weeks, Emma.'

'What has my kitchen to do with it? Nothing would persuade me to go to Berlin.'

'You said that about New York,' Alison reminded her amusedly.

'We know you're a homebird, our Em,' Morton said, winking at Alison. 'And I'm sure Alison appreciates that it's an effort for you to dig yourself out of the nest and go with her on her travels.'

'Indeed I do,' said Alison sincerely. 'I shouldn't relish being alone in a strange city.'

'You'll have the rest of the cast there,' Emma replied.

'A lot of good that will do me! Except at the theatre, I'm unlikely to see them for dust. For some reason, I am never terribly popular with the actors and actresses I work with.'

'I wouldn't put it that way, darling,' said Morton.

'Then how would you put it?'

'They are probably a little in awe of you, Alison. The young ones, anyway.'

'Nonsense, Maxwell!'

'Be that as it may,' he said, 'one thing is certain – not many people enjoy working with an absolute perfectionist. And that's what you are, Alison.'

Emma watched Alison flick a fly from the skirt of her cream linen dress and absently finger the black patent belt that accentuated her shapely figure.

What Max had just said applied to Alison's appearance, as well as to her work, Emma thought. Even on a picnic she managed to look cool and elegant without so much as a hair out of place. Perfection was the word for her, from the brim of her straw hat to the tip of her high-heeled shoes.

Emma had treated herself to a Marcel wave but was conscious that her hair was flopping limply around her face, and her polka-dot print frock clinging stickily to her back in the heat.

'All right, so I'm not easy to work with,' Alison conceded to Morton.

'So you can't expect to be popular with your fellow players,' he replied.

Alison gave Emma an appealing smile. 'If you hadn't been with me in New York, I'd have died of loneliness, darling. You will come to Berlin, won't you?'

'No, Alison. Not even for you. Dear though you are to me. I am not setting foot in Germany.'

Alison and Morton exchanged a perplexed glance.

'Doesn't either of you read the newspapers?' Emma inquired. 'Maybe you just haven't noticed the stories about how Hitler and his party feel about Jews?'

'But Hitler will probably never come to power,' Morton said uncomfortably.

'What makes you think that, Max? When the German people are already under his thumb?'

'I think that only applies to the Hitler Youth Movement, Emma.'

'And I have it on good authority, Max, that they have been trained to terrorise their parents into supporting Hitler. He has become for them a messiah, and they would betray their own families for his sake. I've also heard that many Germans need no bullying to support Hitler. Because times are bad for them at present, they're prepared to believe that he'll turn the bad times into good.'

Emma's quietly delivered words were like a chill wind, so out of keeping with the tranquillity of the summer day that Alison shivered. Nor did they fit with the pictures of smiling blond youngsters parading in Hitler Youth Movement uniform, that from time to time appeared in the English newspapers. Emma had to be exaggerating, Alison thought.

'I didn't expect to spend our birthday listening to you and Max talk politics, darling,' she said, trying to keep her tone light. 'Pour the wine,' she instructed Morton. 'This is supposed to be a celebration.'

'I hope you're enjoying it, Alison,' said Emma. 'I'm afraid that I no longer am. And the politics Max and I were talking about are, for the German Jews, on their own doorstep. That's why I won't go to Germany.'

'On principle, you mean?' Morton said.

Emma nodded. 'I wish it was no more than a question of principle for those who already feel it necessary to leave there.' She plucked a blade of grass and eyed it pensively. 'According to my parents, refugees have begun arriving in England. There are some in Manchester.'

'Refugees from what, exactly?' Morton asked. 'So far as I know, Emma, nothing has happened for them to flee from.'

'But it's probably going to happen, Max. Many who would be the victims prefer to think that it won't, and are sitting tight, waiting for things to blow over. Others are not taking chances.'

'How do you know so much about this?' Morton demanded. 'I wouldn't have thought you had a political thought in your head.'

'Nor would I,' said Alison.

'And you're both right,' Emma answered. 'What I know is from the horse's mouth. When a Jew arrives in a strange place, he makes for the nearest synagogue – he knows where to find his own. Last week, my father found himself praying beside a gentleman from Berlin, one of the refugees I mentioned. He told my father what's going on in Germany, and Dad told me, on the phone.'

Emma threw the blade of grass away and straightened her crumpled skirt, her expression grim. 'The Nazis are organising big rallies to speak against the Jews. Elderly Jewish people are being intimidated by the Brownshirts, and traders are finding their shop windows smashed when they arrive to open for business in the mornings. The gentleman also told Dad that his children were being victimised by their Hitler Youth Movement schoolmates. That's what finally made him decide to leave.' Emma shuddered. "I can't bear to think about it.'

'Then don't,' Alison advised.

'Because you're not going to, are you, Alison? Even though you are half-Jewish.'

Alison's dark eyes flashed. 'I haven't forgotten that!'

'Actually, you look more Jewish than Emma does,' Morton observed.

'And it might not do her any good, when she gets to Berlin,' Emma said.

'Stop it!' Alison exclaimed. 'Nobody is going to tap me on the shoulder and abuse me when I get to Berlin! But it isn't necessary to be Jewish to be appalled by the things that man told your father, Emma. And I quite understand why you don't feel able to go there.'

'I'm sorry, Alison, that you *do* feel able to go there, to entertain people who want to wipe your father's race from the face of the earth.'

'I am not going to Berlin for the purpose of entertaining the Nazis, Emma.'

A strained silence followed, during which Morton poured the wine and wished the subject of Berlin had not been raised. Alison's excitement about the prestigious international festival had fizzled out. Nor was it pleasant to be the object of her dear Emma's disapproval.

Morton took a monogrammed handkerchief from his blazer pocket and mopped his brow. It was not just the heat that was causing him to perspire. Alison and Emma were carefully not looking at each other, a wasp was dancing above his wine glass and would doubtless sting him any minute, and the atmosphere could be cut with a knife.

"Will you please try to understand, Emma, that I can't allow my personal feelings to stop me from appearing at the festival,' Alison said eventually.

'I'm pleased to hear you have some in this matter.'

'My dear Emma, I am not made of stone.'

But there were times when Emma thought she was. And,

though Emma respected Alison's dedication to her work, putting it before principles was another matter.

'Now may we please talk about something else?' said Alison.

Morton raised his glass to drink a toast to them. But the celebratory mood could not be recaptured. Alison had never felt more misunderstood. Emma had lost some of her respect for Alison. And Morton felt, for the first time, like pig-in-the-middle between them.

# CHAPTER ELEVEN

FROM THE moment she arrived in Berlin, Alison was beset by a feeling of menace.

She told herself it was all in her mind, that the great black swastikas displayed on National Socialist Party posters at the railway station were not the sinister symbols they seemed. But her unease increased when she entered her hotel and saw a group of uniformed Nazis chatting in the foyer. Were they eyeing her with the admiration to which she was accustomed? Or because she looked Jewish?

Morton had accompanied her to attend the opening of the play, and had reserved rooms at the Adlon on the elegant Unter den Linden. It was Berlin's most famous hotel and had an ambience of quiet comfort that reminded Alison of New York's Algonquin. The rest of the company had elected to stay at the Bristol. Probably because I am staying here, Alison thought dryly while she and Morton waited to be shown to their rooms.

She caught the eye of one of the Nazis, and shivered.

'I hope you're not coming down with a summer cold, my darling,' Morton said.

Alison made herself smile, and replied in a Cockney accent: 'Not bloody likely!'

Morton laughed. Their festival production was a revival of *Pygmalion* from Alison's Shaw season.

'Did you know that *Pygmalion* was first performed in Vienna, Alison?'

She shook her head and Morton read in her expression her reaction to the Brownshirts' presence.

'I wonder what that German-speaking audience in 1913 made of Eliza Doolittle's shocking language,' he said to distract her.

94

'The same, no doubt, as English-speaking audiences did when they first heard it,' said Alison, managing to chuckle.

'I've wondered, too, how the play came to be premiered there,' Morton prattled on. 'One day, when I have time, I must make a point of finding out.'

'Shaw seems to pop up everywhere. I heard, when we were in New York, that he had even managed to inveigle himself into the American literary élite,' said Alison, wondering if the group of Nazis was still beside the door. She had turned her back towards them.

'Otherwise known as the Algonquin Round Table,' said Morton. 'I was once staying at the hotel when Alexander Woollcott and Dorothy Parker and the rest of their set were lunching together, and wished I could be a fly on the wall, listening to them boosting their own egos! Though Mr Woollcott's needs no boosting,' he added. 'That man has the power to make or break a production with one critical review – and knows it. Broadway lives in fear and trembling of his pen.'

'But he was very kind in what he wrote about me,' said Alison with satisfaction.

When she turned to follow the porter to the lift, the Nazis had gone and she was able to relax.

'There used to be a literary set who met at this hotel,' Morton was saying. 'But I suppose every capital city has its equivalent to the Bloomsbury Group.'

The sight of yet another Nazi uniform, on a burly young man in the lift, set Alison on edge again. Stop it, she ordered herself. Swastikas were part of the scenery here and she could not spend the next three weeks looking over her shoulder. For that, in effect, was what she had begun doing.

After lunch Morton, who knew Berlin well, took her on a guided tour. The splendour of some of the architecture was to Alison breathtaking. She thought the Reichstag, which was built in Renaissance style, one of the most imposing edifices she had ever seen, while the Fischerstrasse, in the old city, captivated her with its quaint charm.

Later, Morton dismissed the car he had hired and they

paused for tea at the Café Kranzler, which allowed Alison a view of Berlin's busiest corner where Unter den Linden met with Friedrichstrasse.

'I would have liked to visit the Jewish quarter,' she said, absently watching Morton dig into a huge portion of *Apfelstrudl*.

'This isn't as good as Emma's,' he declared. And added lightly, 'I don't even know if there is a Jewish quarter here, my dear.'

'Every big city has one, Maxwell.' Alison had learned that from her father's family.

'In that case, we may have passed through it on our tour,' he replied. 'But I understand that the German Jews are much more integrated – or should I say assimilated – than their brethren elsewhere.'

And Emma would say 'A lot of good that will do them', Alison thought. But was this beautiful city, with its theatres and museums, concert halls and art galleries, churches, and synagogues too, really the setting for the evil scenario Emma's words had conjured up? When tea was over and she strolled with Morton in the bustling Alexanderplatz, beneath a peaceful summer sky, it was difficult to believe.

The Berliners were going about their daily business as ordinary people did everywhere. Were these respectable-looking gentlemen in dark suits, and the placid-faced matrons shopping at the Teitz and Wertheim department stores, really going to put someone like Hitler in power?

In the flesh, the youngsters of the Hitler Youth Movement looked the picture of innocence, Alison registered, watching a group of them leap onto a tram. The uniformed Nazis were, in appearance, clean-cut and pleasant young men, she had noted, not at all like the uncouth thugs Emma's story had led Alison to expect. One could not imagine them perpetrating a reign of terror, nor those youngsters victimising their Jewish schoolmates.

'You're very pensive, Alison,' Morton said when they were returning by taxi to their hotel. She had been uncharacteristically subdued throughout the afternoon.

'I was thinking that every city I've been in has its own

special atmosphere, Maxwell. Paris is sophisticated, and New York frenetic. London is elegant. Bath is genteel.'

'And Berlin?'

'I can't find the right word for it, but there's something about it that disturbs me.'

Morton glanced through the taxi window at the people sauntering beneath the trees on Unter den Linden, which he thought was one of the loveliest avenues in the world. They were approaching their hotel, and those who lived in this affluent area of the city could be expected to look the prosperous citizens they were. But Morton had not failed to notice, elsewhere, signs of the economic depression. The sight of clusters of men loitering despondently on street corners had told its story.

'You must remember, my dear, that we are here in difficult times,' he said. 'The atmosphere you are aware of isn't the real Berlin.'

Alison fingered the clasp of her white kid purse, and stared thoughtfully down at her matching shoes. 'On the surface everything is calm,' she replied. 'But it's like the calm before a storm. If I had to put a word to it, I'd call it sinister.'

'You're letting what Emma told us cause your over-vivid imagination to run away with you.'

'I hope you're right.'


Sinister atmosphere or not, Berlin was renowned as a centre of the arts, and appearing at the festival was an exciting prospect for Alison.

The city boasted four opera houses, and was world-famous for its theatre. The great director Max Reinhardt had made his name here. Reinhardt's spectacular production of *Oedipus Rex* at Berlin's Zirkus Schumann Theatre in 1910 was still spoken of with bated breath. This was the city of Bertolt Brecht, and of the unique actress Elisabeth Bergner.

These were some of Alison's thoughts, as she prepared for her opening night. She had heard that every Berlin theatre-goer was a knowledgeable armchair-critic. How would Alison Plantaine's performance be received?

Though her own distinguished reputation was known here – as it was in New York, before she played there – Alison had the feeling that here she was under the microscope. She had not felt that way on Broadway.

Morton had never seen her so edgy before a performance and remained with her in her dressing room until curtain-up.

'Don't worry, Maxwell. I won't turn tail and run!' she assured him.

'I am not in the least worried. And there is absolutely nothing for you to worry about.'

'So long as I don't forget my lines if I spot some Nazis in the audience!' she joked.

But Morton knew she was not really joking, and felt Emma's disapproving presence as though she were in the room with them. Emma's lecture had really got to Alison, though Alison had not let it show at the time.

'They're going to love you, darling!' he declared when her call came.

About that, Morton was right. *Pygmalion*, and Alison's Eliza Doolittle, proved to be one of the triumphs of the festival. Morton was not surprised. What did surprise him was that Alison was. It was as though her confidence in herself had temporarily deserted her. Was it because, in Berlin, she did not feel secure? Nor, Morton noted, was she able to relax. Had Alison wished to, she could have gone from party to party, night after night, enjoying the adulation showered upon her. She accepted only one invitation, and agreed to do so solely because the entire *Pygmalion* company had been invited, and the host was a prominent patron of the arts.

Not until she arrived did Alison learn that he was also a prominent Nazi. So prominent that among his guests were members of Hitler's Shadow Cabinet. She was introduced to a benign-looking gentleman called Ernest Rohm, and to a barrel-shaped one whose name was Hermann Goering, whom she had seen pictured with Hitler, in the English newspapers. Would they be kissing her hand so courteously had they known she was half-Jewish? A feeling of revulsion for these architects of discrimination against her father's race rippled through her. And, too, a gust of personal animosity so strong that it was all she could do to stop herself from spitting in their suave and smiling faces.

Instead, she put on the greatest performance of her life, maintaining the public image of Alison Plantaine, the distinguished British actress, and was filled with self-disgust because her professionalism had again won the battle with her principles. But wasn't her professionalism a principle in itself? The sole reason she was here?

It was an occasion that would remain carved upon Alison's memory. The palatial mansion, furnished with priceless antiques and awash with Nazis. Blue-rinsed dowagers eyeing her through their lorgnettes. Beautifully gowned girls – not a brunette among them. Champagne flowing and cigarettes stubbed out on platters of untouched food. The hubbub of conversation and laughter, and – drifting from somewhere – the music of Wagner. She would never hear Wagner again without remembering this. And the *Pygmalion* company making merry in the midst of it.

None of them felt as Alison did – why should they? They didn't have Jewish blood in their veins, and Alison's had, tonight, risen to the surface as she would never have thought it could. Suddenly she felt like a small island in a hostile sea. For all she knew, her fellow actors in *Pygmalion* might be anti-Semites. There was no shortage of them in England. Indeed, Alison had cause to believe her own mother was tarred with that brush, even though Hermione had fallen in love with and married a Jew.

Nobody could have divined Alison's painful thoughts as she stood proudly beside Morton, a stately and striking figure in her clinging white crêpe gown. But Morton was, as ever, sensitive to her moods. 'What is it, my darling?' he asked quietly.

Alison linked his arm – they were briefly alone beside the buffet. 'I was thinking that you are the only person in Berlin

I know I can trust,' she replied as her rumination crystallised thus.

*Pygmalion*'s director joined them in time to catch what Alison had said. 'You can trust me, pet,' he declared with the appealing smile that lent his somewhat saturnine face unexpected charm.

'You overheard me being melodramatic,' Alison was constrained to say.

The director glanced around at the peppering of Nazi uniforms. 'And who can blame you, darling?'

They exchanged a smile.

Though she did not know Basil Breen well on a personal level, Alison thought him a nice man. He was known to be what Morton called a 'loner', and she had heard that he was homosexual.

'There is something distinctly Ruritanian about the Nazi uniforms,' Breen opined. 'In my view, a political party that decks people out like that isn't to be taken seriously.'

Alison paused. 'That's what I thought, before I came to Berlin. After being here for a few days, I'm not so sure. There's a sort of – creeping evil about those people, Basil.'

Breen's gaze roved around the room and settled on Hermann Goering's genial countenance. 'There's nothing evil about that face, Alison.'

'That's why I said "creeping". There are things that Maxwell and I know, Basil, but I'd rather not tell you about them here.'

'Everyone knows how Hitler's lot are about Jews, Alison, if that's what you are referring to.'

Alison stiffened. 'My father was a Jew.'

'Then you're bound to be prejudiced, love, aren't you?'

'The word "prejudiced" is better applied to the Nazis!'

Morton glanced anxiously over his shoulder. 'We really shouldn't be having this conversation here.'

'Probably not,' Breen agreed.

'That is part of the feeling I've had since I arrived in Berlin,' said Alison. 'If one doesn't feel free to express one's views in public, then Germany is no longer a free country. Though Hitler is not yet in power, his tentacles already have people in their grip.'

'You're being melodramatic again, love,' Breen replied, 'and also making sweeping statements. Expressing one's views in public is one thing. Doing so when they are insulting to one's host – who happens to be a Nazi – is quite another.'

'I would rather not be the guest of a Nazi. When I agreed to come here tonight I had no idea he was one, Basil.' Would she have made herself accept the invitation, had she known? A refusal would have been letting the company down.

It was then that Alison recognised that a sense of place could not be acquired by the homely means she had supposed; by putting down the roots her childhood and youth had lacked. There was only one way it could be acquired: by knowing who you were and taking a stand.

'Let's get out of here,' she said to Morton, and swept from the room without so much as a glance at her host. And, oh, the joy that was suddenly pervading her spirit! I am my father's daughter, with all that means, and his people are mine, she thought. And the stand I am taking is for me, not just for him. Alison Plantaine had had to come to Germany to find out who she really was.

Morton had followed her, with Basil Breen in tow.

'How would you two like to take me to a night-club? I feel like celebrating!' she said while Morton helped her slip on her cloak.

'How very mercurial that lady is,' Breen remarked to Morton, as they tried to keep pace with Alison's impetuous exit from the house.

Morton, who needed no reminding of that fact, managed to laugh. What had changed Alison's mood, so suddenly, was beyond him, but it was a relief to see her so relaxed after the way she had been since arriving in Berlin.

It was by then 2 a.m. Morton's hired car awaited them in the sweeping driveway. The chauffeur was asleep behind the wheel and had to be prodded awake.

'We would like to see Berlin by night,' Alison gaily told him.

101

'Then I will drive you, *bitte*, to our *wunderbar* cabarets,' he replied. 'Such clubs we have here in Berlin' – he clapped his hand to his face, for effect – 'you have never before seen!'

As they drove down the brilliantly lit Friedrichstrasse where shadowy figures lurked in shop doorways, Morton exchanged a glance with Basil Breen.

'I'm not sure that Berlin nightlife is quite for you, darling,' he said to Alison.

'I,' said Breen emphatically, 'am quite sure that it isn't.'

'In that case, I am determined to see it,' Alison answered – as Morton had feared she would.

What followed was an excursion into decadence Alison had not known existed. They went from club to club, each more *risqué* than the one they had just left, as if their driver, like a showman building toward a grand finale, had planned it that way.

Alison was both fascinated and repelled by the sheer abandon and matter-of-fact style of entertainment that broke all the moral rules ordinary folk lived by. She had never thought to see a woman exhibit her breasts onstage, let alone her pubic hair.

And where nudity was not the motif, the girl dancers straddling chairs – which passed for choreography – turned out to be men. As were some of the evening-gowned members of the audience, Alison's male escorts informed her.

'I always feel terribly sad for transvestites,' Basil Breen said after they had left one such club.

They were in the car, and Alison and Morton carefully avoided his eye. The compassion of one kind of homosexual for another was not within their ken. Both would have been surprised to learn that transvestites were not homosexual in the accepted sense of the word.

But sadness for the artistes in general was Alison's overriding emotion as they continued the round. Many were highly talented, and she thought them wasted in the bizarre twilight world in which they had found their niche.

'Alison should see some of Berlin's political cabaret,

102

to complete her education!' Breen said to Morton with a smile. 'The times couldn't be more right for political satire than they are here, right now.'

'How can cabaret be political?' Alison wondered aloud.

She was about to find out. And, to her joy, that there were in Berlin those who were not afraid to poke fun at Hitler in public.

'I was here in 1929,' Breen recalled, 'just after Werner Finck opened his Katacomb Club. It was when Hitler had begun gaining ground, and more and more of his Brownshirts were on the streets. The night I went to the Katacomb, Finck, who himself acts as the club's master of ceremonies – the Germans call them *conferenciers* – was having a good go at the Nazis in his own inimitable comic style.'

'I can't wait to get there,' said Alison.

'Maxwell and I will have to be your translators, when we do, for it is entertainment largely for the mind.'

'Count me out of the translating,' Morton said. 'My German isn't that good.'

'And we are all three a little overdressed for going there,' Breen remarked, glancing at their formal evening attire and his own. 'It will be packed with the intelligentsia, and they don't dress up.'

'Then we'll make an imposing entrance, won't we?' said Alison.

Morton gave her an admiring glance. 'You always do.'

As they entered the Katacomb, Breen told Alison that there were other clubs of its kind, and that they were probably peculiar to Berlin.

'The political climate here is a great breeding ground for what they purvey,' he declared, 'and for writers like Brecht, who pits his wit against the fascists via the theatre.'

'Is that what Brecht is doing in his work now?'

'You bet!' said Morton.

'And if you'd seen his *Rise and Fall of the City of Mahagonny* – it's an opera with music by Kurt Weill – you wouldn't doubt it, Alison,' Basil endorsed, as they were shown to a table.

The air in the Katacomb was as beery and smoke-fugged

103

as in the other clubs they had visited, and the laughter as uproarious. But the similarity ended there. The *conferencier* was stationed before the curtain telling a witty story, and the absence of uniforms a pleasant change.

The anti-Nazi jokes were the kind Alison would liken to the one about the people who thought they were following a bridal car, but it turned out to be a hearse.

The songs and sketches were of the same genre and their real meaning was not lost on the audience, Alison saw. She had rarely heard such applause.

'Thank you for bringing me here,' she said to Breen. 'It has made me believe there is still hope for Germany.'

A young man seated with a party at the next table overheard, and gave her a smile. 'If I thought there was no hope for Germany, I would go home and cut my throat,' he said.

'And I would not blame you,' Alison replied.

# CHAPTER TWELVE

IN THE week they had been in Berlin, Alison had come to depend upon Morton more than she ever had at home. Except for when she was onstage they had spent almost every waking moment together, she thought whilst taking her morning bath.

But today she must fill in the hours as best she might, without Morton's comfortable presence. He was returning to England this evening, and the business meetings in Berlin which he had delayed in order to spend time with Alison could be put off no longer.

Maxwell was the most kind and considerate of men, as her father had been, Alison reflected, and she loved him dearly. How convenient it would be if there was in what she felt for him the missing element that would make her want to be his wife. But convenience played no part in matters of the heart.

She dried herself and dressed, paced the room restlessly, then was lured by the fine weather to join the Berliners strolling outside on Unter den Linden.

Though it was now September, there was no hint of autumn in the soft breeze caressing the trees. The fashionable women who lived in this part of Berlin had not yet discarded their summer attire, and the broad avenue seemed to Alison, at that moment, a carefree place.

Briefly, she gave herself up to that mood. She would not spend this lovely day brooding about what might be in store for Germany and its Jews. There was nothing she could do about it other than take her stand, publicly as well as privately. The only smile the Nazis whom she encountered now received from her was one of overt contempt. Morton had told her she had better draw the line at treating the theatre manager that way, but she had learned that the man was a Party member, and she would make no exceptions.

But she was thinking of none of this, that sunlit morning, as she once again admired the outer trappings of Berlin. At noon, when her wanderings had taken her near to the Kaiser Wilhelm Gedächtniskirche, she saw that the famous Café Romanische was handily nearby, and decided to pause there awhile.

Morton had mentioned that during the Twenties, the Romanische was an international rendezvous for the writers and artists who had then flocked to Berlin, including Sinclair Lewis, who was Emma's favourite novelist. This will be something to tell Emma, Alison thought while she scanned the shabbily splendid café for an unoccupied table. Among the things she definitely could not tell Emma, she reflected, recalling the bizarre night-clubs she had visited. It would take a good deal less than that to make Emma reach for the smelling salts. Alison's dear, sweet cousin was something of a prude.

There was a time when Alison had been one. But she and Emma had jointly suffered an early disillusionment that had opened Alison's mind, if not Emma's. Clara Stein's first marriage was of the shotgun variety, and Emma and Alison had learned thus that respectable girls could get into trouble.

Alison's youthful affair with Albert Battersby had afterwards caused her to comprehend the temptation to which her cousin Clara had succumbed. But Emma had never had a boyfriend. And continued to view temptation through the eyes of one who had never been tempted, Alison was thinking, when a masculine voice addressed her.

'If you do not mind sharing a table, you are welcome to sit here.'

Alison turned around and looked uncertainly at the bespectacled young man who was quizzically regarding her. He didn't look the kind who would try to pick up a woman.

'You do not remember me,' he said. 'That is not remarkable, as we met in semi-darkness and in any case I am far from memorable. The latter does not apply to you.'

He was the young man who had eavesdropped at the Katacomb Club, who had told her that if he thought there was no hope for Germany, he would go home and cut his throat. Alison returned his smile, which she noticed was engagingly crooked, and sat down.

'I remember you now.'

'My name is Richard Lindemann.'

Alison introduced herself.

'You are Alison Plantaine the actress?'

She nodded.

'I have a ticket to see you in *Pygmalion* tonight.'

'Then you must come backstage after the play.' Now why, wondered Alison, did I say that? She wasn't given to inviting strange young men to her dressing room.

But there was something totally disarming about this one, she thought, studying him while he summoned a waiter and ordered coffee for her. He wasn't handsome, and had a quietly serious demeanour. But the blue eyes behind his spectacles were fringed with thick black lashes that gave him an arresting appearance, and matched his curly hair.

Alison noted, too, that his serge suit was shiny with wear and his shirt collar frayed. At this time of day, if he had a job he would be at work. Was he one of Berlin's unemployed, killing time over a cup of coffee he could barely afford to buy?

'You don't have to treat me to coffee just because I am sharing your table,' she said impulsively. 'It was kind of you to order it for me, as I don't speak German.'

'If you wish to pay your own bill, I shall not argue with you. I am not in the least well off, and went without lunch for a week to pay for my theatre ticket.' He gave her one of his lopsided smiles. 'A person needs food for the soul, as well as for the body. And the opportunity to see *Pygmalion* performed in English is too good to miss. I am a great admirer of your Mr Shaw.'

'Shaw is Irish, not English, Herr Lindemann.'

'But for me, he holds up a mirror to the corruptions in your society. As Brecht does here – though not, of course, in the same way.'

Alison stirred her coffee and recalled what her grandfather had said about Shaw being the Shakespeare of his age.

Richard broke into her thoughts. 'The time may come when Brecht will not be allowed to wield his pen in Germany,' he said quietly. 'If Hitler comes to power it will put an end to free expression in this country, and those of us who are trying to stop it from happening will have our voices stilled.'

The unease Alison had that morning managed to discard returned to chill her.

'I have not yet told you I earn my meagre living as a writer,' Richard went on. 'My father, who is a surgeon, wished for me to follow in his footsteps. But my vocation is to work with a different kind of scalpel,' he added with a smile.

The smile faded. 'This can be highly dangerous in the Germany of today. The fascist poison has already permeated high places.

'There is in Berlin a journal called *Die Weltbühne*, whose editor, Carl von Ossietsky, is one of the most brilliant journalists of his time – revered by those like myself, for whom emulating Ossietsky is our ideal.'

He paused to sip some coffee. 'But Ossietsky's policy of publishing the truth has aroused the animosity of the extreme right which includes the Reichswehr generals. Last year, he was convicted on a trumped-up charge of betraying military secrets in a piece his journal published in 1929. He and the writer of the article were imprisoned, Miss Plantaine.'

Richard returned his cup to the saucer and stared pensively into it. 'God help Germany if that was, as Ossietsky has prophesied, a taste of things to come.'

When he looked up, there was a steely glint in his eyes. 'Though I and my friends are but a group of struggling writers, we are doing all we can to prevent it. As Confucius said, "It is better to light one small candle than to curse the dark."'

Alison remained silent. Part of her mind was wondering

what she was doing here, listening to this political young man talk of his ideals. There was an unreal quality about her re-encountering him in a city the size of Berlin. And why did she fear for him, as though he meant something to her?

The reason to fear was clear enough, but Alison's feelings were hard to explain. She wanted to reach across the table and tenderly ruffle his black curls. Was there something about him that had stirred in her the maternal instinct she had no doubt was there?

Richard was wondering why he had told her the things he had. She was a famous actress and had not come to Berlin to be bored by someone like himself, who was obsessed by Germany's plight.

'I did not mean to depress you, Miss Plantaine,' he said, observing her expression.

'I have been depressed since I arrived in Berlin, Herr Lindemann.'

'I am sorry to hear that.'

Alison changed the subject. 'But I enjoyed the cabaret at the Katacomb.'

'I, also.'

'How many meals did you miss to pay for your night out?' she inquired, noting his hollow cheeks.

'That is the kind of question my mother used to ask.'

Probably, thought Alison. It was a very motherly question and she didn't know why she had asked it.

'Unfortunately, she is no longer alive to watch over me,' Richard revealed, 'and my father has convinced himself that worrying about me and my way of life led her to an early grave. The fact that she knew he has a mistress, in his opinion played no part in it. But my mother was a sensitive woman, and my father – whom I no longer see – a highly insensitive man.'

A moment of silence followed.

Then Alison found herself telling Richard that she no longer saw her mother, but had loved her father deeply.

'Such are the strands of which the family web is woven,' he said wryly. 'I am coming to doubt that there is such a thing as a happy family.'

They exchanged a glance of rapport that Alison would not have thought possible on so short an acquaintance. But the same applied to the things they were saying to each other. For some reason, she was immensely drawn to Richard Lindemann – and, obviously, he to her. In a way that had removed the barriers of convention.

'All my friends' experiences with their parents are variations on the same theme,' Richard said. 'And one friend, whose wife is expecting their first child, says he is looking forward to learning how it is from a parent's point of view.'

'It will be how he makes it,' said Alison.

'Not necessarily. It takes two to make a relationship, so let us hope he has the right kind of child.'

'Is there a wrong kind of child?'

'I meant for his personality,' Richard replied. 'My father would not be the disappointed man he is, if I were his kind of son.'

Again, Alison thought the conversation altogether too intimate between strangers. 'You mix with people old enough to have settled down and married, then?' she said.

'I am old enough for that, myself.'

'You look about nineteen.'

'That is probably the little-boy quality that the women in our group tell me I have. We were celebrating the birthday of one of them, at the Katacomb. Her rich uncle sent her a cheque, so it was not necessary to miss any meals to pay for our night out. And by the way, I am twenty-six, and already have some grey hairs, at the nape of my neck.'

Again, Alison was charmed by his crooked smile. And little-boy quality was right! Not until she went to bed with him, two days later, did Richard become for her a man. But the all-embracing love that was to possess her utterly was kindled in her heart that morning, in the Café Romanische.

# CHAPTER THIRTEEN

WHEN MORTON returned to London he went directly to see Emma.

'What is it?' she asked apprehensively, when she had let him in and he stood silently regarding her. She had never seen him so distressed.

'It's Alison,' he said heavily.

I should have known, thought Emma. Only something concerning Alison could reduce Morton to this state. Simultaneously, anxiety for her cousin had flickered within her. 'Is Alison ill?'

'Would I have come home if she were?'

Of course he wouldn't. 'What has Alison done?'

'Nothing, yet. I'm afraid she's going to.'

'Will you please stop talking in riddles, Max.'

Morton lowered his weight onto the hall chair. 'I think Alison has fallen in love with a young German.'

Emma paused to digest this information. 'But you only think so, Max? You don't know?'

Morton fidgeted with his hat, which he was balancing on his lap. 'She hasn't told me, Emma, but I didn't need to be told. She wasn't in the hotel when I got back from some business meetings. I assumed she had spent the day wandering around the shops on her own, and expected her to return as depressed as she'd been since we arrived in Berlin. But she was positively radiant.'

Morton paused and stared into space. 'There was a sort of glow about her that I've never seen Alison display in all the years I've known her. And with her was this young chap. She said she wanted to introduce him to me before I left Berlin.'

As though I were her father! Morton thought sourly,

as he had then. That aspect of it had really stuck in his throat.

'And this was enough for you to jump to the conclusion you have?' said Emma.

'Together with the way the two of them kept gazing into each other's eyes,' Morton replied. 'They had a farewell drink with me before I left, and it was as if they'd forgotten I was there. The boy is as smitten with Alison as she is with him,' he declared bleakly.

Emma wanted to comfort him, but could not find the right words. She was also struck by the bitter irony of the position in which she now found herself. Filled with compassion for the man she loved, because he was sick with love for Alison – who, if Max was right, had now given her heart to someone else.

Briefly, Emma would have liked to banish love and its painful permutations from the face of the earth. Then she glanced at Morton, and knew she would rather love him and not have him, than be deprived of what his mere presence meant to her. She put a consoling hand on his shoulder – as his friend, this much she was allowed to do.

'I don't want your pity!' Morton flashed.

Emma removed her hand and held her tongue.

'It's Alison you should be concerned about, Emma. Not me. Knowing how impulsive she is, God knows what might come of this. She might even have burnt her boats by now.'

'If you mean a hasty marriage, Max, Alison wouldn't get married without you and me there. I'm certain of that. She would want me to be her maid of honour, and you to give her away.'

Morton winced at that prospect. 'I wasn't thinking as far ahead as that.'

'Then what did you mean by Alison burning her boats?' demanded Emma. 'If you meant what I now think you might have, Max, you ought to be ashamed of yourself. Alison is as respectable as I am.'

Morton surveyed Emma's prim little figure, garbed as usual in brown with a white collar that lent her a puritan touch. But passion can play havoc with respectability – which Emma would never know, Morton thought. 'I'd rather not talk about it,' he said.

'What is this young man like?'

Morton recalled Richard Lindemann's unprepossessing appearance – the very opposite of the Adonis-like designer to whom Morton had once thought he had lost Alison. Nor had she glowed for 'Adonis' as she did for the young German.

'Well?' prodded Emma.

'He's an intellectual, and he looks it. Horn-rimmed glasses, and a serious air. Not the kind you'd expect Alison to look twice at, Emma.'

Emma glanced at Morton's craggy face. 'Since when did looks have anything to do with falling in love?' Infatuation, maybe, she thought, but love was caring for the whole person. What they looked like was only their shell.

'What is more important is, what does Alison have in common with him?' she said sensibly. 'To make what she feels grow. And last.'

'Very little, I should think.'

'Exactly. If he were a theatrical, like her, there'd be more possibility of it lasting.'

Morton got up to pace the hall. 'This isn't one of Alison's casual flirtations, Emma. You may be sure of that. And love isn't something to apply commonsense to – which is what you're doing!'

'Calm down.' Emma took his hat, which he was still clutching, and hung it up.

'A person can't choose who they fall in love with,' he informed her.

You're telling me, she thought.

'And Alison is the last one to apply commonsense to anything!' he exclaimed.

'The worst that can happen is she'll talk the young man into coming to England, Max.'

'She may try to, though I doubt that she would succeed. I only spent a short time in his company but it was long enough to learn quite a lot.'

113

Morton returned himself to the chair. 'It seems that he is the editor of a give-away broadsheet. He and his friends are all writers, of the idealistic kind. They don't have two *Pfennigs* to rub together between them, from what I gathered. But with the help of a Jewish printer they are distributing anti-Nazi propaganda.'

'Good for them!'

'I agree. But it could be a reason for Alison deciding to stay in Berlin. Young Lindemann – that's his name – is absolutely dedicated to what he is doing. The only thing that boy radiates, Emma, is dedication.'

'Then he and Alison do have something in common. Nobody could be more dedicated than Alison is to the theatre. And it's ridiculous for you to fear, Max, that she'll stay in Germany. We both know that the man doesn't exist who she'd put before her career. Love, or no love.'

'My dear Emma,' said Morton, gazing morosely at a pane of red glass in the fanlight above the door. 'You seem to be overlooking that the theatre is international. Alison could continue acting in Berlin. She could branch out into films if she wished, like Lilian Harvey is doing in Germany.'

'If Hitler comes to power, Alison wouldn't be safe in Germany.'

'That is one of the things that's worrying me. In my opinion,' declared Morton, 'it is more than likely that he will. You can't walk a few yards in Berlin without seeing a swastika. One would think the Nazis were already in power! But why are we talking politics?'

'It's giving me the creeps,' Emma said with a shiver.

'We're talking politics for a very good reason.' Morton answered his own question.

And her name is Alison, Emma thought. But wasn't Alison, directly or indirectly, the subject of all their talks?

'The person we care most about,' Morton went on, 'has got herself involved with that horrendous political scene.'

'Come into the kitchen, Max. I'll make you some lemon tea.'

Morton followed Emma to her natural habitat from which she rarely strayed for long, and watched her empty a packet

114

of Red Label into the old tea caddy that had been her grandmother's.

Emma's kitchen was a comforting place, but Morton was beyond comfort. 'Your trouble, Emma, is you think tea is a magic potion,' he said sourly.

Emma put the kettle on the cooker and lit the gas jet beneath it. 'And yours, Max, is you wish you could wave a wand and change something it isn't in your power to change.' She gave Morton a kind smile. 'We can watch over Alison, sure, but we can't live her life for her. You had better accept that, Max.'

'I don't have your accepting nature, our Em.'

'That, I already know. All the same, Max, if what you fear about Alison and the young German is correct, all you and I can do is wait to pick up the pieces – for want of a better way of putting it.'

Morton smiled grimly. 'Whichever way they fall.'

It had not yet struck him – as it had Emma – that picking up the pieces with regard to Alison was their permanent role.

# CHAPTER FOURTEEN

EVEN THE presence in Berlin of the Plantaine twins, who arrived with Charles Bligh during the final week of the festival, could not mar Alison's bliss.

It was as though the love she shared with Richard was an armour against all outside influences, major and minor, that might otherwise have made their mark upon her. She went through the motions of doing what her career demanded, but within herself lived for Richard alone. Everything else was a charade that revolved around him.

Alison was under no illusion that the same applied to Richard with regard to her. He had made no concessions in order to spend time alone with Alison. Instead, he had drawn her into his circle and one afternoon she found herself briefly forgotten, seated in a corner of a small printing works.

The old saying that man's love is a thing apart, but woman's her whole existence, was apparently true, thought Alison with tender amusement. Her beloved was at that moment poring over some proofs, with his colleagues.

Mr Rosenberg, who printed their broadsheet free of charge, adjusted his skull cap on his springy white hair, glanced nervously at Alison, and addressed the others in German.

'What did he say?' Alison inquired.

A hollow-cheeked young woman called Maria replied; Richard had not even glanced up from the page he was perusing. 'That he cannot believe a famous actress is sitting here in his print shop.'

Alison gave the old gentleman a warm smile and saw him blush. 'I wish I could be useful, instead of just sitting here.'

'In that case, you may help me fold the pages when they

116

are ready,' said another of the women. 'If it will not dismay you to soil with ink your hands?'

'I should like to help you, Gerda.'

Since meeting Richard, Alison had spent her days with these young intellectuals. They were a friendly lot, who tried not to let her feel the outsider she was, she reflected now. Fortunately, language had not proved a problem. Most of them spoke English. Gerda and Maria, like Richard, had in their schooldays spent time in England with penfriends.

'The others have gone to contact those who assist us with distribution,' Gerda told Alison, when they were alone together, folding copies of the broadsheet.

Gerda flicked her red hair from her forehead and smiled. 'Richard, he is not deserting you!'

Alison laughed. She had not thought he was. Before leaving he had kissed her cheek, absently. Like a husband departing for the office, she thought. Though they had known each other for less than two weeks, there was between them a bond that required no words.

'Who are the people who help distribute the paper?' she asked.

'They are socialists, Alison, like our group. Some are friends of ours, and others are friends of theirs. That is how such a network functions. It requires very many hands to deliver individual copies to as many homes as is possible.'

She added another folded copy to the pile. 'With our first issue, we placed stacks of *Achtung* by the kiosks on the streets. It was a foolish mistake. They were removed by Nazi sympathisers.'

Alison had not seen the broadsheet until today, and paused to eye its boldly printed name. '*Achtung* means warning, doesn't it?'

'And that is what our little paper is.'

'But what are the chances of the Berliners heeding it, Gerda?'

'*Liebe* Alison, Berlin is not the whole of Germany. We have friends in other cities, all of whom receive batches of *Achtung* which we send to them by train. When you are

117

performing at the theatre tonight, some of us will still be here folding copies. And by morning our fingers will be blistered from the work. Press day is always for us a large operation.'

'I see.' The immensity of the task Richard and his friends had undertaken was just seeping through to Alison. 'But you didn't answer my question,' she said to Gerda.

'About the chances of the people heeding our warning?' Gerda's lips tightened. 'I fear it is too late. But the Communists, who fight the Brownshirts in the streets, and we who are doing so with the printed word, continue to be thorns in the Nazis' side.'

'Then why do you fear it is too late, Gerda?'

'Because in the last elections the Nazis gained much ground. In hard times, *liebe* Alison, people are inclined to believe what they wish to believe. Most Germans already see President von Hindenburg as yesterday's man, and Hitler as their only hope for tomorrow.'

Alison was sickened to hear this.

Gerda observed her expression. 'But let us continue folding the pages, Alison. There is much to do. And better to light a small candle than to curse the dark.'

'Richard said that to me,' Alison recalled as they resumed the tedious chore.

'And all of us are constantly saying it to each other,' Gerda answered. 'Those are the words that nourish our spirits. And they are the official maxim of our group. *Achtung* is our small candle, Alison, and we shall keep it burning until it is snuffed out.'

Though Gerda's words had a terrible finality, her voice was as matter-of-fact as it had been throughout the conversation. Was she made of iron? Alison wondered. And it struck her that the same could be said of Richard and the others in the group. It was as if nothing could move them from their resolve.

Suddenly, Alison was filled with foreboding. 'You'll go on publishing *Achtung* even if Hitler comes to power. That's what you meant, didn't you, Gerda?'

'But we shall have to find a different printer.'

'Because old Mr Rosenberg won't be available, will he?' said Alison with mounting horror. 'He'll be in one of those camps where Richard said that Jews will be incarcerated.'

'If he lives to reach one. It cannot be a secret to Nazi intelligence that he is our printer, though his name does not appear on the paper.'

Gerda wiped her hands on a grimy rag that was lying beside the linotype machines. 'But old *Rosig*, as we have come, so affectionately, to call him, he is a brave man. He prints all our copy at night, with his own hands, and gives his staff time off on our press day — '

'So that's why there's nobody here,' Alison cut in. She had thought the absence of workers somewhat odd.

'They are not Nazi sympathisers, Alison, but old *Rosig* wishes not to involve them in the risk he knows he is taking. That is why I called him a brave man. And worse than a camp could consequently happen to him. To me, too,' said Gerda with a wry smile.

'But you are, at least, an Aryan,' Alison countered, though she disliked using the word that had become so overly-significant in the German vocabulary.

'*Liebe* Alison,' Gerda replied gently, 'if you believe that fact might mitigate what Aryans like Richard and I are doing, it is best that you stop believing it.' Her words removed the straw of hope to which Alison was clinging.

'My father, he is a simple minister of the church,' she went on. 'But he does not wish for *Mein Kampf* to be Germany's new bible, and preaches this from his pulpit. Therefore, he too may one day be — ' Gerda completed the sentence by graphically running her inky forefinger across her throat.

Alison stopped folding copies of the broadsheet and sat down.

'It is better for Richard that you do not discuss this with him,' Gerda advised, observing Alison's ashen face.

'I love Richard.'

'Do you think all of us do not know that? It has made us happy for him. But also it has made us sad.'

'Why should it make you sad?'

'Because what is between you can be only a transient affair.'

Alison stiffened. 'I should like to know why you think that?'

Gerda played with a fold of her printed dirndl skirt. 'It is not what I think, Alison. Simply the way things are. Tomorrow you are leaving Berlin.'

And it would not be for the want of trying if Alison didn't persuade Richard to leave with her.

Gerda divined her thoughts. 'Richard has made his choice, Alison, along with the rest of our group. And we know we are doomed if Hitler comes to power. It is possible that our voices could be stilled before then – one way or another. By now, there is surely in Nazi headquarters a file on each one of us, and —'

'I don't want to hear any more!' Alison cried.

Gerda waited until she had calmed down. 'All that remains to be said is that you have given your heart to a man who loves freedom above all else, and that meeting you at this time has made Richard's choice more painful.'

They continued folding the broadsheets in silence. When Richard and the others returned, Alison was thankful that she was an actress, able to put on a cheerful show.

But Richard was not fooled. 'What did Gerda say to you?' he asked that night, when he and Alison lay together in the cramped privacy of his room.

'You shouldn't be here with me now,' she said, evading the question. 'You ought to be working all night with your friends.'

'Dedicated though I am, not to spend with you your last night in Berlin was unthinkable. Now what did Gerda tell you?'

'Nothing I didn't already know in my heart. You are all in terrible danger, aren't you?'

'Some of us would be anyway, *meine Liebe*,' Richard answered in the same matter-of-fact tone Gerda had employed. 'Karl and Heinrich are Jews,' he went on, 'and Maria, who is a Catholic, would find under a Nazi régime that the drop of Jewish blood she has in her veins,

120

from her paternal great-grandfather, is the only drop that counts.'

Alison sat up in bed and burst into tears. 'Why did you have to involve yourself?' she sobbed, drying her eyes on the sheet. 'You will be carted away and imprisoned on some trumped-up charge, like that editor you told me about.'

'Thank you for comparing me to him, *Liebchen*. But he is an important man.'

'And so are you, Richard,' said Alison with feeling. 'To me.'

He returned her to his arms and kissed away her tears. But Alison's fear for him remained. She wanted to beg him to leave Germany, but knew what his reply would be. Richard had made his choice and Alison must not make it more difficult for him. Gerda's advice had lodged in her brain.

Alison too had a choice: she could stay in Berlin. But she was committed to play Sadie Thompson in *Rain*. Morton had seen the torrid drama when it was premiered in New York ten years ago, and had recently decided that it was a perfect vehicle for Alison. She could not let him down.

For Alison the show must go on, and love had no place in the political scenario of which Richard was dangerously part.

Our time is not now, she thought poignantly. This is just a foretaste of what may never be. 'Do you think you and I have a future together, Richard?' was all she allowed herself to say.

'The hope that we might will help me keep my personal small candle alight. You are the only woman I have loved, Alison, but why you love me is a mystery.'

Alison smiled tremulously. 'Love itself is the real mystery. And a game of chance, with Destiny dealing the cards. How else would we have encountered each other twice, in a city the size of Berlin?'

'What a romantic you are, *Liebling*!' Richard said against her lips. 'And how exhausted I shall be in the morning,' he added, as a hardening in his loins proclaimed that they were about to make love again.

Alison lay with her head on his chest and tenderly stroked his hair. 'I wasn't a whole person until I met you, my darling.'

'But you were a virgin,' he teased her. 'That was a matter of some surprise.'

'So you said. But for me, sex without love would be meaningless; the two are as one.'

'As we are, at this moment, *Herzchen*,' Richard whispered as he took her. 'And in our hearts we shall remain so, across the miles.'

Later, Alison rose to draw back the curtains and stood by the window gazing at her sleeping lover. How peaceful he looked in the moonlight, as though he hadn't a care in the world.

She had not, after Emma's revelations, wanted to come to Berlin, but doing so had added another dimension to her life. From now on, everything she did would be coloured by her love for this man, for he was hers and she his. And how perverse of Destiny, after bringing them together, to allow them but a short interlude before pulling them apart.

# CHAPTER FIFTEEN

THE ALISON Plantaine who returned to London was not the woman Emma and Morton had thought they knew. Both were baffled by the change in her. There was about the new Alison a self-contained quality totally at variance with the tempestuousness she had formerly displayed.

Rehearsals for *Rain* had begun immediately, and Alison would rise early in the morning and eat the breakfast Emma put before her, without demur. Her conversation was never contentious. If Emma advised her to wear a scarf, or to take an umbrella, she did as she was bid. In the evenings, she would curl up by the fire until Emma told her it was time for bed. Docile was the word for her. It was as though a whirlpool had suddenly become a placid pond – and equally bewildering. Neither Emma nor Morton expected the metamorphosis to last.

When it continued to do so, their uneasiness increased.

'How is Alison getting on at rehearsals?' Emma asked Morton, when he came to dinner and afterwards joined her in the kitchen for a private chat.

'While they are working, she is her usual professional self,' Morton replied. 'But Basil Breen, who is directing, told me that during the breaks she just sits staring into space, and that it's giving the rest of the cast the creeps.'

'He was in Berlin with you, wasn't he? Did Alison introduce her young man to him?'

'No,' said Morton abruptly. 'That seems to have been solely my privilege. The company knew there was a young man, of course – backstage grapevines are very efficient! And I understand that Charles Bligh asked Alison to bring Richard to a party he gave at the Excelsior, but she declined with thanks.'

'Like she's done with all the invitations she's received since she got back,' Emma remarked. 'Except for rehearsals, she hasn't been out.'

'And it isn't good for her image,' Morton replied. 'A star must be seen in all the right places.'

'You should tell that to Alison, Max. Not me.'

'I have. Her only response was an absent-minded smile, as if she wasn't really listening to me.'

Emma began putting away the dinner set. 'I get that feeling with her all the time, nowadays. That's why I asked you how she was at rehearsals. I wouldn't have been surprised if you'd said she keeps forgetting her lines.'

Morton stubbed out his cigar in the ashtray Emma kept in the kitchen for him. 'Even when her father was dying, Emma, Alison didn't let worry affect her work. She has a unique capacity for departmentalising her life. And at present, I am thankful she has!'

He watched Emma empty the ashtray and wash it. 'Would you say that Alison is happy at present, Emma?'

Emma paused to think about it. 'No. But nor is she unhappy, Max. I can't find the right word for the way she is. The only way I can describe it is that she seems to be hugging her private feelings to herself.'

'You mean she's brooding about that young man,' said Morton resignedly.

'Probably.'

'But she still hasn't mentioned him to you?'

'Not a word. And I can't mention him to her. It would be like prying.'

'Has she heard from him, Emma?'

Emma shook her head. 'I'm the one who picks up our mail. There's been nothing for Alison from Germany.'

'If he lets her down, I'll shoot him!' said Morton passionately – and to Emma's astonishment.

Richard was Max's rival for Alison's affections, and the end of the affair could be to Max's advantage. But he cared more for Alison than for himself, and did not want her to be hurt. Oh, the sacrifices love demanded! thought Emma from the depths of her own experience.

124

By the end of October, when Alison had still not heard from Richard, a further change was apparent in her. The self-containment remained, but a wounded expression had entered her eyes.

In mid-November, the day came when Emma could be silent no longer. 'If you want to cry on my shoulder, I'm here, Alison,' she said quietly.

They were seated at the breakfast table and Alison buried her face in her hands. When she raised her head, her eyes were dry. But Emma knew she was weeping inwardly.

'Maxwell has told you about Richard Lindemann, hasn't he?' Alison said tonelessly.

'If he hadn't, I'd have asked you why you were behaving so peculiarly since you got back from Berlin.'

'I've been in a sort of trance, Emma.'

'You certainly have.'

'But I'm not any more.'

Emma surveyed Alison's dispirited demeanour. 'Max and I have been very concerned about you.'

'So you two have been discussing me, have you?' said Alison, mustering mock chagrin.

Emma's was genuine. You'd be surprised to know that you are all we ever talk about, she thought.

Alison gave her a wan smile. 'I ought to have spoken to you about Richard,' she apologised. 'But what was between us was so precious to me, Emma – how can I make you understand? – so terribly private that I couldn't share my feelings even with you. You'll have to forgive me, darling.'

Emma replied as always: 'There's nothing to forgive.' And added, 'As Richard hasn't been in touch with you, isn't it time you found out why?'

Alison went to gaze through the window, though all there was to see was fog. 'I've had to stop myself from picking up the telephone receiver and asking for his number, Emma. And I shall continue to stop myself from doing so. My heart I have lost – but not my pride. I can think of no reason for his silence but the obvious one.'

A short silence followed, and Alison bent down to stroke the cat, which was lapping some milk from its saucer.

125

'The fact that Richard is several years younger than me doesn't help me think otherwise,' she added bitterly. 'He has a good deal to occupy his mind and his time – but how long does it take to pen a line? Or make a phone call? There is simply no excuse for his not getting in touch.'

'Have you written to him?'

'Three times, Emma dear. Fool that I am!' Alison laughed sardonically. 'Only I didn't know it at the time, Emma. I let myself be duped and now I am paying for it. I am obviously no judge of character – and I shall never again trust my own judgement. Or a man.'

With that, she left the room.

Harsh words, Emma thought, but the tone in which they were uttered was laced with pain. Alison would go on hoping to hear from Richard.

Emma decided it could not be left this way, and later that morning called Morton's office.

'Is it urgent, Miss Stein?' his secretary asked. 'Mr Morton is up to his ears in last-minute snags. *Rain* opens in three days' time.'

'I'm aware of that, Mollie. How could I not be. But I must speak to Mr Morton – and I pray that you are not going to do to me now what I once did to him and you!'

Mollie chuckled. Like her employer, she had since found that her pre-impression of Emma, formed from their first telephone conversation, was misleading. 'I'll put you through, Miss Stein.'

Emma told Morton the gist of her talk with Alison, and added, 'Instead of rushing off to shoot Richard for letting Alison down, why not do something useful?'

'Like what?'

'Put through a call to Berlin – which Alison won't do. Richard could have been run over by a tram and be lying in a coma, for all we know, Max.' Emma could not imagine any man rejecting Alison. There had to be some other reason for Richard's silence.

'Isn't it just like you to give the rotter the benefit of the doubt!' Morton snorted. 'If somebody spat in your eye, Emma, you wouldn't believe they meant it!'

126

'Calm down, Max. And give me your true opinion of the young man you met in Berlin.'

'He struck me as having integrity,' said Morton grudgingly.

'And you're not usually wrong when you sum a person up.'

'All right, Emma, I'll make the call. It won't be the first time I've made a fool of myself for Alison.'

Emma supplied him with Richard's telephone number, which she had found in Alison's address book, and spent the morning waiting for him to call her back.

Instead, at midday, Morton arrived at the flat.

Emma scanned his expression. 'Is the news so bad you had to come and give it to me in person?'

'It isn't good.' Morton took off his fog-dewed hat and coat, and followed her to the kitchen. 'The number you gave me must be a pay-phone – like they have in apartment houses where the tenants can't afford private phones. The woman who answered didn't speak English, and my German is limited. She said Richard wasn't there – I was able to understand that much. Then she added something, in a whisper, and I wasn't sure if she had said he had gone away, or been taken away.'

'That's all you know, Max?'

Morton shook his head. 'I didn't leave it at that. I called the lawyer who acts for me in Berlin, and asked him to make some inquiries. It was ages before he rang back.'

Emma prickled with apprehension. 'To tell you what?'

'The broadsheet isn't around any more. Nor is Richard,' said Morton grimly. 'He and the others who wrote for it have disappeared.'

He stared at the dead cigar in his hand. 'According to Herr Muller, there must be many such disappearances nowadays. He called it the stilling of small voices. Richard and his friends are not public figures – if they were, for the time being they'd still be safe. Unless you happen to know them personally, you wouldn't get to hear they'd gone missing.'

'Who is Herr Muller, Max?'

127

'The man I spoke to! Who else?' said Morton, emerging edgily from his troubled thoughts.

'I'm a little confused – and who can wonder?' Emma said. 'My flesh has gone goosey from what you've told me. You don't look too good yourself.'

'You'll be offering me a cup of hot sweet tea in a minute!'

Emma put the kettle on the cooker to boil. 'We could both use one.'

'Alison is the one who's going to need treatment for shock,' Morton replied, 'not to mention her distress, for which there is no remedy, when the full significance of all this sinks in. Muller thinks that Richard and his group, and others like them, are probably being held in a secret camp and will be openly classified as enemies of the State if Hitler becomes Chancellor.'

He stopped pacing the kitchen and sat down at the table. 'I gathered, Emma, that one way and another things are reaching boiling-point in Germany. Since the elections this month there's been rioting in the streets. Muller said that everywhere you look you see Brownshirt thugs brawling with the Communists.'

Emma shuddered, and Morton refrained from mentioning the mounting abuse directed against her brethren. Muller had said his Jewish neighbours were afraid to venture out after dark.

While they drank the tea, he relayed to her that Berlin was at present rife with rumour. 'It seems that Hitler has made an unlikely alliance with his old enemy, ex-Chancellor von Papen, who, despite his resignation, is still the President's protégé. A hotbed of intrigue about describes it.

'Muller also told me that many people prominent in the arts are leaving,' he went on. 'That is the most telling sign of all, Emma. When the torchbearers of civilised society abandon their own country to the barbarians, the end is nigh.'

'Alison should have made Richard leave Germany,' Emma declared.

'She probably tried to. But there will always be those who would rather be burned at the stake of freedom than flee the flames consuming it.'

They heard Alison let herself into the flat, and exchanged an apprehensive glance.

'Why is she home from rehearsal so early?' Emma asked Morton.

'There isn't one today. Only costume fittings,' he had time to reply before Alison appeared in the kitchen doorway.

'Having a cosy tête-à-tête, are you?' Alison greeted them. 'You'll be pleased to hear that my costumes are fine, Maxwell dear.' Then she noticed his strained expression, and Emma's. 'What's wrong?'

How were they to tell her? Morton steeled himself to do so.

'I see,' was all she said when he had finished speaking.

Why do I feel numb? Alison was asking herself with the part of her mind that was still functioning. It was as though she had been clubbed over the head and was reeling from the blow, but felt no pain.

She heard Emma cry out, but it sounded distant.

'Catch her, Max! Before she falls!'

Then the room began whirling round, and all was black.

When Alison opened her eyes she was lying on her bed. Emma and Morton were gazing at her anxiously. 'How did I get here?'

'Max carried you,' Emma said.

Alison managed to smile. 'It's a good thing he's a strong man. I'm rather a big girl! Did I really faint? How very dramatic.'

Morton patted her hand. 'Everything you do is dramatic. How do you feel now, my darling?'

Alison sat up and had to return her head to the pillow. 'A little nauseous, to tell you the truth.'

'The doctor will give you something to take,' said Emma.

'You know I haven't got a doctor, Emma. I've never been ill in my life.'

'I called mine,' Morton said.

'That was kind of you, Maxwell dear. But anyone can faint from shock. Why all the fuss?'

'You have a heavy schedule ahead of you, Alison. There's

dress rehearsal to get through. And then your opening night.' He observed Alison's pallid appearance. 'A tonic won't do you any harm, and I'm sure Dr Blake will prescribe one.'

'Don't worry, I shan't let you down,' Alison replied.

How can either of them be thinking of the play, when Alison's loved one has disappeared and is probably in the hands of the Nazis? Emma wondered. But Alison and Max were theatre people. A different breed from Emma, and she ought not to be surprised.

Alison's initial numbness was superseded by a great wave of anxiety for Richard. She wanted to rush to Germany and try to find him. She would surely have done so, were she not committed to star in *Rain*.

Morton divined her thoughts. 'When we get the opening over, I'll go to Berlin, Alison, and see what I can find out.'

Alison gave him a grateful smile. 'Bless you, darling.'

'And will you promise to take what the doctor prescribes for you?'

'I'll see that she does,' Emma said firmly.

But a tonic could not cure what possibly ailed her, Alison thought wryly.

Half an hour later, Dr Blake confirmed her suspicion. 'When did you last menstruate, my dear?'

Emma had remained in the bedroom while the doctor examined Alison. Alison saw her blanch, and her hand flutter to her throat. Was it now Emma's turn to faint? Probably!

'I don't keep a record of the exact date, but my last real period was sometime in August,' she answered the doctor.

'Then your baby will be born some time in May,' he calculated.

'Oh, God,' Emma moaned.

Dr Blake pretended he had not heard her. 'What did you mean by your last real period?' he asked Alison.

'Since then there've been a few spots of blood, which allowed me to suppose I might not be pregnant.'

The doctor cleared his throat and polished his pince-nez

in the short silence that followed. Pregnancy without marriage was a difficult situation for any woman. For Alison Plantaine it was more so. The press would lick their lips over so juicy a scandal. Was Morton the father? Dr Blake allowed himself to conjecture. But that was no business of his. Only his patient was.

He summoned his best bedside manner. 'I have always admired your performances, Miss Plantaine.'

'Thank you, Doctor.'

'Mr Morton kindly sent me first-night tickets for *Rain*. But I am afraid you will be unable to appear in the play now. It would be highly inadvisable for you to pursue your strenuous career during your pregnancy.'

'My mother appeared onstage until the seventh month, when she was carrying me.'

But she was a married lady, Emma thought. Alison had evidently not yet considered that aspect of her predicament. Which wasn't just her predicament, but Emma's and Morton's, too. What would Alison's disregard for the consequences of her actions present them with next? But a baby was enough to be going on with!

'If you follow your mother's example, it will be at the risk of miscarrying,' Dr Blake told Alison. 'The spots of blood you saw were nature's warning, Miss Plantaine. You must take things very easily.'

He smoothed his silver hair, buttoned his immaculate black jacket, snapped his medical bag shut, and avoided Alison's eye. 'If you don't want to lose the child.'

Lose Richard's child? Oh, no. It would be like piling injury upon the insult Alison had, by her mistrust, meted out to her lover. Learning about the baby would be to Richard another small candle lighting the darkness that had now enveloped him, as it was to Alison in the gloom that had overtaken her.

'The baby is very precious to me, Doctor,' she said with a warm smile.

'Then you would be wise to follow my advice.'

'I shall.'

Emma went to see the doctor out. She had not uttered a

word since she said 'Oh, God'. What was she thinking? Alison wondered. That her actress-cousin was a scarlet woman?

Alison ought to have known better.

When Emma returned to the bedroom, she took Alison in her arms. 'You're not to worry. Everything will be all right.'

Morton had entered with her. 'You can leave the worrying to us, Alison,' he said gruffly.

Alison's eyes stung with tears. 'What have I done to deserve such loving friends?'

'You rest now,' Emma instructed. 'Max and I will go and put our thinking caps on. And I'll make you a nice cup of tea.'

'You and your nice cups of tea!' Morton said to Emma when they had left the room. 'I seem to spend half my life following you to your kitchen.'

'And the other half venting your feelings on me,' Emma replied. 'Which I don't do to you.'

Morton ignored the comment. 'Everything will be all right, you just told Alison. Would you like to tell me how?'

'I was hoping you would tell me. You told Alison to leave the worrying to us – which she would anyway. And you're not usually short of ideas.'

'Right now,' said Morton, 'I don't seem to have any. About Richard: when I get to Berlin I'll have to play it by ear, as they say in the States. As for our other little problem! I am still having difficulty taking it in. But your job, Emma, will be to look after Alison, and I suggest that you take her up north to your family.'

'Why?'

'Use your head! We can't have it becoming public knowledge that Alison is pregnant. The scandal would be catastrophic for her career. We must get her out of London before her condition shows.'

Morton absently watched Emma refill the kettle. 'I shall have to re-cast Sadie Thompson – at three days' notice! The understudy we have just isn't good enough to open the play.'

Morton's mind raced on. 'I'll announce to the press that Alison is suffering from strain, due to overwork, and has been ordered by her doctor to take a lengthy rest. Dr Blake won't give the game away. He's a good chap – and it wouldn't be ethical.'

'For someone with no ideas, Max, you're doing remarkably well,' Emma said. 'But how do we keep Alison's condition a secret in Oldham? The neighbours there know her. She can't stay cooped-up in my parents' house until next May.'

'When it becomes obvious you'll have to take her someplace where she's unlikely to be recognised,' Morton replied. 'There must be plenty of isolated country cottages for rent.'

'And what,' pursued Emma, 'do we do with the baby when it arrives?'

'Anything but bring it back to London.'

Emma stiffened. 'How dare you be so casual and uncaring about Alison's child? Or, indeed, about any child!'

'At present it's an unborn child.' Morton rose to stare through the window. 'The fog hasn't lifted yet,' he commented irrelevantly. 'If I am to deal with all that must be dealt with, Emma, I must do so unemotionally.'

'But a child is a person, Max, and you had better start thinking of this one that way. For you, Alison and her career are the number-one priority in all this – as if a career is more important than a baby. I don't happen to see things that way. I shan't allow anything to be done that is wrong for the child.'

She plonked the kettle on the cooker and lit the gas, her expression tense with feeling.

Morton eyed her stiff back. 'I'll bear your threat in mind, our Em. Now where were we?'

'Alison and I were up north, where you'd just put us. I don't know where you were.'

'Briefing the press,' Morton recalled. 'But before I can, I must find someone to play Sadie.' He paused thoughtfully. 'I know who could do it. Alison's stepcousin —'

'If you give the part to Lucy, Alison will kill you.'

133

'Alison knows I'm in a spot – and you underestimate her professionalism, Emma. At such short notice it has to be someone who's played the role before. Lucy has, last year, when she made a guest appearance with the Plantaine Players. She'd jump at the chance of stepping in. I'll mention it to Alison before I leave.'

'I'd rather you than me,' Emma said.


As Morton had predicted, Alison raised no objection to his asking Lucy to take over her role. Professionally, Lucy was no threat to her and she was relieved that Morton's problem was so easily solved.

On *Rain*'s opening night, she sat by the fire with Emma, re-reading the story Morton had released to the press, variously embellished according to the newspapers in which it appeared.

'Lucy finally getting her big break via me is the very opposite of poetic justice,' she remarked to Emma. 'I don't doubt that she thinks she has scored one over me, that I'm sitting brooding about it.'

'Aren't you?'

'I have other things to think about, right now, Emma dear. Like how I'm going to look your parents in the eye, when we go up north!'

'Mam will be busy getting your room ready.'

'I know. And it's wonderful of them to agree to have me.'

'Did it enter your head that they might not?'

'No.'

'Nor mine,' Emma said.

In a family crisis, the Steins could always be relied upon to do what had to be done. Alison and Emma were to travel to Oldham by limousine tomorrow. Conrad Stein was already inquiring about a suitably secluded place in which his cousin could spend the latter months of her pregnancy.

For Alison, there was a dreamlike quality about her immediate future having been taken out of her own hands. It was as though she was drifting downstream on a river of circumstances. All that had yet to be decided was the method by which she could respectably return to London with a child. But she was not thinking that far ahead.

Emma, to Alison's amusement, had already begun knitting for the baby. 'Haven't you finished that shawl yet?' Alison teased her.

'It's a pity you never learned to knit, Alison. It would be something for you to do.'

'But if I were sitting here knitting bootees, right now, and somebody rang the doorbell, I'd have to hide my needles and wool before letting them in.'

'Or they might put two and two together.'

'Exactly.' Alison's expression had shadowed. 'And it distresses me to have to keep my pregnancy a secret, Emma. I am proud to be carrying Richard's baby – not ashamed.'

'You can't have your cake and eat it, Alison.'

'In which respect?'

'The reason for the elaborate subterfuge Max has planned is your career.'

'And to me, it's as distasteful as the hasty wedding your father arranged for Clara. But equally necessary – as social attitudes haven't budged an inch in nearly twenty years.'

'I wouldn't want them to, Alison. What would become of the world if respectability no longer mattered? It would soon mean the end of family life.'

Emma dug in her knitting needle and began another row. 'When our Clara got into trouble, I could never have imagined it happening to me or you.'

'Me neither, Emma dear. But that only goes to show that nobody should be censorious, until they themselves have been put to the test.'

'Is that what you think I'm being?'

'Sort of.'

'I just don't believe in living for the moment, like you do, Alison. No good can come of it.'

'I can think of nothing better than having Richard's child,' Alison declared with a rapturous smile.

'How can you be so cheerful, Alison? After what Max was told by his German friend?'

Alison gazed into the fire, and in her mind's eye saw

again her sleeping lover in the cramped, book-lined room where they had shared such joy. So vivid was the memory, she could see the dent in the pillow where her own head had lain, and smell the kerosene from the stove that heated his humble quarters. It was not possible that they would never be together again.

'Maxwell will find Richard, Emma. I know he will. He has never let me down.'

Emma handed her the glass of milk she had not finished drinking. 'Max isn't a miracle-worker, Alison.'

'But God is.'

Alison was not in the least religious, but in trouble, everyone turns to God for help, Emma thought.

'I've always believed in a guiding hand that maps out our lives,' Alison said. 'I call it Destiny.'

'I know.'

'But isn't that just another name for God?'

'I think the rabbis would say that mapping out our lives is just one of God's functions.'

'So would the Church. But what does it matter, Emma? So long as one believes there is someone up there? Right now, I need to believe it, and that whoever it is is on Richard's side.'

# *Part Two*

> Life will suit
> Itself to Sorrow's most detested fruit,
> Like to the apples on the Dead Sea's shore,
> All ashes to the taste.
>
> *Byron*

# CHAPTER ONE

ON THE last day of January 1933 Alison stood beside the window in her Aunt Lottie's guest room, watching the snowflakes whirl by on the cruel north wind.

Emma entered with a breakfast tray. 'What are you doing out of bed, Alison? You're supposed to rest until lunchtime.' She glanced at the newspaper Alison was clutching. 'I see you've got Dad's *Daily Dispatch*. He thought it hadn't been delivered, and grumbled like mad because he had nothing to read with his tea and toast.'

'I'm sorry, Emma. I woke early and nipped downstairs to get the paper. I meant to put it back in the hall before Uncle Lionel got up – but it went out of my head.'

She handed the paper to Emma. 'When you read it, you'll know why.'

Emma scanned the front-page headlines that would doubtless seal Richard Lindemann's fate. Hitler had come to power.

Alison took off her dressing-gown and got back into bed. Her limbs felt like ice. How long had she stood by the window? But it wasn't just her body that was cold. The fear she had not, until now, allowed to chill her spirit had taken her in its grip.

Emma put down the tray and draped a knitted bedjacket around Alison's shoulders. 'Eat your porridge, Alison. It will warm you.'

'It will take more than porridge to warm me now.'

'We knew it was bound to happen.'

'But I still hoped it wouldn't.'

Emma poured some tea and made Alison drink it. 'You've never been a realist, have you?' she said gently.

139

'But in this case I took a leaf from your book, and hoped for the best.'

'Then you had better take another leaf from my book, Alison, and accept things the way they are, when they don't turn out as you hoped.'

'I shall never accept that Richard is gone from me forever. Unless I know he is dead.'

'I wish there was some way to comfort you, Alison. As there isn't, you may as well eat your breakfast. You need the nourishment.'

'Why must you be so damned practical!' Alison flashed.

'Because you are not. And you're expecting a baby.'

Alison forced herself to swallow down the porridge.

'You still don't look as if you are,' Emma went on. 'You're having what Mam calls an all-over pregnancy. You just look as though you've put on weight.'

'But I shall certainly look pregnant soon, Emma. And where are you going to hide me away then?' said Alison wryly.

'Conrad thinks that one of the small places on the Fylde coast would do nicely. The sea air will be good for you, Alison.'

'But I shall have to wear dark glasses when I stroll on the beach! Just in case.'

'Conrad's already bought you some.'

'Leave it to Conrad!'

'It's a good thing we can.'

'It's no wonder I feel that none of this is really happening, Emma. Sometimes I think: "What is Alison Plantaine doing here, when she should be onstage." And there's another kind of unreality about it – the way what's going on in Germany is affecting my life.'

'There's nothing unreal about that, since the father of your child is a German.'

Alison managed a smile. 'Nobody is better than you, Emma, at bringing a person down to earth.' Her smile faded. 'If it weren't for doctor's orders, I'd be in Berlin now, knocking down doors until I found out where Richard is.'

140

'Please don't say that to Max, Alison. It would make him feel worse than he already does.'


Morton's trip to Berlin in November had been a futile exercise. Though Muller had told him not to waste his time inquiring at Nazi headquarters, he nevertheless went there. An officer who spoke perfect English spent several minutes recalling a cricket match he had seen at Lord's, while Morton burned with impatience. On the subject of Richard Lindemann's detention, the officer uttered only four words: 'Where is your proof?'

Muller, who waited outside for Morton, refrained from saying, 'I told you so,' and said instead: 'Even with an eye-witness, you would get nowhere. They would simply remove him from the scene, as they did your young friend. The matter would never reach court.'

Morton decided to visit Richard's father, whom Muller said was a distinguished surgeon, and not without influence. But Herr Doktor Lindemann had made it plain that, in his view, Richard had got what he deserved for choosing politics instead of medicine. The interview left Morton with the impression of a bitter man who was also a frightened one. On his own behalf, as well as his son's.

But fear was now part of the air Berliners breathed, Morton noted. It was as though even those who had trusted Hitler this far had learned, too late, that the horse they had backed had two heads.

There was, too, an atmosphere of waiting for the worst to happen. And well there might be, Morton thought. If the Nazis could ride roughshod over all who opposed them when they were not in power, what would they do when they held the reins?

He had obtained from Doktor Lindemann a list of the young people who had disappeared with Richard, and visited the parents of Richard's two closest friends, whom the Herr Doktor had said with asperity were Jews.

Karl Kohn's family reminded Morton of Emma, and how he imagined all the Steins to be. Warm, homely, and philosophical, even in their anxiety about their missing son.

Morton had pressed their doorbell wondering if he had chosen the wrong time to call. Their apartment was situated on the Oranienburgstrasse, close to a synagogue, which reminded Morton that today was the Jewish Sabbath.

Herr Kohn had gone to morning service which he did every Saturday, Frau Kohn told Morton in German. When he failed to understand, she repeated it in hesitant English, and added apologetically that she had not spoken his language since learning it in the classroom.

Not for the first time that week, Morton was grateful that his language was taught all over the world. He told Frau Kohn why he had come, and was invited into the living room to await her husband's return.

Over lunch – the hospitable Kohns insisted that Morton share their meal – he acquired some information to take back to Alison.

Pastor Schmidt, whose daughter Gerda had vanished with the rest of the *Achtung* group, had called a meeting of all the parents concerned. A private detective, one of the pastor's trusted congregants, had since been engaged to find their children. It was evident to Morton that few people in Berlin felt they could trust the police.

Later, Herr Kohn, who was a tailor, made a wry joke about tailoring being a Jewish trade because its tools were small enough to carry in your pocket whenever another uprooting became necessary. It had then emerged that the family had relatives in Brooklyn, New York, and that the sole reason for them not having fled there was their elder son's refusal to desert his cause. They would not leave Germany without Karl.

Their frail-looking younger son spoke fluent English, and acted, when necessary, as interpreter for his parents and Morton. Before Morton left, the boy said to him that, with God's help, his big brother would be present at his forthcoming *Bar Mitzvah*.

Morton came away from the Kohns' simple home deeply affected by the unique blend of hope, resignation, and

142

self-deprecating humour which, for him, epitomised God's chosen people. He was to discover that in Germany there were two distinct kinds of Jew.

That afternoon, Morton visited Heinrich Morgenbach's family, in their spacious apartment on the Unter den Linden; Herr Morgenbach was a merchant banker, and Morton would have expected no less.

It soon became plain to him that all that the Morgenbachs had retained of their racial heritage was their appearance. Indeed, they went out of their way to tell Morton how Jewish they were not. Unwittingly, he gave them the opportunity to do so by mentioning the traditional Sabbath luncheon he had enjoyed at the Kohns'.

The Morgenbachs gave him afternoon tea, which Frau Morgenbach declared was nowhere more delicious than at the Ritz, in London. But Morton did not get the feeling that she was trying to impress him. The tastefully furnished apartment, and its occupants' demeanour, bespoke generations of gracious living.

Heinrich's sister was present, with her Gentile husband, and – too casually – revealed that she had converted to Christianity and that the children playing at her feet had been baptised.

Why do they think it necessary to tell me these things? Morton pondered. Or were they trying to convince themselves that dissociation with everything Jewish rendered them non-Jewish to Nazi eyes?

Though the visit was a thought-provoking experience, it was for Morton a waste of time. He had hoped to learn that the Morgenbachs – whom Herr Kohn had said did not attend the pastor's meeting – had instituted inquiries of their own.

If they had, they kept the information to themselves, and spoke little on the subject of the missing member of their family. Herr Morgenbach referred to the matter as his son's latest escapade, adding that sooner or later Heinrich was sure to turn up.

'Like the bad penny he is,' Heinrich's sister had said with curled lips. Frau Morgenbach uttered not a word about her son.

143

Morton would not have expected a left-wing intellectual to have the approval of this affluent, highly conservative family. Heinrich's disappearance had probably confirmed his position as the black sheep. Nevertheless, Morton assumed that Herr Morgenbach, who doubtless had friends in high places, was discreetly pulling strings behind the scenes to try to trace his only son. Morgenbach was not the type to throw in his lot with the other parents. Nor, Morton thought, recalling the man's lack of warmth, the sort to care about anyone else's son.

Before leaving Germany, Morton called on Pastor Schmidt. His pre-impression of the pastor, formed from all he had heard about him, was of a powerful personality, determined to do what must be done.

Instead, Morton found a reedy-looking little man kneeling before the altar in his church. When he got to his feet, and heard why Morton had come to Berlin, a burning light shone from his mild grey eyes. Morton had seen the same light in Herr Kohn's eyes. Its name was Faith.

The pastor confirmed this. There was a purpose in everything God did, he declared with conviction. If his daughter had been chosen to be a martyr, it was God's will.

On an earthly level, he was able to supply Morton with some new information: the detective had established that the *Achtung* group was seen being bundled into a van outside the print shop on the night they disappeared. The printer was with them; Morton had learned from Muller that Mr Rosenberg, too, was missing.

Recalling Muller's words about the probable fate of an eye-witness, Morton had no expectation of this one making a public statement. In the Germany of today, the number-one priority was saving one's own skin.

The pastor accepted Morton's card, and promised to contact him if there was any news. But Morton feared that it would not be good news, and returned to London beset by the futility of his trip. It was as though he had spent the time caught in a revolving door which led nowhere.

These were his bleak thoughts on the steamer carrying

him back to a blessedly free land. He would never again take freedom for granted.

Among his fellow-passengers were some German-Jewish families, whose devoutness was proclaimed by the skull caps on the men's heads. The mounds of luggage they had with them left Morton in no doubt that they were leaving Germany. Even the devout were not always prepared to consign their future entirely to God's will, Morton had reflected. Pastor Schmidt, too, by employing the detective, was offering God a helping hand.

Morton, for whom faith had never been a staff, quickly brushed aside this whimsical cogitation. He was a man who dealt in cold, hard facts. In his time he had moved metaphorical mountains. But he had failed to move the one under which Richard Lindemann was seemingly buried. He had let Alison down.


When Morton saw the headlines in his *Times*, on January 31st, he telephoned Oldham immediately.

'You know there isn't a phone in Alison's bedroom,' Emma said to him, 'and that she stays in bed until lunch-time.'

'I didn't call to commiserate with Alison. It's you I want to speak to, Emma.'

'Have you had some news about Richard?'

'No. But when I last talked to Muller, he'd heard a rumour that immediately the Nazis took over they would put all the minor thorns they've removed from their side officially behind bars. Together with the more distinguished dissenters they are now in a position to round up,' Morton added grimly. 'It's going to be that kind of régime.'

'I told you what was coming, Max, the day we had the picnic on the Heath. I don't think either you or Alison took me seriously.'

And, Emma thought, the water that had flowed under the bridge since then had engulfed Alison. Herself and Max, too. Because Alison had gone to Germany and fallen

145

in love, all three of them were now embroiled in the web of deceit Alison's condition had made necessary.

'I'm thinking of going back to Berlin,' Morton said.

'Why? What can you do there? Didn't you have enough, the last time, of banging your head against a brick wall?'

'If the rumour Muller heard proves correct, I might be able to establish that Richard is alive and in prison. I wouldn't expect Muller to go knocking on Nazi doors for me. It's unlikely that his interest in Richard's disappearance is unknown to them. He found out recently that a girl in his office was a Nazi, and dismissed her immediately. He has also learned that his daughter's gym mistress is a Party member. There's nowhere they haven't infiltrated, Emma.'

Briefly, Emma was assailed by the feeling of unreality Alison had mentioned. The things Morton was saying to her were totally out of keeping with the humdrum security of the Steins' home.

'I shan't go to Berlin until things have settled down a bit there,' Morton said.

'I wish you wouldn't go at all,' Emma replied. The fear for his safety that had suddenly stabbed her was all too real. 'Even a foreigner could find himself in trouble for poking his nose in,' she cautioned, 'and I can do without anything happening to you.'

'Britain has an embassy there,' he reminded her. 'I personally think that in the name of decency the ambassadors of civilised countries should be immediately withdrawn, but I doubt that it will happen. Turning a blind eye seems to be what diplomacy is all about. There's no way that British and American diplomats could live in Berlin and remain unaware of what's going on there.'

'They'd have to plug their ears, as well as turn a blind eye, not to know Hitler's intentions toward the Jews.'

'Exactly.' Morton lightened his tone. 'But it's nice to know you care what happens to me, our Em!'

He would never know how much, Emma thought. 'I was being practical,' she said.

'Me too. With all that you and I have to cope with

146

together, it wouldn't help for us not to be good friends,' said Morton before he rang off.

Lottie Stein glanced up from her baking when Emma entered the kitchen. 'Who was that on the phone?'

'Mr Morton.'

Why, Lottie wondered absently, was her daughter's expression invariably wry after she had spoken to that man? She returned her attention to the dough she was kneading. 'How did Alison take this morning's news?'

Emma filled the sink with hot water. 'Why not pop upstairs to see her, Mam? Then you'll find out for yourself.'

'I'm up to my elbows in flour, aren't I, love? Sorry though I am for my niece, my household routine has to go on.' Lottie watched Emma sprinkle soapflakes into the water, and gently immerse some dainty lingerie. 'Also, I don't find it easy to chat with Alison these days.'

'And I think she's noticed that, Mam. I certainly have.'

Lottie pounded the dough, her usually pleasant expression suddenly tight-lipped. 'Alison is too wrapped up in herself to notice anything, Emma.'

'She has plenty to worry about, right now.'

'If she hadn't she wouldn't be here, would she? And we're all doing our best to help her. My heart aches for her, Emma, but her plight is no excuse.'

'For what?'

'For behaving as if nobody else has troubles. Business is so bad at the moment, your father and Conrad will be lucky to keep their heads above water. In a slump, the people who are out of work, like most are in Oldham, can't afford new boots and shoes.'

'I know how things are, Mam.'

'It isn't you we're talking about. I wasn't going to tell you, Emma, but you may as well know that at present we're living on the cash Dad was saving for his retirement.'

Emma stopped washing the lingerie. 'Alison offered to pay for her keep while she's here. If she knew what you've just told me, she'd insist upon doing so, Mam.'

'Don't you dare tell her! That isn't what this is all about.

And your father would have to be starving, before he'd take a penny from Alison.'

'Then what is this all about?'

Lottie slapped the dough onto her board and dredged some flour on it. 'It's about Alison not being aware of what's going on in our lives, Emma. Mine and your dad's. I don't think she even sees us as people. To her, we're just a port in a storm.'

Emma was shocked by her mother's cold assessment of Alison's character. Nobody knew better than Emma that there was more than a grain of truth in it, but Alison was not the callous creature Lottie seemed suddenly to think her. She was warm and loving, and would not wittingly hurt a fly. But wittingly was the key word, Emma thought. It was Alison's failure to see how she affected those around her that had hurt Lottie.

'You have to live with Alison to really know her, Mam,' she said.

'That's what I've found out.' Lottie began rolling the pastry for the meat and potato pie she was preparing, which these days contained less meat than potatoes. 'When Alison used to come here as a guest, I enjoyed her visits.'

'She's still here as a guest, Mam. And under very difficult circumstances.'

'For us, as well as for her. And you haven't changed, have you, Emma? You always did make excuses for people's behaviour.'

Emma surveyed her mother's flushed face. 'At the moment I'm trying to find one for yours, Mam. Why have you suddenly turned against Alison?'

'I haven't turned against her, Emma. I've simply discovered she isn't the person I thought she was.'

Emma thought it probable that Alison had made a similar discovery about Lottie. She began rinsing the lingerie; and held her tongue.

Lottie did not. 'But when I think back, perhaps I ought not to be surprised.' The memory had just returned to her of fourteen-year-old Alison arriving unexpectedly on Christmas Eve, and sitting here at the kitchen table – like

148

a queen, Lottie had thought then – while Emma waited on her.

Emma was still waiting on Alison, Lottie thought now with a pang, and was no doubt Alison's unpaid servant in London. Lottie recalled having prickled with foreboding on that frosty morning, nineteen years ago. She could remember ticking Emma off for putting sugar in Alison's tea for her. As if she had feared then what the future might bring: that Emma would live in Alison's shadow all her life.

'I don't like to see you doing Alison's washing, Emma,' Lottie exclaimed.

'The doctor ordered her to take things easy, didn't he?'

'Sloshing a few pairs of camiknickers in soapsuds is not heavy work. You spoil Alison, Emma.'

Emma smiled. 'I enjoy spoiling people, Mam.'

'And Alison, of course, was made to be spoiled.'

A strained silence followed.

'I think it might be best if Alison and I don't wait until her condition shows, before moving from here,' Emma said.

'And what is that supposed to mean?' Lottie asked sharply.

Emma, who had never exchanged a cross word with her mother, was unable to hide her distress. 'Well, our being here is causing trouble, isn't it, Mam?'

'If you mean between you and me, love, we mustn't let it. This is your home, Emma, and I want you always to remember that. If ever you want to come back to live with us, Dad and I would be overjoyed to have you. And Alison is welcome here. I told her when she was a kid that she always would be, and I meant it. There's no question of you and her leaving before it becomes necessary.'

Lottie dusted her hands on her apron and dabbed her eyes, which had misted with tears. 'The baby Alison is carrying is my dead brother's grandchild. I think of him all the time, Emma. And I'll always do my duty by his daughter.'

No more was said. But Lottie's final words gave Emma food for thought. She had not, until now, construed her

149

parents' standing by Alison as a duty. For Emma, it was a labour of love. It struck Emma then that much of what passed for love in the Stein family, the sacrifices they made for each other, was in truth the obligation imposed by their blood tie.

Alison had arrived at that conclusion gradually, as the time under her relatives' roof dragged by. It was a disillusionment she would never have experienced had circumstances not brought her into their midst, day in, day out.

Like Lottie, she had found this protracted visit quite different from the short sojourns in Oldham she had relished in the past. When the rot began to set in – this was how Alison painfully thought of it – she had attributed it to the reason she was here, and to the effect of the economic depression upon her relatives' lives.

Lottie's harsh judgement of Alison, in the latter respect, was quite wrong. When Lionel Stein came home from his store at night, bowed down with anxiety, Alison wanted to comfort him. Nor had she failed to note that her aunt was serving less costly meals.

But Alison had inherited the Plantaine reticence, in matters she knew were privately distressing to those close to her. In her childhood and youth, she had thought the Plantaines uncaring people. Only with maturity had she realised that trait was present in herself.

There were times when it seemed to her incongruous that she was capable of making what Morton called 'a production number' about a meaningless incident, but could not bring herself to make known her feelings about something that really mattered. But Alison was still discovering her own complexity, and at thirty-two had a good deal yet to learn about herself.

About the Steins, she had now learned what she would rather not have known. Once, they had seemed to her the ideal family. Though she was born to the stage, and would not have changed places with them, she had envied her cousins what they had that she had not. Home, hearth, and the special warmth of Jewish family life epitomised it.

Alison could remember the mixed emotions with which

she had, as a youngster, journeyed from Oldham back to the lodgings in whichever town the Plantaine Players were appearing. With her had gone the memory of the Steins seated around the kitchen fire. It was a memory that had sustained her in her bleakest moments – but would do so no more. Nor would she ever again wonder how her father, who was born into that kind of home-life, could have brought himself to leave it, stage-struck though he then was. Until recently, Alison had concluded that he had put his ambition to become an actor above all else. Now, she was not so sure.

Though Alison cared for her relatives no less than when she arrived in mid-November, living under their roof had demonstrated that in such a close-knit family there was a thin borderline between love and duty – and it was sometimes debatable on which side of it the family members stood.

Alison's mind had lately returned to an occasion in 1916, when a little of the gilt had been chipped from her ideal image of the Steins. She had thought them incapable of quarrelling and had been dismayed when they did.

The blow-up occurred when her cousin Clara told the family she was pregnant. Lottie and Lionel had afterwards brushed aside their feelings and forgiven Clara her trespass, and Alison had thought what a wonderful thing family love was.

Recalling the episode years later and with a perception she had not possessed then, the atmosphere that had pervaded the house was in retrospect similar to that pervading it at present. Like it or not, everyone was doing what was required of them – including Conrad, who lived close by and dropped in regularly. Only this time it was for Alison, not Clara.

On the day Hitler's rise to power was announced to the world, Alison was more concerned with the atmosphere in Berlin. Emma could not stir her from her despondency.

At lunchtime, Lottie went upstairs to her. 'Get dressed and come down, Alison.'

'I don't feel like it.'

151

'I don't suppose you do, love. But it's time to eat.'

'I'm not hungry.'

'The baby is.'

'Everyone thinks of the baby! Nobody thinks of me!'

Lottie sat down on the bed and took Alison's hand. 'That isn't true, Alison. And I hope you believe me.'

Alison looked into her aunt's warm brown eyes. Affection for her was still there. 'I do believe you.'

Lottie took the opportunity to counsel her niece, and thought how sad it was for Alison and her mother that their strained relationship had deprived Hermione Plantaine of the privilege. 'But the baby has to come first, Alison, and after it's born, even more so. You had better accept that being a mother is going to change your life.'

'I'm not thinking that far ahead, Aunt Lottie. At present, it's difficult enough for me to go on living day by day.'

Lottie tingled with alarm. While she had been busy resenting Alison's seemingly careless attitude, what had been going on in her niece's mind? Lottie had allowed herself to forget that Alison was an actress, able to hide her feelings behind a convenient mask.

'If Richard doesn't come back to me, I shall want to die,' Alison declared.

Lottie gathered her close and gave her a motherly kiss. 'But you won't. Sorrow is part of living, and if you have to, you'll live without Richard. And you'll still have something to live for. His child.

'You remind me so much of myself when I was your age,' she went on, fingering a tendril of Alison's silky hair. 'But only in looks!' she added.

Alison managed to smile. 'That goes without saying, Aunt Lottie. If I were asked to describe a paragon of all the virtues, I would describe you.'

'That, I'm not. But I'd be lying if I pretended I don't disapprove of you and your headstrong ways. Look where it's landed you. It was the same with our Clara. Some people would say that getting pregnant was God's way of punishing both of you.'

'Would you agree with them?'

152

Lottie shook her head. 'I'd say He couldn't have blessed you with a greater gift than a child.'

The intimate chat with Lottie was to Alison as though a soothing salve had been applied to her sore heart. It was the first time she and her aunt had talked together without strain since Alison's arrival, and she had begun to think they never would again.

# CHAPTER TWO

When Alison and Emma went to dinner at Conrad's house, Alison recalled her aunt's words. Conrad's wife, Zelda, had not yet been blessed with a child, though they had been married for five years.

Neither Alison nor Emma felt at ease in Conrad's home, each had confided to the other. The house where they had once visited their grandparents was a different place since Conrad inherited it.

Zelda's over-furnishing was partly responsible. But it could not have retained its former charm for Alison and Emma without the old-fashioned pieces and the bric-à-brac, now in London, that had transformed Alison's impersonal apartment into a home.

When Alison first met Zelda, she had teased Conrad about having married the girl of his dreams. In his youth he had had a penchant for blondes, but had been unable to find himself a Jewish one.

Emma had feared her brother might follow in Alison's father's footsteps, and fall in love with a Gentile blonde. But Conrad Stein was a good deal more conventional than his Uncle Horace. He had been attracted to the girl who was now Albert Battersby's wife, but had resisted temptation.

At thirty, Conrad was still single, and the family had resigned themselves to his remaining so. Several Jewish blondes had by then crossed his path, but in other respects they were not what Conrad sought in a wife. He had wanted that rare combination, a glamour girl who was a home-bird at heart, and had found it in Zelda whom he met at a wedding in Leeds.

Zelda was not just blonde, but ash-blonde, and fetchingly

curved in the right places. She had told Conrad early in their acquaintance that she preferred reading and listening to the wireless, to dancing. But he had already discerned that she was his kind.

When they met, Zelda was just eighteen. Conrad had hastened to put a ring on her finger before someone else did. 'Marry in haste, repent at leisure,' his family had warned him. But the old adage had not proved correct in his case. He enjoyed spoiling his young wife, and she adored him. No couple could have been more content with each other. Only their childlessness marred their happiness.

'You don't know how much I envy you, Alison,' Zelda said at the dinner table.

'You're only twenty-three, Zelda. You have plenty of time,' Emma comforted her.

'And my position is not entirely enviable,' Alison added with a rueful smile.

'It certainly isn't,' Zelda replied kindly.

Conrad spread his hands in an exaggerated Jewish gesture. 'But as my dad would say, what can you do? Girls who get into trouble seem to run in our family.'

Alison stopped eating her dessert. 'Did Uncle Lionel say that?'

'Of course not,' Conrad answered with a grin that reminded Alison of the cheeky lad he had once been. 'But who could blame him if he thought it? What with you and our Clara. All we need now is for our Em to throw her hat over the windmill!'

'That will be the day!' Emma exclaimed. 'And who would I throw my hat over the windmill with?' she said wryly – and to the astonishment of the others. Emma's primness was legendary in the family.

Zelda went to fetch the cheese from the sideboard.

'It's remarkable that you and Conrad are not immensely fat, if you eat like this every evening,' Alison said.

'We don't,' Conrad replied. 'Zelda put on this big spread especially for you.'

'And I'm enjoying every morsel of it.'

Zelda pulled down her pink jumper and fingered her

pearls. 'But I'm getting worried about you, Alison. You're not fat enough, where you should be.'

'Every topic of conversation leads eventually to my condition,' said Alison with chagrin.

Conrad's expression shadowed. 'In this house, babies are the usual topic. My wife is overly interested in them and talks about little else.'

'If I had one of my own, I probably wouldn't,' Zelda said defensively. She gave Conrad a hurt glance, then addressed Alison and Emma. 'I want to have an operation to help me conceive – but Conrad won't let me.'

'Because I don't believe in interfering with nature,' he declared, 'to make something happen that wasn't God's will.'

Suddenly the air was tense with feeling. To Alison, it was as though an invisible barrier had risen between Conrad and his wife. And the look they were exchanging was hostile on Zelda's side.

'We know a woman who had that operation,' Conrad told Alison and Emma. 'It worked. But her baby was born with something wrong with it. So if you two think I'm turning into an old-wife, saying what I did, I'm not.'

'You seem to be thinking like one,' Alison said.

'Because I won't take the risk of my wife having a deformed child?'

Zelda burst into tears. 'But without a child, we'll never be a real family, will we? I would rather have a baby that isn't perfect than no baby at all.'

She calmed down and offered her guests the cheese and biscuits. Alison forced herself to make small-talk. But the evening was ruined.

After the meal, Emma helped Zelda clear the table and went with her to the kitchen to wash the dishes.

Alison wasted no time before tackling Conrad. They had gone into the sitting room, and he stood gloomily with his back to the hearth.

'It's now my turn to remind you that we once promised always to be honest with each other,' Alison said.

'So, fire away.'

156

'I'm going to! And to put it briefly, Conrad, I think you should respect Zelda's wishes, instead of laying down the law to her.'

'I see.'

'If she's prepared to take the risk involved, then you should agree to her doing so.'

'That's the sort of thing I'd expect you to say, Alison. And without pausing to consider the possible consequences – which you haven't had time to do.'

'But Zelda has. And your opinion of me isn't relevant to your wife's predicament,' Alison replied.

'Nevertheless, I think I'll give it to you. Leaping without looking is you to a T, Alison, and events have proved how disastrous that can be. I wasn't in the least surprised when I heard you were in trouble — '

'Now you're beginning to really sound like an old-wife!'

Conrad ignored the interruption. 'Another instance of your failure to think ahead, Alison, was your brief engagement to my pal Albert. You never consider the outcome of anything until you are faced with it – though, in that case, I had warned you that Albert wasn't the kind to agree to his wife continuing her career.'

'May we return to the subject of your wife?'

'We haven't really left it,' said Conrad with a weary smile. 'I was about to say, Alison, that your impetuously made and broken engagement caused Albert pain that could have been avoided if you'd paused to think in advance.'

'It was painful for me, too,' Alison recalled. 'But I got over it. So did Albert.'

'The same wouldn't apply if my wife gave birth to an imperfect child. And it wouldn't be you, Alison, who'd have to cope with the consequences of your ill-considered opinion that I should let Zelda take that chance.'

In the moment of silence that followed, Alison noted the sadness in her cousin's hazel eyes, and the premature sprinkling of silver in his hair. Conrad had always resembled her father, and as he grew older the likeness had become more marked.

157

Conrad was, too, a devoted husband, as her father had been. Her mother had demanded too much of him, chipped away at his personality. Zelda was asking only this one thing. But it was all-important to her, and Alison feared their happy marriage might founder if what Zelda yearned for did not come to pass.

'I haven't finished being honest with you,' she said.

'I didn't think you had!'

'There are some women, Conrad, for whom motherhood is their *raison d'être*. I don't happen to be one of them but Zelda clearly is – and I'm afraid she will become neurotic if her maternal instinct remains unfulfilled.'

'For someone who hasn't any, you seem to know a great deal about it!'

Alison felt the child in her womb remind her of its presence and a surge of tenderness for it rippled through her. 'What I meant, Conrad, is that maternity isn't my sole *raison d'être*. As for the latter part of your remark, it requires no special skill to discern that something is very wrong with Zelda – and what that something is.'

'But I can't let her have that operation, Alison.'

He stirred the fire to a blaze, and Alison knew he was avoiding her eye. Then he gave her an anguished glance and sat down beside her on the sofa.

'There's something I know that Zelda doesn't, Alison. If I tell you, will you promise to keep it to yourself?'

'Of course. But you don't have to tell me,' said Alison with the Plantaine reticence Conrad's expression had aroused in her. If it was too painful for him to talk about, she would rather he didn't.

But for Conrad it was a relief to unburden himself. 'If my parents had known what I'm about to tell you, they would have tried to stop me from marrying Zelda. There's a hereditary congenital disease in her mother's family. Her parents are straight people, and they gave me the option of backing out. Whatever the disease is – they spared me the details – my mother-in-law's sister, who died before Zelda was born, had it.

'Even if Zelda had normal children, our descendants

158

would be at risk, wouldn't they?' Conrad went on. 'Zelda has no brothers or sisters. Nor has she any cousins on her mother's side. That's why I think her failure to conceive could be God's way of allowing an unhealthy family tree to die with her.'

'How lyrically you put it, Conrad,' Alison was moved to say. 'But since when were your thoughts so godly? I can remember your father having to drag you to synagogue when you were a lad.'

'And I'm still not what you'd call religious, Alison. But a person doesn't have to be, to believe that God has the power to influence our lives.'

Alison was reminded of her conversation with Emma the night before they came north. 'I agree. But we were brought up to believe that God is merciful, weren't we? And it's hard for me to believe that my lover's disappearance was wrought – via the Nazis – by a benign hand.'

They shared a silence, each with their own bleak thoughts.

'Remember when we were youngsters, how we used to talk to each other like this?' Conrad said. 'For some reason I was always able to talk more openly to you than to anyone else in the family.'

A hint of the old, teasing Conrad was in the smile he now gave Alison. 'Though you're not really my kind.'

'Nor you mine.'

'But it hasn't stopped us from being friends, as well as cousins.'

'And I trust it never will.'

Later that night, when Emma took a mug of hot milk to Alison's room to help her sleep, she asked what Alison and Conrad had talked about.

'You and my brother were looking very thoughtful, when Zelda and I joined you in the sitting room.'

'We'd been discussing family matters, Emma.'

'That could mean anything.'

'Yes. And there are some family matters that are not related to the family as a whole.'

'That isn't possible, Alison.'

'Not in your family,' said Alison wryly.

159

'Which is yours, too.'

'But I wasn't raised in the midst of it – which enables me to see things differently. A family is made up of individuals, Emma dear, each of whom is entitled to their personal privacy. And like any other group of people, each has the right to be selective about to which of the others they tell what.'

'If you want to accuse me of curiosity, I would rather you just said it,' said Emma, sounding hurt.

'My darling Emma, you are the least curious person I have ever met. I haven't construed your question about my private chat with Conrad as prying. But I may as well tell you that since we've been up north, I've been affected by the way everything that occurs in the life of any of us is immediately and automatically a family affair, be it a simple cold in the nose, or a complicated problem like mine.'

'Some people would call it caring.'

'And in one way it's very comforting.' Alison refrained from sharing with Emma her recent conclusion that duty played a major part in what they were discussing. 'But in another way. . . .'

'Yes?' Emma challenged her.

'The only way I can put it, Emma, is that I sometimes feel I am suffocating beneath the weight of the family's united interest in my welfare.'

And where would you be now, without it? Emma thought. 'You used to complain that the Plantaines weren't interested in you enough,' she said.

'They were the opposite extreme. And I didn't mean to upset you, Emma. If I have, you must forgive me.'

For once, Emma did not say there was nothing to forgive.

They bade each other goodnight. Alison switched off her bedside lamp and lay sleepless in the dark. At the back of her mind, as always, was anxiety about Richard. In the forefront remained her conversation with Emma.

Tonight was only the second time they had crossed swords in all the years they had known each other. The exchange could not be described otherwise, though neither had raised her voice or uttered a sharp word.

160

The previous occasion had concerned Alison's going to Berlin. And it struck Alison now that her placid cousin would defend to the last the principles she held dear. Of which family unity was number one on the list.

And Emma probably now thought Alison ungrateful, though nothing could be further from the truth. Alison had said too much, and it could not be unsaid. Nor was it possible for Emma, who was conditioned to the Steins' way of life, to comprehend its claustrophobic effect upon one who was not.

# CHAPTER THREE

THE DUTY aspect of the family's rallying around her was confirmed for Alison by a visit from her cousin Clara. The fact that they had never cared for each other did not prohibit Clara from turning up at the Steins' home one Sunday afternoon, with a parcel of expensive garments she had bought for Alison's baby.

'I'd have come sooner, Alison,' she apologised, 'but I'm on a committee that's raising funds to help German-Jewish refugees. Some of them are children without their parents, and we're trying to get as many more out as possible.'

'The people next door to us have taken a boy to live with them,' said Clara's son Percy, who had accompanied her. 'I'd like Mam to do the same. But she won't.'

Alison appraised her cousin's elegant appearance, and the shallow prettiness of Clara's over-made-up face. Clara wasn't the kind to open her heart and her home to a refugee child. She would leave that to others, while devoting herself to the less onerous task of helping to raise funds.

'I've got enough on my plate with you and your little sister, Percy,' Clara said, confirming this.

'So you keep saying, Mam,' the boy replied resentfully.

Resentment seemed to colour everything Percy said, Alison noticed as the afternoon wore on.

'Why didn't you come to my *Bar Mitzvah*?' he asked her in the same tone.

'In the theatre, we have to work on Saturday, Percy.'

'But you could have got an understudy, couldn't you? If you'd been ill, they would have had to get one. Only I don't suppose you thought it was worth the trouble of travelling to Manchester just for my sake, Cousin Alison.'

162

Alison was surprised that he had noticed her absence. This was the first time he had set eyes on her since he was a toddler. 'I wouldn't have thought it so important to you to have me there, Percy,' she said.

He glared at her with the beady brown eyes he had inherited from his dead father. 'Well, it would've been. I haven't got that many relations who are really mine.'

His mother put down her teacup and stiffened. 'And what, may I ask, is that supposed to mean?'

Percy did not reply.

Tea was, as usual, being served in the kitchen, which to the Steins was a living room, too. Lottie was presiding at the table, and Lionel seated in his chair beside the fire. Both had long-suffering expressions on their faces.

Clara glanced at Emma, who was seated beside her, then addressed the air. 'When it suits them, my family know how to act *shtum*!'

Alison had gathered in advance that Clara's rare visits were invariably stressful occasions, and could now see why. The undercurrents Clara had created years ago were again rippling in the air.

'If Dad were here, you wouldn't have said what you just did,' Clara reprimanded Percy.

'Of course I wouldn't, because he's very good to me, and I wouldn't want to upset him. But he isn't my real dad.'

Lionel intervened. 'All the same, Percy, he treats you exactly as he does your sister – and Lila is his blood child.'

'But I'm not allowed to see my other grandparents, am I? Just because my mother doesn't like them. So nobody can say I'm not being deprived of something?'

'Like them? I absolutely detest them!' Clara flung at him. She addressed the others, two patches of scarlet staining her cheeks, and her bosom heaving. 'Since my son learned the word "deprived", he hasn't stopped using it to me about not seeing his father's parents!'

She rose from the table and paced the room furiously. 'And coming to Oldham – because they happen to live

163

here – always makes him worse. In case nobody realised it, that's why we hardly ever come!'

She stopped pacing and stared into the fire. 'Oldham has such terrible associations for me.'

Lionel's lips tightened. 'And who made it that way?'

Lottie gave him a warning glance but he did not heed it.

'Wasn't it enough that your poor, first husband died in the war, Clara? Without you inflicting upon all concerned the extra sorrow that you have?'

'But you and Aunt Lottie supported what Clara did, and is still doing, to Percy's other grandparents,' Alison could not stop herself from reminding him.

'How could we not?' he answered resignedly. 'Clara is our daughter.'

In for a penny! thought Alison. 'That doesn't mean you have to help her to do something you know is wrong.'

Clara treated Alison to a baleful stare. 'For a person who is at present getting the benefit of how we never let each other down, you have a strange idea of what family loyalty is about.'

'I would question its value when it upholds enmities that affect the next generation,' Alison answered coldly.

She received a grateful smile from Percy. 'So would I, Cousin Alison.'

Alison returned his smile, but switched it off before addressing Clara. 'Remember, Clara, that what you are doing to Percy was done by my mother to me. And it didn't exactly make me happy.'

Percy looked taken aback. 'I didn't know that.'

'Well, now you do, Percy. I'll leave you to find out the details from someone else.'

Lottie poured them all some more tea, and Percy moved to the chair Clara had vacated, next to Alison. He remained at her side for the rest of the afternoon.

'When your Aunt Emma and I return to London, Percy, you must come and stay with us during your school holidays,' Alison said impulsively, when Clara had gone to put on her coat before departing.

'I'd like to. If Mam will let me.'

164

'Don't count on it,' said practical Emma. The last thing Clara would want was Alison influencing her son.

But she had already done so. The smile Percy and Alison were exchanging told Emma that her nephew knew he had found an ally in the family.

# CHAPTER FOUR

ALISON'S SON was born on a balmy May evening in 1933.

Emma assisted at his delivery, and afterwards gazed at him with the same wonderment that was visible in Alison's eyes. The prospect of Alison being a mother had seemed real to neither. Suddenly, they were confronted with a living child.

Emma had bathed the lusty infant and wrapped him in a flannel blanket. She held him close for a moment, then placed him in Alison's arms.

'What shall we call him, Alison?' she asked.

As though, Alison thought with affection for her, he were hers too.

And so, from then on, it was to be. Emma had established her place in his life from the moment of his birth.

The doctor snapped his bag shut, reminding them he was still present, and about to take his leave. 'Whatever you call him, ladies, don't forget to tell him he's a Lancashire lad!'

As his maternal grandfather was, Alison thought while Emma saw the doctor out. And how sad it was that her father had not lived to see him.

The baby's other grandfather was alive and well in Berlin, but would not be given the pleasure of knowing his grandchild. Morton had relayed to Alison Doktor Lindemann's attitude toward Richard, and that the Herr Doktor had not raised a finger to help secure her lover's release from the prison he was now, officially, in.

It had not yet occurred to Alison that her ill-feeling toward Richard's father was comparable with Clara's refusal to let Percy visit his paternal grandparents, and also with her own mother's attempt to keep her away from the Steins. But she had never viewed her own actions dispassionately,

166

nor applied to herself the same yardstick she applied to others. It was as though she wore blinkers when seeing herself – as Emma and Morton could have told her.

'We'll call the baby Richard,' she said when Emma returned to the bedroom, 'and Maxwell will be his middle name.'

'That's very fitting,' Emma answered with a smile.

'And you and Maxwell will be his honorary godparents. Then he'll have one who's Christian and the other who's Jewish. As he is my son, that is fitting too.'

'I'm sure Max will be as happy to have that honour as I am, Alison.'

It was the only kind of parenthood they were likely to experience, Emma thought wryly. And how ironic, that they were to share it.

'The baby looks rather like your father,' she said, studying the tiny face nestling against Alison's breast.

'And not at all like his own father.'

Alison had scanned the infant countenance hoping to find in it something of the man she loved, to no avail. Richard junior had the same mousey colouring as Alison's late Grandma Shrager, from whom her father had inherited it. Emma and Conrad, too.

'He looks more like your child, Emma, than mine.'

'I don't mind if you don't, Alison.'

'If he has your good nature, too, I'll have no complaints,' said Alison.

They regarded each other with sentimental tears in their eyes.

Emma pulled herself together. "I haven't wished you *Mazeltov*, Alison.'

'Nor I you.'

The traditional Hebrew congratulation reminded them both that in Jewish circles a birth was unarguably a family matter.

'I must go and ring everyone up and tell them the good news,' said Emma.

'And you can tell your father I intend to have the baby circumcised.'

Emma looked astonished. 'But he isn't Jewish, Alison.'

'Nor am I. But part of me feels Jewish.'

'The part of you that is, I suppose.'

'It wasn't until I went to Berlin that I let myself feel it, though. Until then, I would feel insulted on my father's behalf if I heard an anti-Semitic remark. Now, it's on my own behalf.'

'That's no reason to have your baby circumcised, Alison.'

'All the same, I intend to do so.' The baby was Alison's son, and the grandson of a Jew. Though the circumcision could not be performed by a rabbi, it was for Alison a continuance of establishing her sense of place.

'I'll phone Max first,' Emma said, departing downstairs.

Alison's expression shadowed as she cuddled the baby close. Though neither she nor Emma had yet put it into words, they knew that the next stage of Morton's carefully engineered deception must part Alison from her child. Miss Alison Plantaine could not return to London from her lengthy rest with a baby in her arms.

Don't think about it, Alison ordered herself. But the ache already pulling at her heartstrings was impossible to ignore. The feeling that she was being swept along on an irrevocable tide again overwhelmed her.

It was as though, since she fainted in the flat last year, only her private thoughts had been her own. Her bodily progress from that point to this had been charted by Morton and Conrad, and Emma had steadied her course.

When Alison's condition could no longer be concealed, Emma had packed their bags and called her brother. Conrad had appeared with his car, to transport them to a rented cottage on the Fylde coast, where a Blackpool gynaecologist would be at hand to deliver the child.

In retrospect, it was remarkable to Alison that all had been accomplished so easily and efficiently. And, too, that she had lent herself so passively to what was required of her, which she must continue to do, if she was to return unscathed to where she had formerly been.

Briefly, she allowed herself to imagine a life of domestic bliss, wherein this cuddlesome bundle snuggled against her

168

would grow into a boy and find his mother awaiting him when he came home from school.

But the scene Alison was envisaging, herself in an apron ministering to a child's daily needs, was less credible to her than the fictional parts she played onstage. It would be like playing a part for which she knew she was wrongly cast.

She brushed the fanciful notion aside. Her child would have to accept her as she was, as everyone close to her must. And so would his father – who didn't yet really know her.

The time they had spent together was like a slowly receding dream. Though love for him continued to burn within Alison, her interlude in Berlin had by now merged with the general feeling of unreality by which she was beset.

Morton had returned there in late February, and had managed to establish that Richard was, as Muller had predicted, now officially a political prisoner. But Morton was not allowed to see him, nor had Alison received a reply to any of the letters she had since sent.

Nevertheless, knowing Richard's exact whereabouts had comforted her. When the Reichstag was burned, she had seen it as a hopeful sign that those anti-Nazis not yet silenced might still contrive to dismantle the barbaric régime.

Morton, who was in Berlin when it happened, had said he felt he was witnessing a last stand – a feeling confirmed for him when he later learned that Bertolt Brecht and other free spirits in the arts had left Germany the following day.

During the final months of her pregnancy, Alison had spent much of the time walking alone on a stretch of beach near the cottage. Occasionally, she had encountered other solitary strollers, and they had greeted each other as they went on their way, as strangers do when uninhibited by the strictures of a town.

Alison had, at Emma's insistence, worn the dark glasses provided by Conrad, which had lent a cloak-and-dagger flavour to her present role. Even without the disguise, she had thought, who would recognise the lumpy woman, windswept and carelessly clad in a shapeless raincoat, as the glamorous actress Alison Plantaine?

She no longer felt like that Alison Plantaine. And the less so with a baby in her arms, she was thinking when Emma returned from making the telephone calls.

Emma put down the mugs of cocoa she had made for them, and settled the baby in his crib. 'We mustn't get him used to being nursed, Alison.'

'The little darling is only two hours old!'

'But we had better begin as we intend to carry on. Tomorrow, he'll begin taking his bottle. And I'd like to get him on a regular routine. He isn't going to be one of those spoiled babies who gets fed whenever he cries.'

Alison laughed. 'Who's his mother? You or me?'

'Talking of which, are you quite sure, Alison, about not breast-feeding him?' Emma observed Alison's blue-veined breasts, their fullness revealed by the lacy nightgown into which she had changed after the birth. 'You obviously have plenty of milk, Alison. And even if you only fed him for a short time, it would be good for the baby.'

'But it would be bad for me, Emma. I shall find it easier to be separated from him – for however long – if I don't put him to my breast. For once I am being sensible.'

On your own account, thought Emma, not the child's. She sipped her cocoa and surveyed Alison's glowing appearance. Her satiny hair, which Emma had brushed for her, made a striking frame for her lovely face.

'Nobody would think you'd spent the evening giving birth, Alison. Tonight, you look like your old self again.'

'My public would be pleased to hear it! Only I wouldn't have a public, if they knew the truth.'

The announcement of Alison's prolonged absence from the theatre had brought forth so many sympathetic fan letters, Morton had to engage someone to reply to them all.

'I owe it to all the people who flock to see me perform, and who've written to wish me well, to hasten to make what Maxwell calls my comeback,' Alison declared.

'He told me on the phone that he's already looking for

a vehicle for you,' said Emma, to whom a vehicle had once been something that travelled on wheels.

'I can't wait to get back onstage,' Alison answered fervently. Then she glanced toward the crib. 'But on the other hand — '

'You don't have to tell me. I know.'

Flickering in Alison's expression now was the conflict between motherhood and career that was to dog her, in varying degrees of intensity, for the rest of her days. And Emma would grow accustomed to seeing her face briefly shadow, as the tug-o'-war within her made itself felt.

# CHAPTER FIVE

CONRAD WAS the first of the family to visit Alison after her baby's birth. He arrived on a Sunday afternoon, when Alison was resting and the infant being fed by his sister.

'You're at it again, are you, our Em?' he said, watching her deftly wield the feeding bottle.

Emma kept her gaze on the baby's face. 'I don't know what you mean, love.'

But Conrad knew that she did. Why else was she avoiding his eye?

For both, it was as though time had swung backward to the fraught period, fifteen years ago, when their war-widow sister had lazed around the house, while Emma took care of her child. In all but name, Emma had been a mother to Percy during the first few years of his life. Clara's remarriage had left a great gap in the pattern of Emma's days. Emma had accepted it in her usual philosophical way, but Conrad had not needed telling how painful for her losing her small charge was.

Emma put down the bottle and wiped the baby's mouth. 'All right, so I do know what you mean, Conrad.'

'And you're leaving yourself wide open for it to happen to you again.'

Emma shrugged and resumed feeding the child.

'Alison isn't going to be able to take him to London, is she?' Conrad persisted.

'And it's going to hurt her more than me.'

'I wouldn't be too sure about that. Alison will have her career to absorb her. What will you have, Emma?'

'Neither of us is thinking that far ahead.'

'Then it's time you did. And the baby's immediate future must be decided, Emma. It can't be left hanging in the air. Have you and Alison discussed it?'

172

Emma shook her head.

'Are you saying you have no ideas on the subject?'

'I leave it to Mr Morton to have the ideas. He's a lot brainier than me.'

Conrad got up from the window seat and stood gazing into the back garden. Though it was not yet full summer, the apple tree beside the whitewashed wall was heavy with blossom, and a bed of red tulips had opened their silky petals to be kissed by the sun. The sweetness of wallflowers drifting in through the open lattice brought a poignant ache to Conrad's heart. It would take more than sunshine to lift his spirits.

He turned to face his sister. 'Zelda and I are thinking of giving a home to a refugee child.'

'That sounds like a good idea.'

'But I've just had a better one.' Conrad's gaze moved to the baby on Emma's lap.

'Are you out of your mind?' she said.

'Somebody is going to have to foster him, aren't they? We could legally adopt him.'

'Alison would never agree to that.'

Alison appeared in the doorway, looking fresh and sparkling after her nap. 'What wouldn't I agree to?'

She had on a smart beige linen dress, with a coral scarf tied in a bow at the neck. She had not lost her flair for making an entrance, Conrad thought, while contrasting her appearance with his sister's pinafored dowdiness.

Alison went to give Conrad a kiss. 'How lovely of you to come!'

'I'd have been here before now but Mam said you shouldn't be bothered by visitors before the baby was ten days old. That's why she hasn't been to see you yet.'

Alison laughed. 'Ten days must have been the official lying-in period when she gave birth! But why isn't Zelda with you?'

'She didn't feel up to coming,' Conrad said awkwardly.

Poor Zelda. She can't bear to see me with a baby, Alison thought. 'I understand,' she said.

Conrad handed her a parcel. 'She sent you this.'

173

'Our baby will soon have more shawls than there are days in the week,' Emma said when Alison opened the parcel.

Alison was admiring the beautiful circular one that Conrad's childless wife had spent so many hours knitting. 'But this will be his special-occasion one, Emma, because Zelda made it.'

Conrad was touched by the depths of Alison's understanding. What an incongruous mixture this cousin of his was! There were times when he thought her hard, and selfishly blind to anyone's feelings but her own, and others, like now, when she displayed a sensitivity and softness of which he wouldn't have thought her capable.

'You can hold the baby, if you like, Alison,' Emma said.

'Thank you, Emma dear!' Alison smiled with amusement. 'As you can see, Conrad, I require your sister's permission to hold my own child!'

'If I didn't watch her, she'd spoil him rotten, Conrad,' Emma declared.

Conrad marvelled at their easy relationship. The one so mercurial, and the other so prosaic. But he had known when his sister went to live with Alison that Emma would make it work. The credit – if not the benefit, he thought with a pang – was all hers.

Alison sat down on the shabby chintz-covered sofa, the baby on her lap. 'I bet this little house could tell some stories,' she remarked irrelevantly, 'about all the different people who've rented it over the years.'

'Which reminds me,' said Conrad, 'that you girls must be out of here by the end of June. The holiday season begins in July, and the agent told me the cottage is booked for the whole summer.'

'If I had to spend many more months here, I should go mad,' Alison answered. 'I've added my chapter to the house's story,' she said pensively.

'And I imagine it's one on its own,' said Conrad.

'You still haven't told me what I won't agree to.'

Conrad cleared his throat and straightened his tie – which usually precipitated something he found difficult to say.

174

'Out with it!' Alison prodded him. 'I am getting more curious by the minute,' she said with a smile.

'To Zelda and me adopting your child.'

Alison's smile faded.

'I told him how you would react to the suggestion,' Emma said.

'And you were right.' Alison held the baby closer. 'I wouldn't agree to anyone adopting my child.'

Conrad fidgeted with his watch chain. 'I didn't really expect you to.'

Alison gave him a hostile glance. 'Then why did you suggest it?'

Emma saw the mute misery on her brother's face, and intervened. 'Conrad and I were discussing the baby's future, Alison.'

'But I didn't mean to mention adoption,' Conrad added. He paused. 'When a person is worried stiff, they sometimes say things off the top of their head.'

'Apparently,' said Alison.

'But there's no reason why Zelda and I can't foster the baby, is there?'

Alison thought about it. 'That is a better suggestion.'

'No, it isn't!' Emma exclaimed. 'From Zelda's point of view, it's a much worse one.'

'Not if she knows from the outset that it is just a temporary arrangement,' Conrad countered.

On this occasion, he wouldn't allow himself to think ahead, unwise though it might prove to be. Fostering an older refugee child would not give his wife an infant to cuddle to her breast, and Zelda's desperate need must be assuaged.

Desperate was the word for it, Conrad thought. 'I am going to confide in you two,' he said to Alison and Emma, 'but nobody else in the family must know about this. Last weekend, when Zelda and I went for a stroll in the park, she lifted a baby out of its pram, and walked off with it.'

'What did the mother do?' Emma asked, when she found her voice.

'She didn't see it happen. The pram was outside the

ladies' toilet, and she must have been inside. I'd gone into the gents'. When I came out, there was my wife heading for the park gates. I could see the edge of a white shawl flapping in the wind against Zelda's coat – then I saw the empty pram,' said Conrad, re-living what had been for him a nightmare.

'It only took a split second for me to put two and two together,' he said, collecting himself. 'Fortunately, I was able to put the infant back where it belonged before its mother found it was gone. I've never run so fast in my life.'

He gazed through the window as though he could not bear to see the compassion in his listeners' eyes. 'Zelda says she didn't realise what she was doing.'

He turned to face Alison and Emma. 'And I believe her. After I returned from putting the baby back, she still had the same dazed expression on her face that was there when I snatched it from her.'

'And how has she been since then?' Emma inquired.

'Afraid to go out,' Conrad answered tersely, 'in case it happens again.'

Alison rose to put her own sleeping child in his crib. But it was Emma who turned him onto his side and tucked him in, Conrad absently noted.

'You may tell your wife that she'll soon have a little one in her own home,' said Alison decisively. 'It will give her something to look forward to and end the necessity for her fear. When Emma and I return to London, we'll leave the baby with Zelda. He couldn't have a more caring foster-mother.'

Emma quelled her misgivings about the outcome of Alison's decision. 'About that, I agree.'

Conrad hugged Alison. 'I don't know how to thank you.'

'There are many reasons for me to say that to you,' she replied, 'and this will be another. What I've agreed to do is for my sake, as well as Zelda's.'

'But where will you and Zelda say the baby has suddenly appeared from?' Emma asked her brother. 'Your friends and neighbours are bound to ask. Zelda's family in Leeds, too.'

It had struck Emma how one deceit leads inevitably to another and that all the Steins were now inextricably enmeshed. Alison's pregnancy had initiated it, and Zelda's childlessness had just woven a further strand.

'You also have the task, Conrad, of making Zelda realise that the arrangement is only temporary,' Alison said. 'Sooner or later, I shall somehow find a way of having my child with me.'

Conrad brushed both problems aside. The first could be resolved with a few white lies – to Conrad, lies were white when they served an honest purpose. The second would cause no trouble until some distant day. For the moment, it was enough that his pressing dilemma was solved.

'I'll cross my bridges when I come to them,' he said lightly.

'That's what my Grandfather Plantaine used to say,' Alison told him. 'When he didn't want to face the facts – which he rarely did.'

'But our Conrad isn't that kind of person,' Emma declared. 'It worries me to see him suddenly taking that attitude.'

Conrad gave her a weary smile. 'I don't have much option, do I, our Em? Now be a good girl and make us all a nice cup of tea.'

While they were drinking it, Morton arrived.

'You ought to have let us know you were coming,' Alison said while he embraced her.

'We'd have laid a red carpet on the garden path!' Emma joked.

It was evident to Conrad that both were overjoyed to see Morton – though Emma was doing her best not to show it. Nor was it difficult to discern that Morton's interest in Alison wasn't the fatherly one Conrad had supposed. He watched Morton stand for a moment, drinking in the sight of her. And fatherly his expression was not!

By the end of the half-hour Conrad remained after Morton's arrival, he had become aware, too, of where his sister's heart lay, and was sick with the knowledge. Emma had finally fallen in love, with a man who had eyes for nobody but Alison, and was a Gentile, to boot! Conrad thought, pitying her.

Morton thanked Conrad for all he had done to smooth Alison's path.

'She's my cousin, and our family stand by each other,' Conrad replied brusquely.

'I already have an inkling of how staunch the Steins are, from knowing your sister,' Morton said. 'Anyone would be fortunate to have our Em for a friend.'

Conrad was ruffled by Morton's use of his own pet name for Emma. But Emma addressed Morton as Max – which Alison did not. There was obviously an intimate relationship of some kind between the two, and it was plain that they respected each other. But what had this sophisticated man in common with Emma?

Emma told Morton what Alison and Conrad had agreed about the baby.

'Well, that's a load off our minds!' he said.

'For the moment,' Alison put in.

Conrad saw Emma and Morton exchange a glance.

'Max will put his thinking cap on,' Emma assured Alison.

'He better had,' she answered.

To Conrad, it sounded like a threat.

'I haven't taken it off since the day you fainted in your flat,' said Morton dryly. 'Nor Emma her worry cap, I shouldn't wonder!'

Again, Morton and Emma shared a glance of rapport.

Alison – and nothing else – was their common bond, Conrad realised then. What a sore situation it must be for his dear sister, who surely knew it. He had better take his leave, lest his feelings in the matter begin to show on his face.

After Conrad had left, Morton went outside to fetch from his car the gifts he had brought: a white silk scarf and red roses for Alison, toys galore for the baby, and lavender water for Emma.

Emma was not surprised that he considered her the lavender-water type. At Christmas, he had sent her bed-socks – glamorously trimmed with swansdown, but she had got the message all the same.

178

Alison opened the box of toys and picked up the baby. 'Your godfather is playing Santa Claus in May,' she told him. 'Though he hasn't yet acknowledged your presence in the room.'

Morton gazed, with mixed feelings, upon Alison's child by another man. Though he had missed her unutterably, he had been relieved not to have to witness the increasing evidence of her pregnancy. He had, too, dreaded seeing the child when it was born.

'Allow me to introduce you to Master Richard Maxwell Plantaine,' Alison said to him.

'Good God!' Morton exclaimed.

Emma quailed and Alison stiffened.

'If you would rather your name was removed from his, it is easily done,' Alison said coldly. 'His birth has not yet been registered.'

'I'm honoured that you've given him my name, Alison. It's yours I am concerned about, my dear. His birth certificate was the one thing I didn't think of.'

'That proves you're human,' said Emma. 'Even you can't think of everything.'

'Even if he had, this is one thing he can't manoeuvre to suit his purpose,' Alison declared in the same cold tone.

It was as though she were being deliberately cruel to Morton, and reminded Emma of the evening Alison had made him grovel on his knees to brush up the spilt sugar. After speaking to him in a manner tantamount to twisting a knife in his flesh, Emma recalled.

'What are you punishing Max for, Alison?' she asked quietly. 'None of this is his fault.'

Suddenly, the strain with which Alison had lived since returning from Berlin was bearable no longer, and her self-control snapped. 'I am sick and tired of Maxwell's concern for nothing but my star status and my public image! Its importance is not lost on me, but it's time he realised that I am a person, too!'

'To me, you are a very dear person,' Morton told her.

'There is no point in my being so, unless my child is to be dear to you, too. I've done everything you asked of me,

179

Maxwell, to protect the career you helped me build. But even if it were possible, I would not deprive my son of his mother's name on his birth certificate. His father's will be written there, too. It will be shock enough for the child when he grows up, and learns what society would call the awful truth.'

'I'm not sure that you can put his father's name on the birth certificate, as you're not married to him,' Emma said practically.

'Be that as it may, Emma. Mine will definitely be inscribed. Even Maxwell can not alter that fact.'

Morton went to kiss Alison's cheek. 'Let us say no more about it, my darling girl. And if you don't know by now how deeply I care for you, you never will.'

'In that case, you may hold your godson.'

'Sit down on the sofa, Max, and Alison will put the baby carefully into your arms,' Emma instructed. 'For you to drop our precious bundle on the floor is all we need!'

Morton did as he was bid, and a moment later found himself for the first time in his life with a child upon his lap.

'I wish we had a camera, Emma!' Alison said, so incongruous was the sight.

Morton, despite his jealousy of the baby's father – whom, ironically, he also admired – felt the layer of ice he had placed around his feelings begin to melt. When the infant's tiny fingers closed around his thumb, Morton knew he was sunk. 'He's a nice little chap,' he said gruffly to Alison.

'Thank you for saying so. Emma and I agree. But he doesn't look very comfortable, Maxwell. Shall we put him back in his crib?'

'Not yet.'

'Then mind his head on your watch chain, Max,' Emma implored.

Morton surveyed the two women, hovering beside him lest he damage the darling of their hearts. This boy would need a man in his life or, between them, Alison and Emma would make a sissy of him. The thought brought Morton full circle to the purpose of his visit. He could not put off any longer telling Alison why he had come.

180

'I received a phone call from Muller early this morning,' he said quietly. 'I'm afraid it wasn't an encouraging one.'

He saw the colour drain from Alison's face.

Emma, too, had paled. If Max thought it necessary to tell Alison in person, it had to be dire news.

'Why did you bother bringing us gifts?' Alison demanded harshly. 'And roses, too! To sweeten the bitter pill?'

Harshness was sometimes Alison's defence mechanism, as Morton well knew, and in this case, a lashing out in advance against something she knew was going to hurt her.

He glanced absently at the silk scarf which was on the table with Emma's lavender water. 'I had the parcels in my flat, Alison, to give to you when you returned to London. So I tossed them into the car this morning. As you've always liked roses, I bought you some from a stall, *en route*. They're hothouse ones, of course,' Morton rambled on, delaying the moment when he must relay Muller's news.

Alison cut him short. 'Never mind. It doesn't matter.' She had the feeling that from now on, nothing would. Morton's expression was stiff, and Alison was sorry for him. Nobody enjoyed being the bearer of bad tidings. 'You had better tell me, and get it over,' she said, steeling herself.

'A horrendous act, Alison, was recently perpetrated in Berlin. But you must have read about the burning of the books — '

'We don't get newspapers delivered here,' Emma interrupted. 'Alison sometimes walked to the village to buy one. But since the baby arrived we haven't even switched on the wireless set.'

'If you had,' said Morton, 'you'd have heard that the Nazis lit a funeral pyre in the Opernplatz. Centuries of literature and learning was the corpse.' He paused grimly. 'May 11th 1933 will go down in history as the night Hitler's barbarism was symbolically unleashed.'

'It was also,' Alison reminded him, 'the night I gave birth to my son. What has this to do with his father?'

'The event would not have been hidden from political prisoners, Alison. On the contrary, their jailers must have enjoyed describing it to them. And I am sorry to have to tell

181

you that some of the *Achtung* group are said to have consequently hanged themselves in their cells. It is not difficult to
imagine the burning of the books putting an end to their
lingering hopes.'

The baby cried out in the silence that followed. As
though, Alison thought, he was sharing her pain. She lifted
him from Morton's arms and soothed him in her own.

But it was still the pain of uncertainty, with which she had
lived for so long.

Emma found her voice. 'If it's only a rumour, Max, what
was the point of you coming here and distressing Alison
about it?'

'Muller obtained the information from a reliable source –
though a rumour it will doubtless remain. The Nazis are
unlikely to issue a statement which implies that to some
Germans death is preferable to the new régime.'

Alison was gazing through the window into the twilit
garden, the infant gathered to her breast. Her hair, which
the whims of fashion had never persuaded her to cut, was
drawn back into a chignon at the nape of her neck. The
stillness of her posture, and the profile she and the baby
presented, softened by the dusk, was to Morton like a
sculpture of the Madonna and Child, and brought an ache
to his throat.

He had not noticed the golden afternoon darken to
amber, only its changing pattern. Alison's delight when he
arrived. Her violent emotion when the baby's name was
discussed. The women's protectiveness toward the child.
And Alison's self-protective harshness on learning why
Morton had come. The silences that said more than words,
punctuating the conversation like exposed thread in a link
of beads. And the too-calm façade Alison was displaying
now.

Alison was recalling the first words Richard had ever
spoken to her – when they were just two strangers, who
happened to be seated at adjoining tables in a night-club.
He had overheard a remark of Alison's and capped it with a
terse one of his own: *If I thought there was no hope for
Germany, I would go home and cut my throat.*

Had the burning of the books caused his small candle of hope to flicker out? For such an act to be possible in his beloved country would have seemed to Richard Lindemann like civilisation going up in flames.

The friends incarcerated with him would also have seen it that way. To which of them would life itself, in the final analysis, have lost its worth on that terrible night?

Alison did not know them well, but felt that Gerda Schmidt and Karl Kohn were capable, like Richard, of making the ultimate gesture. The suicides were not, to Alison, the futile act they seemed, but martyrdom to a cause.

Morton exchanged a glance with Emma. Alison's unnatural calm was becoming unbearable.

Emma switched on a table lamp, and ended the long silence. 'That's better!'

But nothing can brighten my inner darkness, Alison thought. Then the infant stirred in her arms, and she knew that even if her lover was dead, he was not gone from her, but would live on in their child.

# CHAPTER SIX

ALISON'S RETURN to London, announced by Morton to the press, was not accorded so much as a mention.

An actress could not rest upon her laurels for long, she reflected. But if the reason for Alison's lengthy absence from the limelight had leaked out, her return would be pictured on every front page, was her cynical afterthought.

In the meantime, the newsworthy aura attached to the name Plantaine had transferred to her stepcousins. Lucy's sensational last-minute takeover of Alison's role in *Rain* had rocketed her to stardom. But she had not remained loyal to Morton.

Instead, after only a short run, Lucy had utilised a get-out clause in her contract. She was now starring in a revue which Morton's rival, Charles Bligh, had built around her. Her brother had directed it with a flair which did not go unnoticed by the critics, and had subsequently directed two more productions for Bligh.

During her sojourn up north, Alison had managed to put the twins from her mind. On re-entering her working world, it was less easy to do so, and the funereal-looking lilies they sent to 'welcome her back' were a sinister reminder of their ill-will.

The flowers arrived while Emma was out shopping for groceries. Alison dumped them in the dustbin but their scent, and its depressing significance, lingered on. The twins were now riding high: Alison had never felt at a lower ebb.

Morton did not allow her to remain so. Alison's emotional problems were out of his hands, but the same did not apply to her career, of which her image was an essential part.

He began by insisting that she accompany him to the

opening of Ivor Novello's *Proscenium* at the Globe Theatre. It would be some time before she appeared again onstage, but the offstage performances required of her must start immediately.

For Alison, the occasion was like the re-enactment of a scene she had played many times, in another life. The oohs and ahs, when she stepped from the limousine onto the thronged pavement. The familiar stir, as she entered the theatre foyer. Morton, immaculate in evening dress, saying all the right things. Herself, wearing a white fox cape over a silver-sequined gown – and a smile that felt as if it was cemented onto her face.

Briefly, she recoiled from the gushing that greeted her on all sides. Then a question from Novello about what her next play was to be reminded her that this was her real life. It was the interlude up north that was another life – and the sooner she got things in their right perspective the better.

Morton lost no time in mounting a production for her. In the weeks that followed, Alison tried to switch her mind from her own troubles to those of the character she was portraying. But hovering beside her always was the shadow of Richard Lindemann, and of the child she had borne, now being mothered by another woman.

During rehearsals, she became aware that she was just going through the motions of playing her role. Try as she would, her feelings remained unengaged. She could not have cared less when the play flopped, though she was sorry for Morton and the playwright.

Once again, Morton had taken a chance on a new dramatist. But nowadays, he reflected, what the theatre-going public wanted was anyone's guess, as some of the offerings currently showing in London indicated.

The instinct for what was right for the moment, upon which impresarios relied when selecting plays, seemed to have fled. Never had Morton known quite such a pot-luck assortment – ranging from *Fly Away Peter*, at the Embassy, and *Clear All Wires*, at the Garrick, to Shalom Aleichem's *If I Were You*, at the Shaftesbury.

*The Writing On The Wall*, now on at the Royalty, was a

185

title that summed up Morton's gloomy feelings about the current scene. It was as though the theatre was marking time, waiting for a new trend to emerge and jolt it from the doldrums. Nothing of the kind had happened since Noël Coward was hailed as the spokesman of his generation in the Twenties. Meaningful theatre must, one way or another, reflect the times, Morton thought. But no contemporary English play had yet mirrored the economic depression gripping the Thirties.

Before too long, *Love On the Dole* would do so – and introduce to the theatrical scene an immediacy which some would consider the opposite of entertainment. But Morton could not have foreseen this. Meanwhile, managers of integrity, of whom he was one, to whom theatre meant more than a living, waited impatiently for whatever the next new trend would be.

For them, the hazardous unpredictability of their business was part of its excitement, and kept them chewing anxiously on their cigars, while the adrenalin coursed upward and downward within them like a built-in barometer of their fortunes.

Charles Bligh was of another ilk, unscrupulous to a high degree. He had arrived late on the scene, after marrying his wealthy wife whose money financed his initial productions. His instinct for box-office winners had since made him rich in his own right. Some said that Bligh saw himself as another C. B. Cochran, but would never catch up with that great showman. There were few in the business who wished Bligh well. His cunning was legendary. His caution, too. It was no secret that Lucy Plantaine was his mistress, but he had not risked his capital on starring her in a West End production, before her success in *Rain*. Nor had he exhibited a scrap of conscience when Morton had to close *Rain* after Lucy's early departure to appear in Bligh's revue.

These were Morton's assorted ruminations in the cab taking him to Alison's flat, to discuss with her his plans for her next play. He did not like her lethargic demeanour since her flop, and wanted to get her back onstage as soon as possible.

It was a bleak, winter afternoon and Emma led him into the drawing room, where Alison was curled up by the fire.

'I am thinking of staging *The Trojan Women*,' he said to her without preamble. 'How would you like to play Hecuba again?'

Alison had played that demanding role with the Plantaine Players. Re-creating it, years later, would be a stimulating challenge – which Morton felt she needed.

'You'll be pleased to know that Basil Breen has agreed to direct, if we do the play,' Morton told her.

'That would be lovely, Maxwell. I enjoyed working with him for my Shaw season,' Alison replied, and added flatly, 'My Hecuba would be compared with Sybil Thorndike's, of course.'

It was the role with which Miss Thorndike had, more than a decade ago, ensured herself a place in English theatrical history.

Morton was dismayed by Alison's reaction. 'The Thorndike St Joan is legendary, too,' he reminded her, 'but you didn't let that stop you from playing it, nor other parts for which Sybil, who made her début long before you did, was acclaimed when she played them.'

Alison made no reply.

'You are a brilliant actress,' Morton declared, 'but you are not yet thirty-four. It takes time, as well as brilliance, to achieve real stature. But the time will surely come when your interpretations of the classical roles will be retrospective yardsticks in the theatre.'

'Thank you, Maxwell dear. But there is no need for you to lecture me.'

'Nor for you to suddenly lose your confidence, Alison. Just because your last play flopped.'

'It was as much my fault as the play's,' she countered. 'My heart wasn't in it. But if you want me to play Hecuba, I will.'

Morton rose from the sofa to stir the fire, which did not require stirring. His dismay had deepened to alarm. 'I am getting the impression you couldn't care less what you play, Alison, that your career has ceased to matter to you.'

'I'm afraid that is true, Maxwell.'

'But it won't last.'

'Of course it won't last. The theatre is in my blood. I am an actress born and bred. But it is no longer the whole of what I am. I am now a mother, too. It isn't easy for me to muster enthusiasm for anything – not even for my work – when there is still no prospect of having my baby with me.'

Alison's eyes brimmed with tears.

Morton gave her his handkerchief.

'You'd do better to find a way of making it unnecessary for her to weep!' Emma told him with feeling.

'Meanwhile, why not go north and visit the baby?' Morton said to Alison, 'while you are between plays.'

'I'm afraid to,' she replied, 'lest I'm unable to tear myself away again. Why do you suppose I haven't been?' She dried her eyes. 'He's nine months now, Maxwell. Old enough to have grown attached to his foster-parents.'

'Not to mention,' said Emma, 'how attached they are to him. And the longer he remains with them, the worse it will be when they have to give him up. So you had better put your thinking cap on, Max, and come up with a way Alison can present him to the world.'

'That isn't a problem,' Morton answered. 'She will simply decide to adopt a child. The problem is to avoid her decision to do so being connected with her lengthy rest. We must allow time for her absence from the stage to recede from the public's memory.'

A month later, the time lapse was ended by Destiny – or so it seemed to Alison.

For her cousin Conrad, it was God's will when his wife conceived a child.

'*Mazeltov*, Conrad!' Emma said when he telephoned to tell her. 'It's wonderful news.'

'Yes, isn't it,' he replied, hiding his disquiet. 'I'd like to speak to Alison, Emma.'

'She's at rehearsal. Can you call back this evening?'

'No. If I ring up from home, Zelda will hear what I have to say, and she won't like it. So I'll tell you, and you can pass it on to Alison. I think this is the right time for her to take her son.'

'Why? Is Zelda unwell?'

'She isn't a strong girl, Emma, and I don't want her to overdo things. Little Richard, bless him, is quite a weight to carry around. It will upset us to part with him, but Zelda can now look forward to a little one of her own.'

'I understand, Conrad. But I must discuss it with Mr Morton.'

'What has Mr Morton got to do with it?'

'He's Alison's manager, isn't he?'

'And she doesn't move a muscle without him! Nor without it getting into the newspapers, it seems. Her picture, lately, seems to be on the front page every other day.'

'That's because she's about to open in a new play.'

'How do you stand it, our Em?'

'Stand what?'

'Living in that world of let's pretend! It worries me that little Richard is going to have to. Thank God he'll have you, Emma, to keep his feet on the ground.'

Emma required no reminding that this would be her job.

'Has there been any news about his father?' Conrad asked.

'I'm afraid not. Alison hasn't given up hope entirely, but I think she has prepared herself for there being only one Richard in her life.'

'A boy needs a dad.'

'But if he hasn't one, a godfather will have to do. Mr Morton is Richard's, remember, and he isn't the kind to shirk his responsibilities.'

You neither, Emma, Conrad thought. But Alison didn't think twice about doing so.

Conrad was telephoning from the store while his father was out at the bank, and gazed through the window at the familiar Oldham street scene while Emma continued to sing Morton's praises.

Conrad's impression, from his brief meeting with Morton, was that everything Emma was saying about him was true. Morton, like Emma, would become a pillar of Alison's

189

son's life, while Alison flitted gaily betwixt and between – like the butterfly their Grandfather Shrager had fondly called her.

'This phone call will cost you a fortune, Conrad,' Emma said guiltily.

He switched his mind from little Richard's future to the present. 'Mr Morton can tell the press the same fib Zelda and I – for Alison's sake – told everyone. People know that German Jews are fleeing from Hitler. Alison can get valuable publicity from adopting the orphan refugee baby her cousins were temporarily fostering,' Conrad added dryly. 'A bonus Mr Morton will not fail to recognise!'

'Why are you being so nasty about him, Conrad?'

Because you're in love with him, my dear sister, and he's too besotted with Alison to know what he's missing, Conrad thought. 'I'm being practical,' he said.

And here we go with another lot of lies, thought Emma with distress. Lies which an innocent child's life would be built upon.

Accordingly, on an April afternoon in 1934, Miss Alison Plantaine, currently starring in *The Trojan Women*, waited at Euston Station, surrounded by press photographers, there to record for their papers her heartwarming real-life act.

But it was a loving and grateful mother who took the baby from Emma who had gone north to fetch him. Nor was it without a pang of shame that Alison posed for pictures with the cuddly bundle in her arms. The last thing she would have chosen was to make a public appearance out of her private joy. But it was the price of fame.

# CHAPTER SEVEN

IN THE winter of 1938, Alison returned from the theatre one night and found Morton comforting Emma.

'My dad dropped dead at the store this evening,' Emma said tremulously. 'Conrad phoned to tell us, just after you'd left for the theatre, Alison. So I rang Max and he came round.'

Alison was trying to take it in. Uncle Lionel gone? It didn't seem possible.

'Your supper is in the oven,' Emma said to her.

'I couldn't eat it, Emma.'

'Me neither.'

'Then I'll take a leaf from Emma's book, and make us some tea,' said Morton, putting the kettle on to boil. 'Then we must all try to get some rest. We have a long journey up north ahead of us tomorrow.'

He got out the cups and saucers. The incongruity of his busying himself with this domestic task was to Alison as unreal as the news she had just heard. Emma's allowing him to do so added to Alison's feeling that this was not really happening.

Emma's next words were evidence that it was. 'Can you lend me something black to wear, Alison? I shan't have time to go and buy a dress.'

'Conrad called back later, to let us know the funeral will be tomorrow afternoon,' Morton told Alison. 'I said I would drive you both to Oldham, and make sure you arrived in time, so we must leave very early.'

Morton made the tea, without bothering to warm the pot. Emma was too preoccupied to notice.

'I'm amazed at the speed with which the funeral arrangements were made,' he remarked.

'It's always that way in our religion,' Emma explained. 'We bury our dead immediately,' she added with a shudder.

Alison sat down beside her at the table, and held her hand. 'It would do you good to weep, Emma darling.'

'But I don't seem able to, Alison.'

Morton heaped some sugar into a cup of tea and made Emma drink it.

'I don't like sweet tea,' she protested.

'Now you know what it's like to taste your own medicine.'

'When my father died, I wept buckets,' Alison recalled.

'But it wasn't a shock to you,' Emma reminded her. 'Uncle Horace had been in bad health for years. My dad was never ill.'

'Nor mine,' Morton said, 'and he went the same way that yours did, Emma. Without suffering, which isn't a bad way to go.'

'But not being prepared for it,' said Emma, 'makes it harder for those who bear the loss.'

Alison changed the subject. 'You may borrow one of my black frocks, with pleasure, Emma. But my clothes will swamp you. You'll look ridiculous.'

'I don't care how I'll look.'

'But your mother will. And she'll remind you that your father would.'

Emma managed a wan smile. 'Probably.'

Neither Emma, nor Alison, could remember ever seeing Lottie Stein look less than immaculate, even when she was standing at the stove, frying fish.

'I'm sure Aunt Lottie would rather you wore a brown frock that fits you, than a black one that's flapping around your ankles like a tent,' Alison advised. 'I'll lend you a black scarf, to drape around your shoulders, and — '

'How can we sit here discussing clothes, when my father is lying dead?' Emma burst out.

Then a tear rolled down her cheek, and Morton thought it time he left. He did not want to see the tower of strength Emma was to him disintegrate, however briefly.

'I should get her to bed, Alison. Yourself, too. I'll be back to collect you at the crack of dawn. And Richard

192

will have to miss kindergarten tomorrow. We'll have to take him with us, as there's nobody here we can leave him with.'

It was a sombre journey, made more so by the dismal November weather. The two women sat pensively in the back of the car. By now, the unbelievable had become for them a cruel fact. Emma was steeling herself to see Lionel in his coffin. For Alison, that the man who had welcomed her into his family in her youth was no more, was like a sturdy oak being suddenly lopped from a familiar landscape.

Richard was beside Morton, fidgeting with the brass buttons on his reefer coat, affected by the adults' silence.

Morton glanced down at the troubled little face beneath the peaked sailor cap. What was going on in his inquiring mind? Five was too young to understand that life did not go on forever. And Morton had no doubt that this highly intelligent child was puzzling about the little he had been told, when he was awakened at an unusual hour, dressed, and bundled into the car.

'Help yourself to a sweet from my coat pocket, Richard,' Morton said to distract him.

Richard glanced over his shoulder at Emma. 'May I have one, Auntie?'

It did not strike any of them as strange that the child had asked Emma's permission when Alison was present. By now, the role each played in Richard's scenario was firmly established.

Emma had become the mother-figure – though Alison would have been shocked, had she realised it. Her own relationship with her son had, from the first, lacked the solid everyday quality that Emma's constant, reassuring presence had for him.

If he grazed his knee, it was Emma who bathed it and applied the stinging iodine, while Alison kissed away his tears. Emma, though she too petted him, would scold him when he was naughty. Alison did not.

To Richard, Emma spelled security. About Alison, his feelings were a good deal more complex. It would be some years before he was old enough to examine them.

193

Meanwhile, she was to him a perfumed presence who came and went, lighting up his day when she was there.

His Uncle Maxwell, who had taught him to swim, and took him to the zoo, was Richard's hero. It was to him Richard took his childish complaints, when his aunt would not allow him his own way about this or that. And vice versa, if Morton ticked him off. Richard sometimes, too, played Emma and Morton against each other, as a child cunningly does with its parents. But it would not have occurred to him to involve Alison in such domestic by-play. Though he was, in effect, being raised by all three, the one he called 'Mummy' was not of that everyday realm.

His coming had, of course, changed all their lives. It had, too, caused yet another shift in their triangular relationship. Though Alison remained the focal point, her child had fulfilled a primeval need in the other two. Richard had become the nearest thing to a son Morton and Emma were likely to have. And both would have laid down their lives for him.

The boy could not have been raised by people who cared for him more, but his was, nevertheless, a hazardous situation. Two of the three who loved him were haunted by the fear that the one who had the power to do so might suddenly whisk him from their horizon.

Remote though the possibility was, Richard Lindemann might still be alive, and one day claim Alison and his child. Or Alison, unpredictable as ever, could lose her heart again – to some handsome stranger who would make her and the boy his own by the simple act of putting a wedding ring on her finger.

These hypothetical eventualities were never discussed by Emma and Morton, though the vulnerability of each *vis-à-vis* the boy was evident to the other.

Most of the time they managed not to think about it. And neither was doing so on the day they travelled to Oldham for Lionel Stein's funeral.

'Conrad told me on the phone last night that Dad will lie beside your father,' Emma said to Alison.

Alison patted her hand. 'Then he won't be lonely, Emma.'

'Do people lie down in heaven?' Richard inquired. He gazed through the windscreen at the bleak sky. 'It does look rather a lonely place.'

'It's only our souls that go there, Richard,' Morton supplied. He had almost said 'supposed to go there', but Emma would have told him to keep his heathen notions to himself.

In Emma's opinion, the little that Morton had said was too much. 'What are you telling Richard things like that for, Max?' she said scathingly.

'If I don't, some well-informed youngster will. I don't believe in filling kids' heads with too much nonsense.'

'And I,' said Emma, 'believe in letting children keep their illusions as long as they can.'

Richard helped himself to another sweet during the heated debate on child-rearing that followed. He wanted to ask what illusions were, but had learned from experience that when his uncle and aunt were discussing something concerning himself, interruptions went unheard.

Alison closed her eyes and let them get on with it. Their preoccupation with Richard's welfare was sometimes amusing, and occasionally irritating. Whose child is he? Alison had initially found herself thinking, when they did not allow her a say in this or that. But she had long since stopped trying to wield her influence in the matter of how her son was raised.

Recollection of her cousin Clara using Emma as Percy's nursemaid, but not letting her discipline him, had helped Alison accept what she must. Her career prohibited her from undertaking the mundane tasks of motherhood, nor was she suited to them. Emma had filled the breach willingly, and was entitled to the authority that went with the job. Morton, too, had assumed responsibilities he could, had he wished, have eschewed, which allowed him the entitlement he claimed.

If I died tomorrow Richard would still be taken care of, Alison reflected. But what a morbid thought on the way to a funeral!

Emma and Morton had now fallen silent.

'What is our soul?' Richard inquired.

195

'I'll be glad when this lad is able to use a dictionary!' Morton said.

'What's a dictionary, Uncle Maxwell? And I should like to know what an illusion is, too.'

His retentive memory for words was, to Morton and Emma, a constant source of amazement. Recalling her intellectual lover, Alison was less surprised.

Physically, Richard's resemblance to his father had remained nil. It had once seemed to Alison that his endearing, lopsided smile was all he had inherited from the man who begat him. As he grew older, though, he was displaying other characteristics etched upon Alison's memory. A deep frown of concentration, when he was turning something over in his mind. A way of pulling at his lower lip, when he was not certain. And a doggedness, when he was. There was about the little boy, too, an innate gentleness which Alison thought could equally well have come from her father or her lover. Both, in their dealings with others, had been the kindest of men.

Richard chose that moment to illustrate his mother's final thought. 'Would you like me to come and cuddle you, Auntie Emma?' he said kindly. 'To stop you from feeling sad because your daddy's gone away to heaven?'

'I'd like that very much.'

A moment later he had scrambled over the seat and was in Emma's arms.

Alison experienced a pang of jealousy. She stamped it out. The least that Emma deserved was the affection Richard had for her, and Emma had never been more in need of comfort than she was today.

The same applied to Lottie, Alison thought when they arrived at the Steins' house and she saw her aunt's desolate appearance.

'I'm sorry to be meeting you on this unhappy occasion, Mrs Stein,' Morton said after they had shaken hands.

'If it weren't for this unhappy occasion, Mr Morton, we might never have met,' Lottie replied, surveying the worldly stranger whose machinations had embroiled her simple family from afar.

It was he who had plotted the complicated deception surrounding Alison's pregnancy – but Emma had carried the load, Lottie thought. Conrad and Zelda had also served their purpose. And all to protect Alison's career – so Mr Morton could profit from it!

In her personal grief, Lottie's long-harboured grudges rose to the surface in simple terms of black and white. The grey areas between, in which lay the emotional needs and complexities of all the individuals concerned, did not exist for her.

There was, too, within her a sense of bitter injustice that a man of her husband's goodness had been suddenly cut down. Until today, Morton had been only a name to her. In the flesh, he had become the villain of the piece. All her resentments centred upon him and she wanted him out of her house.

'Make Mr Morton a sandwich and some tea,' she instructed Emma. 'I'm sure he is in a hurry to get back to London.'

Though the words were inoffensive, Lottie's tone was not. Emma cringed with embarrassment. Alison was glad they had dropped Richard at Zelda's, and that none of the family's friends were present.

Conrad and Clara were seated on the sofa, with Lottie.

'You'd better do what Mother says,' Conrad said to Emma. This isn't the time to argue with her, his accompanying glance signified.

Morton hid his discomfiture. 'I'm in no hurry to leave. It's my intention to attend Mr Stein's funeral.'

Lottie gave him a hostile look. 'You didn't know my husband.'

'Nevertheless, I should like to show my respect for you and for him. I am a close friend of your daughter, Mrs Stein. And I shall remain in Oldham until my passengers are ready to return home.'

'This is my daughter's home, Mr Morton,' said Lottie crisply.

Emma hastened to soothe her. 'Of course it is, Mam! And I'll be staying for the week of *Shivah*, of course. That's

197

what we call our period of mourning,' she explained to Morton. 'You and Alison can leave immediately after the funeral. I'll come back by train, next week.'

'You're not going back at all,' Lottie said.

The silence that followed was like the aftermath of a pebble being dropped into a pond. Alison could feel the ripples all around her. Would the troubled waters her aunt had just created ever be smooth again?

# CHAPTER EIGHT

ZELDA STEIN smiled down at her small daughter, and the assured little boy whose foster-mother she had once been.

'You'll be good for Mrs Payne while I'm out, won't you, my loves?'

'Your Janet is always good, Zelda,' said the buxom neighbour who had offered to mind the pair while Zelda was at her father-in-law's funeral.

'And I shall be especially good today,' Richard declared, 'as my great-uncle's soul has gone to heaven and everyone is extremely sad.'

'What a quaint little lad you are!' the neighbour exclaimed.

'What does quaint mean?'

'Old-fashioned,' Zelda supplied.

'And what does that mean?'

'Goodness gracious! You'd better be off, Zelda, luv – or he'll 'ave you standin' 'ere answerin' questions for t'rest o' t'day!' said Mrs Payne.

Zelda kissed the children and departed, quelling the apprehension which always beset her when her one ewe lamb was not under her eye. Mrs Payne was kind and trustworthy – but Zelda was unable to rid herself of the fear that some unforeseen mishap might befall Janet. Conrad had warned her that her over-anxiety would communicate itself to their daughter, but to him, too, Janet was a precious blessing, whose coming had lit his life.

Despite her parents' adoration, Janet was not a spoiled child. In appearance, she was a miniature version of her lovely blonde mother. Her obliging nature reminded her elders of her Aunt Emma. But she was more animated than

199

Emma had ever been, and occasionally displayed a mind of her own.

She did so the moment Zelda had left the house. 'I want to show Richard my doll's house,' she replied to Mrs Payne's instruction that they play in the kitchen.

'It's a big, 'eavy thing, luv. I can't be fetchin' it down from your room. It teks a man to lift it, Janet.'

'But Richard and me can go upstairs, can't we?'

'Richard and I,' he corrected her.

'There's a pile o' your toys on t'kitchen floor, Janet luv,' said Mrs Payne. 'You can show them to Richard.'

'But why may we not go upstairs?' Richard wanted to know.

'' 'Cause I'm 'ere to keep my eye on you. An' I've fetched me ironin' to do. It's washday on a Tuesday in our 'ouse. I can't do me ironin' upstairs.'

'Why isn't your washday on a Monday? My Auntie Emma's is.'

'Mercy me! You want to know everythin', don't you, luv? Because me daughter's just 'ad twins. On Mondays I go to 'elp 'er with 'er wash.'

'I'd still like to show Richard my doll's house,' Janet persisted.

'I'm afraid you can't,' he told her. 'We promised to be very good, didn't we?'

'Would going upstairs be very bad?'

'Unless we get permission to.'

Janet giggled. 'But we'll get it when we want to go to the lavatory, won't we?'

Mrs Payne ushered them into the kitchen. Enough was enough!

'Now don't either of you come anywhere near this red-hot iron,' she warned the children, transferring it from the glowing coals in the grate to an upside-down enamel plate on the scrub-top table.

Richard watched her dampen and fold the pile of fresh-smelling laundry she had brought in her basket. 'My Auntie Emma's iron doesn't look like that,' he observed. 'It's nice and shiny. And she plugs it into the wall, to get hot.'

200

'So does my mam,' Janet said.

'But I don't hold wi' them new-fangled electric ones,' Mrs Payne declared. 'Who wants to give theirself an electric shock?'

'What's an electric shock?' Richard asked – as she had feared he would.

'Never you mind! You'd know if you got one. And what an inquisitive little lad you've turned out to be. Don't ask me what that means!'

'I know. It is often said about me.'

'That doesn't surprise me, luv. I expect you'll end up a professor or summat. An' to think I 'elped Zelda bath you, when you were a babe! Right 'ere, in this kitchen, in front of t'fire. She were nervous o' tacklin' you on 'er own, till she got used to it.'

'My mam is always nervous,' Janet piped. 'I heard my daddy say so, to my grandma.'

'I haven't got a grandma,' Richard said. 'Nor a daddy.'

Mrs Payne gave him a smile. 'But you've got a luvly mother, 'aven't you?'

Richard's face lit up. 'Oh, yes.'

'What the good Lord takes away wi' one 'and, He gives back wi' t'other,' the simple woman declared.

The children exchanged a puzzled glance. Then Janet added a red wood block to the multicoloured tower they were building.

But Richard felt that what Mrs Payne had just said somehow concerned him, and was staring thoughtfully into space. There was the other thing she had said, too.

'What's goin' on in that brainbox o' yourn now?' Mrs Payne inquired. She had never met such a serious child!

'I was wondering why you and Janet's mummy were bathing me, when I was a baby.'

Only then did Zelda's well-meaning neighbour realise she had said too much. The recollection had slipped off her tongue, and she had thought nothing of it. You had to watch what you said to a child who didn't know it was adopted – but she hadn't been thinking of that.

'I expect you were staying with us, Richard,' Janet said.

Mrs Payne clutched at the handy straw. 'That must've been it.'

'But where were Mummy and Auntie Emma?' Richard persisted.

'They probably had to go on an errand,' Mrs Payne answered.

But she had avoided his eye, and Richard did not believe her.

Mrs Payne was aware of his piercing gaze. 'All this fuss about nowt, lad,' she said uncomfortably.

But it was not 'nowt' to Richard. Why had this lady told him a lie? A moment later, he had toppled the tower of blocks to the ground.

Janet burst into tears. 'Why did you do that?'

'I don't know,' he replied truthfully.

He had sensed a mystery surrounding himself and, intelligent though he was, was unable to comprehend the feeling that had suddenly surged within him.

It was similar to Alison's, in her childhood, when the seeds of mistrust of her mother were first implanted in her. And it was against Alison that Richard had lashed out. Though Emma attended to his physical needs and he loved her dearly, emotionally, Alison alone had him in her power.

He apologised to Mrs Payne, like the well-mannered child he was, and helped Janet rebuild the tower.

All's well as ends well, Mrs Payne said to herself with relief.

But for the little boy playing at her feet, the uncertainty that was to dog him from now on had just begun.

# CHAPTER NINE

AFTER THE funeral, Alison asked Morton to fetch Richard.

'I would rather he didn't come here, my dear,' Morton said. 'Why don't we collect him from your cousin's when we leave?'

Ten minutes ago, the Steins' house had been crammed with people paying their respects. Their departure had served to heighten the depressing atmosphere, which Morton thought unsuitable for a child.

'My aunt wants to see Richard,' Alison replied. 'And he must say goodbye to Emma, mustn't he?'

Morton voiced their mutual anxiety. 'Let's hope it will be only a temporary one, despite what her mother said.'

'Emma has a big decision to make, Maxwell.'

'Yes.'

Alison fingered the jet brooch at her throat. 'I daren't let myself think that she may not come back. But I shan't try to influence her. And nor must you.'

'Of course not.'

They were conversing quietly in the hall. Emma was in the front parlour with her mother and Conrad and Clara.

Why do I feel like a conspirator? Morton thought. The feeling was strengthened when Lottie opened the parlour door, and by the glance she gave him. Morton swallowed hard and managed to smile. What had she got against him?

He wanted to believe that her attitude was an illogical manifestation of her overwrought state, but felt there was more to it. It was as though some long-standing grudge she had harboured could no longer be contained. Like a festering boil that had suddenly burst.

Were it not for his inextricable relationship with her

niece and daughter, he would not, after the way she had greeted him, have re-entered her house.

Or be embroiled in this ritual, he thought, conscious of the weight of his hat upon his head. Alison had told him it must remain there, in a Jewish house of mourning.

He caught a glimpse of Emma and her brother and sister in the parlour, seated on the low chairs decreed for the next of kin. All three had a jagged cut at the neckline of their garments, as their mother had, put there by the rabbi to signify the severance of their living bond with their departed loved one. For Morton, it served to emphasise the starkness of all he had witnessed today.

At the cemetery, Conrad had introduced him to a family friend from Manchester, a Mr David Sandberg – whom Morton was unlikely to forget. Though he had not succeeded, Mr Sandberg had endeavoured to stop Morton from feeling the outsider he was.

When Morton evinced surprise that Lionel Stein's coffin was of simple unpolished wood, and that no flowers adorned it, or the grave, Mr Sandberg had told him this was customary. And had added – as though he wanted to make a point – that Jews, whatever their bank balance, are laid to rest vested with no more riches than those with which they came.

What had he really been saying? Morton had wondered, noting the cryptic expression on the man's sallow face. His tone had been verging on the defensive, as if Morton's remarks were Gentile criticism of his own race.

Morton was not without Jewish acquaintances in London. But today was his first experience of their ancient rites, he was thinking, when Alison went with her aunt into the parlour, and he was left standing alone in the hall.

He saw her sit down on a high chair beside Emma's low one, and felt her grief merge with the pall of sorrow blanketing the room.

Clara's son Percy, and her daughter Lila, were seated solemnly on the sofa, completing the picture of a Jewish family mourning their dead in the way their forebears had, that would remain etched upon Morton's memory.

The remains of the ritual mourners' meal stood on an upturned wooden box, used today instead of a table. Two flickering candles, placed beside a pile of well-worn prayer books, lit the close-knit group, and enhanced Morton's feeling that only the biblical sackcloth and ashes were missing.

Such was the aura emanating from the scene he was viewing from the hall. But Morton would not have expected Alison, nominally a Christian, to fit so naturally into it. He had not realised how strongly her father's blood ran in her veins; that her link with the Steins was not just with them, but a primeval one with the race Mr David Sandberg had felt it necessary to defend.

'Why are you standing there, Maxwell?' she said to him quietly. 'Please go and fetch Richard. He must come and pay his respects.'

Morton emerged from his thoughts, cleared his throat awkwardly, and left. It was a relief to do so; he had never felt more of an intruder. Suddenly, both Alison and Emma were like mysterious strangers to him.

Driving the short distance to Conrad's house, he wondered if Alison knew how Jewish she was. She had once remarked to him that at times she felt like a child of two worlds. When had she said it? When she was still little more than a girl. Morton had asked her what she meant, but she had been unable to explain.

Now, no explanation was required, he thought. Her theatrical upbringing had conditioned her to be a Plantaine but beneath her polished surface she was, too, a Shrager, as her father had been, as at home amid his ancient heritage as she was with her mother's thespian one, onstage.

Zelda Stein had gone home to give the children their tea, and was washing their sticky hands at the kitchen sink when Morton arrived to collect Richard.

'Why can't Richard stay here with me?' Janet asked.

Morton ruffled her fair curls. 'He has to go to kindergarten tomorrow, my dear.'

'It's been a long day for the children,' said Zelda, watching her small daughter stifle a yawn. 'Janet is usually fast asleep in bed by this time.'

'Richard, too. We shall have to tuck him up on the back seat of the car, as we'll be travelling for much of the night.' Morton smiled at the apple of his eye. 'Quite an adventure for you, eh, my boy?'

Richard did not reply, and Morton thought he was probably too exhausted to do so.

He watched Zelda give Richard a warm hug, and thought – correctly – that Richard would always occupy a special place in Zelda's heart.

'I don't want to go home. I want to stay in Oldham, with Auntie Emma,' Richard said to Morton in the car, when he learned that Emma would not be returning to London with them.

He was still saying this when they entered the Steins' house. Morton halted him in the hall.

'You are not to make a fuss about this when you go into the parlour, Richard. It will distress your mummy.'

The instruction was not heeded. Richard ignored Alison and flung himself into Emma's arms. 'I don't want to leave you, Auntie,' he said forlornly.

Alison and Morton waited for Emma to assure him that it would be only for a short while – and exchanged a glance when she did not. Emma was not the kind to make promises she might be unable to keep, and least of all to a child. She had not made up her mind.

Meanwhile, she held Richard close and seemed unable to speak.

'Mummy will take care of you, darling,' Alison said to Richard.

'I want Auntie Emma to. Like she always does.' Richard glared at Alison. 'And I don't love you any more.'

Morton removed him from Emma's embrace and gave his wriggling bottom a spank.

This was all Lottie Stein needed to see, to compound her resentment of Morton's effect upon her family. 'How dare you do that to my great-nephew?' she blazed, giving Richard his official title to emphasise her own rights in the matter.

'He is also my godson,' Morton politely reminded her. 'And occasionally, some disciplining is required.'

206

Emma raised her voice at last. 'Come here, Richard. I want to speak to you.'

Richard went to her like a lamb.

'That's a good boy,' Emma said gently. 'And I want you to go on being good. For Mummy and Uncle Maxwell.'

To Alison and Morton, it was as though she were preparing the boy for her removal from his scene. This, coupled with her son's statement that he did not love her any more, was enough to make Alison feel that the ground was slipping from beneath her feet.

'I'll speak to you on the phone, every day,' Emma told Richard.

'A nice bill we're going to have!' Lottie exclaimed.

The remark was so out of keeping with her kind and generous nature that Conrad sprang to his feet.

'My mother is not herself right now,' he apologised to Morton.

'Nor,' declared Lottie, 'shall I ever be the mug I always was, again.'

'Who have you been a mug for, Grandma?' Clara's teenage daughter inquired.

Lottie quivered with the feeling of injustice by which she had been beset since her husband was taken from her. 'Everyone and anyone, Lila. Including your mother.'

'Why bring me into this?' Clara shrilled.

'Why not, Clara? You've used me no less than some of the others in this room.'

She was staring accusingly at Morton. How, he wondered, could what she was saying possibly include him? He did not wait to find out – and recalled someone once remarking to him that funerals were often followed by soul-searching and recrimination. They were right!

'I'll get your coat,' he said to Alison.

'It's hanging up in the hall.'

Alison, too, wanted to flee the family fold. It was as though grief had caused her aunt to reveal aspects of herself none of them had known were there.

Conrad viewed his mother's behaviour somewhat differently. She was a woman who had lived for her children.

When they had all left the nest, her husband was still there to engross her. Without him, she was suddenly able to do what she had never done before – concentrate upon herself.

Conrad hoped it would not last. Whether or not it did was probably dependent upon Emma, he thought, glancing at her. He could not ask his wife to have his mother to live with them, when Lottie had two daughters.

Clara was too selfish to offer her mother a home, and Lottie would not want to live with her. Only Emma – the most selfless of her three children – was capable of ensuring that Lottie Stein did not become the embittered old woman she might, if she lived alone.

But his mother's gain would be little Richard's loss, Conrad reflected, watching the boy kiss Emma goodbye. He had refused to kiss Lottie – which did not surprise Conrad. The gentle, grandmotherly figure Lottie normally was had momentarily metamorphosed into the dragon-like sort that frightened children away.

'You still haven't visited us in London,' Alison reminded Percy, with whom there had not been time for her to chat.

'But he has been to see his other grandparents – thanks to you, Alison!' Clara flung at her.

'Good for him.'

Alison took Richard's hand, said her farewells, and escaped from Clara's wrath. But it was Emma's resigned expression that remained with her during the long journey south.

'How shall we manage, Maxwell, if Emma doesn't come back?' she said, when she was sure that Richard was asleep.

'It won't be too easy to find you the right housekeeper,' he replied.

Alison was shocked by his practical approach to the matter. 'Is that all Emma means to you?'

'No, as a matter of fact. I have grown very fond of her.'

'I'm glad to hear that, because Emma's companionship is absolutely irreplaceable to me.'

To me, too, Morton thought wryly. He and she often differed, but one way and another they had become a team.

Alison noted his smile. 'What do you find so amusing about this situation?' she flashed.

'I was thinking of how much I disliked our Em, when we first met.'

'It was mutual,' Alison recalled. 'And the two of you gave me a bad time because of it.'

Morton thought of all the bad times Alison had, over the years, given them, and of the staunch friend Emma was to him. 'If she does return to London, I'll welcome her back with open arms.'

'But I fear she might not, Maxwell. And I can imagine the struggle that's going on inside her. There is no doubt about what Emma would prefer to do but family duty is so strong in her, she is likely to sacrifice herself on that altar.'

'We shall have to wait and see. Now why not try to have a nap, Alison? There is no need for us both to suffer a sleepless night,' Morton said.

Alison rested her head on his shoulder, but was unable to doze off. Instead, her thoughts roved to Berlin – which these days she rarely allowed them to do. Was her lover dead or alive? There was no way of finding out. Hitler's tentacles had now spread to Austria. This did not bode well for a return to freedom in Germany in the foreseeable future.

On the contrary, Alison reflected grimly. Morton had said the dictator's hunger for power could lead to war in Europe; that Hitler was setting his sights further afield. It was hard to believe, she thought as the comfortable limousine sped through the quiet English lanes, that the twisted politics of one man could change millions of lives.

Her own included. Her son's, too. Because of Adolf Hitler, Richard might never know his father. Those far-away politics, which to most English people were not their business, had become personal for Alison. It struck her now that politics were never the impersonal machinations they seemed, that if people realised this, they would take more interest in what the politicians were doing. And try to stop them, as Richard Lindemann had, from playing the power games that eventually made havoc of human lives.

Though Alison's eyes were closed, Morton knew she was not asleep, so well was he attuned to her. 'What are you thinking about, my darling?'

'If I told you, you probably wouldn't believe me. What are you thinking about?'

'That I must be careful not to drop off at the wheel.'

That thought was certainly in Morton's mind, but others, too, were present, centring upon Alison and the sleeping child on the back seat, both of whom he wanted for his own. But he did not dare yet again to ask the woman he loved to marry him. She still hoped to be miraculously reunited with her lover. In our Em's vernacular, thought Morton, for proposals this wasn't the time.

'I wonder why my son said he doesn't love me any more,' Alison said pensively.

Morton chuckled. 'Moody ladies ought not to be surprised if their children inherit their temperament, my dear!'

'But what did I do to deserve his saying that?'

'You've parted him from his beloved Auntie Emma, haven't you?'

As Morton knew nothing of the doubt implanted by Mrs Payne in the little boy's mind, this seemed to him the likely reason for Richard's outburst.

'Are you saying, Maxwell, that Richard loves Emma more than he does me?' Alison asked coldly.

'Of course not. But Emma is the one who is always there for him, isn't she? That enables you to pursue your career,' he reminded her, 'which is what you want.'

'I want to come first with my son, too.'

Morton patted her hand, as he would with a feckless child. 'Even you, my darling, can't have the ha'penny and the bun. And that's what you are asking for, isn't it?'

'I suppose it is,' Alison had to admit.

'But for the time being, you'll have Richard to yourself, won't you?'

'I'm looking forward to it,' she declared. 'Though I shouldn't like coping with a child to be my life's work.'

# CHAPTER TEN

ALISON DID not intend to waste the opportunity that Emma's absence presented. The chance to have her child to herself might never come again. How she would cope with the practical aspect of her maternal interlude, she did not pause to consider.

When did she ever? About anything? Morton and Emma would have said. But neither was around to say it. Morton, too, was suddenly whisked from the scene by a problem affecting a production he had transferred to Broadway.

'I shan't stay in New York a minute longer than I need to,' he assured Alison, when he telephoned to tell her he was required there. 'Trust something like this to happen, when Emma isn't with you,' he added edgily.

It was noon on the day after their return from Oldham. Alison had just risen from her bed. 'You wouldn't be here cooking Richard's meals, et cetera, if you were in London, Maxwell dear,' she said with a yawn.

'But I'd be making sure that you remember to do so,' he replied. 'How shall you get him to kindergarten tomorrow? If I had been there, he would have gone today, too sleepy to get up or not!'

'What an old fusspot you've become,' Alison said. 'As for how I shall get him there – it is not far away, and I have legs. I am as capable of escorting him as Emma is.'

Morton grunted. 'Well, don't forget he has to be fetched home again at three-thirty in the afternoon.'

After she had replaced the receiver, Alison went to the kitchen, where her pyjama-clad son was daubing jam on a slice of bread.

'I'm glad to see you are so capable,' she said, giving him a kiss.

'Auntie Emma and Uncle Maxwell don't think I am.'

'They have the same opinion of me, my love.'

'But with you, Mummy, it is probably true.'

Alison had to laugh. Even the child had her well weighed up! 'Nevertheless,' she said to him, 'you and I will get by on our own, for as long as we must.'

Richard gave her one of his crooked smiles, and her heart warmed with love for him. How like your father you are when you smile, she wanted to tell him. But it was not possible to share that precious remembrance, and how sad for him, as well as for her, that it was not.

'Why haven't I got a daddy, like the other children at school?' Richard asked, as though he had divined Alison's thoughts.

It was a question she had known must come sooner or later. Now that it had, she was unprepared for it. 'Why have you never asked before?' she stalled.

'I asked Auntie Emma. She said I am too young to understand, and that I'm not to bother you about it.'

Good old well-meaning Emma, Alison thought with affection for her. And no doubt she had afterwards discussed it with Maxwell, and they had decided not to mention it to the one it most concerned – herself. There were times – and this was one of them – when Alison wished they would stop protecting her. Allow her to make the important decisions that affected her life and her child's.

Richard had poured himself some milk and was observing her over the top of the glass while he drank it.

'Why did you disobey Auntie Emma, and ask me that question?' Alison asked quietly.

'Because you are my mummy. And mummies always have a daddy with them – like Auntie Zelda has Uncle Conrad. I want to know why we haven't got a daddy living with us.'

Alison took a deep breath and plunged in. 'Of course you do, my love. So let's go and make ourselves comfortable in the drawing room and Mummy will do her best to explain to you.'

Richard then displayed that he was Emma's boy, as well

212

as Alison's. 'We haven't cleared away the breakfast things,' he said, eyeing the messy table. 'And Auntie would have kittens if I sat in the drawing room in my pyjamas.'

Alison took his jammy hand and led him there. 'Auntie isn't here, so we can be as naughty as we like, can't we?'

'So long,' said Richard, 'as we make sure everything is neat and tidy when she comes home.'

They shared a smile that made them conspirators, which would have hurt Emma had she known. Alison experienced a pang of guilt on that account but stamped it out. Richard was her child. And for the time being hers alone.

She switched on the electric fire, absently patted the cat which had followed them, and sat down on the sofa with Richard on her lap. How was she to tell him what he needed to know? For needed was surely the right word.

But it must be done little by little. This was just the beginning – and she must weigh every word. What she said to Richard now would be the foundation upon which the rest of the story would be built. It was like erecting a house of cards, Alison thought, and just as precarious. One day it would fall apart when her son was old enough to be told the whole truth.

What she must tell him now was the fiction her predicament had made necessary. 'Have you ever heard the word "adopted", Richard?'

'Yes,' he replied.

Alison had expected him to say no.

'A girl in my class is adopted,' he said.

'Did she tell you she was?'

'No. She told Miss Robinson. She's a very naughty girl, Mummy, who keeps wetting her knickers, and has to stand in a corner of the room to be punished for it.'

Alison felt that the teacher required punishing, not the child, but refrained from saying so.

Richard went on with the pitiful tale. 'One day, when Miss Robinson said she would tell Anthea's mummy how bad she is, Anthea said, "Please, Miss Robinson, don't! My mummy loves my baby sister better than me, because I am adopted."'

213

Richard paused for breath after his melodramatic rendering of his classmate's plea. 'Is being adopted awful, Mummy?'

'Certainly not, darling.'

'What does it mean?'

'Sometimes, Richard, when God doesn't give them a child, people who passionately want one find a baby who has no parents, and make it their own.'

'How can a baby have no parents? Not even a mummy?'

'Very easily, sweetheart. If its parents die, like poor Uncle Lionel has. Or there could be a reason why they are unable to take care of their baby, and think it best to let it be adopted by people who can, and who will love it as much as they do.'

Alison saw the familiar thought-frown appear on her son's face, and held her breath. How long would it take him to connect the information he had just received with himself?

Only a moment. 'If I had a baby sister, like Anthea has, would you love it more than me?' he asked.

Oh what a clever child he was – and how careful with him Alison must be. 'I could never love anyone more than I do you,' she told him.

Richard did not reply.

'And I am sure your little friend is mistaken in thinking she is loved less than her baby sister,' Alison went on firmly.

'Then why did she say that to Miss Robinson?'

'It isn't uncommon, Richard dear, for an older child to be jealous of a little newcomer. Babies are kissed and cuddled more, because they are such tiny, sweet things. So they appear to be loved more – but that doesn't mean that they are.'

'Did I become your little boy because Janet's mummy couldn't look after me?' Richard asked out of the blue. 'Was I once Auntie Zelda's little boy?'

Who had been saying what to Richard? Alison thought. What had enabled him to put two and two together and make five? Only then did she realise how inextricably she was caught in this web of pretence.

While she was trying to collect herself, Richard told her what he had learned from Mrs Payne – which answered her question.

'Auntie Zelda looked after you for a while, darling,' Alison said, managing to stop her voice from trembling. 'Then you came here, to me.'

'Why?' Richard demanded.

'Because I wanted you.' That, at least, was the truth! 'And as I am not a married lady, you have no daddy,' she added, arriving full circle at the point from which the inquisition had begun.

She gave Richard an appealing glance. 'Do you mind not having a daddy?'

He flung his arms around her neck. 'Of course not, Mummy. I have you.'

It was a moment Alison would cherish in her memory, and she put from her mind the thought that her explanation was unlikely to satisfy Richard indefinitely. As he grew older, he would want to know more about himself, but she would think about it then. Not now.

'I'm hungry, Mummy,' he said, wriggling from her embrace. 'Is it lunchtime yet?'

'It's long past, my love. You had breakfast at lunchtime.'

'But not the kind of breakfast Auntie Emma gives me.'

'Which you won't get from me,' said Alison with a smile of chagrin.

'Why can't you cook, Mummy?'

'Because I've never had to. Nor did my mother have to. She wouldn't have had time to, anyway, she was too busy acting, like me.'

'Is she in heaven now? Like my Great-Uncle Lionel?'

He knows nothing about my background, Alison reflected. And oh, how much there was to know. The Plantaine family history would intrigue any child, but she had told Richard none of it. He did not even know that his grandmother was alive and still treading the boards.

Richard forgot his hunger-pangs when Alison informed him that he had relatives in Hastings, her mother included among them. When she added that Hastings was by the sea, his face lit with delight. 'Then I can take my bucket and spade, and make some sandcastles on the beach, can't I, Mummy? When you take me to visit them.'

If I ever do, Alison thought.

'And now may I please have something to eat, Mummy? Or must I wait until Uncle Maxwell's secretary comes to stay with me while you are at the theatre?'

Morton had asked Mollie to undertake that task until Emma returned. But, Alison decided impulsively, that kindly lady would not be needed.

'How would you like to come with me to the theatre, Richard?'

He regarded her with astonishment. 'Tonight? Instead of having my tea and going to bed?'

Alison nodded.

'Auntie Emma *would* have kittens!'

'There is no need to keep telling me that, darling. It will become monotonous – so many things we shall do while she is not here would cause her to.'

Again, they shared a laugh at Emma's expense. But as they both loved her, what did it matter? Alison said to herself. What mattered was that Alison and her son were enjoying each other's company, which they had not had the chance to do until now.

'What will I do if I come with you?' asked Richard, who had not yet set foot in a theatre. The place his mother went to in the evenings was called by that name, and words like 'backstage', and 'drama' and 'comedy' were familiar to him, but he was unable to attach an image to them.

'You'll do the same as I did, when I was your age,' Alison told him with a reminiscent smile. 'Sit on a stool in the wings, and watch me acting onstage. Like I watched my mummy and daddy, many years ago. And when I felt tired, I curled up on a sofa in the dressing room until it was time to go home.'

Richard's eyes were sparkling with excitement. 'How absolutely marvellous, Mummy!' Then he considered something Alison had said. 'But wings are to fly with.'

'In a theatre, my darling, the word means something

quite different. You'll see when we get there. I must phone Mollie to tell her she needn't come to stay with you this evening. Then I'll make us both a cheese sandwich, to eat before we go.'

'Will the sandwich be our lunch, or our tea?' Richard wanted to know, when Alison had made the telephone call and they returned to the kitchen.

Alison laughed and sliced the bread. 'Just think of it as food, darling. Which meal they are eating is something that theatre people quite often don't know! I rarely did, before Auntie Emma came to live with me and set up her routine. You and I can have a little holiday from it this week.'

'Shall I be going with you to the theatre every evening while Auntie's away?'

'Why not?'

'But I'll be too tired to get up for school in the mornings, won't I?'

'You can have a holiday from school, too,' said Alison recklessly.

Suddenly she was bubbling with pleasure at the prospect of introducing her son to her working world. The thespian heritage was Richard's, as well as hers. But he had not yet imbibed the atmosphere that would surely cause his Plantaine blood to tingle, as Alison's still did when the mixed scent of backstage dust and greasepaint rose to her nostrils.

She would not want her child to experience the seedy aspects of the theatrical life she had known at his age. But the glamour and the excitement had been there, too. The glittering footlights, and the wigs and costumes that transformed their wearers into creatures of terror or charm. The last-minute bustle and tension, and the expectant hush in the darkened auditorium when the curtain rose. And the bow-taking and bouquets and applause, when it fell.

Would this be Richard's working ethos when he grew up? Or would he tread his father's intellectual path? Alison wondered, surveying his intent little face. It was already plain that her son was a thinker – and he might become a

217

playwright, she thought. A writer had begotten him, and an actress carried him in her womb.

But why was she considering his adult occupation, when he was still only five! Like Lionel Stein had planned that his grandson would be an accountant and be useful to him in his business, when Percy was just a babe, Alison recalled. Instead, Percy was now studying medicine. And Lionel dead. A child's future was as unpredictable as life and death. Only Destiny would decide what Alison's son would one day be.

Meanwhile, he would briefly taste the theatre's flavour while his godparents – who would not approve – were away. Both would be livid with Alison when they learned she had disrupted Richard's routine. But she did not care.

Nor did she give a thought to the unsettling effect the disruption, and all that went with it, might have upon the boy. But that was Alison Plantaine who, like her mother before her, had never quite grown up. Hers was not the impulsiveness of a wayward woman, but of a charming child who rushes headlong into this adventure or that, armed with the certainty that those who love it will make everything all right, come what may. What Alison had decided to do was an adventure for herself, as well as for Richard.

'We are going to have a marvellous time together this week,' she told him as they left the flat, hand in hand.

'We've never been out together before without Auntie Emma,' he remarked.

Which is distinctly odd, thought Alison, for a mother and son. 'Would you like us to do so more often?' she asked, and was not surprised by Richard's reply.

'I wouldn't want Auntie to feel left out.'

What a thoughtful little chap he was. A well-mannered one, too, Alison registered, when he stepped aside to allow her to precede him into the lift. But his Uncle Maxwell had made sure he was. A boy needed a male image upon which to mould himself, and Richard could do worse than emulate Maxwell Morton.

Alison hailed a cab and put Morton from her mind. She

218

had left home earlier than usual, to give Richard a short sightseeing tour.

'May we go and see Buckingham Palace, Mummy?' he asked as they trundled down Park Lane with the late-afternoon traffic.

'It would be better to go there in daylight, darling. Then you can see the Changing of the Guard.'

'Like Christopher Robin and Alice did?' he said with delight. Emma read to him each night, and the A. A. Milne poems were his favourites. 'Oh I am going to have a splendid time, Mummy! I'm having one already!'

Alison feared he would wrench a muscle in his neck, from turning his head back and forth lest he miss something interesting along the route.

They alighted from the taxi at Piccadilly Circus. Richard gazed raptly at the statue of Eros. 'Is that an angel, Mummy?'

'No, Richard. It's the god of love.' Who hasn't looked too kindly upon me, she thought, or I would not have been parted from my lover.

Richard glanced up at her, and entwined his small fingers with hers. It was as though he had sensed her momentary bleakness and was silently comforting her.

'Bless you, darling,' Alison said to him with feeling. There was more than one kind of love – as she had learned from her closeness with her father, and was now re-learning from her son.

'Come on, Mummy!' Richard tugged at her hand impatiently. 'I want to see everything.'

For the boy, this part of the West End was a magic place he had not known existed, and the brightly lit theatres fairytale palaces. Until now, he had inhabited with Emma the homely island she had created for herself, and had thought that all there was.

Alison could feel the wonderment emanating from him as he trotted beside her. She was glad her son was seeing theatreland for the first time when it was garbed in its night-time glitter. This was when her territory, and those who were of it, sprang to life. Theatricals were night people, which Richard would come to understand. Little by little, he would learn, too, what lay behind the glamorous façade presented to the public.

Richard was drinking in everything with his mind as well as with his eyes. Badgering Alison with questions, as always. And pausing outside each theatre they passed, to be told what was on there – and what the title meant.

'We shan't get to my theatre in time for curtain-up, at this rate!' she said with a smile, when he halted outside yet another playhouse. She read him the title, which was: *The Milkman's Round*.

'The things that pass for plays, nowadays!' she exclaimed with Plantaine thespian snobbery. 'Shakespeare would turn in his grave, if he knew.'

'Who is Shakespeare, Mummy?'

It seemed inconceivable to Alison that a child of hers did not know. She spent the next few minutes enlightening him. Oh, how sadly she had neglected her maternal task!

But she would, in that respect, make amends from now on, Alison vowed as they headed toward the Comedy, where she was appearing in *The Sacred Flame*.

'Did Mr Shakespeare write the play you are in, Mummy?' Richard asked.

Alison smiled at the respectful appellation. 'No, darling. A gentleman called Somerset Maugham did. But a Shakespeare play called *As You Like It* is on at the Adelphi, at present. If there's a matinée this week I'll take you to see it.'

'How absolutely splendid!'

'Provided it doesn't coincide with my matinée day.'

When they reached the Comedy Alison led Richard across the street, so he would get the full effect of her name written in lights.

'Shall I read to you what it says there, Richard?'

'Yes, please.'

'Alison Plantaine.'

'Really and truly?'

Alison nodded, and would not forget the expression upon his face.

'Is it really you, Mummy?' he said in an awed voice.

'So far as I know, there is only one Alison Plantaine.'

'And only one Richard Plantaine?'

Who but for Hitler would be Richard Lindemann junior, Alison thought. She had never doubted that, had the Nazis not intervened, her lover would have made her his wife. 'I know of no other Richard Plantaine,' she said, managing to smile.

Bleakness had again assailed her. When she entered her dressing room it would, as always, be filled with the roses that symbolised her success. But along with their sweet scent, she would taste the ashes of the happiness she had known in Berlin.

She stemmed the depression threatening to overwhelm her and led Richard to the stagedoor.

'Why can't we go in the front way, Mummy? It's much nicer.'

'Because the actors never do, Richard. It would be breaking the rules.'

'So is giving me a holiday this week,' he countered smartly.

'That's different, my darling.'

'Why?'

'What I mean is that I never, ever, break theatre rules,' Alison said emphatically. 'And you must never expect me to.'

It was then, though he did not yet know the meaning of the word, that his mother's dedication to her art was first communicated to Richard, and he would come to think of that winter evening in 1938 as his introduction to the real Alison Plantaine, for whom nothing and nobody came before her work. Meanwhile, he was a wide-eyed little boy, privileged, because he was her son, to enter her exciting working-world. The gravity with which Alison had briefly chilled him fled away as he followed her into the theatre.

All whom they encountered greeted Alison with a respect that enhanced Richard's reverent image of her. She had always been for him more of a presence than a person. A beautiful, perfumed creature who, though she petted him and kissed him goodnight, remained remote from him. Though Alison was unaware of this, she had sensed that their relationship was not what it should be, and hoped that the experience she was now giving him would draw Richard closer to her.

Instead, she had entrenched herself more firmly on the pedestal she already occupied. All was, that night, touched by magic for the child at her side. The wardrobe and props rooms seemed to him like Aladdin's caves. The garishly lit mirror in Alison's dressing room, where they went first, added to the fairytale quality of the experience. And the stage spotlights, which an obliging electrician switched on for him, were a dazzling finale to his backstage tour. As if she had waved a wand, his mother had made it all happen for him. It was not surprising that Richard attached the magic to her.

'You're the most wonderful mummy in the whole world!' he said ecstatically, when he and Alison were alone on the set.

'I hope you will always think so,' said Alison, who had once had that opinion of her own mother.

'Why did you ask that gentleman if it was all right for you to show me around?' Richard asked.

'Because he is the stage manager and backstage he is the boss. That's another rule, darling.'

Richard was examining the set. 'It's only a pretend window,' he said, inserting his hand where the glass should have been.

'But it looks real from out front,' Alison assured him. 'The theatre is a let's-pretend place,' she added, preparing him for the sight of his mother onstage, being someone else – and very convincingly.

'A play is a story come to life,' she explained. 'Instead of reading it, the audience sees it happen. And the actors pretend to be the people whose story it is,' she simplified her art for her son.

'But they know it is you they are really watching, don't they?' Richard replied.

'I make them forget it's me, once the lights go down and

222

the play begins. That, my darling, is what good acting is all about.'

'I shan't forget it's you, when I watch you from the wings.'

'Nor must you forget that all I say and do onstage is only make-believe.'

Alison showed Richard where he would sit, and warned him that silence backstage, after curtain-up, was also a rule.

'Now come and watch me make up, darling.'

Thankfully, her current role did not involve a drastic change in her appearance. Richard would not get the childhood fright Alison had, when she saw her father transformed into an ass to play Bottom in *A Midsummer Night's Dream*.

This, and other such poignant memories, flickered like lantern slides beamed across the years, while Alison applied greasepaint to her face. And how different everything seemed when seen through a child's eyes. Before the film of illusion had been removed from them, she thought, noting her son's rapt expression.

Later, when Alison settled him in the wings, he declared excitedly, and to the amusement of all within hearing distance, 'I can't wait to see you playing let's-pretend, Mummy!'

It would be a long time, Alison thought wryly, before Richard realised that her profession was not a light-hearted game.

'I'll keep an eye on him, Miss Plantaine,' said one of the stagehands.

'Please do, lest he doze off, and topple from his stool. Like I once did when I was little, in a theatre up north!'

'Did the stage manager get cross with you, for making a noise?' Richard wanted to know.

'Nobody heard the crash, darling. In my grandfather's productions, somebody was usually beating a drum onstage!' Alison said with a reminiscent laugh. The drums and bugles and colourful settings were what she remembered most vividly from her childhood with the Plantaine Players.

When the curtain rose, Richard was riveted by the atmosphere flowing toward him from the stage, and affected, too, by the pool of darkness beyond the footlights, where ghostly faces were visible in the front stalls.

Was the beautiful lady talking to the gentleman in the bathchair really his mummy? he thought, as the first act progressed? It was hard to believe, though the lady had his mother's face. Maugham's searing drama was, of course, beyond Richard's understanding, and much of the dialogue double-Dutch to him. But the all-enveloping theatrical tension he could feel around him raised goose pimples on his flesh.

'I got such a funny feeling, Mummy, when the curtain went up,' he told Alison during the first interval.

Alison could have jumped for joy. 'I get that feeling every night, Richard, and I've seen a lot of curtains rise, in my time.'

'But what does the feeling mean?'

She gave him a kiss. 'That the theatre is in our blood, my darling. And don't ask me what that means! There is plenty of time for you to find out.'

Richard stifled a yawn.

'Are you tired, love?'

'Not in the least,' he replied. Then he curled up on the sofa and promptly fell asleep.

Alison covered him with a rug, as her parents had done with her long ago. It was as though she were re-living her own childhood, thinking of her mother, as well as her father – which she preferred not to do.

When the final curtain fell, Richard was still sound asleep.

'I am absolutely starving, Mummy,' he said when Alison wakened him. 'And oh dear, Auntie Emma isn't there to make our supper when we get home.'

'We'll go to a restaurant,' said Alison, reverting to her pre-Emma routine.

Late-night dining was not for a child, Alison's sensible cousin would say with horror. Morton, too, no doubt. Heaven help Alison, when they found out. But in for a penny, she thought with the recklessness that had impelled her to begin this adventure. This week, Richard was hers to do with what she would, and they would have a splendid time together.

'May we go to the Ivy, Mummy?' he asked. The place where his mother often dined had lodged in his mind. And its name had a pleasant ring.

Alison smiled. 'I think Lyons' Corner House would be more your style.'

She had not eaten there for years, but recalled that it was the sort of place to which people took their children for treats.

'They serve delicious ice cream,' she told Richard, and watched his face light up.

Her son's delight and interest in all he experienced was for Alison the most rewarding aspect of the days and evenings that followed. They would rise late, breakfast on bread and jam, then take a cab to one of the fascinating places little boys yearn to visit. Alison discovered that Richard's favourite food was egg and chips, and that his thirst for knowledge was equally insatiable.

At the Tower of London, he wanted to know exactly *why* two little princes had once been imprisoned there. His reaction on seeing the Changing of the Guard was similar. Though he was captivated by the spectacle, he afterwards asked *why* the soldiers were guarding the palace. Alison, who had never considered the practical aspect, was at a loss for an answer, and told Richard he had better ask his Uncle Maxwell.

At Madame Tussaud's Museum, it was necessary for her to ask an attendant to satisfy Richard's curiosity about how the waxwork effigies were made. It was the same wherever they went. Through her child, Alison became aware of the gaps in her own knowledge. That her horizon was limited to the insular confines of the theatre. Why had she not realised this until now? Because hers was not the kind of mind that delved beneath the surface of what she saw, as Richard's did. But he was his father's son, as well as hers, Alison was increasingly reminded as the week wore on.

'I wish I could tell Auntie what a lovely time I am

having,' he said one afternoon, after he had spoken to Emma on the telephone.

She had kept her promise to call him every day, and the telephone always rang promptly at 5 p.m.

'Auntie thinks I shall soon be going to bed, and that I've been to school,' he said guiltily.

'But she would be upset, if she knew what you are really doing, Richard. As she has just lost her father, I prefer not to give her any more distress, just now. We'll tell her everything when we see her, darling.'

'And what a ticking-off we shall get!'

That she was deceiving Emma was the only thing that marred Alison's interlude with her child.

The following day, another shadow loomed beside it. Alison and Richard were in Fortnum's, buying shortbread to stave off Richard's nightly hunger-pangs in the dressing room, and encountered the Plantaine twins.

'What is it, Mummy?' Richard asked, when Alison blanched at the sight of her stepcousins.

Before she had time to assure him that nothing was wrong, Luke and Lucy had joined them.

'How nice to see you, Alison darling!' said Luke.

'And this is your adopted child, I presume?' Lucy added, surveying Richard from head to toe.

Alison was thankful she had prepared Richard for such a thoughtless remark.

'It's time we met you, young fellow,' Luke said to him, 'as we are members of the same family. Aren't you going to introduce us to him, Alison dear?'

Alison had no option but to do so.

'There seem to be an awful lot of Plantaines,' Richard declared, 'though I haven't met the others yet.'

'So we understand,' Luke replied, giving Alison a reproving glance. 'When are you going to take this boy to Hastings?'

'When the opportunity presents itself,' she said coldly.

'If you are too busy to take him, darling, he could come along with Lucy and me. We visit our mother regularly.'

This, too, was a rebuke to Alison. She carefully ignored it.

Lucy pressed her brother's point home. 'Your granny misses your mother very much, Richard.'

'She is very lonely since your grandpa died,' Luke added.

Alison was inwardly squirming. They were the same old double act and, as always, using the technique to good effect. They didn't care a toss about her mother. What they were doing was turning their knife in the wound of Alison's estrangement from her, and painting her black in her child's eyes.

'My mother is not the lonely kind,' she said curtly.

'But we ought to visit her, Mummy.'

'You tell her, my lad!' Luke applauded.

The crafty pair were using Richard to get at her, Alison saw.

Luke's next remark caused her to steady herself against the counter where the shortbread and other such goodies were temptingly displayed.

'How interesting that Richard has such a finely chiselled profile – like the Plantaines.'

Alison had not noticed this before, but did so now. Because the Plantaines, apart from herself, were striking, blue-eyed blonds, and Richard's colouring indeterminate, she had not seen in him any resemblance to them. But he had lost the baby-pudge that had blurred his features, and the Plantaine profile was definitely there.

Lucy, too, was studying Richard. 'He reminds me also of Alison's cousin Emma, Luke.'

Alison latched on to Lucy's comment, 'Emma is the one Richard spends the most time with. And it is said that people can get to look alike, when they are always together.' Did this sound as lame to the twins as it did to herself?

Luke laughed teasingly. 'Are you sure you're not pulling the wool over everyone's eyes, Alison dear?'

Lucy joined in the teasing. But was it just teasing? Alison wondered, feeling herself go cold.

'You did have that long rest in 1933, didn't you, Alison,' Lucy was saying with a wink.

'If I hadn't, you wouldn't have got your break. And would probably not be more than a supporting player now,'

Alison countered cuttingly. Attack, she decided, was the best form of defence.

A nasty gleam entered Lucy's eyes. Luke kicked her ankle – which Alison did not fail to note.

'You never could take a joke, darling,' he said smoothly to Alison.

Lucy gave her a treacly smile, and asked casually, 'How old is your little boy now?'

'I was five, on May 11th,' Richard supplied. 'So I am now five-and-a-half, aren't I?'

'We must remember his birthday, and send him a card,' Luke said to his sister.

'I'll make a note of it, Luke, when we get home.'

Had they been joking? Alison thought not. Though their light tones had made it seem so, it was much more likely that the germ of an idea with which they might harm her had seeded in their minds.

Alison selected her shortbread and turned away to watch the assistant wrap it, so she would not have to look at the twins. They were now chatting to Richard about the family in Hastings. He would give her no peace until she took him there, after this.

'We're off to see the folks next Sunday, Alison,' Luke said, reiterating his offer to take Richard with them. 'He'd enjoy a ride in my new sports car, I'm sure.'

'I've never had a ride in a sports car,' said Richard excitedly.

Luke knew how to lure a small boy away from his mother, Alison thought. And what an opportunity it would provide for the twins to glean from Richard innocent details, which pieced together by minds like theirs . . . Alison dared not let herself think to what it might lead.

She watched Lucy ruffle Richard's hair, and the boy smile up at her.

'How about it, Alison?' Luke said.

'Please say yes, Mummy!' Richard implored.

'No!' Alison exclaimed. A red mist had risen before her eyes, and her legs were trembling.

So violent was her reaction, Richard stepped close to the

twins, as though for protection. Luke put a reassuring hand on his shoulder. 'Your mother is what we call a temperamental lady, Richard.'

'But we who love her understand, don't we?' said Lucy.

Richard nodded. And Alison saw the twins share a knowing smile with him – at her expense. She took Richard's hand and pulled him away from them.

'There she goes again,' said Luke with a laugh.

'You poor child,' Lucy commiserated with Richard.

Alison led the bewildered little boy out of the store.

'You weren't very nice to them, were you, Mummy?' he said when they had emerged on to Piccadilly.

Alison hailed a taxi and ushered him into it.

'Where are we going to, Mummy?'

'Home,' she replied, giving the driver the address.

'But you promised to take me to see the Houses of Parliament today.'

'I don't feel up to it, darling. If you don't mind, I shall rest for the remainder of the afternoon, as I have a performance to give tonight.'

An all-pervading malaise was the aftermath of Alison's encounter with the twins. The mere sight of them had, in recent years, had a jarring effect upon her, reminding her of their threat to pay her back for her refusal to help them get ahead. They had since succeeded without her help, but had left Alison in no doubt that their threat was still there. Had she doubted it, the funereal lilies with which they greeted her return to the stage would have confirmed it. But even that had not caused her to feel as she did now.

Richard could not have lived under the same roof as Alison without being aware of her flashes of temperament. But, like the rain showers on a summer day, they did not last long and he quickly forgot them. They were offset by her charm – and never directed at him. Nor did he feel that her sudden outburst at Fortnum's was.

He noted her tight-lipped expression while the taxi carried them homeward, and saw her shiver.

'Are you cold, Mummy?'

Alison drew her fur coat closer around her. 'Yes, my

love.' But it was a menacing chill, as if the twins' vindictiveness was touching her from afar, and she longed for the comforting presence of Emma and Morton, with whom she always felt safe.

'You don't like our cousins, do you?' Richard said. It was a statement, not a question, and he did not wait for a reply. 'I think they are very nice.'

'You will learn when you are older, Richard, that people are not always as nice as they seem. Now may we drop the subject, darling? I would rather not talk about the twins.'

The following day, the subject was reopened by the arrival of a toy car, for Richard.

'Sorry you can't come for a ride with us. This will help you not to be too disappointed', said the accompanying note.

'How absolutely marvellous!' Richard's face was alight with pleasure. 'And now I like the twins even more than I did yesterday, Mummy,' he added. Defiantly.

'I'm afraid we must send the car back to them,' Alison replied. 'I can't allow you to accept gifts from people I don't like, and who don't like me.'

'But they like me, don't they?' Richard countered. 'Or they wouldn't have sent me the car.'

'You already have the one Uncle Maxwell bought for you last Christmas, Richard.'

'But it isn't as big as this one – and I've grown since last Christmas,' he said, climbing into the shiny red vehicle and honking the horn. 'Oh, please let me keep it, Mummy darling!'

Alison's resolve to return it whence it came was no match for the appeal in her child's eyes. 'All right,' she capitulated, and was rewarded by Richard clambering out of the car to cover her face with kisses. The toy could do no harm, she told herself. It was those who had sent it who were harmful – and she would not allow them anywhere near Richard.

As usual, Alison was not thinking ahead, and did not see the expensive gift for what it was – the twins' opening gambit in a bid to win Richard.

Their teasing innuendoes had led her to think they might ferret out the truth, and it was this with which she was now obsessed. If they could obtain proof, they would not hesitate to use it to slur her reputation and damage her career.

But her stepcousins were even more treacherous than Alison supposed. The family resemblances they had noted in Richard confirmed the suspicion they had already harboured; they had not forgotten her romance with a young German, which was the subject of gossip during the Berlin festival. Seeing Alison with the child – and maternal love was written on her face – had supplied the twins with a way of hurting her where she was most vulnerable. It would not be for the want of trying if they did not cause trouble between Alison and her son.

# CHAPTER ELEVEN

THE STEINS' week of mourning had dragged to a close. For Emma and her brother and sister, the period of concentrated gloom imposed upon them by their religion had seemed endless, and it was as though they had suddenly emerged from a claustrophobic cavern into the light.

On the morning they rose from their low mourning chairs, Clara stood by the parlour window, massaging the small of her back which ached from the experience.

'It will be a relief to go home to my normal routine,' she declared with a smile.

'Shopping for clothes, and having tea with your pals, you mean,' said Conrad unkindly. 'Not to mention the card parties you and your husband go to, night after night.'

'If you envy me my life, why don't you just say so, and have done with?' Clara retorted with a toss of her blonde hair. 'And the card parties are to raise money for refugees – as you know very well. Though the government are restricting the number allowed in, not all those who are allowed to come to England have relatives here. They have to be helped.'

'Save the speech for someone who needs preaching to, Clara!'

'Will you two please stop this,' Emma intervened, 'before Mam comes into the room.'

Conrad smiled sourly. 'I don't think Mam would be surprised that after a week of our Clara's company, I'm on edge. I'd forgotten what my elder sister is like to live with. And, almost, what she looks like,' he added with sarcasm, 'as she graces Oldham with her presence so rarely.'

'I'm surprised to know you miss me,' Clara replied in the same tone.

'I don't. But I'm sure Mam and Dad did. And now Mam is alone, I hope you'll bear that in mind, Clara.'

'She won't be alone. Our Emma will be here. Mam's asked her not to go back to London, hasn't she?'

'But Emma is not obliged to do what she is asked to do.'

Clara glanced at her sister. 'I had this out with Emma a long time ago, Conrad. She can't say I didn't warn her that she'd have to face up to it sooner or later.' She headed for the door. 'Now, if you two will excuse me, I'm going home.'

'What you mean is you are abdicating from your responsibility,' Conrad said. 'Mam is your mother, as well as Emma's.'

Clara stopped in her tracks and turned to give him a cold stare. 'Like I reminded Emma that day I went to London to try to make her see sense, I have a husband and children. She hasn't. A married daughter can't be expected to turn her life upside down to fit in with these kind of circumstances when she has a single sister.'

'What you're saying,' said Emma, 'is that unless a woman is married she isn't entitled to a life of her own. I don't happen to agree.'

'And I still think that's our cousin Alison speaking, not you.'

Emma went to gaze through the window at the tree-lined avenue in which she had lived for most of her thirty-eight years, and envisaged what the rest of her life would be like if she remained here. She had not been discontented before she left home, but a person did not miss what they had never known. And her mother's house no longer felt like home.

Home was the place where a little boy depended upon her. Where the man Emma loved dropped in for a chat and a glass of lemon tea. Where Alison, who could fend for herself little better than Richard could, had come to rely upon her too. Emma's home was no less a ménage than her married sister's was; that it did not include a husband was beside the point.

'Possibly, what I just said does sound like Alison talking,' she conceded to Clara. 'It was she who made me realise I didn't have to resign myself to there being only two alternatives for me – an arranged marriage, or staying put in the rut I was in.'

'So you put yourself in another rut, in London! Being Alison's unpaid housekeeper,' said Conrad, voicing the opinion he had, until now, kept to himself.

'Our Emma has been under Alison's thumb from the day Alison first set foot in this house, when we were all still kids,' Clara declaimed.

'If that's what you think, you are both wrong,' Emma said quietly. She smoothed the wrinkled skirt of her wool frock, and raised her head high. 'It may have been that way once, but it isn't any more. The relationship between Alison and me is on quite a different basis, now.'

Emma's demeanour at that moment, and her assured tone, made it difficult to imagine her ever having been under anyone's thumb. To Conrad, it seemed, then, that the family sparrow was no more. In its place was a bird, though still drab in appearance, capable of making its presence felt. Also of sharpening its bill, he thought a moment later.

'And you had better stop poking fun at me, Clara, about the sort of person it has always suited you to think I am, or I shall be provoked into telling you the sort of person everyone but yourself knows you are,' Emma said.

Clara was momentarily speechless. 'Living in London has gone to our Emma's head!' she exclaimed when she found her tongue.

Conrad would not have put it that way. But, he thought, Emma had not just grown older with the years. She had grown, and strengthened, as a person, too.

Only then did he realise that the uprooting had been good for her. That she moulded her life to Alison's in practical ways, Conrad still had no doubt. But on another level, Emma had become her own person, as though the spell Alison had once seemed to have cast over her had finally snapped like a slender thread, as Emma's own personality stretched.

I ought not to be surprised, Conrad thought. Spells were not built to last. But Emma's loyalty to Alison was. Her attachment to Richard, too, and, Conrad feared, her unrequited love for Maxwell Morton.

Clara glanced at the clock. 'If I don't get a move on, I'll miss the next train to Manchester. We've lost our father, and Mam's lost her husband, but life has to go on. And I've made a hairdressing appointment for this afternoon,' she added – which for the other two epitomised the shallowness of Clara's life.

'Have you made up your mind what you're going to do?' Conrad asked Emma when they were alone.

'It isn't easy,' she replied, going to stir the fire to a cheerful blaze which did nothing for her dilemma.

'I didn't think it would be, our Em.'

Lottie chose that moment to enter the room. She had just bidden an emotional farewell to her elder daughter, and was drying her eyes.

'Thank God I've got you, Emma,' she said.

A moment of silence followed, during which Emma gazed into the fire. Then she turned to look at her mother. 'What would you do now if you hadn't got me?'

'As I have, I don't have to think about it, love.'

'But you might have to,' Conrad put in, 'if Emma goes back to London.'

Lottie gave him a frigid stare. 'Whose side are you on? Mine, or that man Morton's?' she added irrationally.

Emma and Conrad exchanged a glance. Morton's name had not been mentioned since he and Alison left the house on the evening of the funeral, but Lottie's son and daughters had not forgotten her strange behaviour towards him.

Why she resented him – and so bitterly – had remained a mystery. During the ritual mourning period, when the pain of her sudden bereavement was exacerbated by the stream of visitors coming to commiserate, Emma had not questioned her. She could refrain no longer.

'What have you got against Mr Morton, Mam?'

But Lottie could not express her churning – and confused – feelings in words.

235

'Max is a fine person. And I won't have him insulted,' Emma declared when she received no reply.

Lottie gazed at her piercingly and spoke the thought that had just slotted into place in her mind, like a missing piece in a jigsaw puzzle. 'What, exactly, is he to you, Emma? It's time I knew!'

A memory of Emma's expression after speaking with Morton on the phone, during Alison's pregnancy, had preceded Lottie's question. Her animosity toward the man had sprung from the uneasiness she had felt then. But she hadn't known it until now, she thought, as she waited for Emma's answer.

Emma found it necessary to collect herself. Her mother was more perceptive than she had supposed. 'Max is a dear friend, Mam.'

'But you'd like him to be more, wouldn't you?'

Emma avoided her eye.

'Wouldn't you?' Lottie persisted.

'What if I would?' Emma said with a shrug. She could not bring herself to lie to her mother – and her blush had given her away.

'But he isn't Jewish!' Lottie exclaimed.

'Even if he were, nothing would come of it. He's in love with Alison. And always will be.'

'How do you like what we are hearing?' Lottie said to Conrad. 'It's like something you read about in a book!'

Conrad did not add to his sister's embarrassment by revealing that he had long since divined the triangular situation for himself.

'I'm sorry for all three of them,' he said truthfully. 'But how our Emma, who is such a sensible person, could have let herself fall for someone who's of a different religion, I will never understand.'

*Let* myself? Emma thought. Anyone who believed that falling in love could be avoided by being sensible didn't know what love was! Why was she wasting time having this ridiculous conversation with her mother and brother? Part of it was hypothetical, and the rest concerned ideas and attitudes she could no longer relate to herself.

A sense of déjà-vu overwhelmed her. With it came remembrance of countless family conversations about what might never happen. Emma had not thought them ridiculous then, nor the Steins' attitudes narrow. Why did she now? Because her own horizon had broadened, and the yardstick with which she now measured human behaviour was not convention, as it was once. Living with Alison, and loving Morton, had taught Emma a lot!

'I'm going back to London today,' she said as the decision to do so crystallised in her mind and her heart.

Suddenly, this house and all it stood for seemed part of her past. Emma had changed and her mother had not. Though they loved each other dearly, they would be at each other's throats if Emma remained here.

'You can't stay away from that man, can you?' Lottie said. 'And I won't have a wink of sleep when you've gone – now I know.'

'I've told you nothing can come of it, Mam. But if you prefer to worry in case it might, that's your pleasure. If I didn't go back, I would have a real worry – about what would become of Richard without me.'

'So that's why you're going!' Lottie pounced.

Emma's only reply was a smile.

Now she had decided, it was as if a heavy weight had been lifted from her, and a new lightness had entered her spirit. Since leaving her parents, her conscience had from time to time pricked about her desertion, but would do so no more.

Lottie surveyed her expression. 'How can you smile, when you've just lost your father?'

'Probably because, as our Clara reminded Conrad and me, life goes on. Smiling is as much a part of it as everything else. I can remember you saying that to Grandma, Mam, when Grandpa died.'

'And now my daughter is saying it to me,' said Lottie with a resigned sigh.

'I'll go and pack, Mam. And leave you to make up your mind whether you think I'm going back to London because of Richard or Max!' Emma said with another smile. She paused in the doorway. 'But the real reason is because I want to.'

'And that's what matters,' Conrad declared. 'Zelda and I are only a stone's throw away, and we'll keep an eye on Mam.'

This was all it took to restore Lottie Stein to her normal, ebullient self. 'Since when did I need anyone to keep an eye on me? I shall go on keeping my eye on the rest of you – like I've always done!'

Emma glanced at the clock. 'I might just arrive back in time to put Richard to bed. I've missed him terribly.'

Conrad gave her a word of advice, though he doubted she would heed it. 'But you mustn't let yourself forget that he isn't your child, our Em.'

# CHAPTER TWELVE

IN THE spring of 1939, Richard became aware that the three pillars of his life were deeply troubled. When he asked what was wrong, which he frequently did, they said that nothing was. But the sensitive six-year-old was not reassured, nor did it help to dispel his uneasiness when he noticed that one or the other of them was always glancing at him with anxious eyes.

As spring turned to summer, tension was present in the air he breathed. His elders would break off a conversation when he entered the room, and begin talking with forced brightness about something else. It was not surprising that Richard divined that whatever was worrying them concerned him.

He was too young to know that since Hitler's invasion of Czechoslovakia in March, England had been gripped by war jitters, or that contingency plans to evacuate children from London and the big provincial cities had been laid even before then. There was now little doubt in the minds of even the most hopeful that war was imminent.

Though Alison's personal knowledge of Nazi treachery ought to have prepared her, she, like most others, had believed what she wanted to believe – that the Munich agreement Chamberlain and Daladier had made with Hitler and Mussolini last September was not the empty document some said it would prove to be.

When Chamberlain returned triumphantly and confidently to England, she had shut her eyes and ears to the word 'appeasement', and put the possibility of war from her mind. Now that she could no longer do so, she was haunted by fears for her child.

This war would not be like the last one when, apart from

the odd Zeppelin raid, England had remained unscarred, and civilians unharmed. Bombs would rain from the sky and people would be killed. Was Alison to lose her son at Hitler's hands, as well as his father?

These were her thoughts on the occasions when Richard noticed her looking poignantly at him. Needless to say, Emma and Morton shared her parental anxiety. In all but name, parents to him they were. It was an anxiety to which every parent in the land was prone, and its cause could not be kept from older children. The day came when Richard told Emma that a 'big boy' had said in the playground that there was going to be a war.

'Will it be like when I play with my toy fort?' he asked excitedly. 'But with real soldiers?'

They were walking home from school, and Emma shivered despite the warmth of the June day. 'Not quite,' she replied. 'Now tell me how you got on with your lessons today, love,' she said to distract him. 'Are you still getting ten out of ten for your sums?'

When they arrived home, Alison had just returned from a costume fitting for her next play.

'Did you know there's going to be a war, Mummy?' Richard said to her.

Alison and Emma watched him enter his room and begin playing immediately with his toy soldiers and fort.

'Damn the Plantaine twins for giving him that thing!' Alison vented her feelings, as she followed Emma to the kitchen. 'Since he got it for Christmas, he has played with nothing else.'

'He thinks war is a game,' Emma said grimly. 'But who can be surprised? Things like that fort – and the soldier's cap and toy rifle Max gave him – make little boys think a battlefield is an exciting place.'

'But some who grew up thinking that are about to be disillusioned,' Alison replied.

'Including my nephew Percy,' Emma reminded her. 'He'll just qualify as a doctor in time to sew up wounds in a military hospital.'

'Stop it!' Alison cried.

'What's the point of being an ostrich, Alison?' Emma filled the kettle with water. 'I doubt that our Clara is able to be one, having lost her first husband in the last war.' She paused with her hand on the tap. 'Our concern about Richard's safety shrinks into insignificance beside what Clara must be feeling about Percy. We must be thankful that our boy is still only a child.'

'And oh, how thankful I am. But hearing Richard mention the war made my blood run cold.'

Emma laid the table for Richard's tea. 'He was bound to hear about it sooner or later, Alison. Everyone is talking about it.'

'And Richard will soon have to be told he is to be sent away — ' Alison glanced up and saw her son standing in the doorway. He had changed into his soft-soled house shoes and they had not heard him walk down the corridor.

'Where is she sending me to?' he demanded stridently of Emma.

Alison blanched at the word 'she'. It was as though his mother had suddenly become his enemy.

Richard's face had paled, and panic was in his eyes. 'I won't go! You won't let her send me away, will you, Auntie?' he implored, rushing to Emma's arms.

A moment later, he was weeping bitterly.

'There, there, love,' Emma soothed him.

'Don't come near me!' he cried as Alison took a step toward him.

She stopped in her tracks. 'If you would rather I didn't, I won't.'

'He's only a child. He's confused,' Emma said quietly.

'Then why don't you say something to straighten things out? Instead of standing there stroking his hair?' Alison flashed from the depths of her hurt.

'He's in no state to take in lengthy explanations, Alison. Let him calm down first,' her sensible cousin replied.

But Alison did not heed her advice. 'You overheard me say something, Richard. Now let me tell you what it is all about.' She could not wait to put things right between herself and her child.

241

'I know without you telling me. You don't love me any more.'

'My darling boy!' she said with distress.

'I am not your darling boy. I'm your adopted one. And now you're going to send me back.'

Oh, the consequences of deceit, Alison thought.

Then Richard pulled out of Emma's embrace and began pummelling Alison with his clenched fists. Emma dragged him away and told him to go to his room. 'I'll come to you in a minute, love,' she said calmly. 'And we'll have a little chat before you have your tea.'

Richard did as he was bid, without giving Alison a glance.

'I warned you to say no more just now,' Emma said when they were alone. 'But in you plunged, the way you always do, Alison. And what you know about handling kids could be written on a postage stamp!'

Alison lowered herself on to a chair. Her legs were trembling. 'Comfort, not a lecture, is what I need right now. When Richard said what he did about being adopted, I had to bite my lip to stop myself from telling him the truth.'

'Do you think he'd believe you, if you could and did?' Emma replied. 'Richard isn't the kind who just accepts things, Alison. He's an exceptionally intelligent child.'

'Tell me something I don't know. He's quicker on the uptake than I am.'

'And if you suddenly told him he wasn't adopted, after telling him he is, he would soon be wondering — '

'Which was the truth and which the lie,' Alison cut in, finishing the sentence for her.

They knew their boy.

'You look terrible,' Emma said, eyeing Alison.

'You don't look too good yourself.'

'After what we've just been through! And I'm not looking forward to telling Richard what I must, Alison. I wish Max was here to explain to him why it's necessary to send him away from London – in that man-to-man way he has with Richard. But it can't be delayed,' said Emma, steeling herself and leaving the room.

Alison felt drained of energy and went to lie on her bed. When she next saw her son, Emma was bathing him.

'I'm sorry for the way I behaved, Mummy,' he said.

'And do you understand now?'

Richard nodded. 'But I hope there won't be a war, then I shan't have to go.'

When he stepped out of the bath, Alison took the towel to dry him.

Richard and Emma exchanged a surprised glance.

'Aren't you afraid your lovely frock will get wet, Mummy?' Richard said. 'You used to change into your dressing-gown before you bathed me, while Auntie was in Oldham.'

'About what went on while I was in Oldham, I'd rather not think,' Emma disapprovingly said. 'Your mummy is so careful with her appearance and her clothes, Richard, it's a wonder she didn't wear a raincoat to protect her dressing-gown from the wet!'

'But she always looks beautiful, doesn't she, Auntie?' the child replied.

Though an hour ago his idol had rocked on her pedestal, she had not fallen off it. All was now apparently well. But such was Richard's vulnerability to Alison, overhearing what he had from her lips had reawakened in him the mistrust implanted in his mind some months ago. The same inexplicable emotion had caused him to hit out at her. This time, he had done so physically. But the act was in effect no different from his violent toppling of the tower of wood blocks, in Zelda Stein's kitchen.

Had Alison known that the ground was laid for Richard's love-hate relationship with her, would she have abandoned her career and devoted herself to him? As she did not know, her maternal love was not put to that test. But it is doubtful that anything would have changed the quality she had for her son, as elusive as her perfume even when she was with him.

Meanwhile, she had breathed a sigh of relief when Richard's tantrum subsided, and in her ignorance attributed his display of temperament to the Plantaine blood in his veins.

A few days later, he displayed it again.

'How would you like a trip to America?' Morton, who had joined them for Sunday lunch, asked Richard.

Richard's knife and fork clattered onto his plate.

'On a great big ship,' Morton added enticingly.

In other circumstances, Richard's eyes would have sparkled at the prospect. Now, they were bright with suspicion. He turned his gaze upon Emma, whose explanation about children being evacuated from London had included the comforting mention that Richard would be going to the family in Oldham.

'Don't look at me like that, love,' Emma answered his unspoken accusation. 'It isn't me who wants to send you so far away.'

Richard looked at Alison, his expression hostile.

'Uncle Maxwell thinks you will be safer out of England, darling,' she said carefully.

'But I don't know anybody in America, do I?' said Richard, trying to stem his panic.

Morton gave him a reassuring smile. 'Americans are very friendly people. I have lots of friends there – and it's to one of them you will be going, Richard. He has children of his own, and they won't mind in the least sharing their mummy with you.'

Morton had said the wrong thing.

'I don't want to share their mummy. I want to stay in England, with *my* mummy!' Richard exploded.

Then he knocked over his glass of water and rushed from the room.

'What did you expect?' Emma said with feeling to the other two, as she dealt with the sodden tablecloth, and mopped the drips from Richard's empty chair.

'You'd better go and calm him down, Emma,' Morton advised. 'When you've calmed down yourself,' he added, eyeing her expression.

Emma had just lifted Richard's plate from the table and paused with it in her hand. 'I don't know how you can agree to what Max has arranged for Richard, Alison!'

'So you said. At length, when Maxwell told us it was

possible to arrange it. But I did agree to it, and I haven't changed my mind.'

Emma put down the plate with a slam. 'And I can only conclude that you have no motherly feeling at all! But I have – and my life will be an empty vessel, with Richard so far away.'

Alison was shaken by the intensity of her cousin's feeling. She had not, until now, paused to think that unlike her own life, which centred upon the theatre, Emma's revolved solely around Richard.

'I've been more of a mother to him than you ever were, or shall be!' Emma declared emotionally.

Alison could not deny this, and was moved to compassion for her. 'But it was I who gave birth to him,' she had no option but to remind Emma, 'and what he means to me, I ought not to have to tell you.'

She gazed at the full-blown roses adorning the table and said quietly, 'For once, Emma, I am not thinking of myself. Only of my child. And I am prepared to part with him in order to preserve him.'

Tears were stinging her eyelids. She blinked them away and managed to smile. 'Isn't there something in the Bible about that being the sign of a true mother?'

'It's the judgement of Solomon,' said Morton gruffly.

Emma could not have remained unaffected by Alison's poignant words, and went to kiss her cheek. 'Solomon was right.'

# CHAPTER THIRTEEN

RICHARD'S TRUE mother was not subjected to the sight of a sullen little boy gazing down from a huge ocean liner, as the *Queen Mary* set sail for America on a cloudy August day.

He was travelling with the wife of Morton's accountant, who was escorting her own children to safer shores, and would be handed over in New York to his Massachusetts hosts.

Though war had not yet been declared, its inevitability was emphasised by the evacuation of children having begun. Some of Richard's schoolmates had already been transferred to the country by their parents, and Emma and Morton had not failed to note the number of British children boarding the ship.

That Alison had not come to see him off was, for Richard, more evidence that she did not really love him. She had explained to him that she would have been unable to get back to London in time for curtain-up. But her professionalism was beyond the understanding of a child. Of Emma, too, on this occasion, accustomed to it though she was. And Emma, who would have died for Richard, had cause to question whether Solomon was, after all, the good judge the Bible declared him to be. Only Morton, of the theatre himself, understood what theatrical professionalism meant. And that Alison Plantaine, though her heart might be breaking, would honour her code to the end of her days.

Thus it was that Emma and Morton stood together on the quayside, waving farewell to the child who had become for them a son. In wartime, transatlantic travel would be curtailed, and it was unlikely that they would be able to visit Richard. How old would he be when they saw him again?

Alone in her flat, while the hands on the drawing-room

clock moved toward the moment when the *Queen Mary* would sail away, Alison was no less affected than had she witnessed Richard's departure.

She continued to watch the clock until she knew the ship would no longer be visible from the quay, then went to Richard's room and allowed herself the luxury of weeping, with his pillow cuddled in her arms.

Emma had accused her of having no maternal feeling at all – but the emotion within Alison now was the most powerful she had ever known. Briefly, she was a mother and nothing else.

Then a telephone call reminded her that she was an actress too. Would Miss Plantaine be available to occasionally entertain the troops?

'Certainly,' Alison replied without hesitation. 'If you think that a monologue or two would entertain them.'

'My dear Miss Plantaine, if you read to them from a laundry list, they would be entertained by you. If you could manage to put in an appearance, from time to time, at some of our services canteens – just to say hello to the lads – you would be doing your bit for England,' the refined female voice went on.

Like my mother did in the last war when I was a girl, Alison recalled. Hadn't they called that the war to end all wars? But hope was no match for power-drunk dictators and weak politicians like Chamberlain, she thought.

'You may count on me to do what I can,' she told the lady from whichever organisation it was – she had not registered its name. Only what the call signified: that the women of Britain were preparing, in their own way, to support their men and boys.

When she had replaced the receiver, Alison went to close Richard's bedroom door, which she had left ajar. And it was as if she were closing it upon a chapter of his life and her own.

When he returned they would begin another chapter together. In the interim, Alison would continue to do what she had always done: entertain the public, in good times and bad.

# Part Three

'If love were all.'
*Noël Coward*

# CHAPTER ONE

IN THE summer of 1944, Alison went to France to entertain the troops. It was for her a traumatic experience. Even the devastation and misery inflicted by the Blitz had not prepared her for the battle-scarred scene in which she was fleetingly playing her part.

Though she was here to cheer up the lads with some amusing monologues, she did not easily maintain her smiling veneer in some of the circumstances in which she found herself. And she wondered how some of her audiences could manage to smile.

Would she ever forget the mutilated soldiers for whom she had performed this afternoon, in a military hospital? she thought, *en route* to the camp where she would top the bill tomorrow. Or the weary, young-old faces of the doctors and nurses tending them?

Most of the medical staff had looked as though they had aged overnight. Emma's terse remark that her nephew Percy would just qualify in time to sew up war wounds had echoed in Alison's ears. But Percy was now out of the war, captured in Crete in 1941. Several months had elapsed before the family learned he was alive, a prisoner in Germany. His mother's hair had turned white in the interim. It was the first time Alison had ever been truly sorry for Clara – probably, she reflected now, because she herself was a mother. And thankful that her own son was safe in the United States.

Alison gave her attention to the Normandy countryside. Her driver was whistling Vera Lynn's 'We'll Meet Again'.

'Nothing like tanks for ruining a road,' he said whimsically, as the jeep traversed the pot-holed lanes south of

Caen. 'If we'd been around here a couple of weeks ago, we might have seen Monty directing the bridgehead operation,' he added. 'But don't say that to the Yanks – they think it was all done by General Bradley. Or Patton,' he said as they passed some US army vehicles travelling in the opposite direction.

Alison had responded with a friendly wave to the inevitable wolf-whistles she received from the American drivers and their passengers as they sped by. At forty-four she was still an attractive woman, and even at close quarters looked ten years younger than her age.

Her driver was brooding about the remark he had just made, and declared, 'The Yanks would think their generals had won a battle even if no American soldiers were there!'

Alison had not failed to note the intense rivalry that existed between the Allies. She thought it likely that what the British corporal at her side had just said also applied in reverse.

'What does it matter which wins which battle? So long as between us we win the war,' she said.

The distant rumble of gunfire as they neared their destination reminded her that the war was far from won, though General Patton was said to be approaching Paris.

Alison alighted from the jeep in a field full of grimy tents and vehicles. Her one-man reception committee, a bespectacled, young lieutenant, awaited her in the dusk.

'Welcome to our Field Ordnance depot, Miss Plantaine,' he said, giving her a boyish grin. 'There's an ENSA show here this evening, that's why there's nobody else around to greet you, but me.'

Alison could hear laughter issuing from a marquee nearby. 'Who have you got on the bill? Tommy Handley? Or Bob Hope?'

'Only the Yanks get Bob Hope! But do come along and see the show.'

Alison was longing for a shower and a cup of tea. This was the first free evening in her strenuous ten-day tour, and she would rather spend it sleeping than watching an ENSA show. But she allowed herself to be ushered into the big

252

tent. She did not have the heart to say no to the lieutenant. If she did, he would have to escort her to her quarters, and would miss the show.

Alison perched with him on a bench at the back of the tent, and stifled a yawn. The stand-up comic on the improvised stage – whom she did not recognise – had a line of patter that kept his audience rolling in the aisles. Next came a magician, whose act was nothing special, but who nevertheless received a standing ovation when he pulled the final rabbit from his hat. The same treatment was accorded a soprano whose voice matched her faded appearance. But ENSA shows varied in quality, as commercial ones did, Alison reflected. Some of Britain's top artistes appeared with ENSA. Tonight's fare happened to be a third-rate bill, but its audience was not critical. They wanted to briefly forget the war; be entertained.

A voice Alison recognised – from her past – jolted her from her thoughts. Surely that ageing gentleman, now seating himself onstage, could not be her Uncle Oliver? But it was. And the two ladies now making their entrance together were his wife and his sister.

Alison was so affected by seeing them that she afterwards had no recollection of the sketch they had performed. She had read in *The Stage* that they had closed the Plantaine Playhouse for the duration of the war, and had joined ENSA. And now, there they were, the pathetic remnants of the family company of which her grandfather had once been justly proud.

Though the content of the sketch escaped Alison, the pathos of those feebly performing it did not. She doubted that the Plantaine Playhouse would ever be re-opened. The riveting stage presence Alison's mother, and her uncle and aunt, had once possessed was no more. Had they lost it somewhere along the thorny path that had led them, finally, to close the family theatre? Business could not have been good for the company during the depression that preceded the war. And with Alison and Luke and Lucy gone from the fold to pursue their careers elsewhere, what was there for the elder Plantaines to strive for?

253

Alison experienced a pang of guilt and wanted to flee from the three onstage, from the memories seeing them had stirred in her. Her unhappy childhood and youth. Her mother's disloyalty to her father during the last war. The dire changes wrought in her grandfather's Shakespearean repertoire when Oliver married the erstwhile melodrama-queen, Ruby May.

Her officer-escort noted her pensive expression, and whispered with a smile, 'I didn't mention that the Plantaines were appearing here tonight. Thought it'd be a nice surprise for you.'

Alison summoned the brilliant smile that was her public mask. 'It is certainly a surprise.' But nice? Oh no!

As she had anticipated, after the show all the artistes were given drinks in the mess-tent. Alison was sitting with a ginger-beer in her hand when the other Plantaines entered. She needed a stiff whisky to cope with the reunion, but had decided in favour of keeping a clear head.

All three stopped in their tracks when they saw her. Then Oliver, who bore her no grudges, found his voice and greeted her warmly.

'My dearest niece!' he exclaimed, giving her an affectionate kiss.

The greeting Alison received from Ruby was no less theatrically delivered – but a good deal less sincere. 'How absolutely marvellous to see you, darling!' she declared, depositing a lipstick cupid's-bow on Alison's cheek. Though Ruby was not by nature the hard-nut that circumstances had caused her to become, Alison was no friend of the twin darlings of her maternal heart.

From her mother, Alison got the reception she had expected which did not include a kiss. Hermione Plantaine was as practised in the art of hypocrisy as her sister-in-law Ruby, but did not bother to demonstrate it for her daughter's benefit.

'So you have finally taken a leaf out of Gertrude Lawrence's book, Alison,' she said coolly. 'But there is not yet a wartime Alison Plantaine Company,' she added with a smile that barely touched her lips.

254

Alison stiffened. Was her mother taking the opportunity to belittle her, comparing her status to Miss Lawrence's, because ENSA had given Gertie's name to the company she toured with?

'I'm not part of a wartime company,' she informed Hermione. 'I just do what I can for the troops when I am between plays, and have since the war began.'

'I see,' Hermione replied.

To Alison it sounded like a rebuke. 'Appearing in London where servicemen and women on leave are, these days, a large percentage of the audience, helps the war effort, too,' she felt constrained to say.

'There is no need to be defensive, Alison. I haven't accused you of anything.'

Well, not in so many words, thought Alison, but innuendo was Hermione Plantaine's speciality. She had never had the courage to say what she really meant.

Ruby changed the subject. 'Luke and Lucy tell me they hear regularly from your adopted son, Alison. Last time they visited us, they brought a picture postcard to show to us, that Richard had sent to them from Cape Cod.'

So he was conducting a correspondence with the twins, though he did not write often to her, thought Alison with chagrin. It was Emma to whom his letters home were usually addressed – and who replied to them immediately. Alison preferred to maintain contact with Richard by telephone, but when she called him, she always had the feeling he could not wait to get her off the line and return to whatever he was doing when the phone rang.

Richard was now eleven, and it struck Alison that he had been gone from her for almost half of his life. It would not be easy to re-establish their relationship when he returned.

'Richard's American hosts have a holiday home in Cape Cod,' she said, collecting herself. 'Before the war, my cousin Emma used to take him to Blackpool for his summer hols. The family always rent a flat there — '

'Your other family, you mean,' Hermione crisply interrupted. The mere mention of her in-laws was anathema to her.

Alison was well aware of this, and quietly applied some salt to her mother's self-inflicted wound. 'My Aunt Lottie adores Richard, and has been like a granny to him. And he and Janet – she's my cousin Conrad's little girl – always got on well together. Emma used to take them for donkey-rides on Blackpool sands. I was always too busy working to go with them on holiday — '

'As you were, no doubt, when my parents were laid to rest,' her mother again interrupted – too casually. 'Though I would not have expected even a Plantaine to put professional commitment before her grandparents' funerals.'

Alison controlled her anger. 'Believe it or not, Mama, I did not know that either of them had passed away, until I read their obituaries in *The Stage* – later.'

Gregory had succumbed to influenza in the winter of 1940, on the eve of his ninetieth birthday. In the spring, Jessica died peacefully in her sleep. As though, Alison had thought poignantly, she had just stopped trying to live without him. Her Plantaine grandparents had always seemed to her perfectly matched, like the pair of Victorian silver candlesticks someone had given them for a wedding gift, which they had willed to Alison.

The candlesticks were the only material possession Alison had ever known her grandmother to cherish – or they would surely have been pawned long ago, when the Plantaine Players hadn't two pennies to rub together, she thought now. And recalled, too, the occasions in her child-hood when she had watched Jessica take them from their box, to polish them, then re-pack them in readiness for the company's next journey to yet another theatrical lodging.

Like their owners, the candlesticks had never had a real home. The old people had ended their days as they had begun them, in rented furnished rooms; in the seaside boarding-house in which what was left of the Players still lived, and called home, Alison reflected glancing at them. But it wasn't a home, and she wondered how they could bear not having one. She herself had proved that the glib

256

saying, 'What you've never had, you don't miss,' was not true.

Oliver broke the silence. 'I'm sure that dear Alison would have attended her grandparents' funerals, had she known in time to do so,' he said to Hermione.

'And I am unlikely to forget, Oliver, how loyal to Alison you have always been,' she replied.

Oliver patted his niece's cheek. 'I don't deny it, Hermione. Alison is very dear to me.'

'Then why didn't you bother to let me know when Grandpa and Grandma died?' Alison inquired. The twins' failure to do so required no explanation, but Oliver's default had led Alison to believe that he no longer cared about her.

'Because your mother forbade us to let you know!' Ruby flashed. 'So don't you go blaming your uncle for it, Alison!'

Ruby folded her arms and rested them upon the table of her bosom – always a buxom woman, she had become more so, with the years – and gave Hermione a frigid glance.

'Note what a devoted wife your aunt has become – in her old age, Alison,' Hermione said cattily.

'Ruby has always been devoted to me,' Oliver interceded.

Protective would be a better word, Alison thought. Devoted, when applied to a wife, implied a physical fidelity not present in Ruby's relationship with Oliver. Alison had, in her youth, been shocked by her aunt's extra-marital *affaires*, which Ruby had not tried to conceal. But Oliver had seemed not to mind, as though his wife was to him all he required of a woman; a comfortable and comforting presence, with whom he felt secure.

Only with maturity, and in retrospect, had Alison divined the true nature of their relationship: that her uncle was a homosexual whom convention and circumstances had propelled into settling for love without sex. There was no doubt that Ruby loved him; affection shone from her eyes whenever she looked at Oliver. He had given her his distinguished thespian name, and had enabled her children to embark upon their chosen path. But her love for Oliver was

257

not that of a woman for a man, Alison reflected now, and Ruby's sensuality, in her younger years, was as strong as her perfume. Alison doubted that the marriage would have lasted, had Oliver not had the good sense to turn a blind eye to his wife's finding elsewhere what she could not get from him.

Ruby was still glaring at Hermione. 'I almost did let you know about your grandparents' deaths,' she told Alison. 'And to tell you the truth, I am ashamed that I didn't. But I kept quiet for Oliver's sake. He and I have to live with your mother, don't we, Alison? I'm a match for her – needless to say. But your uncle isn't. And if we had gone against her wishes in the matter – well, we'd never have heard the end of it.'

'I hope you can forgive your aunt and me for not doing what we ought to have done, Alison dear,' Oliver added. He sighed and glanced at his sister. 'When a person gets older, all they want is a peaceful atmosphere around them.'

'That's all right, Uncle. I understand,' Alison replied. 'But you still have some way to go before you are really old,' she said lightly, to relieve the tension.

'I am almost fifty-seven, Alison, and, lest you hadn't noticed, my hair has turned from gold to silver!' he answered with a dry smile.

'But your wife's has turned from silver to gold – with the aid of that dye she uses,' Hermione said contemptuously.

'It wouldn't be a bad idea if yours did the same,' Ruby countered. 'The way you've let yourself go, Hermione, the only part anyone would cast you for is one of the three witches.'

'Now, now, girls — ' Oliver intervened.

'Don't you "now-now" me,' Hermione said.

'If you didn't make it necessary, by being such a bitch, he wouldn't have to,' Ruby told her. 'And perhaps your daughter can now understand what we have to put up with from you.'

Gone were the days when her mother and aunt had hidden their mutual antipathy beneath a sugary veneer,

258

Alison thought. Possibly they still did so when necessary, to protect their public image, but there was nobody except her uncle and herself within earshot at present.

Oliver was fidgeting despondently with his watch chain, and Alison was filled with compassion for him. His lot could be likened to that of a lamb caught between two snarling lionesses. But it would never occur to him to take the one to whom he was incongruously wedded, and escape. Oliver wasn't the kind to shirk the responsibility his widowed sister was to him.

She is also your mother, an inner voice reminded Alison. I owe her nothing, Alison silently replied to it. How lovely it would have been to have the sort of mother she could have brought to London, to live with her. At sixty-odd, Hermione was still capable of playing character roles, and Morton would have made sure she was not without work.

Alison pricked the bubble that impossible dream was. Impossible because Hermione had made it so, allowing her bitterness toward her Jewish in-laws to erode her relationship with her daughter. It seemed to Alison now that all her mother had ever given her was pain.

Simultaneously, she was filled with regret that her estrangement from Hermione had caused her to neglect Oliver and her grandparents. From time to time she had telephoned them, but had kept away from Hastings to avoid a confrontation with her mother.

But Destiny – which always has the last word – arranged for us to meet in an army camp in France, thought Alison wryly, glancing at her elders. What the others were thinking was anyone's guess. They had lapsed into silence after Hermione and Ruby's insulting exchange.

The family quartet was seated in a corner, sipping drinks. This unexpected reunion had opened the floodgates of memory for each of them, and its reflective aftermath was like a small pool of silence in the noisy mess-tent, where the officers were making the most of their chance to flirt with the ENSA company's troupe of comely chorus girls.

Alison noted that her uncle, who had once been an alcoholic, had maintained his abstinence and was, like herself, nursing a glass of ginger-beer. Her aunt, never more than a social drinker, was making a small cognac last. But her mother, Alison observed, was drinking heavily. Hermione had just downed her third brandy, and was holding out her empty glass to Oliver.

'Would you mind getting me a refill?' she requested. 'The steward seems to be busy at the bar.'

'You don't need another drink, darling,' Oliver said.

'But I do. It will help me sleep.'

Oliver exchanged a glance with Alison. 'Your mother has not slept well since your father died, Alison.'

Her conscience must be keeping her awake, Alison thought.

'We're here to cheer up the lads, not to sit in a corner getting each other down!' Ruby said, flouncing off with a rustle of her black taffeta evening frock. But Oliver remained beside his sister, as though he must watch over her. As Mama watched over him, in the days when he drank too much, Alison recalled.

She had noted that Ruby was still an attractive woman, and as animated as ever, but Hermione's fragile beauty had faded like the fleeting bloom on a summer rose, and she seemed to spring to life only when unleashing her bitterness.

This, Hermione was about to do again. 'Lonely though I am, I don't need a keeper!' she flashed to Oliver. 'You and my daughter are free to join Ruby. Don't let me stop you from enjoying yourselves.'

Alison rose from her chair; she had had enough! Then she saw her mother blink away a tear, and heard herself say, 'Come, Mama. I'll walk with you to your quarters.'

Hermione looked surprised, but did not protest when Alison took her elbow and helped her to her feet.

What have I done? Alison thought, when they were alone together in the tent Hermione was sharing with some other ladies from the ENSA company. Allowed an impulse to catapult you into a situation you had so carefully avoided, Emma would say. But short of fleeing from the tent, there was no going back.

'It was kind of you to escort me here,' Hermione said stiffly.

Alison smiled wryly. 'Only Hermione Plantaine would be so formal with her own daughter – whom she hasn't seen for years!'

'As my daughter has, in the interim, made no attempt to see me, she obviously did not wish to,' Hermione replied. 'Formality is not unusual between strangers – which is what you and I have become.'

Alison could not deny that, and was assailed by sadness because it was so. She watched Hermione unpack a dainty pink nightdress and wrapper, and lay them on the camp bed she would occupy tonight. Daintiness had always been part of her mother's nature, she recalled, and neither war nor widowhood had changed Hermione in that respect.

'Are you finding your overseas tour tiring?' Alison inquired, to break the awkward silence.

'At my age, of course I am.'

'And at your age, you ought not to be sleeping under canvas – and all that goes with it,' said Alison with feeling.

Hermione turned from the bed to look at her. 'You sound as if you care about me, Alison.'

'I do.'

'And I about you.'

'I have never thought you didn't, Mama, but I doubt if that applies the other way round.' Alison waved a fly away from her face and watched it settle, for a moment, on her cream linen skirt.

'Your skirt is terribly creased,' Hermione remarked irrelevantly.

'Never mind my skirt! We're talking about you and me, Mama.'

'And where will it get us?' said Hermione resignedly.

'I think about you often, Mama – though I try not to.'

'Why do you try not to?'

'Because you've hurt me more than you could possibly know.'

'As you have me, Alison. By allying yourself with your

261

father's family, which resulted in your cutting yourself off from me, and mine.'

We'll be quarrelling in a minute, Alison thought. Pursuing our private battle, with the sound of distant gunfire echoing in our ears. Lads were losing their lives at this very moment – and oh, how wasteful it was that she and her mother had spent so many years of their lives on either side of a rift.

But its cause was a subject about which their minds would never meet, though their hearts longed for the rift to be healed. The best Alison could hope for was that they might one day lose their rancour toward each other. Only then could they be reconciled.

And what daughter would not hope for the reconciliation Alison now admitted to herself that she yearned for? Nor did she doubt that her mother felt the same way. Alison's feeling for her son had taught her that no bond is stronger than the emotional one forged by giving life to a child.

She looked at the woman who had given life to her, but whom she could not respect. Which wasn't to say she didn't admire Hermione's pluck, she thought, eyeing her mother's frail figure. Like her pink satin nightwear, Hermione seemed out of place in this stark, military ambience.

She had unpinned her hair, and was seated on the bed, absently brushing it with the old tortoise-shell brush she had used when Alison was a child.

'With your hair down, you look like you did when you played Titania,' Alison told her.

'I have only played Titania once,' Hermione replied with a wan smile. 'In your grandfather's memorable production of the *Dream*, in 1912.'

The production had been memorable to Alison's father because it was a financial disaster. She could remember him looking weary with anxiety at the time, though she was too young to understand why. But to her mother, only the artistic aspect was memorable; her sole concern, as it was then.

Her parents were as ill-matched as her grandparents were like two peas from the same pod, Alison reflected with

262

the benefit of hindsight. Yet the same could be said of herself and her son's father. If she and Richard Lindemann had married, would they have ended up with daggers drawn, as her parents often were?

Alison cast that hypothetical thought aside. Marrying her German lover was unlikely ever to be more than hypothesis. But when the war was won – she could not conceive of an enemy victory – she would return to Berlin. Find the man, or exorcise the ghost.

'I wish we could turn back the clock to when I played Titania,' her mother said, 'to when you were still my little girl, Alison.'

You mean to when I still didn't know I am half-Jewish, Alison thought, that I am part of the Shrager and Stein clan, not just a Plantaine. 'But we have to live with the clock moving forward, don't we, Mama?' she said. And added, 'I have the greatest admiration for what you are doing here, right now.'

Hermione took a flask of brandy from her valise. 'It takes Dutch courage, Alison,' she said with bravado. 'And a little drink really does help me sleep,' she added, giving herself a comforting sip. 'But thank you for saying you admire my insignificant war effort. I should like you to know that I am extremely proud of all you have achieved.'

A moment later, they were holding each other close.

This has happened before, Alison thought, in exactly the same way – but when? On the evening she was to make her Plantaine Players début, at the tender age of sixteen. Hermione had come to the dressing room to wish her luck. Though by then the seeds of their estrangement were sown, a brief, emotional coming-together had occurred. Alison had not expected it to last, and did not fool herself that this one would, or could. Though there was love between them, and always had been, neither trusted the other. Nor, thought Alison, when they afterwards stood regarding each other awkwardly – or was it warily? – was there anything but trouble to be gained by raking up the past.

She averted her eyes to the hurricane-lamp, bade her mother goodnight, and left the tent. Hermione had not asked her to stay in touch, or suggested that they try to see each other from time to time. But why would she? Alison reflected, as she trod the stubbly path to find her own quarters. Her mother knew as well as Alison did that the only way to maintain the uneasy peace they had established tonight was for them to stay apart.

# CHAPTER TWO

'THE FIRST thing I want to do,' said Alison to Emma when she returned from France, 'is speak to Richard.'

'You haven't even taken your hat off yet,' Emma replied.

Alison obliged her by doing so, before picking up the telephone receiver.

'Why the urgency to speak to him?' Emma inquired after Alison had booked the call.

'I just want to hear his voice, Emma.' The encounter with her mother had emphasised for Alison how much she missed her own child – and, too, the great gap in their relationship their five-year separation represented.

'Not that he'll have much to say to me,' she added wryly. 'He never does, when I call him. When he was little, he talked non-stop. Now he's eleven, I have to do all the talking to keep the conversational ball rolling.'

Emma, to whom Richard told all his doings, when she telephoned him, refrained from saying so. 'It's only seven o'clock in the morning, where Richard is,' she reminded Alison. 'As he's on holiday, he might not be up yet.'

'But he will be by the time the call is put through. Transatlantic lines are always busy these days.'

'Well, there's a war on, isn't there?'

'You don't say!' Alison replied in the vernacular of the American soldiers Londoners now encountered everywhere.

While they waited for the telephone operator to call back, Emma made some tea, and Alison told her about her meeting with the Plantaines in France.

Alison had kept her tone light, but Emma knew that the reunion had been a moving experience for her. Emma could not remember her ever before talking about her mother. Nor, Emma sensed, was she finding it easy to do so now.

'Mama looks dreadful, Emma. She was never a robust-looking lady – she's tiny, like you. But there used to be a sparkle about her that isn't there any more. And she seems to have taken to the bottle. I fear she will become ill.'

'And who'll take care of her, if she does?' practical Emma inquired.

Alison, who had not paused to consider that aspect, did not reply.

'As her only child, it will be your responsibility,' her cousin informed her.

Then the telephone rang, and Alison switched her mind to her own child.

'Hi, Mom,' he said casually.

Alison laughed. The sound of his voice was balm to her troubled heart. 'What an American boy you have become, Richard!'

'Well, I've lived in the States for almost half of my life, haven't I, Mom?'

And his thought processes were as logical as they had always been, Alison thought. 'How are you enjoying being in Cape Cod, darling?'

'It's like a second home to me, I guess. Coming back here each summer, like we do.'

'Don't you mean a third home, darling? England is your real home, isn't it? And Massachusetts no doubt feels to you like your second home, by now.'

Richard did not reply.

Why had she gone through that ridiculous verbal rigmarole with him? Alison asked herself. Because she didn't want him to forget where he belonged.

'How are your foster-family?' she asked him. 'Mrs Baxter rushed away to bring you to the phone. I didn't have time to exchange a word with her.'

'Aunt Mary and Uncle Josh are just fine.'

'And the children?'

'Mike and Maggie and I are having a real good time on the beach.'

'Has Josh junior been drafted yet, darling?'

'He didn't wait to be drafted. He volunteered.'

'I see.'

Alison listened to the static, crackling on the line, as her son waited for her to say something else.

'I don't have time right now for a long talk, Mom,' he said when she asked how the weather was in Cape Cod. 'Aunt Mary's making buttermilk pancakes for breakfast. If I don't move fast they'll all be eaten up.'

'Then you better had move fast!'

After Alison had replaced the receiver, she stood gazing at the photograph of Richard aged six, which was on the hall table. The youngster to whom she had just been speaking was not that boy. The recent snapshots of him that were pasted into her album told her what he looked like, but that was all. And Alison was beset by the feeling that she no longer knew her son.

'I must bath and change, and go to the read-through for my next play,' she said, collecting herself. Emma was dusting the front door, not that it needed dusting but Emma cleaned the entire flat, every day.

'Why don't you give yourself a rest?' Alison said to her.

'And what would I do if I did?'

Alison laughed. 'From you, that's a good question!'

'What play are you doing next by the way?'

'By the way is right! As my career comes second in this household to your domestic chores,' Alison teased Emma. 'But I'll take advantage of your rare interest in my work, if I may. I need to get my disappointment off my chest. I wanted to play Nora, in *A Doll's House* — '

'That sounds like a children's play,' Emma cut in.

'Oh, what a philistine you are!' Alison said with a laugh. 'It is one of Ibsen's stark dramas, Emma dear. I've hankered after playing its tragic heroine since the days when I was too young for the role, but because *Peer Gynt* is on at the New Theatre, Maxwell has said no. He thinks a plethora of Ibsen's plays is not what wartime audiences need. They're too gloomy, he says. People want to be cheered up.'

'He's right, Alison.'

267

'I know he's right, Emma. But I wasn't thinking of the audiences. I was thinking of me.'

'You should be thinking of Max, too. If he is to make his living, he must give the public what they want.'

'That's what most impresarios are now doing,' said Alison with a snort, 'and some of the play titles speak for themselves. *Is Your Honeymoon Really Necessary*, and *A Bird In Hand*. Trite's the word for it, Emma. And *Keep Going*, which is on at the Palace, just about sums up the current scene. Superficial entertainment seems *de rigueur* nowadays.'

She paused only for breath. 'But, conversely, evening dress at the theatre no longer is. And I sometimes wonder if the special occasion a night-out at the theatre was, before the war, will ever be that again.'

'Why are you getting so het up about it?'

'Probably because the theatre is so special to me. I grew up in it, didn't I? And cut my acting teeth on the finest plays ever written. I can't bear to see it debased. And I am coming to see that I don't take kindly to change. I can't accept the war as an excuse for it.'

'Well, the war hasn't changed you, has it? You still put on an evening gown when you go to the theatre.'

'And I always shall,' Alison declared. 'When Alison Plantaine goes to see a play, or is seen emerging from the stagedoor of a theatre where she is appearing, it will never be said that she is unsuitably attired.'

'Bravo!' Emma said with a laugh. Alison standing on her dignity was always amusing to Emma. 'But what will you do when your dozens of evening frocks are worn out, and all your clothing coupons spent?'

'Wheedle some coupons from you and Maxwell, of course.'

'As if you hadn't already! So which play has he chosen for you to do next, Alison?'

'A good one, thank heaven. Maugham's *Home and Beauty*. The only thing that bothers me about it is I shall be playing a woman about twenty years younger than myself.'

Emma scanned Alison's unlined face. 'You'll get away with it, Alison.'

'Onstage!'

They were beside the hall mirror, and eyed their two reflections.

'Nobody would guess your age,' Emma said. 'Nor would they believe you and I are the same age.'

Alison did not deny the evidence of their eyes.

'Your looks aren't your living, Emma dear,' she said dryly. 'But the day will soon come when mine limit the roles I can play to middle-aged mums. And the next stage after that will be blue-rinsed dowagers!'

They shared a glance that said more than words. This time next year they would be forty-five. The tick-tock of the grandfather clock, that had lived in their grandparents' home when they were young, increased the feeling that life was passing them by.

Alison, who had allowed no man to touch her since her love affair with Richard Lindemann, was aware of her passionate womanhood, on which she had turned the key. Remembering his embraces still brought a flush to her cheeks. But a memory was what he now was, and it was as if she had remained faithful to someone in a receding dream.

Emma had not expected life to treat her any better than it had, and said wryly, 'Why are we standing here like a couple of lemons! You've got your read-through to go to. And I've got my housework.'

'And meanwhile, the years are flying by,' Alison answered. 'And are gone without one noticing it happening.'

'There's nothing a person can do about that.'

'Except make the most of every minute.'

Emma was still clutching her duster, and used it vigor-ously on the hall table. 'The life you lead, Alison, you are certainly doing that. Compared with my life – not that I'm complaining — '

'But yours is now the empty vessel you said it would be without Richard, isn't it?' Alison interrupted. 'It doesn't have to be, Emma. There are things you could be doing that are just up your street, like helping at a services canteen.'

Emma smiled. 'Could you see me among those upper-crust ladies who were at that canteen where you made an appearance? I felt like a bumpkin, that day! I was sorry I'd let you drag me along.'

She gave the already gleaming table top another rub. 'And they make ham sandwiches at services canteens, don't they?'

'Spam sandwiches,' Alison corrected her.

'Ham or Spam, it's all the same to me, Alison. It isn't for a Jewish woman of my age to suddenly start handling non-*kosher* food.'

'If you can find a reason for not stirring out of this flat, you will, Emma!' Alison exclaimed.

The rut in which Emma had entrenched herself since Richard's departure was a source of anxiety to Alison. Though not exactly a trough of despondency, it was the next best thing. As though Emma was just marking time until the boy returned.

'And if no reason for not stirring out exists, you'll invent one,' Alison went on. 'Like you just invented two! Not all of the ladies who help at services canteens are upper-crust. Far from it. And if you didn't wish to handle the Spam, or whatever, you wouldn't have to. And you know it.'

'I don't know it. And I'm not prepared to offer my services and then have to back out on religious grounds.'

'You are being ridiculous, Emma!'

'And you are trying to browbeat me, Alison! If there was a Jewish canteen in London, I'd offer to help there,' Emma said, confident that there was not.

Alison, who knew her all too well, smiled. 'I'm sorry to disappoint you, Emma dear, but there is one in the West End. I think it's in Portland Place. It's called the Balfour Club.'

Emma tried to wriggle off the hook on which she had impaled herself. 'With a Jewish community the size of London's, the boys and girls who use that place don't need me.'

But you need them. Alison thought. 'You said that if there was such a canteen, you'd offer to help there. And I expect you to keep your word, Emma – as you always do.'

'All right, Alison! I know when I'm beaten.'

# CHAPTER THREE

RICHARD'S TELEPHONE conversations with Alison were no less a strain for him than they were for her. Their long separation had heightened the remoteness she had always had for him. There were times when he had to look at her photograph to remind himself that she existed in the flesh. But when he dreamed of her, which he did frequently, he smelled her perfume, and it was as if she were in the room.

'How are things in England?' Mary Baxter inquired while the family was eating breakfast, after Alison's call.

'OK, I guess.'

'Didn't you ask your mom about the buzz-bombs?' young Mike Baxter quizzed him.

'I guess I forgot to.'

'I bet he didn't ask if she got the food parcel Mom mailed to her,' little Maggie Baxter wagered, through a mouthful of bacon and buttermilk pancake. 'Rick never asks his mom anything, does he?'

Her father laughed. 'Which considering all the questions he's forever asking me, is mighty odd!' Josh Baxter had thought his own children had over-inquiring minds, until he met Richard.

He glanced down at his *Boston Herald*. 'It says here that your mother has been entertaining soldiers in France, Rick. That's a brave lady.'

Richard experienced a surge of pride but it did not make Alison more real for him.

'If my big brother gets sent to France, and Rick's mom goes there again, maybe she'll run into him,' Maggie chimed in.

Her other brother licked some maple syrup from his

fingers. 'I wonder if Junior will remember to bring me a German helmet, if he gets to Europe.'

'He might bring me a grass-skirt, if they ship him to the Pacific,' Maggie said.

Josh managed to smile though his heart was heavy. 'You kids sure know your war zones!'

'If the war's still on when I'm old enough to enlist, I hope they'll ship me to Europe,' Mike declared.

'Get on with your breakfast!' his mother said – more sharply than she had intended. One soldier son was enough worry to be going on with.

Josh junior's enlisting had, for the elder Baxters, blighted the family's annual vacation at their summer home, but they were not allowing their anxiety about their elder boy to communicate itself to the younger children.

Mary had inherited the waterfront house in Dennisport from an aunt, when she and Josh were a young couple struggling to get by on a newly-qualified lawyer's salary. Josh junior had learned to walk here, she was recalling while she sipped her second cup of coffee, and such cherished family remembrances had become for Mary and her husband as much a part of the house as its faded clapboard walls, and the sagging porch where they sat in the evenings. Josh was always talking about strengthening the porch and about giving everything a lick of paint, but it would be like changing the appearance of an old friend, Mary thought with a smile.

'If the war's still on when I grow up, I guess I'll join the WACs,' her small daughter was telling Mike and Richard.

Mary put down her coffee cup. 'If you kids have finished eating, it's time you were all out on the beach.' She had heard enough war-talk for one morning.

Fostering Richard had brought the war in Europe closer for the Baxters and their children long before their own country became involved in it. You could not have an English evacuee in your home and put from your mind the reason he was here. Would it have been easier to do so, if Richard had not, when he arrived, been such a miserable child? Mary ruminated while she washed the breakfast dishes. In those days, every time she looked at him his forlorn expression had caused her heart to ache because the war had separated him from his mother. But that lonely little boy was no more. Through the window above the sink, Mary could see Richard and Mike racing along the beach, and Maggie trying to catch up with them, her ginger pigtails flying behind her in the strong, Cape Cod wind. A happy family sight for Mary's motherly eyes.

'Do you remember the day we met Rick off the *Queen Mary*?' she said to her husband with a reminiscent smile. 'And brought him back here to Dennisport?'

The family had interrupted their summer vacation to fetch Richard from New York.

'I think I'd rather forget it,' Josh replied, 'but I guess I never will. My over-riding memory of that day is of a nightmare drive back to the Cape with a carful of squabbling kids – ours – and an English one who wouldn't speak to them or us! Let me not forget to remind you that I didn't have a cooling system in that car. And oh boy, was that day hot!'

Mary laughed. 'And when Rick finally did utter a word or two, our kids poked fun at his British accent – which clamped his mouth shut again for the rest of the vacation.'

'And for some time after it. When I look back on his first few months with us, Mary, I don't know how we lived through it. He used to depress me so much, I kept thinking, "Oh God, what have we done?" After a weekend at home with that kid it was a pleasure to get back to the office – and you know how I love the office. How long is it going to take him to stop being homesick? I asked myself every day.'

'Me too, Josh. But I no longer think that homesickness was all it was.' Mary paused with the dishcloth in her hand. 'Or should I say, what it *is* – because something is still bugging that boy.'

Josh put down his newspaper and eyed her thoughtfully. 'Now you mention it, honey, I have noticed that occasionally he still behaves as if the cat has got his tongue.'

'You're more observant than I gave you credit for. Have you noticed when those occasions invariably occur?'

274

'He clammed-up during breakfast today — '

'And not because his mouth was full of pancake.' Mary watched Josh unfold his lanky figure from the rickety rocking-chair she had inherited with the house, and go to fetch his favourite briar from the pipe-rack on the New England dresser. 'Why do you always bring all your pipes, when that's the only one you ever smoke?' she said impatiently.

She waited for him to take some tobacco from a jar and return to his chair. 'When you're ready, Josh, we'll resume our discussion.'

'Oh. I thought we were just having a conversation!'

'Call it what you like. But I require your undivided attention.'

'Then you must wait till I've filled and lit my pipe – like my partner has to, when we're discussing a case.'

'But I don't suppose he minds, as lawyers do everything at a snail's pace.'

'I guess I asked for that!'

'Anyways, I do mind so let's get on with it.'

Josh stopped filling his pipe. 'What the heck's with you, this morning?'

'I have to get this thing about Rick off my chest. He was his usual self when he got up, wasn't he?'

'Yes.'

'But not during breakfast. So why the sudden change in him, Josh?'

'You're beginning to sound like a private eye, honey!'

'A person doesn't have to be a detective, Josh, to see Rick isn't the same after getting a call from his mother. Or that something comes over him whenever she's mentioned, which she never is, by him – and that is another thing.'

Josh surveyed the troubled expression on Mary's freckled face, and noticed that her nose was peeling. His red-haired wife and kids had the kind of skin that wasn't beautified by the sun, he thought absently.

'Why are you scrutinising my nose?' she demanded, 'when I'm talking to you about something that worries me.'

275

He went to put a comforting arm around her plump shoulders. 'You mustn't let it, Mary. Though I know how much you've come to care for the boy – me, too – you have to see things in the right perspective.'

'And what might that be?'

'Giving it to you straight, honey, we're providing him with a temporary home while his country is vulnerable to enemy attack. We've made sure he's comfortable and happy with us, and we can do no more for him than that.'

Mary put down the dishcloth and gazed through the window at the familiar vacation scene. Families like her own were arriving with picnic baskets, to spend the day on the shore. A fat lady in a bright yellow frock stepped out of her shoes and emptied them of sand. The old gentleman who lived next door was wading in the sea with his grand-children. And a bevy of small girls, their eyes riveted to the beach, passed back and forth in front of Mary's window, meticulously searching for seashells. Maggie, Mary noted, had joined them – and would doubtless later want her mom to help her make yet another shell bracelet or necklace.

'What are you thinking?' Josh asked her.

'That I'm running out of thread for homemade jewellery.'

'And with the part of your mind that wasn't thinking that? As if I didn't know.'

'Then why bother to ask?' Mary could see Richard clambering on the rocks that fringed this section of the beach, with Mike and some other boys. He looked as carefree as the rest of them but Mary knew that within himself he was not.

She thrust her hands into the pockets of her simple cotton dress and turned to face her husband. 'What you said to me about Rick, Josh – about seeing things in the right perspective. You meant that how he feels about his mother isn't our problem, didn't you?'

'I guess I did mean more or less that.'

'You don't think we should talk to him about it?'

'Certainly not.' Josh returned to his chair and puffed thoughtfully at his pipe. 'We don't know how he feels about his mother, do we, Mary?'

276

'Only that he gets a fit of the blues, whenever she's called him up!' said Mary with asperity.

'But it doesn't last long.'

'By now, the kid must be an expert in willing his blues away. And I've wondered from the start what kind of woman his mother is. She couldn't spare the time to see him off to the States.'

'I understand from my friend Morton that she's charming,' Josh pointed out.

'Possibly. To a man!'

'And crazy about her son, Morton said.' Josh relit his pipe, absently, after a few seconds of futile sucking. 'How you can take a dislike to someone you've never met, Mary – and you obviously have – beats me!'

'Because you are a lawyer, and lawyers deal only in facts. You're not endowed with my intuition, Josh.'

'Nor with your imagination! But please don't let it run away with you about Rick and his mom any more than it already has. It isn't fair of you, honey. Alison Plantaine isn't here to defend herself, and you're unlikely ever to meet her and form a valid opinion of her.'

'There goes the lawyer again! I have no desire to meet her, Josh. But I love her son. And what's the betting that Rick will always stay in touch with us?'

'It would surprise me if he didn't.'

'Me too.'

'When he's older, he'll look back on his time in the States as an interesting experience,' Josh said.

'I think he'll see it, in retrospect, as more than just that,' Mary replied. 'Putting two and two together — '

'And, as usual,' Josh laughed, 'making five!'

'I think that living with us has given Rick his first taste of real family life.'

# CHAPTER FOUR

As 1944 approached its end, and the war in Europe intensified, an atmosphere of defiant gaiety pervaded London's West End. It was as though the Londoners who spent their nights sleeping in the Underground, and went about their business by day, buzz-bombs or not, were thumbing their noses at Hitler.

The city's uniformed transients had about them the same devil-may-care air, thought Alison, who rubbed shoulders with them on the thronged pavements of theatreland. She noted, too, the preponderance among them of GIs, whose coming had enhanced the wartime change in the capital's historic face.

In Piccadilly, the Stage Door Canteen, with its garish façade, was a testament to the new American influence upon the British way of life. Rainbow Corner, in Coventry Street, was another. It was at these clubs that the GIs in London introduced their British girlfriends to hamburgers, peanut butter, and other US culinary delights.

A stone's throw away was the spacious Nuffield Centre, London's most popular rendezvous for those whose uniform was not American; where dancing was still dancing, and the jitterbug imported from across the Atlantic held in contempt.

Theatre had remained as available as it had always been. Apart from a brief period of government-enforced closure in September 1939, there was no shortage of entertainment in wartime London. The list of playhouses damaged during the Blitz, and after, had included the Duke of York's, the Queen's, and the Piccadilly, but somehow curtains in the capital had continued to rise. When night air raids were at their height, Shakespeare was performed at the Strand at

278

lunchtime, and ballet at the Ambassadors. The Ballet Rambert had even presented after-tea performances – which Alison had dryly thought could not be more British. It would take more than a war to put the entertainment business out of action, she had frequently reflected with pride.

Nor did London's opportunities for wartime pleasure end when the theatres and service clubs closed. A plethora of so-called night-clubs had mushroomed for the benefit of those who could afford an exorbitant membership fee and the bottle of black-market liquor it was obligatory to order at the table. It was at one of these shoddy places, in Knightsbridge, that Alison and Emma found themselves rounding off the evening on their first double date.

For Emma, the date itself was her first, and for Alison it was a blind one, which Emma, incongruously, had arranged.

Emma had kept her promise to offer to help at the Balfour Club. 'You're not going to believe this, Alison,' she had said after returning from there one evening, 'but a man wants to take me out!'

'Why shouldn't I believe it?'

'Because I don't, myself.'

She had rushed into the drawing room to tell Alison her news, without pausing to take off her hat and coat. And had a dazed look on her face, Alison noted with fond amusement.

'I mean it's never happened to me before, has it?'

'How could it, Emma dear? Before I forced you to venture forth, where did you ever go where you might meet an eligible man? The grocer and butcher are both married!' Alison teased her. 'And apart from them, and the milkman – and Maxwell, of course – how many men do you know?'

The mention of Morton blunted the edge of Emma's excitement. But Max was not for her and never would be.

'Tell me about your admirer,' Alison teased her again.

'He's an American major, who is in their equivalent of our Army Catering Corps. And he's stationed in London for the duration.'

Alison could not resist saying, with a laugh, 'So your date won't be what the Yanks call just a one-night-stand.'

Emma blushed to the roots of her greying hair. 'Really, Alison!'

Then they shared a laugh, and Emma curled up on the hearthrug beside Alison, to toast herself by the fire.

With the blackout curtains shutting out the dismal November evening, and the small but cheerful blaze in the grate, momentarily they were able to forget the war.

'This is like when we were girls,' Alison recalled, 'and your mother let us light a fire in your bedroom.'

'Which she only let me do when you came to stay.'

'And we'd sit beside it, telling each other our secrets.'

'I don't remember having any, Alison.'

Alison smiled. 'Any more than you have now. Oh, what an open book you are!'

Emma thought of her unrequited love for Morton, which she would keep secret from Alison to the end of her days.

'But I hadn't known you very long before I was telling you mine,' Alison went on. 'We've been through a lot together since those days, haven't we?'

'And knowing you, Alison, I don't doubt that there is more to come.'

'But meanwhile, it's you who is on the brink of an adventure,' said Alison with a grin.

Emma pictured the bespectacled little butterball of a man her American major was. 'I shouldn't think Major Wiseman has an adventurous bone in his body.'

'Then he's just right for you, isn't he, Emma dear?'

'Don't start planning my wedding reception, Alison! Al's a lonely widower who wants some company. I've only met him a few times, when he's come to the club for a Jewish meal. He misses his *gefilte* fish and chopped liver, he told me.'

'The dear man sounds right up your street. So when is the big night out to be?' Alison inquired, mimicking her Aunt Lottie. 'And what shall you wear? I'll scream if you say your best brown dress.'

'So shall I, Alison, if you don't stop teasing me. And

280

behaving like my mother. Can't you see I'm a bag of nerves about the whole thing? I've promised to have dinner with him at the Savoy, next Sunday night. He wants to hear the Carol Gibbons orchestra.'

'I doubt that they'll be playing on a Sunday night.'

'That's why I made the date for Sunday. It's a dance orchestra, isn't it? And I can't dance.'

Alison hooted with laughter. 'What a cunning creature you've turned out to be!'

'When it comes to men, I've never needed to be, have I?'

'But you're learning fast.'

'And there's nothing wrong with my best brown dress!'

'Except that you've had it for years. I haven't used those coupons you gave me, yet, so you can have them back. The ones Maxwell gave me, too. Buy yourself something fetching to wear.'

'I appreciate the offer, Alison. But you know as well as I do that the word fetching could never apply to me. And,' Emma added, 'if it did, I don't think Al would have asked me out. He said that what he likes about me is I'm not the showy type.'

An understatement if Alison had ever heard one! 'In that case, he wouldn't fancy me,' she said dryly. 'I can't wait to meet him, nevertheless.'

She was to do so sooner than she had anticipated. On the day of his date with Emma, Major Wiseman telephoned to tell her that a friend of his from home had turned up in London. Was it possible for Emma to bring along the cousin she lived with?

Alison was in the bath when the call came, and Emma pounded wildly on the bathroom door.

'If you refuse to come, I may have to go out with the two of them,' she panicked, when she had told Alison about the major's request.

'Calm down, Emma! And if you've left your boyfriend hanging on, go and tell him your cousin will come. I was going to Maxwell's cocktail party this evening but I don't mind in the least sharing your adventure, instead!'

'It will certainly be one for the two men, when they

find out my cousin is the famous Alison Plantaine,' said Emma before she fled to tell the major that his friend had a date.

Thus it was that Alison, after twelve sexless years, encountered the next man in her life. Major Wiseman's friend was as tall as the major was short, and as sensual-looking a male as Alison had ever seen. His immediate reaction to her was the same as hers to him. They knew they would end up in bed – and the sooner the better.

The physical attraction each had for the other crackled in the air from the moment their eyes first met. Emma and Major Wiseman could not have been unaware of it, and looked on uncomfortably while the pair they had brought together shook hands after being introduced. Even when they were not looking at each other the tension they gene-rated remained, though during dinner the conversation could not have been more prosaic.

Al Wiseman, whose family owned a catering business, provided a detailed account of what could go wrong when arranging a banquet. Colonel Clark, who was an advertis-ing agent in civilian life, reminisced about their shared schooldays in St Petersburg, Florida. Alison contributed some backstage anecdotes, and noted that Emma had retired into her shell.

But she emerged from it after the meal, when she and Alison went to powder their noses.

'You find the colonel attractive, don't you, Alison?'

'Who wouldn't?' Alison replied, too casually. 'And don't be so formal, Emma dear. His name is Donald.'

'What I'm scared of, Alison, is that you're not going to be formal enough; that before the evening is over, you're going to be calling him Don, and arranging to see him again. On your own.'

Alison was putting on lipstick, and paused with it in her hand. 'What's the matter with you, Emma? In the years we've lived together, I have gone out with lots of men. You've never tried to be my keeper – until now.'

Emma snapped her powder compact shut. 'Donald is married, Alison. Al told me on the phone this morning.

282

But I didn't think it mattered as we were going out in a foursome.'

'And it still doesn't,' Alison declared truthfully. The feeling Colonel Clark had aroused in her had nothing to do with permanence.

'I don't trust him, Alison.'

'You don't trust me, either, when it comes to men. Do you, Emma?'

It occurred to Emma then that, deep down, she – and Morton, too – had been waiting with trepidation for something like this to happen to Alison. Something like what? Emma asked herself. Something that could mean trouble for all three of them. And given Alison's impulsiveness, and her passionate nature, trouble in the shape of a man.

'What I don't trust is your judgement, Alison,' she replied.

'I'm not making a judgement,' said Alison lightly. 'What we are discussing isn't – in this case – important.'

Emma found this hard to relate to the sight of Alison and the colonel locked together on the small square of parquet that passed for a dance floor, at the club where they later found themselves.

Major Wiseman, who, like Emma, was the opposite of a nightbird, managed to stifle a yawn. 'I wonder who told Donald about this place? Me, I've been in London for months, and I didn't know dives like this existed here.'

But his friend was the sort who would know, Emma thought.

'Would you like a drink?' Al asked, glancing at the bottle of Vat 69 on the table, for which Donald had, without batting an eyelid, paid five pounds.

'I'm not one for drinking, like I told you at the Savoy.'

'That's something else you and I have in common,' said Al. 'You wanted to go straight home after dinner, didn't you, Emma?'

'How did you know?'

'Because you're my kind, hon. Which I knew the day I met you. And you oughta have let me get us a separate cab, like I wanted to, and see you home. Instead of feeling you had to do what Donald and your cousin wanted to do. I'm a softie myself, Emma, but not that much of one.'

Emma shrugged and smiled. She could not tell him that the only reason she had agreed to come here was to chaperone Alison, lest her wayward cousin lose her head and spend the night with the colonel. But Emma knew she was waging a losing battle; it was remarkable that Alison had remained faithful to Richard Lindemann for so long.

What she did not know was that Alison had, that evening, discovered that it was as possible for a woman, as for a man, to divorce her sexuality from her emotions; that the heart may remain true – as Alison's was to her son's father – though the body be traitorous. These were her thoughts while she enjoyed the sensual pleasure that Donald Clark stirred in her.

When, the following afternoon, she went to bed with him at the old-fashioned Bloomsbury hotel where he was spending his short leave, she did so without a pang of conscience about his wife, or the man whom she still loved. Never again would Alison Plantaine regard fidelity as a physical matter.

Her fleeting affair with Donald was to her a sexual education. Unlike her young German lover, Donald was a skilled and experienced one, and roused Alison to heights of passion she would not have thought it possible to bear without crying out.

'I envy your wife her sex life!' she joked to him one day, when they lay together panting with exhaustion.

Donald reached for his pack of Lucky Strikes, and lit one. 'To tell you the truth, sugar, I don't do with her the things I do with you. And that goes for smoking in bed, as well as everything else!'

He put his cigarette in a handy ashtray, and ran his tongue along Alison's satiny thighs. 'They say that for-bidden fruit tastes better, and I guess it's the truth.'

Alison laughed at his earthiness, though it would have seemed distasteful to her under other circumstances.

Then they heard the drone of a buzz-bomb, and held their breath. Would the missile stop buzzing while it was poised above the hotel roof? If it did, they would soon be blown to bits.

'In case this is the last chance I get to tell you, you're the best lay I've ever had,' Don said, while the bomb droned on, getting louder and louder.

'Thank you for the compliment,' said Alison, who had not heard the word 'lay' used in that context before.

The buzzing stopped abruptly and he pulled Alison against him.

'What's this? One more time before we say goodbye?' she said with bravado.

'Personally, I can't think of a nicer position to die in.'

When, a minute or two later, the explosion came, they were thrown out of bed, but suffered no damage. Donald helped Alison to her feet and went to straighten a framed print of an illustration from *Oliver Twist* that had swung sideways on the wall. 'I'm sorry for the poor devils who got it. But I'm sure glad it wasn't us!'

It struck Alison that what Donald had just said was probably the feeling experienced by every soldier who witnessed the death of his comrades on the battlefield; where lament for the fallen must surely mingle, like blood with the morning dew, with thankfulness for still being alive. But she refrained from sharing this thought with the colonel, whose few days of leave marked the end of his recuperation from a battle wound. He had made light of the slight limp that was its legacy, and had not allowed it to stop him from dancing.

'Why are we wasting time?' he said now. 'Before I know it, I'll be back riding in a tank!'

He swept her into his arms and returned her to the bed.

'The bomb interrupted our conversation,' she recalled.

'That wasn't all it interrupted,' he said, silencing her with a kiss.

'But I'd like to know why forbidden fruit tastes better,' she said when he allowed her to speak.

'I guess the answer to that, sugar, is that a guy just doesn't feel as free'n easy in bed, with his wife.'

'But why shouldn't he?' Alison turned to lie on her stomach, and cupped her face in her hands. 'Could it be because he is emotionally involved with her?' she said thoughtfully.

Donald was stroking her bottom. 'If you say so, sugar. But let's not get too cerebral, huh? We're here to have ourselves a good time.'

While he proceeded to teach her that making love was equally pleasurable when the participants were not face to face, Alison's mind detached itself from her body, and allowed her to analyse their uncomplicated physical delight in each other, though in every other way they were strangers.

It's because we are strangers, she thought, unimportant to each other's lives, that we are free to be our animal selves. And what they were so uninhibitedly doing was not lovemaking: love didn't enter into it. They were plainly and simply having sex.

The US Army allowed them to do so for only two more days.

'I guess it'll be a relief to you, not to have to put on your camouflage and come perform in my hotel room!' Donald said with a laugh, when he telephoned to tell Alison that his orders to proceed immediately to his new command had arrived.

'That cute little chambermaid I told you about asked me if I had a blind girlfriend,' he added.

Alison had put her dark glasses to good use again, to avoid being recognised when she entered and left Donald's hotel. 'You did plenty of performing yourself,' she said reminiscently.

'But who with, will go with me to my grave.'

'And I thank you for that.'

Their farewell had been as lighthearted as their *affaire*, Alison thought when she replaced the telephone receiver. There was a lot to be said for the philosophy Donald and his kind called 'no strings'.

No strings, no heartache, she reflected with satisfaction, and returned to the dining room humming a merry tune.

The two anxious faces that greeted her caused her to change the tune to 'Oh dear, what can the matter be?'

'What are you so happy about?' Emma asked her suspiciously.

Morton, who had joined them for a late supper, waited with bated breath for Alison's reply. Had that colonel chap just proposed to her? Emma had answered the telephone; the caller's identity was no secret.

Alison stopped humming and laughed ruefully. 'With you two, I can't win, can I? If I'm too cheerful, it worries you as much as it does when I'm in the depths of gloom!'

'And some of the things you've been overly cheerful about have, in the past, resulted in all three of us being consigned to the depths of gloom,' Morton answered. If the fellow did want to marry Alison, he would first have to divorce his wife – and not the least of it all was that Alison's reputation would be sullied in the process, Morton thought.

Then Alison went to kiss his cheek. Emma's too.

'Conscience kisses, no doubt,' Emma said.

'Call them what you will,' said Alison, who felt like dancing an exuberant jig. 'But for the information of my darling fusspots, that colonel chap – which Maxwell has insisted upon calling him since he learned of his existence – rang up to tell me he's been posted from London. And I'm unlikely ever to see him again.'

She had to laugh at their relieved expressions. 'It was just a pleasant interlude, my dears,' she said airily. 'Nothing more than that. Good while it lasted.'

She sat down at the table and helped herself to a large portion of stew, which she ate with a relish she had not displayed for years.

That 'cat that's been at the cream' look on her face could mean only one thing, Morton thought, studying her. He was looking at a woman sexually fulfilled.

Emma too recognised the signs and carefully avoided Morton's eye.

'I know what you are thinking,' Alison told them. 'I also know that I couldn't have more loyal and loving friends than you are to me. But there are some matters in which I must live my own separate life. The only man to whom I have ever totally belonged is long gone. And I am a normal, healthy woman.'

She poured herself some water and quaffed it as if it were wine. 'I have no intention of becoming habitually promiscuous, so have no fears on that account, but I can't promise you that I shall never do again what I have just done. If and when I do, it would be best for you two to turn a blind eye and let me get on with it.'

# CHAPTER FIVE

'DON'T FORGET about mother's seventieth birthday party next Sunday,' Conrad said when he telephoned for a chat with Emma.

'I'll be there, Conrad. I don't need reminding.'

'I thought perhaps you did.'

'Alison will be there, too. And what sort of remark is that?'

'The kind I sometimes feel impelled to make to you, nowadays, our Em. Unfortunately.'

'I see.'

Emma listened to the crackling on the long-distance line in the moment of awkward silence that followed, and visualised her brother's censorious expression. Since their father's death – was it really six years ago? – Conrad had assumed the role of head of the family and did his best to maintain family unity, as Lionel had.

'A person could be forgiven for thinking it's out of sight, out of mind, with you these days,' he said.

'I speak to Mam on the phone regularly.'

'But when did you last visit her? If my memory serves me correctly, it was before D-Day that you came.'

'And I've hardly had a spare minute since Alison got back from France. I was planning to come to Oldham then – but afterwards, it seemed more important to work at the canteen.'

'I see.'

'Don't keep saying I see! You don't see at all. When I'm not at the canteen, we do a lot of entertaining at the flat.'

'That doesn't mean you have to forget you've got a family,' said Conrad before he rang off.

It was with the bitter aftertaste of her brother's rebuke that Emma went north for the family celebration.

'He made me feel terrible,' she said to Alison on the train. 'I couldn't make him understand.'

'And you never will, darling. Conrad wears blinkers when he views family commitment. For him, everything stands or falls by it. He hasn't the slightest idea of the inner conflicts people like you and I suffer because of it. I used to think you were like him, Emma, but you're certainly not any more.'

'Well, Conrad stayed put, didn't he? The conflict you're talking about couldn't arise for him. But I think it began in me when I had to decide whether or not to come and live with you in London.'

'And in me,' said Alison, 'when Maxwell offered me my first West End role and it meant leaving the Plantaine Players. If you ask me, Emma, the choice between family and self probably accounts for more unhappiness and guilt than anyone would imagine. And in the end, what is it all about? A family is just a group of people who happen to be related by the accident of birth, some of whom may not even like each other; yet they're called upon to make sacrifices – and feel guilty if they don't – on each other's behalf. It doesn't make sense.'

'Tell that to Conrad!'

'If he makes any snide remarks to you on the subject, I might. And I'm absolutely determined, Emma, that no such pressure shall be put on Richard. I want our boy to feel that his life is his own. That in that respect he need show no loyalty to us.'

'I get the impression from his letters, Alison, that Richard is already a very independent child.'

Emma's impression of her niece Janet was quite the opposite and Alison shared it when she chatted with Conrad's daughter at the party. There seemed to be no activity, apart from school and elocution lessons, in which Janet engaged outside her home.

'Don't you ever go and play with your friends?' Alison asked when the little girl, whose organdie frock she had admired, revealed that she and her mother had made it together, and that they spent their weekends either reading or sewing.

'I don't let her,' Zelda chipped in. 'Her friends live on the other side of the main road.'

'Mam's afraid I'll get run over,' Janet explained. 'But Katie and Beth don't get run over when they come to my house to play with me.'

Was there a rebellious streak in this outwardly placid child? Alison wondered, and hoped that there was.

Lottie, who had somehow managed to blow out all the candles on her cake, had had time to recover her breath and told Janet, 'Your mother knows best.'

'I wish I had a pound note,' said Clara's plain-faced daughter, 'for every time Grandma has said that to me.'

'And it's a pity you need telling, Lila,' was her mother's retort. 'The last time was when you wanted to volunteer for the ATS the minute you were eighteen.'

'And Dad would have let me.'

Clara gave her portly husband a despairing glance. 'He never did know how to say no to you.'

'So what can you do?' Lew said mildly. It was his stock reply.

'Instead of being in uniform, I'm spending the war clerking in a hospital, which exempts me from the Forces,' Lila told Alison. 'And the only boys I get to meet are ill in bed!'

'My grand-daughter Lila,' said Lottie, 'is boy mad.'

And made up in vivacity for what she lacked in beauty, Alison thought. Despite her plainness, Lila would not find it hard to captivate a man. Janet, on the other hand, was a lovely looking little girl who radiated nothing. Where was the liveliness that had once been present in her? It was as though something had stifled the child.

Alison watched Lottie cut a large chunk of birthday cake to be sent to Percy in his prison camp, and listened to a discussion on how best to pack it so it would not arrive in crumbs. But her mind remained on Janet, to whom she was inexplicably drawn. Inexplicably because Janet had aroused no special tenderness in her until now. But it was a long time since Alison last visited the family. She had been to Oldham only once since the war began.

In the interim, apart from Percy's removal from their midst, nothing had changed. Lottie had lost none of her matriarchal ebullience. Nor Clara her mercenary attitudes; her admiration of the garnet brooch Alison had given Lottie for her birthday had included a remark about how much it must have cost. Conrad and Zelda seemed as devoted as they had always been. But Alison sensed that they sometimes quarrelled about their child, and it was not difficult to understand why. She could not envisage Conrad approving of his wife's keeping their daughter tied to her apron strings.

That's why I feel for Janet, Alison thought now. Because once, though the reason was different, I too was the cause of quarrels between my parents. But I didn't get diminished by it. I did what I wanted to do – and became my father's girl.

She glanced at Janet, who was beside Lila at the piano, turning over the pages for her as she played 'Home Sweet Home'. Janet, Alison instinctively knew, was the kind who thrived on peace. A good little girl who would fall over backwards not to upset anybody, and especially not her own parents. But Alison had the feeling that she was, too, a child with a mind of her own.

'Cut me another bit of birthday cake, Janet,' Lila requested when she finished playing the tune and the adults were applauding.

'I'll do it,' Zelda said.

'Why can't I, Mam?'

'Grandma's cake knife is very sharp. You might cut yourself — '

'Don't be ridiculous, Zelda!' Conrad thundered.

'It's all right, Daddy,' Janet said. 'I don't mind letting Mam do it — '

'But I mind, Janet! Pick up the knife and slice your cousin a piece of cake.'

292

Janet did as she was bid. Zelda hovered anxiously over her. Conrad looked on, tight lipped.

'My brother's turned into a tyrant,' Emma whispered to Alison. 'I pity poor Zelda, if he's like this all the time.'

Janet's the one to pity, Alison thought, recalling the times she had been caught up in her parents' verbal flak. Though she agreed with Conrad – a girl of ten did not need protecting from a cake knife – scenes like this were bad for a child.

'Mind how you carve through the icing – it's like rock, Janet,' Zelda said nervously.

'And don't break it to pieces, it cost me a fortune on the black market,' Clara added.

Then Janet let the knife slip and cut her finger, and Conrad and Zelda began a shouting match.

Emma took a handkerchief from her cuff and bandaged the cut.

'It needs iodine on it, Emma,' Zelda briefly paused to say before continuing to tell her husband what she thought of him.

'Is this my birthday party, or a madhouse!' Lottie exclaimed as Lila departed to rummage in the first-aid box.

'Bring the lint and the scissors and some sticking plaster, as well as the iodine,' Zelda called after her. 'And perhaps this will be a lesson to you!' she flung at Conrad.

'What will it take to give a lesson to you?'

'If you'd listened to your mother, you wouldn't have had an accident,' Lottie told Janet.

'But my daddy said I should slice the cake, and I never know which of them to listen to.'

After Emma had dealt with the injury to Zelda's satisfaction, Lottie rapped her knuckles on the table and called for order. 'Can we get on with the concert, now? Lila's played her piece on the piano and it's Janet's turn to entertain us. She's not getting out of doing a recitation because she's got a plaster on her hand.'

'I don't want to get out of it, Grandma. I love doing recitations.'

Alison was enthralled by what followed. Janet's rendering of a comical Lancashire monolgue was not just a recitation but a performance. With a table napkin tied mill-girl fashion around her fair curls, and an antimacassar slung about her shoulders to serve as a shawl, she planted herself on the hearthrug and displayed a drollery that reminded Alison of Gracie Fields. For an encore, she removed her improvised costume, fixed her gaze tragically upon the window, and gave them Juliet's balcony speech.

'I played Juliet in a reading we did at my elocution class,' she said afterwards when Alison congratulated her.

'And it wouldn't surprise me if you followed in my footsteps, young lady.'

'God forbid!' was the family's united response.

'My daughter on the stage is the last thing I need,' Conrad capped it.

'But an actress is what I want to be, Daddy. When we had to write a composition called "Myself Ten Years Hence", that's what I wrote about.'

'You must come to London, as soon as the war is over, and watch me from the wings,' Alison encouraged her.

'She'll do nothing of the kind,' Conrad declaimed.

Alison saw Janet's brief animation fade, and put a hand on her shoulder. 'If she's destined for the stage, Conrad, nothing will stop her. Not even you. And in my opinion, Janet has what it takes.'

'Over my dead body she'll be an actress,' Conrad replied.

'Mine, too,' Zelda said with feeling.

'Haven't you done enough damage in the family, Alison?' Clara demanded. 'Taking my sister away from us?'

'I wasn't taken away. I went of my own accord,' said Emma.

'But who put leaving home into your head?' Clara flashed. 'The same person who put it into my Percy's head that he should go against me and visit his horrible other grandparents, that's who! Not to mention how the whole family was embroiled in the cover-up, when she made her big mistake.'

Lila pricked up her ears. 'What cover-up?' she inquired, but received no answer. 'What big mistake?'

'As you did the same,' Alison crisply told Clara, 'you are not in a position to rebuke me.'

'You were old enough to know better. I wasn't thirty-two.'

'This is like a Sherlock Holmes mystery!' Lila exclaimed. 'What did they both do?'

Let themselves be seduced, Lottie thought with a reminiscent shudder. 'Who can remember?' she lied to Lila. 'In a family, things get buried with the years.'

'I don't think of it as a mistake,' Alison declared. 'I've never regretted it – how can I? And how, Clara, can you?'

Each of them had gained from it a beloved son and their eyes briefly met.

Clara's husband, who was reading the Talmud with which he distracted himself on such family occasions, glanced up from the book. 'Will someone please tell me what my wife and Alison are talking about?'

'Go back to your book, love,' Clara said to him with a tolerant smile. She had not told him that her first marriage was the shotgun kind and nothing would be gained by telling him now.

'Can we stop digging up the past and talk about the future?' Conrad interceded. 'I'd better make it clear to Alison, here and now, that I won't have her influencing my daughter.'

Zelda drew Janet close to her and said belligerently, 'Alison had better not try.'

'When I was your age, love, I fancied being a fireman,' Conrad told the child. 'Like nearly every little boy does – those who don't want to drive a bus or a train when they grow up!'

But not every little girl was endowed with the talent Alison had discerned in Janet. Would she one day do what her great-uncle, Alison's father, did? Break free of her conventional Jewish background and enter Alison's theatrical world? If she did, she could rely on Alison's support. Meanwhile, Alison would hold her tongue.

Emma was relieved – and surprised – that Alison had the good sense to do so, but was beset by a feeling of family trouble to come. Here we go again, she said to herself. And, as always, Alison would be in the middle of it, though several years might pass before it came about.

# CHAPTER SIX

EMMA'S RELATIONSHIP with Major Wiseman, though he had not so much as held her hand, progressed to his becoming a regular visitor to the flat. With time, he warmed to Alison. There was nobody whom she could not charm if she set out to do so, though she had to work hard to counteract the major's initial impression of her.

The American uniform was not the only one seen at the flat at that stage of the war. Casual invitations to drop in, issued by Emma to the young people she befriended at the Balfour Club, were not forgotten. Alison also offered hospitality to the assorted soldiers, sailors and airmen she encountered here or there.

'This place is getting to be like a Forces canteen!' Morton grumbled one Sunday evening, when he arrived uninvited and could not find a vacant chair.

'Who is the officer who let me in?' he inquired, glancing at Al Wiseman who was now dispensing drinks. 'He looks as if he owns the place!'

'He's someone I met at the club,' said Emma, turning pink.

'So you've got a boyfriend, have you, our Em? Don't tell me you are going to end up a GI bride!' Morton joked despite a sudden stab of alarm.

'When you stop being ridiculous, Max, I'll introduce you to him. He's a nice man. I'm sure you and he will hit it off.'

On the contrary, Morton and the major took an immediate dislike to each other.

Though it was Alison with whom Morton was in love, Emma had become part of his life. The possibility that she might not return to London, after her father's death, had brought home to him how much he valued her. That Emma

297

might one day be removed from his scene by family obligations up north had remained his abiding fear. But he had not expected her removal to be effected by a man, and Major Wiseman posed that threat.

Al resented Morton's proprietary air with Emma. Nor did he like the way Emma bowed to Morton's judgement. As though, Al thought, Morton were some kind of god. He had not, of course, witnessed one of their heated differences of opinion, but even if he had, Morton's taking it for granted that Emma would do this or that for him was sufficient to cause Al's hackles to rise.

They had initially done so with regard to Alison, for the same reason, but Al had by now resigned himself to the inequity of the cousins' relationship. Alison clearly adored Emma, and actresses were too busy feeding their own egos to consider others, Al had finally said to himself. A person had to make allowances for Alison. But there was no way he could countenance Morton. The guy was nothing special, though Emma did not seem to agree.

The day came when Al realised, with a sinking heart, just how special Morton was to Emma. He happened to be in the vicinity of the flat, and decided to drop in.

Emma did not seem too pleased to see him.

'So I've caught you with a duster in your hand,' he said with a grin. 'So what? I've just had a good idea – why don't you let the chores go hang, Emma, and come have lunch with me? I'll take you to a good "deli" I've found.'

'Thanks for asking me, Al. But I like to potter around at home, on the days when I'm not at the canteen.'

'OK. You can give me a sandwich here.'

'The jar of peanut butter you gave us is all used up.'

'So for once I'll make myself swallow some of that scrambled dried egg. The way you British eat it, on toast.'

Emma smiled, then avoided his eye.

What's the matter with her? Al thought. Emma was usually the most hospitable little lady he'd ever met. He suddenly had the feeling she was trying to get rid of him. Since he got here, she had glanced three times at her wristwatch.

'You're expecting someone else, aren't you?' he said in his direct manner. It had to be that.

'Not exactly.'

'But you want me gone? Just in case?'

'Don't be daft,' said Emma, though it was true. 'It's just that Max said he might pop in. His dentist is near here, and he has an appointment today. And you don't particularly enjoy his company, do you?'

'You can say that again! What time is his dental appointment?'

'He didn't say.'

'Are you telling me you're gonna stay cooped up here all day, when you don't even know for sure the guy is coming? Boy! Do you let him mess you around!'

The reason she had given for not going out for lunch was just an excuse, Al registered in the silence that followed. He allowed himself, now, to see what he had not wanted to see: Emma was in love with Morton. And the guy didn't even know she was around! Except when it suited him.

Suddenly, Al was filled with compassion for her, and his animosity toward Morton rose within him until he thought he would burst with it. If the guy were here now, Al would sock him on the nose!

Oh, no, I wouldn't, he thought, and forced himself to simmer down. It could mean 'curtains' for himself and Emma, if he brought matters to a head now. But the war was not yet over. Al still had time to show Emma where her happiness lay – in Florida, with him. But he mustn't rush things. And would keep to himself what he'd just tumbled to.

# CHAPTER SEVEN

ALISON WAS still playing in *Home and Beauty*. Maugham's comedy was a fast-moving romp, which left Alison and her two leading men drained every night. By the end of November, when the play had been running for three months, all Alison wanted to do after the curtain fell was go home and get some sleep.

'There's a Yank askin' to see you, Miss Plantaine,' the stagedoor-keeper told her, while she was removing her make-up on the last Saturday of the month.

Alison sagged at the prospect of seeing anyone, right now. 'Did you get his name?' It could be one of a score of young GIs whom she had rashly invited to have a drink with her backstage. She could not even remember their names.

'He said to tell you he's Josh Baxter Junior.'

Alison sprang to life. 'Please ask him to come in!' She had not known that the Baxters' son was in England.

She wiped the cold-cream from her face in double-quick time, put on some lipstick and was standing waiting to greet the lanky red-haired youth when he entered the dressing room.

For a moment, neither spoke.

Alison was choked with emotion, though she knew not why.

Josh Jr was overwhelmed by her presence. Rick's mom was as gorgeous close-up as she was when you saw her on the stage, he thought.

Then both spoke at once and laughter followed.

'Welcome to London, Josh!' Alison said. 'When did you arrive in England?'

'I'm not allowed to say, Miss Plantaine.'

'Of course you're not. And I ought not to have asked you.'

'But I can tell you I'm based not too far from Salisbury Plain. And I guess I never expected I'd get to see Stonehenge! London, either. I oughta have let you know I was coming to town. I sure have a nerve, walking in on you this way!'

'I'm delighted to see you, Josh.'

'I oughta have called you. But when I got given a thirty-six-hour pass, out of the blue, I just hoofed it to the train station, fast, with the rest of the guys.'

'Did you call my flat, when you arrived in town?'

'Sure. Rick gave me your phone number, in case I found myself in England after I was shipped out. I called you several times, but there was no reply, which didn't jell with what Rick told me.'

'Who is Rick?'

'Your son, of course.'

Alison had thought it must be a young GI she had perhaps met somewhere and given her phone number. 'I see,' she said with a smile.

'Here's me coming to give you the lowdown on him, an' all, and his mom has forgotten who he is!' Josh said.

'I had no idea Richard had abbreviated his name — '

'Obviously,' Josh said with a grin. 'I was joking, Miss Plantaine.'

'But you can give me the lowdown on him, all the same.'

'Could we go someplace to eat, while we talk? I grabbed a frankfurter at Rainbow Corner before the show, but my innards are growling again. I sure did enjoy the show, by the way. Rick never told us his mom was a great comedy actress.'

Alison went behind the screen to change. 'She isn't. But a good actress can play any role. I was brought up on Shakespeare, Josh, which, of course, includes comedy. But I prefer dramatic roles, and have always felt more at home in them.'

When Alison rejoined him, the boy gaped. 'We are sure going to cause a stir, if I take you to eat at the Stagedoor Canteen in that get-up!'

Alison's svelte black velvet evening gown had taken his breath away; the cleavage it exposed, more so.

Alison patted her chignon, and draped a white fox cape around her shapely shoulders.

'If you would like to take me there and cause a stir, fine, Josh, but wouldn't you enjoy a home-cooked meal, more?'

'Are you kidding? Rick told us that his Aunt Emma is a great cook. He also said she's always home – that's why I was surprised when nobody answered your phone.'

'My cousin is on duty at a services club tonight,' Alison explained. 'But she will have prepared some supper for me before she left. I expect my son also told you that his mother can't cook,' she added with chagrin.

'I don't recall him mentioning that.' Josh then recalled that Rick rarely mentioned his mother at all. If she were mine, I'd be bragging about her all the time, he thought.

'Emma's casseroles for one are invariably enough to feed three,' Alison assured him, 'so please don't think that inviting you home to eat with me will mean I shall go hungry. There won't be much meat, of course, but Emma does wonders with vegetables.'

Outside the stagedoor, Josh watched Alison sign programmes and autograph books. Was this really the mom of the boy who had become like another kid brother to him? It was as hard for Josh to believe as was his own awkward presence beside her. When he told the folks back home how people had waited on the sidewalk in the rain, just to get a glimpse of her leaving the theatre, they'd be as awestruck as he was. Rick sure had come from a different world than the Baxters'! Josh thought, helping his famous companion into a cab.

'What are you smiling at?' Alison wanted to know.

'It's just dawned on me why Rick didn't find it easy to settle down with us.'

'Didn't he?'

'No. But he's fine and dandy by now.'

Alison gave the cab-driver her Albion Gate address. 'It's a relief to know that, Josh,' she resumed their conversation. 'One can't really know from telephone calls and letters.'

'You don't have a thing to worry about, Miss Plantaine. Though I guess you won't recognise him when he gets back and not just because he's grown!'

Josh recalled what Alison's son had been like when he arrived in America. A little 'square' wasn't in it! he thought with a reminiscent smile. Though the Baxter kids had been raised to know their manners, and like their parents spoke with the Boston accent other Americans called 'snobby', they had seemed uncouth beside young Richard Plantaine. And Josh, who was then the age Rick now was, had sure felt it, he remembered. He had forgotten how posh Rick's accent once was, until he heard Alison speak. He'd also forgotten how unmercifully he and his kid brother and sister had teased Rick about it – and now wished that they hadn't. But Rick had not been too nice to them, either.

Alison was pointing out places of interest, *en route* to the flat. But she was thinking her private thoughts.

She had learned, via the comings and goings of the soldiers she and Emma entertained at the flat, that a sudden short leave invariably, nowadays, preceded being sent into battle. The war was still far from won, and rumour had it that casualties in Europe were so heavy, a constant supply of replacement troops was required.

Alison had little doubt that Josh Baxter Jr was headed for that supply line. The word 'replacements' had caused her to shudder when she first heard it employed in that sense. Surveying the vulnerable lad who was surely to be one translated it all the more for her into human terms, and she was stricken by the horror of war as she had not been even when she toured the army camps in France. Though visiting the wounded soldiers at the hospital near Caen had broken her heart, she had not then seen their plight in its wider context, as she did now. Nor appreciated the expediency and expendability with which a whole generation of young men – German ones included – were being fed into the cold machinery of war.

Impulsively, she reached out and took Josh's hand. He looked surprised, but allowed her to hold it.

303

'I guess being with me brings Rick closer to you,' he said with an awkward smile. 'I mean him living with my family, an' all.'

This had probably accounted for her emotion when he entered the dressing room, Alison thought, and allowed him to think it was why she had taken his hand in hers. She could not tell him that she was comforting him in advance for what might be in store for him, or how thankful she was that her boy was too young to fight in the war.

'You will stay with Emma and me while you're in London, of course,' she said.

'I was hoping you'd invite me to. But I'll only need a bed for tonight. I have to return to Base by midnight tomorrow.'

'Then we must make the most of your short leave, Josh. If you'd like to do some sightseeing tomorrow, that's what we'll do. There's been a lot of bomb damage, of course, but Buckingham Palace and the Tower of London are still there!'

Emma returned from her stint at the club to find Alison eating supper in the kitchen with Josh. She was unable to stop herself from embracing him when she learned who he was.

'I guess you're just like I knew you would be, ma'am!' he said with a grin, when she released him.

'Is that a compliment, or an insult?' she wanted to know. 'What has our boy been saying to you about me?'

'Never you mind!' he teased her. Rick's aunt was the kind you teased. His mom definitely was not.

Though Josh no longer felt awkward with Alison, he was unable to relax with her entirely. She was what his mom would call a personage, and had not lost that aura even when she changed, before supper, into her housecoat.

'And am I as you expected me to be, Josh?' Alison inquired as though she had read his thoughts.

Josh was putting away his second helping of Emma's apple pie, and paused to consider the question. 'I guess I didn't know what to expect,' he said eventually. 'I mean, Rick keeps a photo of you on his bed-table, like he does of his aunt. So I knew you were a beautiful lady —'

'Thank you,' said Alison when he paused.

Josh glanced at Emma, who was donning her pinafore. 'Rick didn't actually describe either of you. As people, I mean. But somehow I built up a picture of his aunt – which included what she's doing right now,' Josh added with a smile, when Emma began washing up. 'Homey is the word for it, I guess.'

Josh turned to look at Alison. 'I knew you were an actress, of course, Miss Plantaine. And I can remember my mom seeming quite excited when she told us whose child was coming to be our wartime evacuee. A friend of hers had seen you in a play on Broadway, Mom said. I was only a kid, but which American kid hasn't heard of Broadway? From then on, I guess for me you were surrounded by bright lights!' Josh said with a laugh. 'But it didn't help me to know what you were really like.'

Alison laughed too. And hid her chagrin. What Josh had just said doubtless was so for his parents, too. To the family with whom her son had lived for more than five years, his mother had remained a glamorous myth. It was possible that by now she was no more than that to Richard. Unlike Emma, she had never been part of the everyday fabric of his life. When Richard, all those miles away, suffered a pang of homesickness, it was Emma of whom he would think, for Emma, not Alison, reminded him of home. What other interpretation could Alison put upon what she had just learned?

Later, when their young guest was enjoying the luxury of a civilian bathroom, Alison shared her thoughts with Emma.

'You can't have your cake and eat it, Alison – as they say up north,' Emma declared.

Alison smiled wanly. 'They say it down south, too.'

'Then you shouldn't need telling, should you?'

They were in Richard's room, making up the bed for Josh. Emma paused with a pillow case in her hand and surveyed Alison's forlorn expression.

'If love were all, you'd be the perfect mother, Alison.'

'Thank you for saying that, Emma.'

305

'I said it because it's true. I know what a sacrifice you made when you sent Richard to America.'

'And if love were all,' said Alison pensively, 'I'd have let Maxwell down and let my career go hang, and stayed in Berlin with Richard's father. Or he would have abandoned his political activities, and come with me to England. But love is only one aspect of life – albeit the most painful – as I've learned too well.'

Alison left Emma to tuck in the sheets, and absently fingered a china rabbit, which with her son's other nursery ornaments was still on his chest-of-drawers.

'Acting is part of me and my life, as his idealism was of Richard Lindemann and his life. And, love or not, a person cannot be other than what they are.'

Emma smiled dryly. 'They can't change their nature, if that's what you mean. Or you wouldn't have wandered off and left me to finish making the bed.'

'Is that some kind of crack, Emma?'

'How could it be, Alison? After we've lived together for so many years. I was just illustrating – unnecessarily – that you are one kind of person and I'm another.'

'And what has that to do with what we are discussing?'

'It returns us to where we started from: that if love were all, you'd be the perfect mother. But as you said, Alison, a person can't be other than what they are, and there's more to motherhood than you are equipped to give.'

Emma put the blankets on the bed and tucked them snugly into place. 'Don't look so downcast, Alison. It isn't your fault that it isn't in you to give Richard the undivided attention you give to your work.'

'For which I am now paying the price.'


The following morning, Alison telephoned Morton, who immediately placed himself, his car, and his petrol allowance at Josh Baxter Jr's disposal. This fitted Josh's pre-impression of Morton. Nor was he surprised when Emma declined the invitation to accompany them and stayed at home to cook lunch, or that Alison had said after breakfast that if nobody minded she would go back to bed.

*My Uncle Maxwell is a great fixer*, Josh recalled Rick once saying, and throughout the time he was in Morton's company, Josh was aware of that quality in the man. Morton had called a parliamentary acquaintance, who gave them morning coffee at the House of Commons. And, though the Albert Hall was closed that day, Morton was allowed to enter to show Josh its splendid interior. Josh had the feeling that had he asked to be shown around Buckingham Palace, or to meet Winston Churchill, it would have presented no problem to Morton.

Morton had arrived to collect Josh, bearing delicacies to supplement the luncheon menu – including some fresh eggs, which rationing had put in the rare-delicacy class. Only Emma gave a thought to how much it must have cost him to give the boy a feast, at black-market prices, and to how incongruous it was to start a meal with egg mayonnaise and smoked salmon – which Josh said Americans called 'lox' – when the main course was the make-do, wartime fare she was able to provide.

After lunch, Josh elected to spend the rest of the day beside the fire. If this was Rick's family, he thought, though it wasn't the usual kind it sure was a fine one. Then thoughts of his own family in faraway New England brought an ache to his throat.

Morton went to chat with Emma while she made them some tea, leaving Josh briefly alone with Alison in the drawing room.

'I guess my folks will be sitting down to breakfast right now,' he said, glancing at the clock.

Alison saw yearning for home written in his expression, and put a comforting hand on his shoulder.

'You're a nice lady, ma'am,' he said gruffly. Sitting cosily with her like this, he was able to forget she was a famous actress, to think of her as just Rick's mom.

'And you are a brave lad,' Alison replied.

'I guess that's how it looked to everyone back home – me volunteering, an' all. And I have to admit I thought I was brave. But I don't feel that way now it's coming to the crunch.'

Alison recalled thinking during the last war, when her cousin Conrad was on embarkation leave, that if she were a boy and had to be a soldier she would not find the courage to go into battle. But somehow the boys had, and were doing so this time.

'At least in this war you know what you are fighting for,' she said to Josh. 'Those who fought in the last one didn't.'

'That's what my dad told me, Miss Plantaine. On my last furlough, before I was shipped out. He sat up late talking to me one night, like as if I wasn't just one of his kids any longer, as though he was suddenly seeing me as a man.'

Josh gazed into the fire and saw again the big, shabby kitchen that was the most lived-in room in the Baxters' house. His father could afford to buy new furniture and everything, as Mr Aaronson, his partner had, over and over again, in his home in Brookline. He could have moved closer to Boston where his office was, but Josh's parents preferred to live quietly in the small-town atmosphere of West Newton as they always had. Josh couldn't imagine his mother being happy without the shabby old furniture she would never throw out, any more than he could imagine Mrs Aaronson *not* throwing it out. And that included the ancient deal table with kids' names carved on it, where he and his father had sat drinking root beer and talking, on the last night of Josh's furlough.

'What are you thinking?' Alison asked him gently.

'That happiness means different things to different people,' he said, recalling Mrs Aaronson arriving for dinner with the Baxters wearing one of her two fur coats. Mary Baxter had never wanted one.

'And of what my dad said to me, that night: "You're fighting for a free world. So go to it, Junior!" Even though he called me Junior, like he always has, I felt he was seeing me as a man.'

'He must be very proud of you, Josh. Your mother, too.'

The wintry afternoon had darkened to dusk and Alison went to draw the blackout curtains and switch on the lamps. 'At this time of year, the days seem to get shorter and shorter. It's certainly fireside weather.'

'It's great to sit beside a fireside again, Miss Plantaine.'

'But it isn't much fun for a soldier on leave, is it? We're touched that you chose to spend your leave with us, instead of finding yourself a pretty girl and having some fun.'

'I've got me a nice little ATS corporal, where I'm based,' Josh replied, with a wink. 'So don't give it another thought. It was Rick's folks I came to London to see, and I'm sure glad I did. And I thank you for all your kindness, ma'am.'

'I need no thanks, Josh. At the weekends, this flat is often full of young people like yourself to whom we enjoy offering hospitality. So don't be surprised if, later, some of them drop in and make themselves at home.'

'What happened to your cat?' he asked irrelevantly. 'Rick told me you had one.'

'It finally died of old age. We didn't upset Richard by letting him know. The reason we didn't get another is that Emma is out a good deal more these days than she used to be. She doesn't think it fair to leave a domestic animal so much on its own.'

'That sounds just like her.'

'And I have to confess,' said Alison ruefully, 'that it was a very lonely cat before Emma came to live with me.' Nor was it just the cat that had been lonely, she reflected. Emma's coming had changed both their lives – which were by now so interwoven, it would take something drastic to tear them apart.

'I was about to say – when you asked me about the cat – that you are a very special guest to us,' she said, emerging from her thoughts and giving Josh a warm smile. 'Compared with what your family is doing for our boy, having you for a weekend is nothing at all.'

'I wish you could meet my mom,' Josh said.

'Maybe, one day, I shall.'

'She's a beautiful person, Miss Plantaine.'

And that's a beautiful way for a boy to feel about his mother, Alison thought. The snapshots of Mary Baxter which Josh had shown them were of a dumpy-looking little woman. But Josh had meant the woman herself, not her shell, and Alison could wish for nothing better than that her own son would, when he grew up, feel that way about her.

# CHAPTER EIGHT

WHEN NEWS of the Battle of the Ardennes, that had preceded Christmas 1944, filtered through to England, Alison feared that Josh Baxter Jr might have been in its midst.

'He said he would call us,' she reminded Emma and Morton, 'but we didn't hear from him. And now we know why.'

'What we actually know is nothing,' Morton said, though he shared her fear.

'Where else would he have been sent? And what a bloody battle that must have been.'

Morton saw that Alison's eyes had filled with tears, and handed her his handkerchief. 'You could be weeping for no reason, my darling.'

'And let us hope she is,' Emma said.

'I am weeping for all the boys,' Alison told them. 'The German ones, too. Every one of them is somebody's son.'

'But on the Germans, I wouldn't waste my tears,' said Major Wiseman, who was wishing he had chosen some other time to drop in.

'They might be our enemy, but they are still human beings, Al,' Alison said quietly.

'Tell that to the Jewish refugees, Alison! Also to the people in the occupied countries who've stood up to them – and been tortured for it.'

Al's face had coloured with feeling and Emma put a hand on his arm. 'That's enough of that, Al.'

She was not surprised when he gave her an astonished look. Al did not know that a German had fathered Alison's child; that she had learned, first-hand, that not all Germans were Nazis; that for Alison the war was against Hitler and his disciples, not the whole German people.

311

'The fire's going out,' said Morton, after sharing a glance with Emma that told her that he was thinking what she was.

Al got up from his chair and put some coal on the fire. If he weren't here, Emma would have done it, he thought with disgust; Morton would not deign to lift a finger!

Alison returned the conversation to Josh. 'I felt so drawn to that boy.'

'How could any of us not have felt drawn to him,' Emma said, 'when our boy is with his family?'

'Exactly,' Morton endorsed.

'While Josh was with us, it was as if we had joined hands with them across the miles,' Emma declared.

Al Wiseman, who was made by this intimate exchange to feel even more superfluous than Morton's company always made him feel, managed not to show it.

'I guess this war has brought our two countries close like never before,' he said, 'Being based here has sure been an eye-opener to me. I used to think the British were cold and unfriendly.'

'How many had you met?' Morton inquired crisply.

'I hadn't met any.'

'Then how could you possibly form an opinion?'

'An opinion it wasn't. It was acceptance of a legend.'

'We're not short of legends about Americans,' said Morton with a crusty smile. 'And one of them has, for me, been proved true.'

'Like which, for instance?' Al rapped.

'The one about you chaps thinking just because you wear American uniform, every English woman you meet will fall at your feet.'

'I should only be so lucky,' said Al, looking at Emma.

Emma was, as ever, distressed by their animosity, and embarrassed on her own account. 'If you two men are going to argue – again – I don't want to hear it,' she told them.

Alison came to her aid. 'And what are such legends, but hearsay?' she declared with derision.

'Which prejudices people in advance,' said Emma. 'The one time I was in New York — '

'New York is not America,' Al cut in. 'As I've told you before.'

'But it could have been Timbuctoo, for all I cared, and the people I rubbed shoulders with were just the natives to me.'

'Don't say that to a New Yorker,' Al advised her. 'Though I can see how that city would seem like a jungle to a lady like you. But Florida — '

'About Florida you have already told me enough to write a travelogue, Al! I feel as if I know personally every palm tree on your local beach. And every street in St Petersburg — '

'But mine is the nicest.'

'I am trying to say, Al, that if I ever go to America again, I'll see the people as individuals, which I certainly didn't the last time. I won't think that because they're American, they are bound to be over-friendly. Or that everyone lives like the people do in a Hollywood film.'

'Again I should be so lucky,' Al said. 'I've wanted a swimming pool all my life.'

'Don't make fun of what Emma has said,' Alison rebuked him. 'It's quite true that films are where the British get their impressions of America and Americans from.'

Al rolled his eyes, comically. 'Do you mean she mistook me for Eddie Cantor?'

'Eddie Cantor has a waistline,' Emma said, eyeing the place where Al's had once been.

'But joking apart,' Morton declaimed to Al, 'if the war's done nothing else, it's allowed some of our people to get to know some of yours. And vice versa.'

'Which isn't such a good thing in every case,' Al replied unpleasantly.

'One has to take the rough with the smooth,' Morton countered in the same tone.

'You're telling me!'

'And God help us all,' Emma intervened, 'if you two are a typical example of "hands across the sea"! Fortunately you are not, or how could our two countries possibly fight a war together? And now, if everyone will excuse me, I'm going to make some tea.'

She had gone before the others had time to utter.

Al, who had never seen Emma angry before, looked like a naughty child ticked off by its mother. His chubby countenance had crumpled visibly. He took off his spectacles and polished them, then replaced them and looked at Alison uncertainly.

'I should go after her,' Alison advised him.

'She might throw me out of the kitchen.'

'I doubt it.'

He shot an acrimonious glance at Morton, before departing.

'Why are you so nasty to poor Al, Maxwell?' Alison demanded the moment they were alone.

'You could ask him the same question, with regard to me!'

'But which came first, the chicken or the egg? As Al is such a mild-mannered man with everyone but you, there's no need for you to answer that question!'

Morton smiled sourly. 'Which of us spoke the first sharp word to the other is debatable. But I assure you that our antipathy is entirely mutual. For some reason I am, to the major, as a red rag to a bull — '

'And he to you. I want to know why.'

'I should have thought that would be plain to you, Alison. He isn't good enough for our Em.'

'That isn't for you to say, Maxwell. You are neither her father nor her brother.'

'Her father is dead and her brother is not here. Shall you and I stand by, Alison, and see our dear Emma make what could be the big mistake of her life?'

Morton jettisoned his dead cigar in an ashtray. 'Emma may, as she says, see Americans differently now she has got to know some personally. I myself have great respect for the American people – or I would not have thought it right to send Richard to the States. But that doesn't mean I think Emma would settle happily for the rest of her days in Florida.'

'St Petersburg sounds like a pleasant place.'

'It probably is. I quite liked Miami when I visited it.'

314

'It's nowhere near Miami. Al said it's in what they call the Bay area. But the geography of Florida has nothing to do with what we are talking about!' said Alison impatiently.

'I was about to say that pleasant though the major's hometown may be, the American way of life is different from ours, and Emma, at her age, would not find it easy to adapt to it. But by then she would be Wiseman's wife, and it would be too late. Nor is he worthy of her, as I've already said.'

'Emma is capable of adapting herself to any situation,' Alison replied. 'She's the nearest thing to a chameleon a human being can be. And, as her mother once counselled us – in the days when she still hoped we would both be blushing young brides – it isn't where you live that's important. It's who you live with. I don't agree with you, Maxwell, that Al is unworthy of Emma. In his unassuming way, he is a fine man. But you're jumping the gun a bit, aren't you? Al hasn't mentioned marriage to Emma.'

Morton gave Alison a gloomy smile. 'And what do you think her answer will be, if and when he does?'

'Your guess is as good as mine.'

# CHAPTER NINE

WHEN THE telegram came, Richard and Mike were helping Josh Baxter to clear the snow from the front garden path.

'I guess you're hoping this'll be your last winter in New England, Rick!' Josh said cheerfully. 'What with getting snowed up here, an' all, the way we do.'

'I can't remember what an English winter is like, Uncle Josh. Except for the smell of fog. I remember that,' Richard replied. Then he saw Josh's grin change to a twisted grimace.

'What is it, Dad?' Mike asked with alarm.

But Josh's lips would not move to answer him and his tongue felt paralysed in his mouth. The boys had their backs towards the street, but Josh was facing it, and had seen the bearer of a dreaded envelope heading up West Newton Hill.

Don't let it be for us, he silently prayed. And if it is, let it be anything but what we haven't let ourselves contemplate since our boy volunteered.

Richard and Mike turned around to see what had so frighteningly rooted Josh to the spot. A minute or two later, when neither of his prayers was answered, Josh stood staring sightlessly at the cruel slip of paper in his hand. Then it slipped from his fingers, and Mike picked it up, scanned it, and handed it to Richard, without a word.

Josh made a mighty effort and pulled himself together. 'We are all going to have to be strong, for Mom's sake,' he declared. 'And I guess you guys have just learned what war really means.'

Josh put the telegram into his pocket and retrieved the spade he could not remember resting against the garage door. He must have put it there, when he opened the envelope. 'Now let's get this chore done, before Mom and

316

Maggie get back from doing the marketing,' he said to the boys.

Mike regarded him with astonishment. 'How can we just go on shovelling snow, as if nothing has happened?'

Richard, too, was taken aback.

'The wire says Junior is missing in action. And until and unless he is pronounced dead, all we can do is hope he's alive and carry on as though he is.' Time enough to mourn if we have to, Josh thought with pain.

'So I guess we'll behave as if this is just another Saturday morning, eh, you guys?' he said, giving their shoulders an encouraging slap. 'And it would sure be a help to me if you'd follow my lead, and try not to make a big deal out of it.'

'Whatever you say, Uncle Josh,' Richard replied. 'Maybe this will be a comfort to you: my mother's dad was missing in the last war. But he turned up.'

'And I bet the show went on in the meantime,' said Josh, trying to smile.

'If I dropped dead in the wings, my mother would stride over me and make her entrance onstage,' Richard declared.

Alison's father had once made that harsh assessment of her mother, with regard to himself. Though he was an actor, the theatre had seemed to him a rival. So it was for Richard, now, and a rival that would always win. In his heart, Alison had remained the beautiful, perfumed lady whose presence could light up his day. But in his mind, she was the woman who had once declaimed to a small boy that he must never expect her to break rules concerning her work. And who had illustrated it by not being there to wave him farewell, when he sailed away.

Josh had noted the tight smile that accompanied Richard's flat declaration. 'I doubt that your mom would carry theatrical tradition that far,' he said lightly, though his feelings were leaden.

'You don't know her,' Richard answered. Then he heard himself say, 'I wish I could stay here with you for always.'

'That's like saying you don't want the war to end,' Josh told him gently. He could think of no other suitable reply.

317

And Mary was right; something sure was bugging this kid about his mom.

Josh firmed his voice, which was not easy. 'Now move it, you guys, or we won't get this path cleared before the next snowfall!'

Mike jammed his woollen cap more securely on his unruly red hair, dug in his spade and tried not to think of his soldier-brother, or of what Richard had just said. Richard, too, resumed snow-shifting, but after a while stood staring into space, and Josh pretended not to notice that he had stopped work. Just another Saturday morning this was not!

Richard was gazing up at the maples, oaks and elms that made West Newton Hill a haven of shade in summer, their branches now tinselled with icicles that looked like the trimming on a Christmas tree. Behind him was the sturdy clapboard house he had learned to call home. And it seemed to him now that no other house could ever feel like home to him. He glanced at Josh's tall, lean figure, and Mike's short, stocky one. It wasn't just the house, but the people who lived in it, he thought with a lump in his throat.

Richard swallowed hard. If he didn't get a hold of himself he would be bawling in a minute – and his Uncle Maxwell had taught him that boys were not meant to cry. The thought of his uncle added guilt to the way he was feeling and a remembered picture of his Auntie Emma rose before his eyes. But it wasn't because he didn't love them that he wanted to stay here. Nor was it that he did not love his mother. He loved her and hated her, at one and the same time. Yet he did not feel guilty because of the hate.

He tugged wretchedly at the waistband of the heavy woollen sweater Emma had knitted and sent to him for Christmas. She had made one for Mike, too. Richard's was red, and Mike's blue. But Mike's was too long for him, Richard noticed. Auntie Emma had made them both the same size; she didn't know that Richard was inches taller than Mike. Today was the first time they had worn their new sweaters – and if Aunt Mary had been here, she would not have let them do so to shovel snow.

But why was he standing here thinking about sweaters,

318

when he'd just learned that Junior was missing in action? Because he didn't want to think about that. Or about what the end of the war, when it happened, would mean for him.

Mike gave him an awkward glance. 'What you just said, Rick – about not wanting to go home —'

'That wasn't what Rick said, Mike,' Josh interposed crisply.

'But it was what I meant.'

A moment of silence followed. Then Richard strode off along the path that led to the back door.

Josh and Mike stood listening to his boots crunching on the icy gravel. Then they heard a door slam shut and knew he had gone into the house.

'I don't know what's got into that boy,' Josh muttered. 'This just isn't the way Rick behaves.'

Mike was staring unhappily down at his feet.

'I don't want you telling your mom about this,' Josh instructed him. 'One shock at a time is enough for her,' he added, conscious of the envelope that felt like a heavy weight in his pocket.

'OK, Dad. But hearing Rick say what he did wasn't exactly a shock to me. It didn't take me five months, let alone five years, to figure out that he doesn't like his mother. And I was only a little kid, like he was, when he first got here.'

'How can a boy not like his mother?' Josh replied.

'It beats me. 'Cause I sure love mine.'

The water into which Richard had led them was for both of them too deep. To this uncomplicated father and son, that liking and loving were not automatically twin emotions in a child for its parents was inconceivable.

Mike was even more perplexed by a conversation he had with Richard that night.

It had been for the family a stressful day, though Mary Baxter, like her husband, had managed to remain her reassuring self after reading the telegram. But the determined pursuance of their weekend routine, the ice hockey game in the afternoon to which Josh had taken the boys, and the familiar, steaming tomato soup and grilled cheese

319

sandwiches awaiting them as always when they returned, had served only to emphasise the effort they were making.

The Baxters had sometimes joked to Richard about the British 'stiff upper lip'. But he had never seen a better example of it than he was witnessing here in America. Even his Uncle Maxwell, whose upper lip was the stiffest Richard had ever seen in a crisis, would have expressed his admiration for the Baxters, he thought.

But after supper, when the family sat toasting their winter-Saturday marshmallows by the fire, Maggie let the side down. Mary quietly carried her upstairs and put her to bed, after she had wept for her big brother.

When Mary returned to the kitchen, her attempt to be cheerful was so strained that Josh declared gruffly that it was time they all hit the hay, and put this terrible day behind them.

'I guess Mom will have a good cry herself, now she doesn't have to pretend in front of us guys,' Mike said to Richard, in the privacy of the bedroom they shared.

'But mine would just go on taking her curtain calls, to the bitter end!'

'That's show business, like they say, isn't it, Rick?' Mike felt a need to defend Richard's mother, on behalf of all mothers. But he had never been required to do so before because Rick so rarely mentioned her. 'And don't they also say that keeping a hold on your feelings is the British way?'

Mike took off his flannel shirt, and dropped it absently on the floor.

Richard picked it up and hung it on the back of a chair. The neatness Emma had instilled in him was still there. Mike's room had stopped looking as if a tornado had blown through it since Richard moved in with him.

'It strikes me you seem to've forgotten you're British,' Mike declared while taking off his shoes. 'And boy, what a prissy English kid you were when you arrived! Your folks sure aren't going to know you, when you get back.'

Why did I have to say that? Mike chided himself – remind them both that Rick didn't want to go back? He oughta have kept his big mouth shut – but it was too late now. The smile Rick was giving him was only with his lips, as though he couldn't make it include his eyes.

'My aunt and uncle will soon get used to the new me,' Richard said confidently. 'As for my mother – well I guess I'll be lucky if she has time to notice I'm there.'

The flat tone in which he said it gave Mike a creepy feeling. 'I guess you could say that about all moms,' he said, managing to laugh.

'But not in the way it applies to mine. Your mother is a busy lady, what with us kids to cook and wash for and everything — '

'What she does at the Red Cross, making up packages an' all, keeps her busy, too,' Mike added.

'And she sometimes gets absent-minded at home,' Richard went on. 'But it doesn't give a guy the feeling she doesn't care about him. Need I say more?'

Mike avoided his eye. 'I guess you've said enough.'

But Richard continued to talk about Alison. Why he was suddenly doing so, when despite their brotherly intimacy he had been unable to unburden himself to Mike before, he neither knew nor cared. It was as if his emotions, once unleashed, were pouring forth in words, like water hitherto restrained by a dam.

When he finished speaking, a heavy silence was the aftermath.

'I guess I've embarrassed you, Mike,' he said stiffly.

'Only because beefing about your troubles isn't like you. But don't think I didn't know you'd got troubles. Or what about.'

'Even though I've never talked to you about my mother?'

'I might not get grades as good as you do at school, Rick, but I ain't dumb! It was from you not mentioning her unless you had to that I knew something was wrong.'

Mike's gaze strayed to the picture of Alison, on Richard's bed-table. It was one of the photographs used to promote her career. Even Greer Garson, who since he saw her in *Mrs Miniver* was his favourite movie-actress, could not compete with Alison Plantaine in the beauty stakes, Mike thought.

'How can you not love a mom like that, Rick?' Mike said, affected by Alison's soulful expression. It was hard to believe that lovely lady capable of the unfeeling acts Rick had listed. And Mike would have forgiven her anything.

'I didn't say I don't love her.'

'But you said you wished you could stay here with us for ever.'

'I do.'

'And you wouldn't say that if you did love your mom. So quit telling me lies!'

Richard stared down at a threadbare patch in the rug beside his bed, which had grown more so in the years this had been his bed. How could he make Mike understand what he didn't understand himself?

'If ever a guy talked double-Dutch, Rick, it's you about your mom!' Mike remarked scathingly.

'I guess it must seem that way to you.'

'It sure does!' Mike headed for the door. 'And if you're not going to level with me, I may as well go brush my teeth.'

Later, when they had switched off their lamps, and Mike's gentle snore told Richard his friend would say no more that night, he lay thinking of his mother. Was she thinking of him? He did not need to wonder if his Auntie Emma was. And oh, what a comfort to know that when he returned to England, his aunt would be there.

# CHAPTER TEN

On VE night, Major Wiseman proposed to Emma. The dilemma this presented threw her into a panic. She received the proposal at a noisy victory-party, given by Morton at his Knightsbridge flat – and wished that it could have been anywhere but there.

Al had penned her into a corner before popping the question.

'Couldn't you have waited?' she mouthed.

'What are you whispering for, Emma? Me, I don't mind if the whole world knows that I want you for my wife! And haven't I waited long enough?' Al said, fondly surveying her flushed face.

'It's very hot in here, with all these people milling around,' was all Emma could find to say.

'In Florida, you get used to feeling hot,' he answered, employing some *fait-accompli* tactics. 'But you'll have the sea right on your doorstep, to swim in and cool off.'

'I can't swim.'

'I'll teach you to.'

'Flapping about in water-wings, at my age, I can do without. And I'm scared of water. Since I nearly got drowned at Blackpool when I was seven I only use water for drinking and washing.'

'So you'll watch me swim.'

Emma had a sudden vision of what Al would look like in a swimming costume and had to smile.

Her attempt to prick his bubble of love was not lost on Al. But he would not allow her to do so. 'We'll have beach parties with our friends, like my first wife and I did.'

'I haven't said I'm willing to be your second wife.'

'But you will. I hope.'

323

Emma listened to yet another description of the delights of Florida, and of St Petersburg in particular.

'But it isn't St Petersburg I'd be married to, Al,' she said, recalling, as Alison recently had, her mother's counselling. 'It would be you.'

Al's chubby face crumpled. 'There's something wrong with me?'

It was necessary for him to shout, in order to be heard above the revelry. Champagne was flowing and overflowing, and streamers unfurling as they were hurled in the air. Someone who had just arrived said the same was happening in Piccadilly Circus and Trafalgar Square.

Emma had not meant to hurt Al and said contritely, 'Of course there's nothing wrong with you. But that doesn't mean you're right for me.'

'The streamers think I'm right for you,' he said as a bright green one landed around their shoulders and bound them together. 'Look! Now we're tied up.'

Emma smiled. 'But only by a streamer.'

'For the moment. And I promise you, Emma, that whatever's wrong with me for you, I'll do my best to change.'

What was wrong with him for Emma was that he wasn't Morton, she thought, glimpsing their host's leonine head amid his guests. And, too, that he lived on the wrong side of the Atlantic. Where Richard still was, though not for much longer.


'It isn't exactly a shock to me, Emma,' Alison said dryly, when Emma conveyed the news of Al's proposal as though she were dropping a bombshell. 'It had to happen sooner or later. And nobody could call yours and Al's a whirlwind courtship.'

'It hasn't been a courtship, only a friendship.'

'On your side maybe. Not on Al's.'

They were eating a late breakfast on the day after the party. Emma, Alison observed, seemed to have lost her appetite.

'I don't remember ever having breakfast with you when

you were wearing your dressing-gown before, Emma,' Alison remarked.

'Al's proposal has knocked me off my stroke.'

'Apparently. And I'd like you to consider it very carefully, Emma dear.'

'As it's the only one I've ever had, or am likely to get!' Emma joked at her own expense.

Alison fingered a button on her blue chiffon housecoat. 'That wasn't what I meant. As well you know.' She gave Emma an affectionate glance. 'Nor do I want you wafted from my scene, and you know that, too. I don't know what I'd do without you, Emma. But it's your happiness that we are talking about. I wouldn't want you to sacrifice it, in order to go on devoting yourself to Richard and me.'

Emma was moved by Alison's rare display of selflessness. But she had never doubted that her cousin cared about her, and ought not to be surprised that she was proving it now. 'I'm not in love with Al, Alison. So the kind of happiness you mean doesn't enter into it.'

'But you're very fond of him, aren't you?'

'That goes without saying. He's a lovely man.'

'And marrying him wouldn't be the same as one of those arranged marriages you fled from Oldham to escape.'

'Of course not. Are you telling me to say yes, Alison?'

'I wouldn't presume to, Emma. I just don't want you to say no on my account.'

Emma poured the tea and they sipped it in silence, at ease together, as they had always been.

'How would you and Richard manage, if I said yes to Al?' Emma asked.

'I'd still have Maxwell, wouldn't I? And Richard is no longer a young child who needs attention, Emma. Before we know it, he'll be grown up and won't need any of us.'

'That time is still years ahead, Alison.'

'But the years speed by – and as we said to each other when we last noticed them doing so, a person must make the most of them, Emma.'

'We didn't say it to each other. You said it to me.'

'And I'm saying it to you again. Telling you to do what is

325

best for yourself. To make the most of what's left of your life.'

'I'm not sure that marrying Al would be doing that.'

'Then don't give him your answer one way or the other until you are.'

'He's expecting to be shipped home very soon, now the war in Europe is over.'

'But you'd be foolish, Emma, to let that hasten your decision. You'll be able to think things out more clearly after he has gone. But please promise that you won't consider me.'

Emma smiled. 'What about the promise we made to each other, when you asked me to come here to live with you? We said we'd take care of each other in our old age. Though we were only thirty, then.'

'There was an unspoken proviso written into it, Emma: that if either of us met the right man, the deal was off.'

'Don't look so despondent, Al,' said Alison to the major when he came to bid them farewell. 'Emma hasn't said no to you.'

'She hasn't said yes, either.'

It was a Sunday afternoon, and Al was not the only teatime guest.

He glanced to where Emma was chatting to Morton and an ATS girl, and said vehemently, 'And the one I have to thank for it, Alison, is that man!'

'What on earth are you talking about, Al?'

He turned to look at her and thought how elegant she always was, even in a simple summer frock like the cream shirtwaister she had on today. Her sleek black hair was drawn back into a perfect chignon, accentuating her sculptured features, and the heady perfume she wore seemed to Al, as it drifted toward him, the essence of Alison Plantaine.

'You didn't answer my question, Al,' she said to him. 'And why are you looking me over? You've seen me before!'

'I was thinking that it isn't surprising, Alison, that people forgive you your shortcomings.'

326

'And that is the most dubious compliment I have ever been paid.'

Al glanced again at Emma and Morton, and added, 'But I didn't know your shortcomings included seeing no further than the end of your nose.' He gave Alison a dispirited smile. 'If you'll excuse me, I'll go and have a word with Emma – and leave you to figure out what I mean.'

What could he possibly mean? Alison traced their conversation back to its beginning and stopped short at Al's assertion that he had Morton to thank for Emma's not saying yes to him. As though Maxwell were Al's rival for Emma's affections. Al must surely know that nothing was further from the truth. Which left only one other possible explanation for Al having said what he had. That Emma was in love with Maxwell.

Oh no! Alison thought, and had to lean against the wall to steady herself. She did not want to believe it. But in the few seconds she remained there, a kaleidoscope of recollections, insignificant when they occurred, shimmered before her eyes and settled into a pattern she could not now fail to discern. Emma's face lighting up when Maxwell arrived unexpectedly. Her anxiety about his lifestyle being too onerous for a man with a heart murmur. Her flatness when he was away from London. Her animation when he returned.

Alison's glance locked briefly with Al's, across the room. Then she averted her eyes and went to speak to a couple of RAF pilots who were seated on the sofa, their cake plates balanced precariously upon their laps.

'Sunday tea at your flat will be one of my wartime memories, Miss Plantaine,' one of them said to her.

And she would not forget this particular Sunday, Alison thought, against the background buzz of casual conversation. Though nothing had outwardly changed, a nice little man from St Petersburg, Florida, had opened her eyes to what she would rather not have seen, and still did not want to believe. If it was true, how could Emma not be jealous of Alison, with whom Morton remained ever in love? And how could Emma bear the hopelessness of her

327

own situation? The constant companionship of a man for whom her heart yearned, who took her for granted, though she was to him a valued friend?

These and other such thoughts whirled like snowflakes heading nowhere, in Alison's mind.

While the pilots talked lightly about having survived the war in Europe, and equally lightly of the likelihood of their being consigned to help 'polish off' the Japs, Alison kept a listening expression on her face.

She had always despaired of Emma's unique capacity to subjugate her own feelings to those of others, though it was this that had enabled Emma to adapt to the vicissitudes that came her way. And, as Alison's father had once predicted, the timid girl Emma had been had matured into a woman of strength. Had Alison ever doubted that, she could do so no longer. The manner in which Emma had borne the burden of her secret love for Morton, and maintained her loyalty to Alison in spite of it, required a strength of character Alison knew she herself did not possess.

She saw Al glance at the clock. Then he came to have a final word with her before departing, and they went to stand together by the window.

'I don't know whether to thank you, or curse you,' Alison said.

Al spread his hands and shrugged. 'What's to thank or curse, Alison? The truth is the truth and I guess there's nothing you or I can do about it. Emma will either be sensible, or she won't.'

'Emma is the most sensible person I know.'

'But not about you-know-who.'

'All I can wish for you, Al, is that things turn out the way you want them to.'

The plump little officer, upon whom a uniform had always to Alison seemed out of place, eyed her searchingly. 'You really mean that, don't you?'

'I'm not in the habit of saying what I don't mean.'

Al grinned. 'Except when you're being nice to other actresses.'

'That, darling, is part of the theatrical life.'

328

'And shall I tell you something, Alison?'

'Fire away.'

'This is the first time I haven't felt you're putting on a show for me.'

'This is certainly your day for home truths, Al!'

'Well, I don't have time to play footsie any more, do I? I'll be gone from England by tonight. And I'm sure glad I didn't depart without getting a glimpse of the real you.'

It occurred to Alison, then, that none of the servicemen and women she had entertained in her flat had seen the real her. She had given them what they expected of her: an at-home version of the Alison Plantaine she was on the stage. As though, in the presence of her public, the show must go on – even when the setting was her own home.

But wasn't that the price of being who she was? She could not, as Emma had told her so bluntly, have her cake and eat it. In more ways than one.

'Thanks for everything, Alison,' Al said.

Alison kissed him warmly. 'There's nothing to thank me for. And I'm going to miss you, Al.'

He looked surprised. Did he think people came and went from Alison Plantaine's scene, leaving her untouched by their having been there? Probably. Oh, how wrong was the impression people had of her. Though she was not too good at attaching names to faces, there was nobody who had crossed her threshold during the war whom Alison would forget.

She watched Emma and Al leave the room together to say a private goodbye, and exchanged a glance with Morton.

Would it be goodbye? Or only *au revoir*? If it turned out to be the latter, the threesome that had withstood the test of time and tribulation would be no more. But like the lovelorn major, Alison would have to wait and see.

329

# CHAPTER ELEVEN

'ONE OF the things I'm going to miss when I leave here, is popcorn at the movies,' Richard said on the Saturday preceding his departure, experiencing nostalgia for America in advance.

He had been listing what he would miss since VE Day – with increasing despondency.

'You can take some popcorn home with you,' Mike said.

'But it won't last long.'

'It will if I lend you my trunk.'

'If I was going to take a trunkful of something, it wouldn't be popcorn.'

'What would it be, Rick?' Maggie asked. 'Mike's trunk would fit me in it. Would you like me to come?'

'No thanks.'

'Get on with your breakfast, you kids!' Mary instructed. 'Or you won't get your Saturday apple pie.'

'I'll never get apple pie for breakfast again,' Richard lamented. 'And my Auntie Emma would have kittens if she knew people ate it for breakfast here.'

Josh looked up from his *Boston Herald*. 'I never heard you use that expression before, Rick, and I don't especially care for it.'

'People sometimes say it in England, Uncle Josh.'

'In that case, go right ahead and say it. I'm glad to know you're practising for when you get back.'

'I didn't know I'd remembered it. It just slipped out,' Richard said. 'I guess because it's what I was always saying about Auntie Emma, and I'm going to be seeing her soon.'

'You still didn't say what you'd put in the trunk, Rick,' Maggie reminded him, wiping a splodge of cream-of-wheat from her chin with the back of her chubby hand.

Richard paused to think about it. 'All the things I want to remember, I guess.'

The smile he gave the family tugged at Mary Baxter's heartstrings. 'They'll go with you anyways, Rick. Memories don't have to be packed in a trunk.'

'Why don't we give Rick a family outing to Boston, to remember?' Josh suggested, as Mary refilled his coffee cup. 'It's something we haven't done. Not all of us together.'

But one of us is missing, the glance his wife shared with him said.

'That's a great idea, Dad,' said Mike enthusiastically.

'Is it OK with you, Rick?' Josh inquired.

'Sure. Whatever everyone wants to do is fine by me, Uncle Josh.'

Though Josh commuted to Boston every working day, Mary and the children seldom went there. There was no necessity for them to do so. West Newton had everything they needed.

Richard had enjoyed his first visit to a cinema at the local movie house, where the children who were his classmates at Pierce Elementary School splurged a nickel of their pocket money on a ticket to see Woody Woodpecker cartoons, and another at the popcorn machine. These special Saturday shows were their big event of the week, and they would rush to complete the household chores assigned to them, in order to be there when the movie house opened at 11 a.m. And occasionally, if a Mickey Rooney film was showing, or a Deanna Durbin 'weepie', their parents might take them to the movies on Saturday evening. Mike always pleaded to be taken when his heart-throb Greer Garson was the star, and Richard if it was Betty Grable, who was the pin-up girl not just of the US Armed Forces, but of every American schoolboy old enough to appreciate her shapely charms.

'We can give Mom a treat, and take a walk around Filene's or Jordan Marsh's while we're in Boston,' Josh said to the children, while he lit his after-breakfast pipe.

'Since when was I one for walking around department stores?' said Mary with a smile.

331

'Mom isn't like Mrs Aaronson,' Mike pronounced. 'She gets what she's gone to town for and comes straight home.'

'Mrs Aaronson is a very nice lady.' Josh thought it necessary to defend his partner's wife.

'Sure,' Mike agreed. 'She never comes here without bringing us kids candy, and Mom flowers. But she sure does like dressing up!'

'Well, she's Jewish, isn't she?' Maggie said, as though that accounted for it.

'So is my Auntie Emma,' Richard reminded her. 'But I never saw her all dressed up. Why did you just say what you did, Maggie?'

'Because she's a big-mouth!' Mike exclaimed.

'That isn't a reason for saying it.'

Rick has the makings of a fine lawyer, thought Josh. He hadn't lived with the boy for six years without becoming aware of the clarity of his intellect, nor of his ability to stick to the point.

Josh noted that his daughter was staring uncomfortably down at her plate. His wife signalled him with her eyes to say something to smooth things over, and he was not surprised that Mary was briefly at a loss for words.

So was he. And smoothing things over wasn't good enough. Rick had sensed in Maggie's innocently delivered remark an oblique insult to his aunt and her race, and wasn't the kind to let it go at that. He wanted a logical explanation for what Maggie had said. But logic could not be applied to prejudice. How was Josh to explain society's age-old attitude toward the Jews? And it wasn't just Rick to whom he must explain. It was time he set his own kids, straight, too – if Maggie, at the tender age of nine, was already spouting the poison she had imbibed with the air she breathed.

Josh could recall his father being pleased when his lawyer-son went into partnership with Jake Aaronson. Jewish lawyers were said to have what it takes to succeed in their profession – but, that, thought Josh, was one of the few generalisations about Jews that was true.

'I don't know why I said what I did about Mrs Aaronson,' Maggie said.

'Of course you don't, honey,' Josh replied, emerging from his cogitation. 'It just slid off your tongue. But you mustn't let that kind of remark do so ever again. It's like saying that every cat you encounter will scratch you, just because it's a cat.'

Maggie giggled.

Mary gave Josh a rebuking glance. Did he really have to compare Mrs Aaronson, whom she had never heard say a bad word about anyone, to a cat? But he had made what he meant clear, and that was what mattered. Richard and Mike were smiling. The awkward moment was over.

But Richard knew that Josh had not finished what he had to say, and was waiting for him to continue.

'There are a lot of popular fallacies about Jews,' Josh informed him, 'as though every Jew were the same.'

'I see,' said Richard thoughtfully. When he went back to England, he would ask his aunt to tell him more about it – and why it was so. Meanwhile, he was grateful to Uncle Josh for putting him in the picture, and gave him a smile. 'But I won't let anyone get away with making that kind of crack, Uncle Josh. I'll be like you. And I would be even if I weren't the adopted son of a half-Jewish lady,' he added.

Maggie ventured a few more words on her own behalf – in her appealing, childish way. 'But when we all went to see Andy Aaronson get confirmed, in that synagogue over in Brookline, Mrs Aaronson *was* very, very dressed up, wasn't she?'

'So was Andy!' Mike declared.

'You can say that again,' Richard endorsed.

Josh and Mary shared a smile. The Aaronsons' only son was the apple of their eye – and nothing too good for him. It was not just his mother whose finery had created a stir in the Kehillath Israel Synagogue that morning. Richard and Mike had gaped when they saw Andy in the elegant pinstripe suit his tailor grandfather had made for him.

'I wonder what kind of bird that feather in Mrs Aaronson's hat came from?' Mike reminisced.

Richard laughed. 'It kept tickling her nose!'

'It looked like an osprey,' Mary said, 'and it probably cost the earth.' She smiled at Josh. 'Aren't you glad you're married to me, and not to Dolly Aaronson?'

Mary shopped in Boston only once a year, when she went there to buy a new evening frock, to wear at the monthly dances held at the Neighborhood Club. At Christmas, Josh took Richard and Mike to town to choose their gifts at Shwartz's toy shop. Maggie's still arrived from Santa Claus. Afterwards, the boys would go with him to browse in Goodspeed's bookshop, which he did not have time to do on a working day. Richard had only been once to Boston when there was not snow on the ground. Josh had taken him and Mike to Boston Common on a balmy spring day to sail in one of the little swan-shaped boats on the lake. Then they had strolled up Beacon Hill, where Richard had liked the tall, gracious houses, with their wrought-iron balconies, and the ornamental street lamps that lit the Hill at night.

'Can we eat lunch at Schrafts, Dad?' Mike asked, 'like you'n me'n Rick did, the last time we were there?'

'I'd rather go to Bailey's Ice Cream Parlor,' said Maggie.

'We'll go there for dessert, and have ourselves some nut fudge sundaes,' Josh said, 'as it's Rick's farewell treat.'

'Great!' his son and daughter yelled.

Under any other circumstances, Richard would have joined in. But the charm had gone out of his day with the reminder that the trip to town was to mark his departure.

Only Mary was aware of this. 'Rick can have two sundaes today,' she said. 'Two different flavours,' she added smiling at Richard comfortingly. 'How would that be?'

I don't feel like going to Boston, Richard wanted to say. He would just as soon sit on the porch and read his Dick Tracy comic. By himself. But living with the Baxters had taught him that when you were part of a family, you didn't only think of yourself – and if he said he didn't want to go on the outing, nobody would go, though the others were looking forward to it.

He managed to laugh. 'I guess one ice cream sundae will be enough for me, Aunt Mary.'

334

But the family outing was not to take place. A letter to Richard from the Plantaine twins was responsible.

The letter arrived while the others were waiting for Mary to powder her nose. Had Josh not remarked that it looked shiny, she would not have bothered. And they would have left for Boston, before the mail came.

But as Alison would doubtless have said, such are the ways of Destiny. Richard, whose regular correspondence with Luke and Lucy had convinced him that he was right about them, and his mother wrong, opened the envelope eagerly, and smiled with amusement when he began reading.

A moment later, he blanched.

'What's wrong?' Mike asked, but received no answer.

Josh glanced up from his own mail and saw Richard's face. 'Who is that letter from?'

There was no reply to that question, either.

Richard did not trust himself to speak lest his voice trembled. 'A little bird' had told the twins that his Aunt Emma was probably going to marry an American officer. Wives lived where their husbands did. Richard and his aunt would soon be swopping places, on either side of the Atlantic. And a home with no Aunt Emma would not be a home to Richard.

Mary snapped her powder compact shut, breaking the silence. Maggie, always sensitive to the feelings of others, was eyeing Richard, and looked about to burst into tears. Mike had not shifted his concerned gaze from Richard's face. And Josh, Mary thought, would any second now explode with impatience.

Mary's instinct was to let Richard alone until he had pulled himself together. But patience was not one of her husband's virtues. Josh had had a hard week at the office and his pipe had gone out while he waited for Richard to say something. He fumbled in his pocket for his matches, but they were not there, and that did it. 'Either tell us what's wrong, or get the heck out of here, Rick!' he barked.

Richard did both.

'But you'll still have your mom, won't you?' was Maggie's response to his news.

Richard gave her a tight-lipped smile and left the room, with Mike hot on his heels.

Mary heard the boys go upstairs to their bedroom.

'I guess Boston is off,' said Josh, who was now regretting his outburst.

His wife's reply was a glance of rebuke. But after reading that letter, Rick wouldn't have enjoyed the family outing anyways, she thought.

Maggie was again on the verge of tears, 'Did I say something to Rick I shouldn't have?'

'No, honey,' Mary lied. But you sure did, she thought. And if Mary ever met Alison Plantaine, she would give that woman a piece of her mind! The damage she had done to Rick might never be undone, thought Mary – whose heart was aching for a son of her own who might never come back.

# CHAPTER TWELVE

WHEN RICHARD walked down the ship's gangway, his elders did not at first recognise him. He was uncommonly tall for his age and had on a sports jacket and long trousers. They could not relate him to the little boy who went away.

'In no time, he'll be a young man,' Morton said emotionally, when the bareheaded, lanky lad confirmed his identity with a wave – and a smile that lit his face when he spotted Alison.

It was to her he ran.

And that's the way it will always be, thought Emma with a pang, as she and Morton stepped aside to allow them their private moment of reunion.

'Where has my tiny son gone to?' Alison said when she had released him. But he still had his father's endearing, lopsided smile.

'Well, I sure make Auntie look tiny nowadays!' Richard gave Emma a bear hug. 'But a guy doesn't have to be big to do that!'

'I'm next in the hugging queue,' Morton said.

'As it was you who taught me how guys should behave, if you don't think twelve is too old to be hugged by my uncle, neither do I, I guess.'

'And how very American you have become,' said Alison, as Richard had known she would.

'A good boarding school will change all that,' Morton declared.

'We haven't agreed that Richard is going away to school,' Alison countered. 'It all depends.'

Richard waited until they were on their way to London before revealing that he knew upon what it depended.

'Damn the Plantaine twins!' Alison exclaimed. 'Is there anything those two don't know?'

Richard was seated beside her in the back of the car, and likened her expression to that of a snarling tigress.

'I guess it's no secret if Auntie's been seen around with the guy,' he said to calm her. And added, in defence of Luke and Lucy, 'So why wouldn't they tell me?'

A better question, thought Alison, is why *would* they tell Richard? Her stepcousins did nothing without a reason and Alison was under no illusion that their longtime vendetta with her was over. Their keeping in touch with Richard throughout his time in the States had made her uneasy. She had learned of it from him, not from them, though she had run into them here and there during the war. Her feeling that they were pulling strings behind her back had increased.

The least of it, she thought, was that they were befriending the boy to upset his mother, whom they knew would like to forget they existed.

Now, as though they were present in the car, the twins had contrived to cast a blight for Alison upon her son's homecoming. Richard liked them, and Alison loathed them, and the tension that had produced in the space of a few minutes had no place in a joyous reunion.

Richard voiced the resentful thought that had just entered his mind. 'Why didn't you tell me yourselves?'

'That is what we would have preferred to do, darling. When you've settled down at home again would have been time enough.'

'When I've made my decision, which I haven't yet, would have been time enough,' Emma declared.

Upsetting Richard on his first day back was the last thing she would have wanted, Emma thought in the silence that followed. Nor did she want to be the cause of once again disrupting his life. Why didn't she just say, here and now, that she wasn't going to marry Al? Set the boy's mind at rest? She was tempted to do so for Richard's sake. But as Alison had said, soon he would no longer need her.

To Emma, it seemed only yesterday that she had waved goodbye to a small child. Seeing Richard now had brought home to her – as it had to Max – that before too long he would be setting forth upon his adult path. All that would

338

then be left to Emma was a return to what Alison called their cosy threesome. Me, Max, and Alison, growing old together, Emma thought now, envisaging them sitting by the drawing-room fire, Alison and Emma with shawls around their shoulders, and Max with a lap rug tucked around his knees. And Alison and Max, even in their dotage, would still be discussing plays!

Was that what Emma wanted? To end her days with a bossy man whom she adored, and the temperamental object of his adoration, who would surely become even more so with age?

Part of Emma longed for the peace and stability that marrying Al Wiseman would ensure, to be cherished by someone who loved her, as her mother had been by her father. And the chance she had not expected to come her way was unlikely to come again.

So why was she hesitating? For three reasons – and they were all sitting in the car with her. Around them was woven the tapestry of her life so far. Until she uprooted herself from Oldham she had not really been alive. Now, there was a child who still needed her and his mother, who always would; who would never grow up.

And a man who depended upon her, too. Emma stole a glance at Morton. And who was behaving like a dog in a manger! He didn't want her himself, but seemed unable to bear the thought of her marrying someone else.

She sometimes wished she had never met Max, and marrying Al might help her to forget she loved him. Out of sight, out of mind, the old proverb said. Florida was a long way from London.

While Emma was debating her future, Richard had been considering his.

'If Auntie Emma leaves us, why must I be sent away to school? Mom and I could get a housekeeper,' he said, as they left Southampton behind and a rural scene that he compared nostalgically with New England unfolded before his eyes.

Morton smiled dryly. 'Your mother would be incapable of keeping one! And a housekeeper could not replace your Aunt Emma.'

'I guess I don't have to be told that, Uncle.'

How can I possibly leave him? Emma thought with feeling. But she had to make her decision with her head, not her heart.

'If the housekeeper left, I could fill in until we found another lady,' said Richard confidently. 'I'm very handy around the house, now. At the Baxters', us kids helped out with the chores. I know how to scramble eggs and make French-fries. I'm also a great bed-maker. I could make your bed, Mom, and cook your supper when you get home from the theatre at night.'

His elders could not have remained unmoved by Richard's eagerness to prove his capabilities.

Emma almost told him, there and then, that she was staying put, and had to clamp her mouth shut in order not to let her heart rule her head.

Alison touched Richard's cheek. 'And how, my darling, would you stay awake in school, if you went to bed late every night? And now you are getting older you'll have lots of homework to do, there won't be time for doing household chores. It's lovely of you to offer, and to want to look after me. But it isn't practical, I'm afraid.'

'We could make it work out, Mom. Somehow, we'd get by.'

'For a week or so, my love. But on a permanent basis, getting by wouldn't do. I couldn't give my work the attention it requires if I were worried about your welfare, Richard. Nor could I take you along, if a play I was in transferred to Broadway. Or when I go on tour, which I intend to do now the war in Europe is over.'

'Thank you for telling me, Alison!' Morton chipped in. 'As I'm your manager, it's useful for me to know!'

'I've only just made up my mind to tour, Maxwell.'

'And may I ask why? So suddenly.'

'Because my career seems stagnant to me.'

'Everyone's career should be stagnant the way yours is, Alison! You've reached the pinnacle. Where else is there for you to go?'

'Hollywood,' Emma said, with a dry smile.

'Wherever my art takes me, and I wouldn't rule Hollywood out.'

'Films are a very different art,' Morton declaimed and gave Emma a sidelong glance. Was she trying to lure Alison, too, across the Atlantic?

If looks could kill, I'd be dead! Emma thought, wishing she had not mentioned Hollywood – which nobody seemed to know had been a joke.

'Where was I, before Emma so interestingly sidetracked me?' Alison said.

'About to leap off the pinnacle,' Morton tersely informed her.

'Artistry knows no pinnacles, Maxwell. True artists are never satisfied with what they achieve, but ever striving to perfect their art.'

'Would you like to tell me what you are really saying, my dear?' Morton demanded impatiently. 'Instead of delivering a lofty speech.'

'Lofty it may sound. But true it remains,' Alison replied. 'And for me, stardom isn't enough. While you, Maxwell dear, have been busy coining it in at the box office during the war, and with few exceptions by staging plays I would not deign to call plays, I have grown increasingly disenchanted and dissatisfied, because I was appearing in them.'

'But you too have profited from their box-office success.'

'That, and the need to give wartime audiences the relaxation they needed, was my consolation. But I have become more and more restless, Maxwell.'

Alison paused to gaze through the window as they drove through the New Forest, and was aware of Richard gazing through his window at the towering trees.

'The feeling I have now, Maxwell, is similar to the one by which I was for a long time beset before I left the Plantaine Players. That I was standing still, artistically. My father told me it was because I had outgrown the company, and had lost the stimulus of challenge that had once fired my talent. When you offered me a part, and I made my West End début, I found it again.'

'Are you telling me that you've now outgrown the West End theatre?' Morton exclaimed.

'Keep your mind on your driving,' Emma said to him as the car swerved.

Morton steadied the car, but otherwise ignored the interruption. 'There are some very good plays on, right now, Alison. *Little Eyolf*, and *Duet For Two Hands*, to name but two.'

'Also *Chicken Every Sunday*, and *Alice in Thunderland*, to name two of the other kind!' Alison replied.

'You must never judge a play by its title, Alison,' Morton flashed back. 'Any more than one judges a book by its cover. And *Alice in Thunderland*, for your information, happens to be a political fantasia.'

'And what, exactly, is that?'

'Use your imagination, my dear girl! I haven't yet had time to go and see it, but I expect it will be the kind of satire you and I saw together, in Berlin, at the Katacomb Club.'

Where I met my Waterloo, thought Alison.

'I didn't know you'd been to Berlin,' Richard said to her.

Or that you were conceived there. 'I played there in a theatre festival in the summer of 1932, darling,' she said, managing to keep her tone casual – and aware that Emma and Morton had frozen in their seats.

'Well, I sure hope you never go there again, Mom. I hate the Germans, after what they've done!'

And oh, how shattered he would be, to learn he was half-German, was Alison's reaction. Would she ever tell him the truth about his parentage? Never to do so was to deny him his right to know who he was. But she would not be faced with that dilemma for a long time.

Morton ended the moment of tension. 'Shall we return to the subject, Alison?'

'I can't remember what it was.'

In view of what it had led to, Morton and Emma were not surprised.

'You were talking about the theatre,' Richard reminded her. 'But when aren't you talking about the theatre!'

'It's my work, isn't it, darling?'

'But why do you want to go on tour?'

'A good question!' said Morton.

'To get myself out of the rut I feel I am in,' Alison replied. 'But that is only one reason.'

'Tell us the other; we are waiting with bated breath,' Morton said. How could he be in love with so capricious a woman? But he still was.

'The wartime audiences were not like the peacetime ones,' said Alison. 'Lots of people came to see me perform who would not have been able to, had the war not brought them to London. Now, they'll be shedding their uniforms, and going home to the provinces to be civilians again. And I feel I should take myself to them. Good theatre should be available to everyone, not just to Londoners.'

'Your altruism is touching, Alison,' said Morton.

'My Plantaine ancestors were strolling players,' Alison reminded him. 'They took Shakespeare's plays to the people – and the family company continued to do so – until they settled in Hastings in 1914. I see no reason, Maxwell, why Alison Plantaine should not devote some of her time to continuing that touring tradition.'

'Except that my bank balance will suffer accordingly.'

'I'm not the only star in your galaxy, Maxwell! Nor are the plays in which I appear for you your sole productions – far from it!'

'Don't make yourself out to be money-mad, Max,' said Emma. 'We know you're not.'

Richard was listening gloomily. 'How soon will you be going on tour, Mom?'

Though to Morton it was not yet a *fait accompli*, to the boy it was, and as if he had returned full circle to the point from which he had departed in 1939. His mother was still putting the theatre before him. But he was not surprised.

'We shall have to wait and see, darling,' Alison replied. 'The play I'm appearing in now has only just begun its run.'


That evening before leaving for the theatre Alison went to Richard's room and found him staring aimlessly out of the window.

343

'I wish you didn't have to work on my first night home,' he said, turning to look at her.

'But you know that I must. And that I love you very much.'

'That makes two of us, Mom,' he said gruffly.

'I'm glad to hear that, Richard. When I called you on the phone, and you seemed to have nothing to say to me, I felt I had lost you,' Alison told him, 'that you had become Mrs Baxter's boy.'

A picture of Mary Baxter in her gingham apron rose before Richard. And with it, a yearning for all that Mary epitomised.

It was Richard's good fortune, and Alison's misfortune that the woman who had raised him during so formative a period of his childhood was the earth-mother kind, and her family so secure and normal. Without his years under the Baxters' roof, Richard would have reached manhood lacking the criteria which living with them provided. Mary could not have put it better when she told her husband they had given Richard a taste of real family life. And the ménage to which he had returned, with the possible removal from it of Emma, could not have felt less secure to him.

'I sometimes wished I was Aunt Mary's son,' he admitted. 'But a guy has to make do with the mom he's got.'

'I'm afraid so,' said Alison, with a rueful smile.

Richard surveyed the beautiful woman who was his mother and as unreachable now as she had always seemed to him. He no longer doubted that she loved him but it wasn't enough. He wanted her to belong to him alone, and knew that she never would. But he wouldn't swop her for any other mom in the world.